F

Ea
Gif

JUST BEFORE I DIED

S. K. Tremayne is a bestselling novelist and award-winning travel writer, and a regular contributor to newspapers and magazines around the world. The author's debut psychological thriller, *The Ice Twins*, was picked for the Richard and Judy Autumn Book Club and was a *Sunday Times* No.1 bestseller.

Born in Devon, S. K. Tremayne now lives in London and has two daughters.

Also by S. K. Tremayne

The Ice Twins
The Fire Child

S.K. TREMAYNE

JUST BEFORE I DIED

HarperCollins*Publishers*

HarperCollins*Publishers*
1 London Bridge Street
London, SE1 9GF

www.harpercollins.co.uk

Published by HarperCollins*Publishers* 2018
2

A catalogue record for this book
is available from the British Library

ISBN: 978-0-00-810588-4 (HB)
ISBN: 978-0-00-810589-1 (TPB)

This novel is entirely a work of fiction.
The names, characters and incidents portrayed in it are
the work of the author's imagination. Any resemblance to
actual persons, living or dead, events or localities is
entirely coincidental.

Set in Sabon by Palimpsest Book Production Ltd, Falkirk, Stirlingshire

Printed and bound in Great Britain by
CPI Group (UK) Ltd, Croydon, CR0 4YY

MIX
Paper from
responsible sources
FSC™ C007454

Author's Note

I'd like to thank everyone who assisted me in my research on Dartmoor, in particular Tim Cumming, for his inspiration, and Loic Rich for his company. Likewise I am indebted to: the staff of the Two Bridges, White Hart and Gidleigh Park hotels; the makers of Plymouth Gin and the brewers of Dartmoor Jail Ale; and my editors at *The Times* and *The Sunday Times Travel Magazine*: Jane Knight, Ed Grenby and Nick Redman.

As always I must thank Jane Johnson, Eugenie Furniss and Sarah Hodgson for their wisdom, advice, and professionalism.

There are many references throughout this book to various Dartmoor locations and place-names. A few of these have been altered or invented, by me, although I hope that the book, in general, is a faithful representation of the uniquely beautiful Dartmoor landscape. Any unintentional errors are entirely my own.

My thanks to Seth Lakeman for allowing me to quote from the lyrics of his songs.

For Star, on Kes Tor

Poor Kitty Jay
Such a beauty cast away,
This silent prayer should paint some peace on her
 grave
But something broke her sleep

From 'Kitty Jay', by Seth Lakeman

Huckerby Farm

Saturday morning

The dead birds are neatly arranged in a row. I don't know why they are dead. Maybe they were slaughtered, by a domestic cat, in that cruel, unhungry, feline way: killing things for fun. But I don't know anyone who keeps a cat, not for miles. We certainly don't. Adam prefers dogs: animals that work and hunt and retrieve, animals with a loyal purpose.

More likely is that these little songbirds died from frost and hunger: this long Dartmoor winter has been hard. The last few weeks the ice has bitten into the acid soil, gnawed at the twisted trees, sent people scurrying into their homes from little Christow to Tavy Cleave, and has turned the narrow moorland roads to rinks.

I shudder at the returning thought, as I cradle my hot coffee and gaze out of the kitchen window. Ice had been a danger on the roads for a while. Yes, I should have been more careful, but was it really my fault? I looked away for a moment, distracted by something. And then, it happened, on the dark road that runs by Burrator Reservoir.

It was just a little patch of ice. But it was enough. I went from heading home at a sedentary pace to being in a car out of control, skidding terribly, ramming the useless brakes, in the frigid December twilight, sliding faster and faster towards the waiting waters. All I remember is a strange and rushing sense of inevitability, that this had somehow been meant to happen all my life: my sudden death, at thirty-seven.

The rising black water had always been meant to freeze me; the locked car doors had always been meant to cage me. The icy liquid in my lungs had always been intended to drown the last of my gasps, on this cold, anonymous December evening on the fringes of the moor, where the bony beacons and balding hills begin their descent to Plymouth.

But it didn't kill me.

I fought and swam, blood streaming – and I survived. Somehow, somehow. Yes, my memories are still ribbony, still ragged, but they are returning, and my body is recovering. The bruising on my face is nearly gone.

I survived a near-fatal accident and I am determined to number my blessings, as if I am an infant doing sums by counting her fingers.

Blessing number one: I have a husband I love. Adam Redway. He seems to love me too, and he is still very handsome at thirty-eight: with those dazzling blue eyes and that crow-dark hair. Almost black, but not quite. Sometimes he could pass for a man ten years younger, he has that agelessness, despite the toughness of his job; perhaps it is *because* of his job.

He doesn't earn that much, as a National Park Ranger, but he adores the moors where he was born, and he adores what he does: from repairing walls so the Dartmoor ponies can't range too far, to taking troops of school kids to see the daffodils of Steps Bridge, to guiding tourists, for fun, all the way down Lydford Gorge, spooking them out with stories of the outlaws who lived there, in the sixteenth century, the Gubbins who lived in caves, and became cannibals, and died out from inbreeding, and madness.

Adam loves all this: loves the poetry and the severity of the moor. He likes the toughness and the strangeness; he grew up with it. And over the years he has allowed me to become a part of it: we have a happy marriage, or at least a marriage happier than many. Yes, it is regular, ordinary, even predictable. Right down to the sex.

I am sure my friends from uni would laugh at the homeliness, but I find it deeply reassuring. The world turns: rhythmically and reliably. I desire, and am desired. We haven't made love so much since the accident, but I am sure it will return. It always does.

What else can I give thanks for? What else makes me glad to be alive? I need to remind myself. Because these flashbacks *are* pretty painful.

Quite often I get sudden, frightening headaches: head-aches sharp enough to make me cry out. It's as if something is crunching in my mind, bone grating on nerves.

Like now. I wince. Setting the big coffee cup by the sink, I put a hand to my forehead, to that tender place where I must have hit the steering wheel, cracking bone and brain and a week of memories into fragments, like a shattered pane of winter ice on a moorland dew pond.

Deep breaths. Deep, long breaths.

Focus on the positive, that's what the doctor said. Be

thankful every day. Makes the healing quicker. Mends the mind faster.

I like my job, working in the National Park tourist office. It's not the archaeological job I wanted when I graduated from Exeter University. It's not my dream, and it doesn't pay well, but I get to write the leaflets, to talk about history, to enthuse to day trippers, and the park authorities let me join the digs in the season, slicing into the turf to find Bronze Age barrows or buried kistvaens – sunken chests – of Neolithic skulls and femurs and backbones, the remains of people who lived here when the moors were warmer, and drier. Kinder.

Better than all that: I love this rented granite house we live in, five miles south of Princetown, lost in the high moorland, a mile from the next inhabited building, the Spaldings' farm, and two miles from the nearest hamlet, with its pub and tiny shop that sells processed ham and charcoal briquettes, and little else.

I love the wild remoteness, the deep starry skies and deeper silence. I love the dreaming, arthritic, moss-hung rowan trees that line the lanes. I like that the moorfolk call them 'quickbeams', or 'witchbeams'. I also love the battered, stubborn, obstinate history of it all. Huckerby used to be a proper farmstead, and it still has barns and outhouses crumbling in the Dartmoor rains, sprouting cornflowers and campions in the haze of high summer, but the only intact building is the one we live in, a classic moorland longhouse, possibly six hundred years old.

Once there would have been a sizeable family here: humans at the top of the house, animals down the other end. Cattle warming people under the same Devonshire thatch. Now the house is converted, the roof slated, and the interior modernized. Yes, it's hard to heat and it still gets damp. But it has character. And it is occupied by me, and Adam, and Lyla our daughter, and our two dogs Felix and Randal.

I named the dogs from a poem by Gerard Manley Hopkins. I love poetry, too: I write it occasionally, and never show it to anyone. I hide it away, as shyly as my daughter hides her secrets. I would have liked to be a poet, the way I would have liked to be an archaeologist. But that's OK: because I am happy, I think, and certainly happy to be alive, and I live in a house I love in a place I love with a man I love and two dogs I love and, best of all, with a daughter I wholly adore.

Lyla Redway. The girl who likes to arrange dead birds in rows and curves.

Lyla Redway. The nine-year-old girl out there in the farmyard wearing a blue beanie hat and a thick black anorak, playing on her own as she always plays on her own – or with Felix and Randal, who she probably prefers to any human beings.

I don't mind this. She's a different sort of girl: she is herself, her vulnerable, eccentric, funny, kind, lovable self. How many kids would spend a cold frosty morning in January arranging dead birds?

Sometimes she orders stones, or twigs, or bright blood-red berries. Other times Adam comes home with presents he has found on the tors, things he knows she will like – miniature pink snail shells and delicate bird bones and bleached-white adder skulls – and she arranges these faintly macabre moorland treasures into complex patterns: mandalas, hexagons and zodiacs, intricate visual symbols only she understands, imposing a poetic order on her lonely moorland world. Where she reigns supreme.

And sometimes she does nothing. She stands for hours, listening to an unheard music, seeing things invisible to others, or remembering incidents from her very early childhood. I've read that these strange traits, the acute hearing, and that remarkable memory, are all part of her condition, almost proof of her condition. But we refuse to have her diagnosed, or examined, despite the obvious signs.

Adam doesn't want to label her, doesn't want to put her in a box, and I tend to agree. We don't want to set limits on her, because she seems happy, despite her isolation, her solitude.

Though maybe less happy today?

Lyla is staring down at the birds. And standing absolutely still. This is common for her: she seems to have no middle ground of normal movement. Either she is silent and frozen, as now, or she is dancing and twirling, skipping up the moorland tors, as if she has energy she cannot endure, waving her hands, nodding and rocking, and talking talking talking, chattering like the River Dart under Postbridge, nattering away to herself, a babble of information stored in her brain from all the books she reads.

Hyperlexia, they call it. Another symptom. Reading too much.

How can that be a thing? Reading too much? I let her read as much as she likes. Entire books in a day, thousands of words every hour. Filling up her hungry soul. Because this is, I hope, my gift to her.

She has inherited her father's beauty, the nearly-black hair, the piercing eyes, but she has my love for words. One day she might be the poet I never was. She might have the scholarly life I wanted. And I'm glad she got her looks from her dad rather than me. My looks have always disappointed: brown hair, brown eyes, average height, average face, nothing special to look at, just me, Kath, the woman married to Adam Redway, with the quirky daughter, does something for the National Park, lives way out in the middle of nowhere, over near Hexworthy.

Nearly dying in that reservoir is probably the one exceptional thing to have happened to me, the only thing likely to get me noticed.

Except, I don't want to be noticed.

Opening the kitchen window to the cold morning air, I call out: 'Hey, sweetie, are you OK? Sure you're warm enough?'

Lyla does not move. She is still frowning at the dead birds, some of them arranged in lines like the rows of Bronze Age ritual stones out on the moors.

'Darling,' I repeat, but not impatiently: I am used to having to press things with Lyla, to repeat twice or three times when she is in one of her more obsessive moods. 'Lyla-berry, I want to check you're not cold, it's freezing out there. Where are the dogs?'

Still no answer. I might have to go outside and literally turn her face to meet mine, to make her realize I am talking to her, that I am interacting, that a person needs a response.

Opening the front door, I walk towards my daughter, my arms crossed against the chilly breeze. 'It's interesting that they're all dead, isn't it, Mummy?'

Her eyes are bright like her father's under the blue beanie.

'Sorry, darling?'

'All the birds, so many of them, all of them are dead. I checked. So many, there must be twenty of them.'

'Probably the cold, Lyla. It's a bitter winter, worse than usual.' I place an arm around her slender shoulders.

'Hm.' She shrugs absentmindedly, stares at the birds.

I follow her gaze, examining the pitiful little corpses. They're definitely frozen: beaks rimed with white frost.

I don't know what species they are. I can see a thrush, I think, and a robin. Lyla surely knows: she can identify every bird and every mammal, and most of the moorland flowers.

'Well I thought it was sad, Mummy, sad that they were all dead, so I put them in a special pattern so they could all have a funeral together, and not be lonely.' She stoops and rearranges two of the birds, delicately realigning them. It unsettles me to see her so careful, so precise. She makes such lovely patterns, but these are dead birds. Where did she get them from?

'All right, that's good, that's good. Do you want some lunch?'

'Wait. Wait, Mummy. Nearly finished.'

This elaborate game is spooking me. Dead birds arranged in a pattern I cannot quite grasp. All those glassy little bird-eyes, a trail of twinned black buttons across the frigid mud.

Lyla turns one frozen blackbird this way, and then that way.

'Lyla! Please. Enough now.'

Straightening up, she flashes me a smile. 'Don't you want me to spend the day arranging dead birds? Are you saying this is inappropriate behaviour?'

I am lost for words. Until I realize my daughter is joking, teasing me about my anxieties. Lyla can exhibit startling flashes of adult humour, insightful, surreal, and self-aware. It's one of the reasons we've resisted that diagnosis.

'No, I think it's perfectly fine to arrange loads of creepy dead birds in rows and circles.' I laugh, and hug her again. 'What kind of birds are they, anyway? And what is the pattern, is it a face?'

But now her head is turned, looking down the farm

track, past the conifer plantation, past Hobajob's Wood, as if she can hear something. In the far distance. I've known her to hear cars minutes before they arrive, long before anyone else.

'Lyla?'

What can she hear? A raven makes a cronking sound overhead as it wheels across the dull grey sky. Yet her focus seems to be on something else, further away. What is she sensing, coming towards us, down from the tors? The memories hurt. My head stings with pain.

'Lyla.'

No reply.

'Lyla, what is it, what can you hear?'

'The usual man, Mummy, the man on the moor. That's all.' Her words are a ghostly vapour in the cold. Her anorak is unzipped and I see she is wearing only a T-shirt underneath. She should be freezing, and yet she never seems to suffer from the cold: she likes the fierce Dartmoor winters, same as her dad. They both relish the cold. The snow. The icicles that hang from the splintered granite. 'You know, Mummy, that if you see a lot of crows they are rooks, but a rook by itself is a crow. Did you know that?'

I reach for her once more. 'Lyla.'

She squirms away from my touch. 'Don't touch me, Mummy. Leave me be.'

She is snarling. Lyla does this when she is angry or alarmed or overstimulated, she snarls, grimaces, and waves her hands. She does this at school as well: she can't help it, but it means other children laugh at her, or are scared by her. Isolating her further. She has so few friends. She probably has no real friends.

'Lyla. Stop this.'

'Go away, grrr . . .'

'Please—'

'YARK!'

There's nothing I can do. I step away, watching my daughter as she goes running to the farmyard gate, calling for the real dogs: I can hear them yapping, see our two big mongrel lurchers galloping after her.

She could be gone for another two hours now, half a day even, running across the fields, romping through Hobajob's, hunting for that Saxon cross lost in the nettles by the brook, with Felix and Randal on each side. Adam supposedly bought the dogs for Lyla, but he loves them as much as she does. They hunt, like proper dogs. They bring back dead rabbits, necks lolling, blood dripping from their muzzles. He likes to skin these hot, reeking corpses in front of Lyla, teaching her authentic Dartmoor ways, tossing gobbets of raw meat to the hungry dogs. *Eat them up, you eat them all up.*

Lyla is far away in the distance.

What can I do?

Let them play, I think, let them go. Lyla is clearly still upset about my accident. We've tried to talk to her about it, as gently as possible, I've told her I hit some ice and veered into deep water. We've spared her too many details but she will surely have heard stuff from kids at school, in the papers, on the net. We've also told Lyla that my memories are hazy but that they will return. Retrograde amnesia. Common after car accidents, caused by the brain ricocheting inside the skull.

Back in the kitchen I wash the coffee mug in the sink and gaze out of the window. In the distance I hear barking, getting nearer, louder. Then they come bursting through the door, the dogs happy, big and growling. Lyla lingers in the doorway, oblivious, it seems, to the bitter wind at her back.

'Daddy is on the moor again.'

'What?'

She gives me one of her blank, impenetrable smiles. 'He's out there again like he's watching us, Mummy. That's Daddy's job, isn't it?'

'Yes,' I say. 'He's a park ranger. He has to patrol everywhere, looking out for people.'

Lyla nods and shrugs, and pursues the dogs into the living room. I stare after her, wondering how she saw her father. He's meant to be working in his normal patch, way past Postbridge. What is he doing down here? Maybe Lyla is just confused or upset. And I can't blame her for this dislocation, this bewilderment.

Because her mother nearly died. Leaving her alone, forever.

Princetown

Monday morning

My daughter is silent, my husband is grimly silent, but the car is making that horrible grinding sound as Adam changes gear. I don't care. I'm happy. The winter sky over Princetown is sharp, unmarred, and today I get my freedom back.

I'm buying a car for myself, to replace the one still sitting at the bottom of Burrator Reservoir. This is the most intense relief. Living in Dartmoor – especially somewhere as remote as Huckerby Farm – is almost impossible without transport of your own. There are barely any buses; the railway lines were ripped away in the 1960s, and in winter on the lonelier roads you might not see a car from one cold morning to the next, so you couldn't even hitch-hike.

During these weeks of recovery since my accident, Adam has been driving me around in his knackered old National Park Land Rover, ferrying me to work, helping me do the shopping, and it's been a source of friction. Adam can be taciturn at the best of times but when he's had to take me all the way to the Aldi supermarket in Tavistock I've sensed a certain repressed seething.

But today I'm buying myself a secondhand Ford, from a cousin of Adam's. We bundled together some cash from God knows where, as Adam argues with the insurance people. Adam does everything to do with cars and engines and plumbing and stoves; and I like the masculine way he handles all that.

Turning in the passenger seat I look at Lyla, in her grey-and-white school uniform. She is staring out at the dull housing of Princetown outskirts.

'Hey, sweetpea. From now on I'll be able to take you to school again, isn't that good?'

She says nothing. Her face is averted. She is gently tapping the window with her fingernails. I don't know why she does this. Perhaps it's another sound she likes. She calls them *tinkly-tankly* sounds. Crackling, jingling, light metallic sounds, things like the silvery rattle of coins, or keys.

My daughter once told me, when we stood in the summer hayfields over Buckfast, how she loved the sound of butterflies.

There are also sounds that she hates. City sounds. Traffic. Sirens. The jostle of people in crowds. It's one of the reasons we moved to the remoteness of Huckerby.

'Lyla?'

She turns, her blue eyes wide. Distant. 'Mmm?'

'Did you hear what I said?'

A shake of her head. She offers me a reserved frown: as if I've done something wrong, but she is too polite to say. I feel a pang of pity. She is a nine-year-old girl with troubles and issues and dreams, and laughter I sometimes do not quite hear; she's a girl who has personal names for flies and rocks and frogs, who collects wild lilies and

14

trembling violets from Nine Maidens and Seven Lords' Land and presses them in books. My girl, my only girl. The idea that I could have died and left her behind fills me with a terrifying sadness, that threatens to make me cry, but I fight back the emotion.

I've been getting these sudden spates of sadness, or anger, ever since the accident, but I do think that I am getting the hang of them. Coping. And today I am definitely happy. Or happier. Determined to be positive: yes, it's winter but winter is the womb of spring.

The car grumbles.

'Darling, I said today Mummy is getting a car, so that'll make everything easier, and Daddy won't have to do all the driving.' I turn to him, 'Which will be a relief, won't it, Adam? I know you're bored of carting me around.'

Adam nods, wordless, in the driver seat, and takes the left turn on to Princetown's main road where it descends, literally and aesthetically, from Georgian coaching inns and the glossy new National Park offices, to the grim black outline of the prison, which broods and menaces even in sharp sun.

'Here we go.' Adam yanks the brake hard as he parks outside the school. He turns around, ignoring me, and addresses Lyla. 'All right, Tate and Lyle. Give us a kiss, before you go.' Lyla sits there, inert.

Adam tries again. 'Come on, sweetheart, big kiss for Daddy.'

She shakes her head, and grimaces. This is unlike her. She and Adam are close; sometimes I envy their relationship, exploring the moor together, watching the birds of prey riding summer thermals over Blackslade.

Abruptly, she opens the door. Her hands clutch her *Jungle Book* lunchbox and school bag tight to her chest.

'I'm going now,' she says, without looking at me or at Adam, as if she is announcing this to the world, not to us.

'It's OK, darling, off you go. We'll have a special tea this evening. Those fishcakes you like.'

She nods, blank-faced. Not really looking at us. Then she turns, and walks towards the grey school gates.

Adam puts his hand on the ignition key, ready to move off. But I put a hand on his. 'No, wait. I want to watch.'

'Watch what?'

'You know. How it goes.'

He sighs. 'You always do this.' But he takes his hand off the key and the two of us watch Lyla entering the school gates.

For a second she hesitates.

I've seen this scenario before, so many times. She is trying to be normal. Getting ready to interact as best she can. Perhaps she is slowly improving? In the car, we are helpless observers.

There are lots of kids in the schoolyard, excited by the first day of the week. They are playing and scrapping, boys and girls, dark and blond; they are laughing, chasing, greeting each other: swapping stories and jokes.

Into the middle of them all walks Lyla. Solitary, unnoticed. She pauses and looks around, her pretty face pale and unsure. I know she wants to join in, but she is too shy, too socially awkward to begin a conversation.

And she doesn't understand random play.

So she looks up and down, fiddling persistently with a button on her cardigan. I guess she's hoping someone will simply come up to her, start something off. But the kids run right past her, ignoring her entirely.

'Christ,' Adam says, quietly.

Lyla makes a big effort: she walks back to the gate and looks directly and hopefully at some taller girl who is late arriving. I think I know this new girl. Becky Greenall. Popular, good at games, socially confident; everything Lyla isn't. My pity and anxiety surge. *Don't do the smile,* I think to myself, *please don't do that smile.* Lyla walks closer to Becky and of course she does the smile, that strange rictus grin, that special silent monkey shout that Lyla thinks looks like a smile, but isn't. She gives Becky a thumbs-up.

It makes her look utterly mad.

Becky Greenall stares at Lyla, and she puts a hand to her mouth, trying not to laugh, or sneer.

Lyla tries once more. She does a little jump, up and down, waving her hands like a bird.

I'm her mother, but I have no idea what she is trying to do – be a kestrel?

Becky is now openly laughing, she can't help it; then she turns a sudden shoulder and casually blanks my daughter and shouts to some other girls who wave back. Together, these girls head laughingly for the school door. The day has begun. The whole class has sprinted inside.

Except for Lyla, who is the only one left behind in the schoolyard.

Alone and silent, she watches all the other kids disappear into the school. Only the slump in her shoulders betrays her emotions. The loneliness.

I desperately want to run out of the car and give her the biggest ever hug, to make it all better, but I can't, there's no use: she would push me away. Instead she walks slowly towards the school; and now she too is gone, in through the doors.

'Jesus,' says Adam. 'Jesus Christ.'

I know exactly what he means. Sadness is deep in me,

and for this I have no coping mechanism. I can recover from a car crash, my brain can heal, but there is no convalescing for Lyla.

We are silent. Adam starts the car, turns it and retraces 300 yards, towards the National Park office. He turns off the engine, as if he is prepared to talk. But before he can speak, I say, 'We have to do something. This can't go on. It's worse than last year.'

Adam stares ahead. 'But she laughs at home. She loves the moors. And she loves the dogs. So she's isolated at school, so what? She's a loner. It happens.'

I can see the pain on his face; I know Adam lives for Lyla. Would kill to protect her. He wants only what's right for her. And I usually listen to him, I want to believe. But I think about Lyla and her wariness in the car, and that lonely walk into school, that humiliation in the yard. I imagine her now, sitting on her own in the classroom, not talking to anyone. I picture her during breaks: sitting by the wall in the playground; a strange, eccentric girl with a weird smile, who mutters to herself about ants and newts while her classmates all talk to each other about selfies and music.

I can't pretend any more.

'No, Adam. We can't go on thinking this is acceptable, that she's just quirky, it's not right.'

The muscles in his jaw are flexing: he's grinding his teeth. 'So what are you saying?'

'We have to be proactive, do *something*. Take action. Because I *don't* think she's happy, not really. The other day I found her arranging dead birds in a pattern. She's never done that before. All those dead little birds. Why?'

Adam stares ahead. He is in his Ranger uniform: green fleece, green trousers, hiking boots. On most men it might be unflattering but Adam makes it look good. Masculine.

I think of the sex we haven't had in a while. I want it again, I want him to turn and kiss me, sometimes he still does that, he'll suddenly kiss me, passionately – across a car, while we're walking the moors – and I love it. But his fierce blue eyes are fixed on the far horizon, as if he is looking beyond horrible Princetown.

I can sense the violent yearning in him. He doesn't want me: he wants to be out there, alone on the uplands. Striding the heights of the northern moors: standing on Great Kneeset, gazing at High Willhays, Black Tor, Hangingstone Hill, Cut Hill, Fur Tor, Great Mis Tor, the places he loves, the places he has known since he was a boy. A child of the moors, like his daughter. Unlike me.

'Look at those bloody houses,' he says.

'Sorry?'

He tilts his head at a row of grey drab council housing: accommodation for the wardens in the prison.

'My dad built some of those, when he was a brickie. Imagine that. Imagine if that was your life's work? Building the ugliest fucking houses in Britain. No wonder he turned to vodka.'

His laughter is sour. Adam doesn't get on with his father, who fought and drank and womanized, scattering children from Exeter to Okehampton. Adam loves his uncle much better, Eddie Redway, a tenant farmer near Chagford. That's where Adam did his real growing up, on Uncle Eddie's smallholding, escaping the boozy arguments at home. That quaint little farm was where Adam came to know and love the moor, with his tearaway cousins, scrumping apples at Luscombe, fishing for little trout in the Teign.

The Redways have been a moorland family for countless generations. They've been tenant farmers and quarry workers and turf cutters since there was a church at

19

Sheepstor; they have shaggy cattle in the blood, and buzzards on the brain.

And I am glad my daughter inherits this ancestry. She can claim Dartmoor as I can't. But today this ancestry is irrelevant: right now, my daughter needs some modern therapeutic help, and Adam and I need to talk about that help.

'Adam, please. I really think it's time now, time we went to a doctor. Get her properly statemented? If it really is Asperger's—'

'I'm not putting a bloody label on her. Told you.'

'But I've been researching, talking to people, going online. They say that if you get diagnosed earlier it's better, the earlier the intervention the better the outcome, because you can get real help, therapy for social skills.'

He shakes his head. 'I'm not hanging a sign around her neck. *Look. Here's Lyla Redway. She's hopeless. Take pity.* Hell with that.'

I raise my voice. 'Asperger's kids aren't hopeless! You can't say that. It's a spectrum, we're all on it somewhere, she's just further down that spectrum, where you might need some help, and she's definitely getting stranger – the birds, it was too eerie. Adam! Listen to me, please. She's getting worse.'

Adam straightens his arms and lays his big hands hard on the steering wheel, as if he wants to race away. 'And why do you think that is, Kath? Eh?'

'Sorry?'

His face is turned towards me now: the blue eyes burning. 'Why the hell do you think she might be getting *worse*?'

I flounder. Thrown by this outright hostility. 'Sorry? What? Are you actually blaming me? Somehow it's my fault? It's *my* fault she's getting *worse*?' I have my own anger, now. 'For God's sake, it was an *accident*! It's not anyone's fault. I skidded on some ice.' I search his face for sympathy. 'I don't understand, Adam – you and Lyla – you should be happy I'm alive: I nearly died. I'm alive! And anyway: this is about our daughter, not me. We have to think about *her*.'

'That's all I do think about,' he says, in a low, dark voice. 'And now I have to go to work. Earn some money. For Lyla.' Without another word, he leans across and opens my door, inviting me to step outside.

His stubbled jaw is set, his frown is sombre. He won't be swayed. He is looking at me the way Lyla looked at him. Wary. Distant. Guarded. It feels like our once-contented family is falling into mutual suspicion. And I have no idea why.

'OK, Adam, OK, but I won't let it go. Not this time.'

Climbing out of the car, my bag over my shoulder, I watch him drive away, gears grinding. As I turn towards the Park offices I can sense the great prison, looming behind me.

You can always sense the prison, in Princetown.

Monday afternoon

Two p.m.? I stare at the clock on the wall of the cream-painted National Park offices with a sense of unhappy surprise.

Where did the day go?

I'm used to losing track of working hours if the work is compelling. If I am, say, writing new brochures about the history or archaeology of the park, describing the wistful stone circle of Buttern Hill, the cottage at Birchy Lake where the old witches lived with a dozen black cats, the famous grave of Kitty Jay who killed herself for love, after falling pregnant by some wicked toff – that grave on which people still poignantly lay flowers – when I am immersed in writing these wonderful stories, I can happily misplace an entire afternoon.

The same goes for a busy summer day at one of the visitor centres, in Haytor, or Postbridge, when we can't move for hearty German caravanners and determined French hikers – all looking for maps, loos, Wi-Fi signals – then the hours can fly past.

But it's the depths of winter. No one comes to the moor in January. Half the National Park staff take long holidays around this time, as there is little to achieve – except what I'm doing now. Tweaking, twiddling. Revising the Park's official leaflets and websites. Updating the policy on dogs in National Park tea-rooms. It's deathly boring. The sort of stuff that would normally make the minutes drag by.

And yet I've got myself lost in the assignment.

'What's up, Kath? Having too much fun?'

It's my boss, Andy, he must have heard me sigh. He's a nice guy, blond, younger than me, newish. Been here two years. I sometimes wonder if I should resent him, that I didn't get the promotion. But I don't. I like my more varied employment. Usually.

'Sorry, Andy. Was I sighing a bit loudly?'

'You could say that.'

'Well, I'm updating the rules on campervans in car parks, out of season. Perhaps I'm overexcited?'

I hear him chuckle. He's the only other person in the large, open-plan office today. He is framed by the windows, where the Princetown sky is now as dark and sombre as Dartmoor granite. The winter sun can be so painfully brief.

'You should pity *me*, Kath. I'm doing Section 211 on Tree Preservation Orders, it's practically better than sex.' He clicks something on his computer. 'Jesus, I hate January. What we really need is a massive accident to liven things up. Like, a bus could drive into a lake, up at Meldon, that would help.' He stops, and turns my way. 'Hey, sorry, ah, Kath, I—'

'No. It's OK. I want people to forget, Andy, I'm bored of being The Woman That Had That Accident.' He listens as I go on: 'In fact I want to go back to regular work

23

soon, working proper shifts, doing my job as before, I mean: it's nice you're giving me half days, letting me work from home, but I'm OK now. Can we get back to *normal*?'

'Abso-bloody-lutely. If you really feel you're up to it, that's great. We'll put you back on normal shifts in a few weeks.'

He returns to his work. I gaze at him as he concentrates.

Why won't he let me do proper shifts now? Sometimes it feels as if *everyone* is tip-toeing fastidiously around me, scared I might break. They're not treating me like someone recuperating, they're treating me like something odd. Unusually fragile.

Returning to my work, I scan the words on my own computer. The official Dartmoor Tourism website.

Dartmoor constitutes the largest area of granite in Britain, with about 360 square miles stretching across central Devon, making it the only true wilderness in Southern England. Much of it is covered by marshy peat deposits, in the form of bogs or mires. The moorland is also capped with many characteristic granite outcrops, known as tors (from the Celtic 'tor', meaning tower) that provide varied habitats for wildlife. The entire area is rich in archaeology, from the Neolithic to the Victorian . . .

I want to edit this, make it flow better, liven it up: but the words blur in my eyes. Sphagnum. Carboniferous. Wassailing . . .

I hate this new, enduring haze in my mind, I despise this peculiar sensation – since the crash – that my mind has become one of those vast cupboards in my mum's old kitchen, in the big Victorian house, down on the coast at Salcombe. Those cupboards were dusty and chaotic, and every week my hippy-chick, eco-sensitive mum would reach in and find some pot of organic mustard, or jar of Manuka honey, that she'd clean forgotten, and she'd say, *Gosh I didn't remember we had this*, and sometimes she'd have to throw it away, wasting more of the dwindling Kinnersley cash, and sometimes the jar would go back in, only to be forgotten and retrieved and thrown away all over again . . . and that's what my brain feels like, since the accident. I don't quite know what's in there, and when I put things in there they sometimes get lost, and when I find things in there they are often useless, past their sell-by date, actively unpleasant.

My brain is hiding things from me.

And now it's 3.15. So dark the office lights are on.

I try to relax. Perhaps I am being hard on myself. The stress about Lyla doesn't help, the tensions with Adam, too. Perhaps we all need more time. That's what the doctors repeated from the start: *Be patient, don't expect instant miracles. And remember*, they said: *remember that you are relatively lucky: because you will heal over time.* I was classified with Mild Traumatic Brain Injury, nothing worse; I was apparently unconscious for less than six hours; I was 13–15 on the Glasgow Coma Scale.

Any longer than that, and I'd have been upgraded and they would have taken away my driving licence, for at least a year. At one point in my unconsciousness I was technically dead, flatlining for a minute or so, but the machines flickered into life and I got through. So I was 'Mild'.

MTBI.

As for my retrograde amnesia, the stuff I've forgotten from before the accident, that is expected to recede over the coming weeks, and the misplaced memories will return like 'hills emerging after a flood' as one of the psychologists put it, and eventually the whole landscape will be revealed as the obscuring waters drain away.

'Hey. Is that your new car?'

Startled from this introspection, I look up. Andy is gesturing out of the window: I can see Adam's cousin Harry, standing by a blue Ford Fiesta, parked right outside. The car is a bit battered and scratched, but that's fine, nearly every car on Dartmoor is a bit battered and scratched. And so am I.

Harry waves at me. He has the Redway looks: a handsome young man. They all have these looks, the Redway cousins. The eyes and the cheekbones, they are so distinct. Harry does odd jobs all over the moor, when he's not making a few quid from car dealing. He is a bit of a lad.

But he's also very likeable. He reminds me of a younger Adam. But then Adam, in the right mood, reminds me of a younger Adam. I think I desire my husband as much today as the afternoon I first met him.

Andy says, 'You must be chuffed to get wheels again, don't know how you've been coping without a car.' He flashes me a smile. 'Go on, Kath, go for it – I'll see you tomorrow.'

My kindly boss is making my shortened working day even shorter. I can get my new car, collect Lyla from school, go home to Huckerby, and everything will be fine. My brain will be fine. Lyla will be fine.

'Thanks,' I say, 'You're a superstar,' and I grab my raincoat, and step out into the wintry afternoon. The cold has abated, which means it is probably about to

26

rain. Harry and I sign the documents and he hands me the keys and he says, 'It's not a Ferrari, but it'll give you a couple of years.'

And I offer my thanks as I climb in. And when he strolls off to a pub, I sit here in the driver's seat, holding the cold, hard keys in my hand, suddenly scared that I have forgotten how to drive. I haven't done it since the crash into the reservoir. Since the dark waters tried to turn me into moorland mud.

Key. You put the key in the ignition. You turn it. Then the engine starts. Remember? Come on, Kath Redway: you've done this a million times. You got your licence at nineteen. You've done this virtually every day for eighteen years. It's called driving.

I turn the key. I press my foot down. I steer away. I do not crash into the saloon bar of the Plume of Feathers, I do not smash into the leaded windows, crushing off-duty prison wardens in a clatter of stained wood and beer-bottles. I am driving.

From the anxiety of the afternoon, I feel a kind of elation. *I CAN DRIVE.* It's another sudden mood swing. I get more of them now. Since the accident.

Happy, even giddy, I collect Lyla from school. She looks a little bemused: she thought she was going to After School Club, to be alone in a whole new place, but she also looks content to be going home early, where people will talk to her, where she can play with the dogs in front of the fire.

Or make cryptic patterns with dead birds.

I CAN DRIVE!

But as we aim for the turning that leads to the open moor, to the wild emptiness, I realize I have left my bag in the office. I was so excited by the car, I quite forgot.

Hastily, I park, once again, outside the Dartmoor NP

Office. The day is wintry and dimming, a faint drizzle speckles the windscreen.

Lyla pipes up as I swing open the door, 'Where are you going?'

'Nowhere, darling. Just the office. Forgot my bag.'

'No! Don't go!'

'Lyla?'

I turn, surprised, a little shocked. Lyla is trembling in the back seat.

'Mummy, don't go. Don't.'

This is strange. Lyla worries about odd things, shapes, sounds, or the wrong kind of prickly vest, but she rarely worries about being left alone.

'Darling—'

'No. Mummy! You might not come back! You might not come back!'

'Lyla, this is ridiculous. I'll only be gone a second, really, I promise.' I put out a hand to calm her but she waves it away. She does, however, seem a little soothed. She turns and gazes at the wrinkles of rain on the window, the black shape of the prison.

I seize the opportunity. Scooting out of the door, I run into the office, past my surprised boss. 'Forgot my bag!'

He grins. 'Ah.'

Grabbing the handbag, I head back to the car, but as I do I notice something on Andy's desk. It's a row of roundish grey stones, about the size of large golf balls, or wild apples. They might have been there all day.

They're half hidden by his computer.

All the stones have holes in them. And I've seen this sort of stone before. I know the *type*. And it makes me quietly shudder.

'Hey,' I say, trying to hide the tremble in my voice. 'Where did you get those?'

He glances up at me, the blue light of his computer shining on his spectacles. 'These rocks? Ah.' He picks one up and turns it in the light. 'They were arranged along the window ledges this morning, outside, so I brought them in. Kinda odd, right? Guess some hiker made a collection? Left them here overnight.'

'No,' I say. 'I don't think so.'

His grin is edged with perplexity. 'Sorry?'

'These aren't any old stones.'

Leaning close, I pick up one of the bigger rocks. It is surprisingly heavy: probably it has some metal ore inside. The hole is naturally weathered, which is crucial to its identity. But of course, Andy wouldn't know the identity, the significance of these stones, because he doesn't know the folklore and the mythology of Dartmoor: because all that stuff is my job. I did the archaeology degree, I've read the folklore books, I write all the leaflets. 'These are hag stones.'

His grin is entirely gone. 'You what?'

'Hag stones.' I have a burning desire to throw the stone away. To take all of these stones and bury them far from here, in Cornwall, Ireland, America. I try to disguise my irrational fear. 'Moorland people used to put them on windowsills, or hang them from ropes over doors. You can still see them on Dartmoor farms, in really remote places. They're a kind of joke, but I suspect some people still believe.'

He looks at me, frowning. 'Hags? Old women?'

I turn the stone in my fingers, calming myself. 'They also called them hex stones. Because they were thought to be apotropaic.' I don't wait for his question. 'Apotropaic means they were used to ward off evil, to thwart black magic. People placed them by windows and doors to stop witches getting in.' Even as I replace the stone, very carefully, next to its sisters, I can't help glancing at my desk. 'Or . . . or to stop them from getting out. And somebody arranged these stones, in a line on our window ledge, overnight? That must have been deliberate.'

Andy stares at the stones. The rainy light outside is almost entirely gone. But I can see Lyla in the back of my new car. She is sitting up rigid, and gazing straight at me. Unblinking.

The Lych Way

Tuesday morning

Adam had been walking this path for ten minutes, deep in thought, before he realized he was on the Lych Way. The old corpse road, named for when the Dartmoor villagers were forced to carry the coffins of their dead to the official parish church, right across the moor at Lydford.

In the lee of a biting wind, beside a stand of dark pines, he paused, imagining the scene – a dozen ragged peasants hefting the wooden box from Bellever Tor, over the Cowsic brook, up and down the bleak, shaved hills, Lynch Tor, Baggator Clapper, the Cataloo Steps.

And when the river was running high at Cataloo, what did they do then? They must have waded waist-deep into the freezing water, holding the coffin over their heads, before heading up Corpse Lane to Willsworthy. All so they could deliver their dead to the decreed resting place.

Twelve miles they carried those corpses. Twelve bloody miles.

Walking on, Adam scanned the horizon, watching for

wildlife, seeking solace in the landscape. As he topped a rise, a kestrel caught his eye, hovering in the white winter sky. Instinctively, he stopped to admire the tremendous skill of the bird, that delicate trembling of the tips of its feathers, exquisite, masterful.

Windfuckers, his uncle used to call them, kestrels were *windfuckers*, because when they rode the wild air it looked as if they were fucking the wind – possessing it, owning the breeze, followed by that sudden climactic rush of a dive, a frightening swoop on some prey, then gone.

He paced on, still following the Lych Way, the old way of the dead, guessing that the cross should be along here somewhere, near the Iron Age settlements.

We saw a stone cross had been vandalized, on the road by Sittaford, that's what the hiker who called it in had said.

But it was difficult to focus on the job. His mood was darker than the pines. He was trying his hardest, but today he couldn't lose himself in Dartmoor. The human world pressed around him, the unfurling, uncontrollable emotions he felt for his wife, the sense of resentment he tried to hide for the sake of sanity, for the sake of his daughter. But how was he meant to hide this kind of emotion? What she'd done, and what she'd said, and what she had so conveniently forgotten. How was he meant to cope with that and pretend it didn't matter?

All he'd ever wanted was to live his life and love his family, and be happy in his job, tending the moors, repairing the hedges, helping the tourists, watching the buzzards above Sourton Down, and normally he was happy. They had all been so happy. Yet now his family was crumbling.

Approaching a stile, Adam paused, vaulted, and took

a deep cold breath, before striding on, the squared green conifer plantations falling far behind him. He was trying not to think of his family, trying not to surrender to despair, or to this growing dislike, whirled with guilt. Even as he loved and desired his wife, he felt a surging fury towards her.

Lyla. *What was all this doing to Lyla?*

He closed his eyes to steady his surging emotions, then looked across the landscape once more.

He could see the greener, emerald turf of a bog to his left, the faint sparkle of soggy acid grass, flashing in a break of winter sun. A memory returned: he was eight, or nine, with his Uncle Eddie, crouching to watch a snipe, right here, performing its nuptial display, the bird rising fast and steep in the air, then abruptly stooping and diving with its wings scarcely open, the tail delicately flared, making that strange noise. That sad, thrumming sound of the outspread tail feathers, vibrating in the dive. Once heard, never forgotten.

And on the way home from these days of learning about the birds and rocks and streams, his uncle would teach him the old moorland words:

Dimmity, meaning twilight. *Owl-light*, a darker kind of dusk. *Radjel*, a pile of rocks. *Spuddle*, to mess about. *Tiddytope*, a wren. *Gallitrop*, a fairy ring.

Appledrain, a wasp. How beautiful was that?

Moor-gallop: wind and rain moving across high ground. *Drix*: brittle wood. *Ammil*, a fine film of silvery ice that rimes the leaves and twigs and grass when a hard Dartmoor freeze follows a deceptive Dartmoor thaw, like an ice-storm, but more delicate. That was how precise the farmers had to be: they had to have words to describe the most beautiful and unusual states of frost and thaw and ice. Because lives depended on this precision: knowing when to gather the cattle, shelter the ponies, tend the struggling crops, nurse the suckling lambs.

Another, bigger, stile. Catching his breath before he clambered over, Adam stopped, and gazed to the horizon.

Every inch, every square mile. He'd seen it all so many times, and still he loved it. The grouse over Steeperton in the autumn, feeding on ling, and whortleberry. The glades of Deeper Marsh, with its alder buckthorns, where the yellow butterflies come to feast, heralding the late Dartmoor spring. The caves of Cuckoo Rock, where the smugglers once cached their brandy. And the great empty spaces of Langcombe, where he would tramp on a summer day: out there where you could imagine you were the only person in the world, with a featureless expanse of wafting grass and sedge all around you, mile after mile of nothing, no one to be seen, nothing to be done, the sun beating down, and all you could hear was the whirr and murmur of insects: that, and the silent moving clouds, and your own beating heart.

Those were probably his happiest moments; those, and when he was out with Lyla, teaching his little girl about the ravens and rock basins, the damselflies and purple orchids. She loved the moor as much as him. They spent endless sunny hours, walking the Abbot's way, down to Rundlestone, or looking for the old blowing house, by the King's Oven, or hunting for black-berries, up by Dunstone, and Shilstone, their lips and fingers purple, their teeth bright pink, and laughing – and then, at the sweet weary end of these days, they would drive home to Huckerby, and Kath would have passed by a supermarket, and they'd all sit and have tea, and a plate of fruitcake, and they were all happy. And Lyla would make clever patterns with the pretty petals she'd collected, arraying them on the kitchen table.

Beautiful, complex patterns that only she truly understood. Or patterns she made for Daddy.

They were once so very happy.

And now it was all different. Now Lyla was confused and scared and sad, and often she wouldn't let him – her own father! – hug her like he used to. These days Lyla sometimes gazed at him as if *he'd* done something wrong, all because of Kath, that Kinnersley family. All of them. And yet at other times – before bed, before sleep – Lyla sometimes hugged her dad so very close, so desperately close, it was like she was scared he too would disappear in the night – like her mother.

This was no good. Adam tried to drive the spiralling, dangerous thoughts from his mind. It was as if they were *all* being sucked into a Dartmoor mire: Dead Lake, Fox Tor, Honeypool: the more they struggled to get free, the deeper they sank into frustration, and anger. The best thing was to calm yourself. Not make it worse. Not to do anything rash.

Adam could see the old cross now. A metre high, with a weathered and lichened green-grey granite disc at the top. Probably Anglo-Celtic, probably a thousand years old or more. Someone had hit it pretty hard, knocking it over, probably some fool in an SUV, drunk or skunked, driving offroad and having a laugh. The disc of the cross was cracked and shattered; it had survived so many centuries and now it was grievously damaged, possibly irreparable. Something good had died.

Adam knelt beside the antique stone, stroked the cold granite as if it was the mane of an injured foal. Feeling the scratchy roughness of the lichen under his hands, feeling utterly helpless. Trying not to feel any more futile emotions. Trying to be practical.

Rubbing air between his raw fingers to keep out the

winter chill, he stood up and began the long walk back to his Land Rover, and as he did so he made his decision about the cross. No matter how difficult, they would try to repair it. Because that was his job: to preserve this precious place, from the antiquities to the landscape to the chittering fieldfares at Soussons. To preserve as much of it as possible, and hand it on to the next generation, to Lyla, to Lyla's children.

He would call the archaeology department at Exeter, get them to send an expert. Yes. It could be saved.

If only love were the same, he thought as he headed down the corpse road. If only love could be repaired, re-erected, restored. But once you smashed up loyalty, smashed up a loving family, that was it, wasn't it? And what if that love was replaced by suspicion, even contempt, what did *that* do to you? Where did that lead you? In what dark, dark wood did you wake up? Perhaps the path you took might lead you even deeper into darkness.

Adam had nearly reached the Land Rover. He could see another kestrel, hovering in the cold air, framed by the pale green heights of Hurston Ridge. The bird was so beautiful, so perfect, quivering, elemental, doing precisely what it came here to do. Trembling with intent, with a fierce and irresistible desire to kill; to survive.

What did Kath do that night, and all the nights he was away? The question was simultaneously unapproachable and unavoidable. If he got to the answer he might get the measure of her guilt – and their marriage would be over. If he didn't, he would seethe with speculative rage forever, and their marriage would be over.

And either way, Lyla ended up without a mother. So probably he should let it go; yet he could not. He loved her, he hated her, he loved her, he hated her. The confusion of emotion was like a wet moorland fire, making smoke rather than heat: it choked him. It killed his hopes, smothered things forever.

As he opened his car door, Adam remembered what his uncle used to say about the wilderness of Dartmoor, as they castrated the rams and dehorned the shrieking cows, as they took the frightened, lowing bullocks to the blood-slicked slaughterhouse, where the sheets of blood shone like a gorgeous lacquer, in luxurious swirls of scarlet and purple.

The moor is beautiful, lad, because it is dangerous.

Huckerby Farm

Wednesday morning

Today is another inset day. A training day for teachers at Princetown Primary, when the kids get a day off. These days come around every so often, and it means that one of us – Adam or me – has to clock off work, to look after Lyla, one-on-one. It's always intense, because Lyla has no proper friends; play-dates are out of the question.

But I still, usually, look forward to the chance to bond with her. To take her out on the moors, go for a summer swim, or autumn horseriding. But today is dank, and very chilly. It might even snow.

And my mind is elsewhere, and perhaps Lyla senses it. I am thinking about the hag stones left on the window ledge at my office. Could be it really was a hiker who set them down for a moment, and forgot. Could be it was kids having a laugh. But did they know the stones symbolized the driving away of witches? And why did they choose my office?

As I pensively clear the breakfast plates, my daughter

kicks the table leg. Kick kick kick. *Kick kick kick.* She
wants her mother's attention.

And she deserves it.

'What can we do, Mummy?'

'I don't know, darling, it's a horrid old day. Something
indoors? Like Castle Drogo?' *Kick.*

'It's nice there, Mummy, but they don't like dogs. Can
we please do something else?' She looks at me yearningly.
'With Felix and Randal?'

I struggle to think. Look at a good map or a detailed
guidebook and there are so many enticing places on
Dartmoor, so many places with fairytale names – the
Lost Crosses, Hameldown Daggar, Quintin's Man – but
today I am not enticed. Lyla needs to be entertained,
diverted, though. I don't want her spending the entire
day lonely, lost in books. Not again.

An idea forms.

'I know,' I say, with a studied brightness, 'Let's go
somewhere to see the standing stones you like.'

Her face brightens: she loves Dartmoor's ancient circles
and menhirs.

'Merrivale? Scorhill?'

'No,' I say, slightly mischievously. 'Somewhere you
haven't been before.'

She beams with delight. 'Where? Tell me!'

'Hah. No.'

'Tell me, Mummy!'

'Get ready, and I'll make a picnic and we'll go on a
mystery tour! Put your boots on, and a coat. Everything
else is fine.'

My daughter looks down at herself: she's wearing a
pair of black jeans, and a grey shirt, with a yellow pull-
over. She always mixes up colours wildly, I'm not sure
she understands how clothes go together, yet she usually

gets away with it, with her father's blue eyes, his pale, nearly Slavic cheekbones, and that dark, dark hair. That beauty. I remember the boy I saw in the pub when I was seventeen, the boy I have loved ever since, the blue-eyed boy who gave me this blue-eyed girl. Adam Redway, my childhood sweetheart.

'Do I really need boots? I hate wellies, they're scratchy.'

'Yes, you do. It will be wet in the bogs, and muddy. So go and get your things and I'll pack some sandwiches.'

'Peanut butter? So it's a Special Occasion!'

I laugh. Lyla laughs. Whenever we go on a jaunt we always take peanut butter sandwiches: the comic predictability is a family in-joke. Jumping up from her chair, Lyla runs out of the kitchen, shouting out to Felix and Randal, who are slumbering in the living room, 'Felix! Randy! Going on a walk! Big huge walk!'

I hear her scamper upstairs and the dogs canter after her, their claws skittering on the wooden steps.

Ten minutes later I've packed a hasty picnic in a bag, dropped the bag in the car boot, the dogs are jumping in the back seat, on either side of Lyla, and I have the key in the ignition. We're having a day away from Huckerby Farm. My intent is Grey Wethers, a pair of poetic stone circles on the far eastern edge of the moor. Merely getting there will be a high adventure. It will take up the whole day. A good day outdoors with the dogs, even if the cold and gloom persists.

As I reverse the car, Lyla says, from the back seat, 'You know . . . I saw a man.'

I trundle the car down the lane, towards what passes for a road in remoter Dartmoor. 'Sorry, darling?'

'I saw a man.'

The tension tightens inside me. I slow the car to hear my daughter better. 'When, darling, what man?'

I'm looking at her in the mirror, but her face is averted. She is tickling Felix behind his ear. For a long while she says nothing.

'Lyla?'

I drive at about five miles an hour through the squelch of a wintry Dartmoor day, over tiny medieval bridges never meant for cars.

At last she says, 'It was a man that you know. I saw him at Huckerby. Near Huckerby.'

Who can she mean? It seems important but I don't know why. She could be referring to anyone; she might be recalling a dream.

'When, Lyla-berry? And what did he look like?'

'Two or three times. I don't know, he was far away. He looked . . .' She squirms, 'He looked a bit like Daddy. A lot like Daddy. And I think he was there the night you went to . . .' Her voice is trembly. 'The night. That night. When you left me with Auntie Emma.'

This is Lyla's name for our neighbour, Emma Spalding. Emma was looking after Lyla when I was working late: the night I skidded into Burrator. Emma has been like an aunt, or like the grandmother Lyla never had, because Adam's mum died years ago, and both my parents are gone.

We drive on. The roads are a mess of mud and fallen leaves. What is Lyla saying? That she saw a friend of mine that night, and she's seen him since, near Huckerby? Or does she really mean Adam? It is impossible. My own husband is not following me. Could it be someone that looks like him, though? Harry? Or one of his many other cousins? The Redways are scattered across the moor.

But why would anyone follow me?

I slow the car down, my hands firm yet feeble on the wheel, gazing out of the window, trying to work it out.

42

The trees bend in a cold wind, tatters of grey moss fluttering. Birds hide among the leafless twigs. The only colour apart from dull grey and green is the shivering yellow of gorse flower.

In the mirror, Lyla's face is rigid. I know this mood, what it means: she doesn't want to speak. At its worst she can go into total and prolonged silence. Elective mutism. Another Asperger symptom. But I can't let it go. 'Lyla, this is very important. You say you saw someone I know.' She is mute.

We turn on to the main road to Widecombe and Fernworthy, the faster road. And almost immediately, I slow. Dartmoor ponies, their rich black manes rippling in the breeze, are standing on either side of the tarmac. In this pose they always strike me as guardians of the moor, essential spirits of the place. 'Lyla? Please?' Nothing.

'Lyla—'

'It was the day you left me.' Her blue eyes meet mine in the mirror, and they are piercing, 'The day you left me alone. You must remember that day, Mummy.'

Her face goes still again, still and quiet and pale. Even angry. And I know if I ask one more question she will not say another word for hours, or days. Or a week. Yet I am anxious to interrogate her further. What is she trying and failing to say? Is it something so unspeakable she cannot bring herself to say it clearly?

The words already spoken pain me quite enough. She seems to be *blaming* me for the accident. I want to tell her: *it wasn't my fault.*

Foot down on the brake, I bring the car to a total halt as another pony crosses the road. Heedless of our presence, living in a different world, the pony trots along the verge, then canters away – over the brown crest of a hill, its rich mane flowing like a dark flame on the wind.

The scene reminds me of my daughter: with her black hair streaming on a cold blustery day, running with the dogs, happy in herself. Alone with her thoughts and dreams, and as mysterious as the weather beyond Haytor.

Grey Wethers

Wednesday lunchtime

It's taken us an hour to walk here, through the serried pine plantations of Fernworthy, out on to the expanse of brown moorland.

'There,' I say.

'Where?'

I point to Grey Wethers, the two stone circles, barely visible in the distance, set on a slope, staring at the nothingness all around them. Grey Wethers is one of my favourite places on Dartmoor: there's something poetic about the silent, twinned nature of these circles, raised three thousand years ago by men who knew how to use a landscape, how to adorn it, respond to it, with simple rings of grey moorland rock.

Grey Wethers is as beautiful, to me, as a palace or a castle. The only reason I don't come here more often is that it requires a long and boring walk, first through regimented conifers, then hopping over quaggy ground, boots sinking into unsuspected pools of stagnant, cressy water, shins cracked on hidden moorland boulders.

'What do you think?' I say. 'It's kind of lovely, isn't it?'

I scrutinize her passive face for clues. Who did she see at Huckerby? If it is someone I know, that makes it even more bewildering. I barely have any friends – let alone male friends – who live nearby; my old university friends are mainly in London, or scattered around the world.

So she must mean a relative of mine. And I have so few contenders. My brother is down at Salcombe, in my mother's house. We like the distance between us; it prevents us squabbling. As for my father, he is long dead.

It keeps coming back to someone who looks like Adam, as Lyla said. The man on the moor. Or could it be Adam himself?

No, absurd.

In silence, we approach the nearest of the circles. The dogs are running ahead; for once Lyla is not interested in their romps and explorations.

Instead she frowns gently, puzzled, gazing first at the stones, then at the horizon, alert to something. Finally my daughter walks to the centre of the nearest stone circle. And sits down.

'Are you all right?'

She nods. I sit down beside her, cross-legged. The cold wind has dropped and a feeble hint of January sun pierces the cloud cover. The turf beneath us is quite dry. Apparently it hasn't rained here for weeks. Dartmoor weather is so strange. Adam says that on July days he can leave tourists sunbathing by a moorland river, then walk ten minutes up a tor – and be hit by driving snow; yet when he walks back, the kids in the valley are still swimming in the sunshine.

'Shall we have a sandwich?'

Lyla says a quiet *please*. I unbuckle my rucksack and take out the picnic box and for several minutes we eat our peanut butter sandwiches in companionable silence, listening to the whirr of the gentle wind in the sedge, and the trill of a cold moorland stream in the distance. I can also hear the dogs, barking happily over the next shallow hillside, hunting out rabbits, or hares. Or digging up old human bones from Stone Age cairns. Kistvaens. Those chests containing ancient skeletons, where the bodies were cruelly bent to fit them in: knees pressed to chin, as if the burial was a torture in itself. Perhaps they buried some alive. No one is quite sure.

Setting down her sandwich, Lyla says, 'I'm sorry for what I said about the man. I don't think I saw anyone. Sorry, Mummy. I get scared?'

'Ah . . . OK.'

Confusion settles upon confusion. I begin to fear that one day I may wake up, trapped, snowbound by all this strangeness. But Lyla is still traumatized by her mother nearly dying; confusion would be understandable. Expected.

Taking another bite of bread and peanut butter, she chews diligently, and says, 'I like it here. I like the silence and the forests over there, so far away. I always like the stone circles.'

'That's good.'

'I like Scorhill and Totterton and Sourton and Buttern Hill and Mardon, all of them, but they're not the best ones. Do you know my favourite?'

'No . . . ' I am wrapping the sandwich foil into a ball, putting it back in the box. 'But tell me.'

'Merrivale!' she says, smiling brightly.

I smile in return. We've been to Merrivale several times: it's definitely one of her cherished places on the moor.

47

Merrivale, with its stone rows and burial cairns, arrayed along a bald and windswept crest of moorland.

'Why do you like Merrivale?'

'Because they called it Plague Market! I read that was its name. Do you know why it was given that name? I had to look it up.'

'No.'

Her eyes turn to meet mine, unblinking. 'During the Black Death, the moorland people would leave food in the stone circle. And later the coastal people, all the people who had the plague already, they would come and take the food, and leave gold and silver as a payment, in a trough full of vinegar, then they would go away. And that's how they tried to stop it, stop the Black Death spreading.' She blinks, once, and goes on. 'Isn't that amazing? A special plague market, on the moor, between the stones, where no one had to meet, so no one saw anyone else, like they were all ghosts. And all that gold and silver in the vinegar.' Lyla frowns, toying with a blade of grass, 'But . . . but it didn't work, that's what I read. The Black Death spread anyway, right across the moor. So all the people died. Even when you leave gold in vinegar, Mummy, it doesn't work. Everyone dies.'

The anxious, fluttering wind carries the scent of newly chopped pine from the forest. I'm not sure whether to be disturbed by my daughter's monologue, one of Lyla's Aspergery lectures, or happy that she is, at least, communicating.

'Have you finished with your drink?'

Lyla says yes and hands me her finished carton of apple juice.

'Thanks for bringing me here.'

'Hey. It's nice for me too, Lyla. I love these circles, like you.'

48

She nods, but she also shakes her head.

'What is it?' I ask.

'You're wrong though, Mummy. Wrong.'

'Why? Wrong in what way?'

'You said I'd never been here before. But I *have* been here before. Here to Grey Wethers. I remember it.' As she speaks, she repeatedly brushes non-existent sandwich crumbs from her jeans. *Brush brush brush.* 'I've been here before, with you and Daddy.'

I reply, very gently, 'No, darling, you haven't been here, not with me, perhaps you came here with Daddy, or Uncle Dan, but not me.'

Lyla shakes her head. Stops brushing. 'I *have* been here. You've forgotten.'

'No, darling, I—'

And now I remember. I murmur, out loud: 'Oh, yes, my God.' She's right. Lyla *has* been here before. In fact she was here the very first time I came here. Adam brought me to see the Grey Wethers and I was carrying Lyla on my back, in a harness, because she was *nine months old.*

For a moment I am speechless.

I know that my daughter, like quite a few people on her part of the spectrum, has this ability to recollect way back beyond normal human memory, but it always surprises me. And delights me. My daughter has issues; but she also has gifts. And this is one of these gifts, however unsettling.

Lyla gets to her feet. Picnic time is over. We begin the walk back to the car.

'So you had a nice time?'

'Yes, Mummy, yes, thanks. Look, here's Felix and Randal, can we give them the last of the peanut butter sandwiches?'

The dogs are galloping over the windswept brown turf. Lyla takes the picnic box from my rucksack, unwraps the foil, and hands out the crusts. The dogs eat as if they haven't been fed since they were pups. I'm sure they'd prefer fresh meat, but they would probably eat dust and pebbles from Lyla's hand: their adoration of her is total.

Our long, chilly walk back to the car is quiet, the journey to Huckerby is quiet, everything is quiet, until we are a mile from home and Lyla asks if we can go to Hobajob's Wood. It's another one of her favourite places: she finds rare flowers there – eyebright, fritillary – and the iridescent shells of nameless blue beetles. Flowers and insects and little weathered claws.

I glance at the wintry sky, 'It's getting really dark, sweetheart. We need to get home.'

'Oh please, Mummy. We're so close.'

'Hmm.'

The day has been good. One of our best since my accident. I experience a surge of maternal happiness. Why not indulge her? 'All right, but only for a few minutes. It'll be night in half an hour.' Parking the car in the lay-by, we begin the cold walk along the cold valley to the cold and dense little wood with its twisted, moss-hung oak trees, clawing at the blank winter sky. Hobajob's Wood is like a smaller version of famous Wistman's Wood. Not quite as atmospheric, but not as touristy, either. Hidden away.

Our secret.

The dogs run ahead, leaping over boulders. They know the route well, it looks as if they are keenly following the scent of a badger or a fox. I pat my pockets, wishing I had brought a torch. The daylight will be gone in twenty minutes. Anxiety rises, very slightly. I want to get home, to a nice roaring wood-fire. Whatever timid warmth the day possessed has now gone for good.

It's going to be a very bitter winter night on the high moorland.

The trees surround us, their cold branches scratching my anorak. It must be below freezing now: the perpetual Dartmoor dampness has turned, here at Hobajob's, into a hard-core frost. The twigs and leaves underfoot make brittle, snapping sounds as we pace. Lyla is eagerly pursuing the dogs towards the gloom, towards the little clearing in the middle of the wood, where she always finds her treasures. The clearing was probably a Stone Age hut, many thousands of years ago, or some Neolithic shrine, no one quite knows.

We have to cross a stile, an ancient wall, it could be two hundred years old, it could be two thousand, after that we climb a hill and the woodland deepens again, surrounding the clearing. Cages within cages, no birds sing.

The dogs are already there. I can see them in the frosty gloom, circling shapes, like loping wolves in a Victorian picture book. They are barking wildly, oddly. Making a noise I have never heard from them before. What have they found?

Lyla turns to me, her face worried.

'What's wrong with Felix and Randal? Mum? Something is wrong!'

I have a fierce and overwhelming urge to turn and run back along the deepening shadows of the path to the car. It's freezing cold. It's nearly dark. I am scared, of what I do not know.

But I don't want to show Lyla my fear. *Get the dogs, and go home. Now.*

Lyla runs towards the dogs as their howling gets even louder. I can barely see a thing; the winter evening is falling fast, dark grey and black, and the mossed and gathered trees make it darker still. 'Mummy!'

Lyla's yell cuts right through me.

She is yards ahead, in the clearing; I push icy brambles aside and run into the sombre glade. The dogs are circling and yowling. Fiendish. Perhaps they are simply scared of the weather, and the whiteness: here in the dark cold core of the forest, there's been an *ammil*, that strange Dartmoor phenomenon when an initial thaw in cold weather is turned to ice, once again, as deep winter suddenly returns, devouring and glaciating.

In the slantwise evening light, this ammil, as always, looks beautiful. The special moorland ice storm that makes silent glasswork of the world.

My mother always loved the ammils.

As the dogs raise their eerie lamentations I look around, in something like wonder, an infant on a dark Christmas Day: every twig on every branch on every wizened little tree looks like the finger of a candied skeleton, a slender see-through bone of sugar. All the holly leaves are turned to immobile flames of white frost; through the trees I can see the distant shaggy cattle walking on grass made of tiny crystal spears.

But the dogs won't stop their yowling. What is frightening them?

'Look, Mummy, look!'

Lyla is pointing to the centre of the clearing. I can see a couple of dead birds and a few dead mice, three or four, lying, claws in the air, no doubt killed by the vicious returning cold. They're in a kind of line, but that means nothing. Next to them is a trail of household rubbish. Daily waste. Casually dumped. It makes me so angry when people do this to Dartmoor, it makes Lyla even angrier.

It sometimes makes her cry.

Yet something snags. I look again at the scattered line of trash in the frost. I can see a hairbrush. Incongruously pink, and now rimed with a varnish of frost.

It is mine. I am sure it is mine. I lost it a while ago. And now I step a little closer I can see my own fine brown hairs are still meshed in the prongs, though stiffened to wire by the cold, and there are scrunched-up, mouldering tissues trailing from the brush, red and stained, either kissed with lipstick, or dabbed with blood. I shudder in the freeze. Is this my blood? And there, at the end, under the tree, is that a tampon? One of my used tampons? I have to throw away tampons carefully, in bags: our sewage system out in the wilds cannot cope with these things, but why would my tampon be scattered out here?

Revulsion shudders through me. I feel invaded, or poisoned. Violated. It must be the scent of all this, the blood, the hair, the waste, that is freaking out the dogs, who are now backing away from the clearing, hackles up, growling.

Lyla calls after them. I stare at the tissues daubed obscenely with my blood. Who is doing this? Who has taken my trash, my hair, my brush, and laid them out here in the wood, next to these sad little birds, stiffened and killed by the cold? I look at my daughter, could she have done this, as a joke, or some ritual, making a pattern? Why? This is not her style, she is not sly or conniving, and she looks as shocked and alarmed as me.

'Mummy, what's wrong with the dogs?' Lyla's face is even paler than usual. 'Where are they going?'

53

My blood thumps. I wonder if it was me that dumped this here, or lost this here, and I have simply forgotten. Part of my amnesia. Yet why such intimate waste? Blood, tissues, hair.

Abruptly, Lyla grabs at my hand, her fingers freezing, and lets out a piercing scream.

'Mummy! I can hear someone coming!'

Hobajob's Wood

Wednesday evening

'What? Where?'

I clutch my daughter's hand, very tight. It is so dark now I can hardly see the bare frozen twigs of the dead trees on the other side of the clearing.

'Lyla, what can you hear?'

She shakes her head and tilts her face, listening intently. My words are clouds of mist. The twigs tinkle in a subtle breeze, like sentimental chimes. It could be minus five. We need to get away, get far away from this wood and this sickening trail of trash.

'Lyla, come on.'

Lyla shakes her head at me, almost angrily. 'Listen!'

I strain but can't hear anything unusual. 'There's nothing, no one. Come on, Lyla—'

'No! That's him!'

She's almost screaming. Her hearing is ten times better than mine. Needles of fear prickle my fingers.

'Who? Lyla, who can you see?'

'No one!' she says, whispering now. Hard and low.

'But I can hear him, he's out there, I know it! Mummy, he's watching us, it's him, the man on the moor, in the freeze.'

'Stop this. Let's go! When we get home we can call the police.' I pat my raincoat pockets for my phone. I have no phone, of course, and anyway it wouldn't get a signal out here, but it does have a little torch. But I left it charging in the car. So we don't have any light. We have to leave right now.

'Lyla, come on, we have to go.'

'But what if he sees, Mummy, what if he catches us on the way? He'll do it again . . . He'll take you to the lake.'

'What are you talking about?'

'Mummy, Mummy, look!'

She is chattering with cold, or terror. Helpless, I stare around at the quiet wood. In the gloom, the leafless, frosted, moss-hung trees seem to edge towards us, their dark, frost-rimed fingers lifted to the twilit sky as if they were once a crowd of trapped, imploring people, burned to blackness by an awful fire.

Is that someone, or something, in the trees?

'Mummy, he's so close! That way, over there!'

I look and think, for a second, I see movement. But no, there is nothing here, is there? Just us and the dogs and the dead birds, and my hairbrush, and a hideous used tampon.

My resolve is snapped, by a crackle of frosted twigs, a human footfall.

'Mummy!'

Lyla bolts. She wrenches from my grasp and goes sprinting down the frosty path, out of the woods, towards the distant car. She is a faster runner than me, she runs so much on the moor. But I must not let her out of my sight. I hear the dogs barking wildly as they scatter into the woods, not pursuing us: pursuing someone or something else. Or they are being pursued in turn.

'Felix!' I shout. 'Randal! Come on!'

Lyla is racing away, a dim little figure, getting dimmer in the dusk. Trees and brambles snag at me, lacerate my hands and neck as I stumble on cold, mossy rocks. I urge myself on; it is so dark, I can barely see, but I can hear my daughter. I fall, cracking a knee on an icy tree stump. *Ah. Ah ah ah!* I shout at the sudden sparkling pain, and look ahead. Lyla has stopped, on the path, by a little wooden footpath sign.

She turns in the gloom, and shrieks, 'Mummy, he's coming! He's coming after you! Right behind you!'

'Lyla—'

'Don't look back, Mummy, get up get up!'

I can hear crashing noises behind me, something big emerging from the cold heart of Hobajob's Wood; the dogs, or someone else?

Someone I know.

Pushing myself to my feet, I start running, again. But Hobajob's Wood wants to lock us inside. Dead branches block the path, ice patches crack as I trample my way, breathing chilly fog. I have reached the ancient stone wall, toothed with new icicles. Climbing over, I jump down, the crashing behind me as loud as ever – but I am too scared to look back.

There. The car. A welcome grey shape in the deathly twilight. I see Lyla is already inside, her face pressed to the rear window, her eyes wide with fear.

The cold car door handle stings my hand, I yank it open and fall into the seat and twist the key into the ignition, but Lyla shouts at me, 'Wait, Mummy, the dogs, where did they go?'

'They ran off, but they'll find their way back. We have to go.'

'No! He'll kill them.'

She is right, she is wrong, she is screaming, I open the door again, to the frigid dark air, and see – what? Who? Something? – and there is Felix, crashing over a fence, leaping it in one go, three foot high. He tears towards us, leaps across me into the car, wet and cold and doggy and yowling. He jumps on to Lyla, clearly terrified.

Forcing Felix away from her face, Lyla cries, 'Where's Randal, we can't go without him!'

I can hear something. Getting nearer.

'We can't wait any longer!'

'Over there!'

I stare, helpless, into the dark pillars of the trees and the crouched shapes of bushes. It is now too dark to see anything for sure. It is as if I am drowning again in the black waters of Burrator. Even as it formed, the ammil is beginning to melt. Drip, drip, drip. The black ice dwindles.

'Hide, Mummy. Duck down so he can't see!'

It feels ludicrous. Surely he will see us. He'll have heard us slamming the car's doors. But I don't know what else to do.

Lyla is nearly crying. 'Duck down low, Felix, Mummy, *please* hide.'

I do as she says; cower low in my seat. Maybe he will run past. Maybe he has got Randal. Maybe he's been watching all along, for weeks.

The seconds pass. Felix whimpers. Lyla shushes him, fiercely.

Seconds become minutes. *He is here, he will open the door.*

My fingers and lips are numb from the cold. I try to keep my breathing as quiet as possible. And I wait.

Nothing happens. The silence endures. From crashing and panic to total immobility and total calm. The cold is the only noise, like a steely ringing in my ears.

My limbs ache from this cramped position. I need to stretch. We've been here ten minutes. Nothing has happened. Was there ever anything? I begin to doubt. The brush, I definitely saw the brush, and the dead birds, and the tissues – but was that tampon, stained with blood, really mine? Was any of it really mine? There's no sure way to tell.

Maybe we just panicked. Overreacted. People dump litter all the time in Dartmoor. Adam loathes them. Says he will set the dogs on them if he ever finds them, let the lurchers tear the yobs apart, limb from screaming limb. See how they like their lungs and kidneys being scattered across the tors.

Even as I think this, I hear a friendly, recognizable growling, outside the car.

Kicking open the door, I see Randal, his tongue lolling, smoking cold breath in the dimmity. He jumps casually into the car, and on to the back seat, to be fussed by Lyla, and nuzzled by Felix. He does not seem frightened. He does not act like a dog that was chasing, or being chased. It's Randal. Our dog. Behaving normally.

Lyla's face is blank now, the terror gone.

'Let's go,' I say.

She nods, and shuts her eyes.

I work it through; and I work it out. It really was a simple panic. We *panicked*. It's what people do in woods. In the dark, as the cold and the night kicks in. They panic: they see the Great God Pan. The fabled monster. But the monster is always your imagination, conjuring terror out of rowans and frost and little dead birds. And it was an average plastic hairbrush, iced with frost. Could have been anyone's.

I turn the key and the lights illuminate our drive home. Shadows of trees line the route as we unbend the narrow road and reach Huckerby. We open the door to a warm kitchen, I turn all the lights on and make a pot of tea. Neither of us speaks. The dogs are fed. Lyla is subdued, can't even look me in the eye. It is as if she feels guilty, or is still scared. She sits at the kitchen table, nibbling a biscuit, drinking a glass of milk. I feel a need for one of Andy's hag stones, to hang on the lintel of the door. To keep the witches out, the evil influences of Dartmoor that creep their way along the thorny hedgerows, trying to find a way into your home.

At a beam of car lights, Lyla looks up. I hear the familiar sound of an engine, which is turned off.

Adam has returned.

He opens the door, brushing snowflakes from the shoulders of his fleece. As he shuts the door behind him his expression says it all as he looks at us.

We have mud on our hands and faces. I have scratches on my neck from the twigs and brambles.

'Jesus. What happened to you two?'

I don't know quite what to say. 'Well, there was this load of crap in Hobajob's, rubbish and tissues – anyway, we got a bit scared, and probably it was a joke, or co-incidence, but it was frightening—'

Without warning, Lyla bursts into tears. She waves a hand at me, angrily. 'I don't know, I'm sorry, Mum, I thought I heard him, saw him, I thought he was coming to take you away again.'

Adam steps toward Lyla, but she turns and shakes her head and says,

'Sorry, Daddy. Sorry. I want to go to sleep.'

And with that, she leaps to her feet, and runs up the stairs.

The dogs, as always, rise and follow, cantering noisily up the wooden steps to join her in her bedroom. We hear her bedroom door slamming shut.

Adam looks as if he wants to go after; I raise a hand. 'Wait, please – let her be, for now. She's frightened because, you see, there really was a scare. There wasn't any man, but there were these dead birds—'

'It's freezing, it's Dartmoor, it's winter.'

'Yes, but all the rubbish, strewn everywhere – it looked like it was from our bathroom.'

He regards me, sceptically; I press on.

'And I wondered if Lyla is taking it there, likes she takes stuff to her den? Making patterns. But she's too embarrassed to admit it. And yet, I don't know, because she seemed as freaked out as me.'

'Tell me the whole thing,' he says. There is real anger in his expression, or some other emotion I cannot discern. 'Tell me everything, Kath.'

And so I tell him the whole story, as he pulls up a wooden chair. I tell him about the day at Grey Wethers, the stones and the forest, and the trip to Hobajob's; then the accelerated sequence of the yowling dogs, the tissues, the birds, and pattern of familiar household rubbish made so evil by the setting. My blood, my lipstick, my hair, arranged in lines and circles. In a ring of fine frost. And I admit the panic, the manic fear that gripped us, the sense of an imaginary man. A predator.

Adam stays silent as I explain, he is still in his damp Ranger's fleece, as if he is a passing visitor.

'So that's it,' I conclude, wearily, wanting his understanding, his sympathy. 'Everything freaked her out, I mean it freaked me out, a used tampon? Someone's hair, someone's blood? Possibly mine?'

He gazes my way, his expression undecipherable. 'You can't know it was yours. We get fly-tippers all the time.' He offers me a shrug. 'Probably kids from Princetown. Bunch of tossers.'

'I know,' I say, unsurely. 'Yes, I know all that. But in the middle of Hobajob's, why there? And Lyla is *really* scared of something happening, to me, all over again. She's not herself. So what do we do now?' I want him to come over and hug me. To sort this out, be my husband, to help, to hug, to kiss. 'Will she get over it, Adam? Will we be all right? When she sees I'm not going anywhere, will she stop imagining things?'

His expression is tinged with proper anger now. 'No,' he says. Firmly, coldly. 'No. She won't simply get better.'

Rising, he walks to the sink, and takes down a Plymouth Aquarium mug from a hook under the cupboard. His voice is low and sombre, darker than ever. 'All this lying isn't helping, it's making things worse.' He turns to face me. 'Kath. It's time. The time has come. There's something you need to know. About your accident.'

Huckerby Farm

Adam is getting Lyla ready for school. He's said nothing more since last night, nothing to explain his cryptic words. He's told me I need to meet someone, and she will explain. Later yesterday evening, I heard him make a series of muffled phone calls, outside in the freezing yard, where there is sometimes better reception. It sounded as if he was arranging something.

Now he stands here in the kitchen, helping Lyla into her winter coat. We all turn to the sound of a car, squelching through frost and mud, into the farmyard. Adam goes to the door.

And there she is. Tessa. My brother's wife. My thirty-eight-year-old sister-in-law. The woman we once sought out, for advice on Lyla's suspected Asperger's: because she is a psychologist, teaching psychology at Plymouth University.

Tessa walks into the kitchen and stands next to my fridge, with its magnets spelling *Love You Mummy from Felix*, a joke by my daughter, who likes to pretend Felix

63

and Randal can read and write, as if they are real friends who can talk with her, and understand her.

'Hello, Kath,' says Tessa.

I don't say anything in return. I glare at my husband. He looks back at me carefully, yet rather coldly.

Why has he brought Tessa Kinnersley to Huckerby? If he has something to say, why can't he say it himself? Why involve Tessa, a psychologist?

As if I am mad.

In the distance I can hear the dogs barking happily. The normality makes me angry.

I am not mad. My memory is fragmented and I have odd panics but this was all anticipated. *Mild to moderate brain injury,* they said. *Expect mood swings, sudden anxieties or depressions, difficulty with daily tasks, insomnia, nerves, prickliness, but you should also expect a slow and steady recovery.*

Tessa comes a little closer. 'Kath, I know this must be weird, and I'm really sorry, but I'm here to talk. That's all. Adam thought it might be better if you heard things from me.'

'What things?'

She flashes a glance at my husband. He responds with a subtle nod as he chats quietly with Lyla. Making sure she has everything in her schoolbag. He is ushering her away from the scene, telling her to wait in the car. I gaze at Lyla but she's not even looking at me, as she exits. What is going on? The hag stones, the symbols made of birds, the objects in the forest, maybe it is all imagination and coincidence sending me to the edge. Perhaps Tessa really is the kind of person I need to see. A trained psychologist, who used to work at the prison, and for the police.

'Kath.'

My husband's voice rouses me. How long have I been stood here, lost in pointless thought? 'Sorry,' I say, and immediately regret it. Now I've apologized, I'm on the defensive. I feel a need to protect myself. This feels like a hostile situation. I am the woman who gets panicked in woods. How can she be allowed to drive?

'Kath,' says Adam. 'This is difficult for everyone, but Tessa is a friend and a professional. You know that. So we thought it was the right way to do this. Cos it's really important. There are questions you need to be asked. There's stuff about your accident that you need to hear.'

He comes over and puts a protective arm around my shoulders. And I feel an urge to sink into those arms, forever. My big husband, the National Park Ranger, the guy who rescues drowning tourists from quarries.

But no. Stiffening myself, I ease out of the hug. I mustn't admit to my stirring feelings of disintegration, my fear of stones and brushes and dead animals. I've got to stay sane and sensible. Because, if they take my driving licence away it could permanently fracture my marriage, and really drive me over the edge. A few weeks of reliance on Adam, for transport, left us bickering. What would a year do? We can't move back to Princetown, we all hate it. And park rangers are obliged to live within the Park. And Lyla has to live in the wilds, she loves it here, she hated it in town.

Without a car each, we'd be screwed.

'All right,' I say, forcing a smile. The way my daughter forces a smile, because sometimes she doesn't know how to smile. 'I'll answer questions. I've got some of my own, I think.'

'Good,' says Adam, backing away. 'I'll take Lyla to school.'

The door opens and closes. I hear the rumble of the Land Rover, fading away.

Recalling my manners, I offer Tessa some tea. She nods and says sorry, again, and I feel my hostility melt, somewhat. She is a good friend, or at least one of my few remaining friends, of any kind. She gave us good advice on Lyla. When I was wondering if we should have her assessed, but Adam was more reluctant.

The fat brown teapot is placed on the kitchen table. 'Can I ask you some general questions first, Kath?'

'I suppose so. OK.'

'Would you say you are happy, or were happy, before the . . . accident? Happy in your life, that kind of thing?'

I look her in the eyes. Startled. 'You really think that's a general question?'

She lowers her gaze, apologetically. 'OK, but this is tricky. Let's do it the other way round. Let me build a picture first, for both of us.' She reaches for her fashionable handbag and pulls out a black notebook.

'You're taking *notes*.' I can't help bristling. 'Really? You're not my doctor, Tessa, you're my friend. I saw loads of psychiatrists after the accident. What is the point of this? Who are you taking notes for, the police?'

She opens the notebook. Pen in hand. 'No,' she says calmly, and pauses. I can hear the moorland rain rattling on the windows. 'No, not yet, Kath. We all really want to avoid anything like that.'

Again, I am put on the defensive, and simultaneously alarmed. Avoid the police? Why should the police be anywhere near this? That has all been dealt with. Adam handled all that. I was still in hospital. So why has he asked Tessa here to talk about the police?

I don't know. But I have to believe my husband is doing this for a good reason, acting in my best interests.

He must be. Adam has *always* done what's best for me, and Lyla.

'You met Adam when you were very young, isn't that right?'

I shrug, bemused. Tessa surely knows this backstory almost as well as her own.

'Tessa, you're married to my bloody brother. Why do you even need to hear this stuff?'

'I know some of it, Kath, yes, but—' she sighs apologetically. 'I really want to hear it from you. Please let me run with this?'

More mystery. Things are being hidden. In the back of the kitchen cupboard.

Taking a gulp of tea, I sigh. 'I was seventeen, at a private girls' school in Totnes.'

'OK. Go on.'

'Dan must have told you the story. We bunked off to the pub one day. I was underage, of course, so I was frightened to buy a drink, to break the rules, but then this very good-looking guy came up. It was Adam, he was eighteen. We went on a date the next day, started going steady the day after. He already had a job at the Park, as a trainee, and I went off to uni.'

'Exeter. Yes.'

Her brisk smile is meant to be reassuring, I am not reassured.

'I did archaeology, as you know.'

'You enjoyed it?'

'Sure. Yes. I really liked it.'

'And you stuck with Adam?'

'Yep.' I smile, faintly, at the memory. 'Everyone at university was sceptical, everyone scoffed and said *Oh it won't last, you'll break up by Christmas*, but I knew they were wrong, and they were wrong, and it did last, we stayed loyal, we had fun. Adam would come over to my halls of residence.' I look her in the eyes. 'Some days we never got up, just stayed in bed. After a few terms we got engaged. And when I graduated we got married. A year after you and Dan.'

Tessa takes more notes. Meanwhile, the January weather is at the windows, listening in, rattling panes. I wonder if the weather can hear my deeper thoughts, the occasional recurring doubts about my marriage, that trouble me from time to time: did I ever *really* deserve a handsome guy like Adam Redway? I know I brought the education to the marriage, and the faded poshness of the Kinnersleys: that was my side of the marital contract, but I've always thought I definitely got the best of the deal. Adam Redway: loyal, rugged, sexy – look at him, 100 per cent man. *What did he see in her?* I've watched women openly ogling my husband all the way through our marriage.

Has he stayed loyal? Does something like infidelity lie underneath this oddness? No. *No.* I do not believe that. Adam is loyal, and honest, and he loves me.

'It's around this time,' Tessa says, scribbling away, 'when you went off to uni, that your mother died?'

This is a change of tack. Now I feel vaguely affronted, again. 'Look. I'm sorry, Tessa, and I don't want to be rude, you're always so kind to us, but . . . Can you please tell me why you're here?' I look at the clock on the cooker. 'I've got work to do, too.'

'Yes, I know, I'm sorry, Kath. I totally understand your confusion and irritation. But . . . ' She sets down her pen, and meets my gaze. 'I need to colour in the blanks, and then I'll tell you. It's best we do it this way round. So that, you know—'

'What? What do you have to tell me?' I'm trying not

to freak out. What can be so bad that Adam calls in my sister-in-law who happens to be a psychologist? Why does it need this long preamble, as if I am being prepared for the worst?

Tessa ignores the flush in my cheeks, and puts a pen to her notebook, ready to write. 'Please, Kath, it's best this way. Honestly.'

I look at her: the nice shoes from London, the cashmere cardigan. And I yield, wearily. 'It was my second year at uni. Mum died in an ashram, when she was in India, which was typical of her.'

'How do you mean, "typical"?'

'Because Mum was always, like, *alternative*. Give her a crazy religion, Mum went for it. Reiki, Buddhism, wicca, astrology, shamanism, putting crystals up your bottom. She didn't believe in things, she believed in *everything*. I think at one point she was simultaneously vegan, vegetarian, pescatarian, breatharian, and oddly fond of ribeye steak. And red wine. She always loved wine.'

Tessa smiles. 'You miss her?'

I smile wistfully, in return. Oh yes. I miss Mum, even now. As I gaze across the kitchen I can see, on the shelf, one of the many souvenirs of her solo travels, when she would hare off to far corners of the world, dumping us kids with bemused but tolerant relatives; this particular souvenir is a garish, ancient doll from Greenland, an Inuit spirit-doll, I think, made of feathers and bird bones, with a leering face. Walrus teeth carved very crudely into human teeth. Yellow and awkward.

Adam hates this doll, I like it, because it's Mum's. She always loved eccentric things, quirky, broken, eerie things, stuff no one else liked. And I miss that artiness, that curiosity, and I miss her generous, scatterbrained

69

foolishness, and I miss her wild and waspish wit. I also think I disappointed her. I was so *normal*, so conservative, wanting to fit in; yet in myself I loved her, revered her, despite her egotism, her partying.

I wished I could have showed it to her, more.

Looking back at Tessa I realize I have been lost in silence. For too long.

'Yes,' I say, sighing deeply, 'I miss Mum. I miss her daily, even now. She was great fun, most of the time.' I pause, and look at the smirking Inuit spirit-doll with its yellow teeth, like an old smoker. 'Mum was Mum. Always herself. She grew up rich, I mean – you know we were an old family, the Kinnersleys. She used to talk about a big house in Dorset, long ago sold, but by the time it got to her, or at least me and Daniel, most of the money had gone and she was determined to spend the rest on experiences. She wanted to try everything, go everywhere, Greenland to Zambia, and she did. She used to say no one ever died wishing they'd bought a bigger TV: they died regretting things they didn't do. Which is true, I think. I often wish I could live by those words, but I haven't got the guts. Or the money.'

I take a breath. This is possibly the most I've spoken in one go since the accident. Which in itself is striking.

Tessa nods. Pen poised. 'You never knew your father?'

'Nope. Dan did a bit, but not me. No. He was American, based in London, and he wasn't in her life that long, and never lived with us, never even lived in Devon, and he died when I was barely two, Daniel five. You should ask Dan about the funeral; by all accounts it was mad. Sitars and pentangles – and a Cornish harp. And Dad was pretty soon replaced.' I chuckle, a little sadly, a little bitterly. 'Mum was, you know, never into domesticity, never wanted to be bossed around, with a man around the house. But she certainly loved male attention, and men loved her back.'

Tessa looks at me. I can guess what she is thinking.

'Of course Mum was a beauty, so I am told, but she bequeathed her looks to Dan. I got her intellectual curiosity, I think.'

'I see. I see.'

Tessa squints at her notebook, and then looks at me, and I wonder if I can see embarrassment in her eyes. I sense an awkward question coming.

'Let's talk about your mother some more. The bequests. Does it hurt you that she left the Salcombe house entirely to Daniel?'

I flinch. Because, yes, this does hurt. It hurt a lot, and it sometimes still hurts, now. I look at Tessa's expectant face. 'Yes, that was pretty difficult. Emotionally.' I am surprised at my own honesty; surprised by my vehemence. 'The house was the last major asset Mum owned and she gave it *all* to my brother, supposedly because he' – I do sarcastic air quotes with my fingers – '"always loved Salcombe so much more than me", and Mum allegedly balanced it by giving me shares and antiques.' I stare at the Dartmoor calendar on the kitchen wall, the picture of Kitty Jay's grave, pretty and sad in the snow. 'The shares and antiques turned out to be virtually worthless. Stuff my mum bought when she was stoned. God, she loved weed.' I roll my eyes. 'She used to buy it in Totnes from druids. I hate drugs. Hate them.'

Tessa writes brisk, efficient notes. Like a proper detective. I wonder if it is displacement activity, to hide her own discomfort. She glances at me.

'So you still feel a certain resentment? Towards Dan, and your mother? About our Salcombe house?'

'Yes. No. Oh, I don't know. Yes, a little. But not really

71

– I know there's always that bit of friction between me and Dan, because of the house and all that, but I also *love* my brother. He's an extrovert – not like me. He's funny. And most of all we both endured Mum, together: that's a profound bond, and of course it's not his fault Mum was so scatty.' Our eyes meet; I go on. 'And of course I like you, Tessa, and I totally love your two little boys, and so, yes, sure, Dan has the big house, and yes, you guys get the money and the life, and we have to rent this place – but he's loaned us cash when we've been hard up, you've bought holidays for me and Lyla, and that's helped, Dan's been a big, big help.'

'OK. I see.' Tessa is nearly expressionless. 'And that brings us round to Lyla.' She takes another sip of tea, which must be nearly cold. Mine is. 'Let's talk about that. And after that we're nearly there, Kath.'

Nearly there? Nearly *where*? The tension builds like snow on snow – that snow which piles up and up, until the roof collapses.

'You only had one child. Or have, I should say.'

'Yes. We wanted more, but remember, Adam got Hodgkins, a few years back, and he needed chemo. And so he can't have kids any more. So, as you know, Lyla is it. But it's fine, he's better. And I adore her, I love her, and Adam's illness made us stronger.' I push my mug away, defiantly. 'It set us back financially, it was horrible – but we saw it through. It united us even more, and here we are. A family. A unit. This is who we are, and I like it.'

'OK. This is my last question, Kath.'

'Good.'

'How are you coping with Lyla's, ah, quirks?'

'Her Asperger's?'

'She's still not been officially diagnosed,' Tessa says quickly, 'As far as I am aware?'

'No, but I reckon that's what it is. Anyway, it means our lives are different; she still hates bustle and towns and loud noises, and new people, they make her panic, and she loves animals. So we live here, in the wilds, in the quiet, where we can have dogs, and there are horses. It's fine, it's all fine. Or it was until the bloody accident.'

Tessa nods and puts down her pen. My session, it seems, is over.

'All right, taking all this into consideration, would you say that, on the whole, you were happy – or at least content – at the time of the accident at Burrator?'

'Yes,' I say, with some force: because it is true, and the truth is easy to say. 'Tessa, that's what makes it so awful! What gives me flashbacks, the horrors: I nearly lost it all. I have a husband I love, a daughter I love, a home I love, and I nearly lost it all, because of some stupid ice on a stupid Dartmoor road. I am very lucky. I've been given a second chance. I was actually technically dead for a few seconds!' I shake my head, marvelling at my own luck. 'Yes, life could be better: we need more money, Lyla needs help, it's far from perfect, but what is money compared to life? No one ever died wishing they'd bought a bigger TV.'

Tessa smiles politely, yet I think I detect a faint, sad blush on her face. For a moment we both listen to the wind, knocking things over in the farmyard outside, like a drunk returning home from the pub. I wonder what Lyla is doing now. At school. Sitting alone in assembly, perhaps. Not talking to anyone. Ignored and friendless. Her mind wandering on to the moor, thinking of her newest bird feathers, and that piece of antler-felt her father found.

'Kath, you clearly know you have retrograde amnesia? Because of the brain trauma?'

'Yes. Of course! I know I've forgotten some stuff from before the crash, a week or so, but there are fragments, and the psychiatrists at the hospital say it will all come back. But, Jesus, I wish I could forget the actual crash! I still see the ice, the skid, the water – ugh—'

I close my eyes to dull the mental pain. When I open them, Tessa is frowning.

'Well, the thing is, Kath: what the doctors at Derriford Hospital might not have properly explained about this amnesia is that you can forget that you've forgotten. That is to say, there are holes in your memory that you don't even realize are there, and the mind tries to fill them.'

The wind has stopped abruptly. The whole house is quiet. I realize that the dogs must have gone with Adam and Lyla. All I can hear is Dartmoor rain on the window. A tinkly-tankly sound. I feel a sense of congealing fear. Some kind of horror is approaching. Like a moorland witch, creeping along the hedgerow. And we don't have any hag stones. We have nothing to keep the witches away.

I can't stand this any longer.

'OK, this really is enough, Tessa. Tell me why you are here, in my kitchen?' I am close to shouting. 'I've told you everything. You know most of it already. So now it's my turn to ask. *Why are you here?*'

'Because,' she says, looking deep, deep into my eyes, 'you didn't have an accident, Kath.'

'What?'

'Your mind has invented this. Invented the ice, invented it all.'

'What?' The panic rises in my throat, an acrid, metallic taste. 'What? What do you mean? I had the bruises, I've seen the doctors. The bloody car is at the bottom of Burrator Reservoir. I had to buy a new one!'

'Yes, it is. The car is down there. But that's because you drove it in there, deliberately.'

I sense my life pivot around this moment. A ritual dance. 'You mean – you mean – you can't possibly—'

Tessa Kinnersley shakes her head, and I see the most enormous pity in her eyes. 'Kath, there was no accident. You tried to leave your husband and daughter behind, to destroy yourself, to destroy everything. You tried to commit suicide. We just don't know why.'

Later Thursday morning

Absolute stillness. That's what it feels like. Absolute stillness, as if the beating heart of the world has slowed to a
stop. Nothing. Nothing. Nothing. Then a lash of rain hits
the windowpanes, breaking the quiet, and my words rush
out.

'How can you think that?'

Tessa remains calm, doing her job. She's not here as a
friend, but as a professional psychologist.

'You were observed.'

'Sorry?'

'There was a witness at Burrator. By the reservoir.
Walking his dog. It was night but there was a full moon,
and he saw you drive your car, quite deliberately, into
the water.'

'But—' The panic rises, like that black cold water, the
water I can so vividly remember, and yet I can't? 'But.
No. No way. Can't be. There was ice. I skidded.'

'Check the records, Kath, go back and look.' Her arms

folded, Tessa continues, her voice deliberately low and kind: overtly calming. 'Go online and look at the weather for that night, December thirtieth. It was one of those dry and mild winter evenings we get. Twelve degrees centigrade. A southwest wind. There was no ice. Also . . .' I flinch, inwardly.

'Also, Kath, there is a wall around Burrator, you must remember that. A big, thick brick wall, a solid Victorian construction, far too strong for a car to smash through. You know Burrator well, you must recall this?'

She's right. I do. There *is* a wall. Yet my mind has deceived me, recreated a different place: a place where I might drive in accidentally.

'So how did I . . . I don't get it—' I swallow. I mustn't cry.

Tessa guesses my question. 'They were doing some construction at Burrator, rebuilding part of the wall, leaving a gap, barely wide enough for a car to slip through. The chances of skidding on ice, or whatever, and hitting the right spot would be pretty tiny, infinitesimal. But anyway you didn't skid, and there was no ice, and you simply aimed the car, very carefully.'

'There must have been someone else in the car.'

'I'm sorry, it was you, just one person was seen, driving, and it was you. Only you drove into the reservoir; only you came out.'

'I don't believe it!'

The tears gather now. I stare, blurrily, up at that calendar. Kitty Jay's grave, covered in snow, the flowers so forlorn against the whiteness. This is the famous beauty spot near Chagford, where my mother's ashes are scattered: and I shrink inside. I huddle from the thought, the irony: what would Mum think of me? Of this terrible thing. Suicide? Like Kitty Jay herself? My mum loved life, she devoured it, despised the idea of suicide, and she taught that to me.

The words come again, all too quickly. 'But *why* would I kill myself, Tessa? Why on earth would I do that? It's hateful, suicide: it's so selfish, the most selfish thing, and I was quite happy, I was. Yes, we had problems, with money, and Lyla, but I love her, I love – I love my husband – I love my daughter!'

And now the waters engulf me, and the truth pours in through the car window. Adam obviously knows all this, hence his cold anger, his strange distance, these past weeks. And I don't blame him. What must he think of me? I tried to kill myself, for no apparent reason, I was prepared to leave him without a wife; and, worst of all, far worse, the deepest, darkest water of all, I was prepared to leave Lyla without a mother.

'No,' I say, flatly, defiantly. 'NO. I don't believe it. I would never do that. Never leave Lyla without a mother, never ever, *ever*. I am not that kind of woman, not that sort of mother! I love Lyla to bits. I would *die for* my daughter. Not die and leave her here. Oh God.'

I have to take a huge breath or I will shatter. I am a monster, a gargoyle. I am a leering thing made of dead birds and smeared blood. A horrible Inuit spirit-doll with feathers and yellow teeth. Here I sit in this warm bright kitchen with its ancient walls and the *Come to Dartmouth* tea towels: and yet I am something grotesque, a woman who would leave her lovely, fragile daughter without a mother . . . No.

'I didn't do it, Tessa. I didn't! There has to be some other explanation.'

Tessa looks at me assessingly, as if judging how much I can take; reaching into her bag she lifts out a folded piece of paper, places it on the table. As she unfolds it, carefully, she reveals an image. The image looks scanned, photocopied. There seems to be handwriting on it, and it is small, introverted handwriting: scratchy and spidery.

I recognize this distinctive handwriting, from all the way across the kitchen table.

It is mine.

Tessa advises me, gently, 'Adam has the original. This is a copy.'

I know what I am about to see: it is obvious. It doesn't have to be said. But I also need to see it, to secure the lid on this. To hammer in the iron nails, so that no hope can escape.

Tessa pushes the paper across the table. With trembling hands I turn it around, and read my own handwriting:

I shouldn't have done what I did; shouldn't have let this into my heart
So I am going now. Going away forever
Forget me if you can, I know you won't forgive

The words are mine. I don't remember writing them, don't remember them at all, but this is my handwriting: I wrote this.

I tried to kill myself.

I shunt the paper aside, lean forward on my folded arms, gently rest my head on them. I can smell the clean, honest wood of our kitchen table, where I have spent so much time, with my husband, with my daughter, cooking suppers, drinking wine, laughing loudly, being a family. Here at this table. And now, at this same table, I quietly break into a sob, and keep sobbing.

Tessa says nothing, I stare down at the darkness between my arms, and sob and sob, in my white-painted kitchen. But I am not crying for me, I am crying for

Adam, for my dead mother, for my brother, for this house, for this place around me, for the wildflowers on the high moors in the summer, for the meadowsweet at Whitehorse Hill, for the foxgloves down at Broada Marsh, for the sundews and shepherd's dials and pennyroyals and roses – all the flowers my daughter loves, all the ones that she can name and I cannot, all the one she shows me, all the flowers and rocks and feathers she collects, because I am crying, crying, crying for my daughter, the little girl I was prepared to hurt, to damage, to dismiss, to throw away; the girl I picture, standing alone in the farmyard, listening for the tiny animals, puzzled in her anorak, wondering why her mother tried to run away forever.

To kill herself.

And my God. It is too much. And the rain tinkle-tankles on the window, as my tears run to their end.

How long I sit there, with my head slumped, I don't know. An hour or more. But even the fiercest tears find a cease, as all things must die, and I lift my head. Tessa is sitting there patiently with a look of deep pity on her face.

'Sorry,' I say.

Warren House Inn

Monday lunchtime

Lyla is at school and I should be at work in Princetown. Instead I'm parked down the road at Warren House Inn. The fog is so thick I can barely see the humble old whitewashed building, though it is only a hundred yards away. Normally the inn is visible for miles around – because it is the only building for miles in the rolling, bony moorland. Today, in the Dartmoor murk, Warren House looks like the vague, gloomy idea of a cottage, half-formed in someone's mind.

Stepping out, locking the car door, I pause and stare at my own hand, unnerved. I never used to do this. Locking my car, in one of the wildest places on the moor. We never lock anything on the moor: bikes, cars, houses. And who's going to steal my worthless old Ford? A team of stoats?

One of the shaggy Dartmoor bullocks?

Or the sheep?

I can hear sheep, somewhere around me, also invisible in the fog:

meh, meh meh meh meh, as if they are mocking me.
MEH, Kath Redway, *MEH*.

It was Lyla who first suggested this to me, that sheep say *meh* not *baa*, and once she'd said it I couldn't get it out of my head; because she was right. Sheep are laughing at us, mocking; *meh meh meh*, look at you, what are you doing here, look at this person locking her car door, *meh*, why is she locking it, *mehh*, is she scared she might get back in and *drive into a reservoir?*

Mehhhhhhhhhh!

Thoughts press in on me: I am stuck inside myself. How could I possibly have tried to kill myself? What did I do on that fateful December day? I do not believe it; yet I have to believe it.

As I walk up the mist-swirled moorland road towards the inn, I go over it for the seventeenth time this morning. Yesterday I thought it through two hundred times or more. I've been obsessing like this since Tessa's visit.

I remember Christmas, I do remember that. It was nice. We did what we always do, went down to Salcombe like the poor relatives we are, and feasted at my brother's expense.

We had a roasted goose, like they eat in Dickens. And Lyla actually got to play with other kids, her rambunctious eight- and ten-year-old cousins, Oscar and Charlie – or Foxtrot and Tango, as Dan calls them. Charlie and Oscar tolerate Lyla because they've grown up with her: when she twirls her hands repeatedly or gets phobic about scratchy things or hides shyly under a table with an encyclopaedia, they accept it, and laugh good-naturedly, and that makes Lyla smile and come out from under the table and play with them in her own awkward, funny way, and that's why I like Christmas. Lyla is always happy at Christmas.

And I enjoyed Christmas this year, too. I remember crackers and sloe gin, and luxury chocolate assortments my brother bought from some posh London shop, and then a fat, contented drive home to Huckerby on Boxing Day – and that evening Adam went away for a week, to do up the rangers' hut on the northern moors, leaving me alone with Lyla.

And after that, the horrible fog comes down on everything, like a door closing, and everything is lost in the remorseless mist of my post-traumatic, retrograde amnesia, the vapours of my bruised and useless brain.

From Boxing Day onwards my mind is basically a void. Four days later I tried to kill myself, and I have no idea why.

Meh.

As I get nearer the pub, I see the door is shut and the windows are dark. It looks as if the pub is closed. The peat fire in this pub has, famously, never gone out since 1847. But sometimes they casually close the place in the dead days of winter. But I need this pub to be open: because it is the one place I might find Adam, when I need to find my elusive husband.

It's not his fault he's a ranger. But it means he ranges, across a sizeable tract of moor with all its sparkling streams and clapper bridges, its hidden spinneys and forgotten villages. He is always out and about, usually in remote areas with no mobile coverage, so I can't get hold of him. And right now I want to get a proper hold of him. We've spent the days since Tessa's visit quietly not addressing the massive issue: pretending that this enormous thing isn't there, didn't happen. *Let's have some more tea and say nothing.* I know Adam is resentful but he keeps it pretty much hidden.

This morning my mood changed. I dropped Lyla at

school, went back to the office at Princetown, opened my computer and typed in some words: *The first recorded instance of the word 'swaling' comes from a thirteenth-century poem. It means the spectacular, controversial winter burning of Dartmoor's stubborn gorse and bracken, and can still be witnessed every winter, on the higher moors* . . . And then I stopped writing and looked at my stupid words, so irrelevant to the gaping void in my life, the open wound in everything, about to be infected. So I decided I had to leave the office and talk to my husband: immediately. And I made my excuses and headed out here.

Enough tea; enough denial. Enough imaginary men in woods.

I need the facts.

Turning the rusty handle of the knackered wooden door, I step through. The pub is open, but almost empty. There are a few local drinkers with drams and pints at one end; a huge grey wolfhound snoozes by the undying fire at the other.

I suspect this story about the eternal Warren House fire is a lie, told for tourists, but we all tell lies, to get by. And why not? I wish I had more lies, to tell myself. I would happily lie to myself for the rest of life if I could: I didn't really try to commit suicide, no: I was trying to explore the reservoir. I was trying to see if my car would float. I was in a parallel universe at the time. I never tried to kill myself and leave my daughter alone, *meh meh meh meh meh*. I feel like crying again.

'Hello, Katarina.'

A friendly face: Ron, behind the bar. He's owned this pub for decades, possibly centuries: I wonder if he kindled the hearth fire in 1847. He certainly knew my mum, who loved this poetic little pub with its ghosts and legends and mummified cats buried in the walls, and the stones of the Iron Age village visible from the saloon bar windows. He knew she called me Katarina, and he knows that I shortened it to Kath because I felt it was pretentious. So he teases me.

'Hey, Ron. Call me Kath?'

'Nah,' he says. 'Doesn't feel right. What would your mum think?'

We've probably had this conversation six hundred times. It is comfort food for my soul, right now.

'How are you, Kat? I heard about the accident.'

'Oh, OK. Recovering. Wouldn't mind the odd holiday in the Maldives, you know.'

He ponders. 'Isn't that the place that's, like, sinking underwater?'

'Bit like Dartmoor in January, then.'

He chuckles, and turns to serve another customer, lifting a glass to the optic, draining a shot of Gordon's. I look at him as he works, his weatherbeaten, grog-blossomed face. He probably kissed me as a baby, when I was called Katarina Olivia Mirabel Kinnersley, not Kath Redway.

I am shortened. Abbreviated. Truncated. I have fallen off a social cliff. And I don't mind. Because all I wanted was an ordinary life, with ordinary happiness, and my ordinary and handsome husband and my extraordinary and beautiful daughter, and the happy dogs and the ancient house, and yet I tried to throw it all away? To damn them to a kind of hell, without me?

I must not crack. I must keep a grip.

I wonder if Ron knows the truth about my 'accident'. I wonder how many people know that it was actually a suicide bid. I don't think it appeared in papers, I suspect the local police did Adam a favour, a Dartmoor favour for Dartmoor people. Because Adam is popular, the handsome Chagford boy, one of the Redways, a National Park Ranger, and the moorland people are so tight-knit.

And I am not quite one of them. I'm a well-spoken girl from the coast, with connections on the moor, and I'm always very welcome – but I'm not quite one of them. And never will be.

'So, Kat, love, what can I get you?'

'The usual.'

He chuckles. 'Your husband? I'm not sure if he's been by today, I was out this morning.'

We nod at each other. Ron leans over the bar, and calls out to one of the drinkers at the distant tables, a farmer I'm guessing by his muddy boots. He's drinking on his own. I think I recognize him: yet another cousin of Adam's. He has so many: so many with the very same dark hair, striking eyes and rakish, slanted cheekbones, the looks inherited by Lyla. This particular handsome cousin is on Adam's aunt's side, his dad's sister. And I'm not sure he and Adam get on.

'Jack, you seen yer cuz?'

Jack nods as he drinks his beer. 'Adam? Yeah. By an hour back. He's up at Vitifer, I think, some sheep in a wire.'

Ron turns to me with an expressive shrug which says: *What do you want to do?*

'How far is Vitifer, where is it?' I ask.

Ron shakes his head. 'Half-hour walk, straight across the moors. But you don't want to do it in this fog, Kath, you'd get lost in five minutes, we'd have the air ambulance out. And that goes on my tax bill.' He is grinning. I'm not.

'I really have to see him. It's really, really important.'

'C'mon now, Kath, please—'

'I have to. Please. I have to! HAVE TO.'

I realize, too late, that I am shouting. The wolfhound lifts a lordly muzzle, sniffing the tension amidst the peatsmoke. The pub is silenced: the fire is probably going out. I have caused a scene. I never cause scenes.

For a moment there is deep embarrassment. The silence is shrill. Then someone says, 'Hey. That's all right. I'll take ya.' It's Jack, again. He comes across, puts his empty glass on the bar. Grins at me. 'I've got to go that way anyway, gonna see a mate about some feed. Thanks, Ron.'

Ron looks at the two of us, he squints unsurely at Jack, and he shrugs in my direction. 'You're more like your mum than I thought, Kath. She loved taking risks.'

Jack grasps me by the arm. Ten minutes later I am jumping from tussock to tussock and squelching through the foggy mire, with Jack at my side, guiding me carefully.

Ron was completely right. I wouldn't have had a clue where to go in this mist. I'd have wandered off track immediately, got stuck knee-deep in a marsh, fallen head first in a leat, knocked myself out and drowned. *Oh look, she tried to kill herself again. And this time she succeeded. Meh.*

Jack tells me he farms sheep, though I knew this already. He tells me all about sheep, as we hike through the fog.

'You know they say sheep are stupid,' he says, helping me over a wooden stile. 'Well they're right. Only thing sheep is good at is dying. You name it, they get it. Lice, ticks, scabs, big fat worms as long as a toddler's arm.' He laughs, his hand firm on my arm, or sometimes, rather too warmly, right around my waist. 'Foot rot, braxy, tetanus, pulpy kidney, blackleg, lamb dysentery, black disease, pasteurella. And if that isn't enough, if they haven't managed to kill themselves eating ragwort, or drowned themselves down at Black-a-Tor, they go and stick their heads in wires. I sometimes think they are naturally suicidal.'

I try not to react. Does he know my story? Is he winding me up? I'm pretty sure Adam doesn't like Jack Bryant. Some ancient family argument.

That arm strays to my waist again.

Squeezing.

'Then there's the devil-worshippers.'

'What?'

'Yeah,' says Jack, steering me over a little clapper bridge. 'Get a lot of that all over: weird patterns, burned circles, tortured animals. Adam deals with it all the time.' He pauses, in the mist, looking at me. Smirking. 'There was this one case, with a foal. Jeez. Did he not tell you?'

'No.'

'Guess he doesn't want to bring it home, scare that little girl of yours, Lyla?' His grin is very wide, like he finds it all funny. 'Anyway, yeah. Last autumn he found a foal. Bloody odd, it was surrounded by these patches of charred grass.' Jack chuckles loudly. 'He called me and asked me to help. What a job. That poor bastard foal. They'd cut its tongue and eyes out, and cut off its, you know, genitals, cut 'em all off, and sliced off an ear. And there was this weird white paint on one leg, some symbol, a star or pattern.' Jack is scanning the horizon, though all I can see is fog, then he puts his hand on my hand. 'And the weirdest thing of all was, they'd dragged the bleeding corpse, when the animal was likely still alive, they'd dragged it round and round in circles and stars, making these crazy patterns of blood in the frost. Demon symbols, I heard. Strangest thing I ever saw. Sent a fucking shiver right down me. Happened over near your place, Pete Bickle's farm. Not far from Hobbyjob's and Huckerby.

90

Which I thought was kinda funny, cos your mum would have loved the spookiness, if you see what I mean.'

'What?'

I gaze at him. Those blue eyes so like Adam's, but colder still. 'My mum? You knew my mum?'

'Sure I knew your mum, Kat, way back, when we were all kids, all of us cousins, lads in Chagford. And she was all into that pagan stuff, wasn't she? You do know that? I don't mean she tortured animals, nothing like *that*.' He laughs. 'All I mean is that she was into those symbols. Spells. Spirits, spooks, deadly nightshade, wacky mushrooms, whatever. Dancing naked around stones: all stuff they used to do on the moors back in the day, all the hippies from Totnes. Amazing she didn't die of flu, your mum, amount of time she was starkers up the tors. They did like a party.' He stops abruptly. As if he is teasing me.

'There's Adam.' He pauses. 'At least, I think it's Adam. This mist is a right fucking job.'

Vitifer Leat

Adam emerges through this chilly fog, as we must emerge, to him. He is standing next to a wire fence, his face hard and blank. I see a sheep, panting, lying on its side, its head stuck in horribly tangled wire. There's mud all over the shaggy fleece, there are blood smears on the wool, around its neck, where the wire bites. A back leg kicks, feebly, repeatedly.

Jack steps forward. 'Hello, Adam, your wife was trying to find you. So I delivered her. Hope that's all right with you, like.' Adam says nothing; simply nods.

Jack stares down at the ewe. 'Ah, fuck, these stupid animals. One of Ryan Thorne's, is it? Hard to tell with the mud.'

He stoops to the animal, brushes some of the mud away, showing that it has a purple stain on the fleece.

'Yep, Thorne's.'

This is how they identify sheep on the open moors. Coloured blotches of dye on the fleece. Lyla likes to play games with these coloured sheep, one point for a

93

red sheep, two for a blue, five for a pink. Sometimes we play this game with Lyla simply because it is the only way she will engage when she is lost in her reveries. The only way she will talk is with a very structured game, or with numbers. Making patterns. Like that pattern of rubbish from my bedroom in Hobajob's.

Jack and Adam make small talk. Chat about the weather. I look at the sheep, my thoughts straying back, to Hobajob's, and Huckerby.

I still can't work out if Lyla took the old hairbrush and hid it there. It's also possible I dumped the brush there, along with my tissues and tampons, when my memory was at its worst – yet I have no idea why I would do such a thing, I can't even be *entirely* sure the brush was mine – they sell identical ones in supermarkets.

What disturbs me is the lipstick smear. And the stain of blood. And the hair. Pieces of *me*. It felt ritualistic. I suppose this is mild paranoia, my temporarily unbalanced mind, but it keeps me awake at night, staring at our fifteenth-century ceiling, as Adam gently snores beside me, through the winter nights.

Jack and Adam have stopped chatting. Adam has turned, and is glaring my way. Silent. Jack clearly senses the tension. Offering a forced smile and a brisk cheerio, he strides off into the fog, disappearing in seconds. Even though I'm not taken with Jack Bryant, part of me wants to call out, *Don't go!*

Adam speaks. 'What are you doing here? With Jack Bryant?'

Not even a hello. The hostility is palpable.

'He showed me the way. I came to see you. He was telling me all about sheep diseases, and talking about Mum.'

Adam grunts. I seek his angry eyes, needily.

'I think it's time to talk, Adam. I mean talk *properly.*'

Again, he shows me no warmth, just looks down at the stricken sheep. Assessing.

The politeness of our life in Huckerby is gone, the appearance we keep up, for Lyla, is torn away. This is the first time I've been truly alone with him since Tessa's visit. Now I see the rawness in him. The contempt. And I'm not sure I can blame him. What if he had done this to me, tried to kill himself, for no reason, leaving Lyla without a father, a vulnerable girl growing up knowing her dad didn't love her enough to hang around. I would *hate* Adam for that. Hate him. A part of me would probably wish him dead all over again: that his suicide had succeeded.

But I must think of Lyla, and get through this for her. There *must* be an explanation, for what I did before New Year. I am not mad, and I am – or I was – rarely illogical. I must have had a reason for driving into Burrator. I can't remember because I have mild to moderate brain trauma, Glasgow coma 13–15. Yet the answer will come.

'Adam, please. I can't cope with this, can't cope with pretending it didn't happen. Not one moment more. I know I supposedly did something terrible, but we need to talk about it.'

He shrugs. 'Whatever. Have to deal with this sheep first.' He doesn't look at me. 'It doesn't want to be dying. It didn't *try* to kill itself.'

He is stroking the neck of the sheep, which looks oddly peaceful, its eyes glistening, resigned to being stuck, resigned to dying: the wires are hideously tight and tangled.

'Must have been struggling here all night,' says Adam. His eyes flick my way. 'Spoke to her owner, Ryan, up at the market in Tavistock. He said I must do what I've got to do.'

Now I realize what is happening.

'But – no – you can't. Can't you cut the wire?'

'Could've last night.' His handsome head is tilted, with a hint of pity, but not that much pity. 'But she's too far gone now, she's been fighting it, made it worse. Wires are deep in the neck, half garrotted.' He trudges to the shape of his Land Rover. I hear him open the back door: sorting, seeking, as he goes on, talking loudly. 'Some drinkers down at the Warren said they heard her, late last night. Screaming. You ever heard a sheep scream?' He returns carrying a double-barrelled shotgun, broken over his forearm. His cold blue eyes meet mine, a hint of a smile on his lips. 'Have you, Kath? Ever heard that?'

'Wait. Please.'

'Terrible sound. Very human, like a little child.' The mist is so thick around us, ten yards' visibility at most. 'Sound of real human anguish. A little child hearing that her mother is dead.'

'Stop it, Adam. I'm sorry – that's why we need to chat – to talk this through—'

The sheep bleats, interrupting me. It is fighting for life It surely sees Adam's gun. Perhaps it knows what that means. I kneel next to the gently panting animal, stroke the oddly clean, domestic fur of its bleeding head. To me it seems the metal twine is not so deeply embedded.

'Wait, Adam, I think we can save it.'

'Don't be bloody stupid.'

'No, look – you don't have to kill it. The wires are looser?'

He gestures, angrily. A tall man, with a gun, in the thickening mist. A hand that looks ready to slap me.

96

'Step away. You're always so sentimental. Isn't any hope for it.'

'No, Adam.' My defiance rises. My urge to resist. This sheep doesn't have to die. 'No, I won't.'

'This is my job, Kath, you don't understand. You never understand. This is the moor!'

We stare at each other.

'Get back!'

'No.'

'Get back!!'

I know he isn't really arguing about the sheep. This is his contempt for me, emerging.

Yet for me this *is* the sheep, at least in part. Why does he always have to be so brutal, so ruthless? I know he grew up on a moorland farm; I know he sees the moor as a working place. I know his family history has made him harder. Yet sometimes it goes too far, I've seen the cold glitter of his blue eyes when he's breaking the neck of a pheasant hit by a car up at Houndtor: sometimes the icy glitter looks like a kind of appetite. A pleasure in killing, fulfilling an instinct, a relish for blood.

'Step away. Now. This sheep is suffering. You're only making it worse. You're not yourself. Be logical!'

Now I hesitate. I falter, and wonder, deep inside, if he is right. Am I thinking rationally? I am the one who drove into the water. I am the one who has amnesia. I am the one who did everything wrong.

Meekly, I step away. Adam nods. Halfway satisfied, he steps closer, focusing hard as he swings the gun around, filches two cartridges from a pocket, and slots them into place. He snaps and locks the barrels with a fat-sounding click.

'Stand *right* back. If I get this wrong, it could get messy.'

Adam aims. I still don't know if the sheep is aware

of what is coming: the big, lazy eyes – lashes fluttering, almost flirtatious – look vaguely up at Adam. They do not flinch: perhaps the sheep knows it is going to die. It accepts. Right at the end I wonder if we all accept.

The muzzle of the gun barrel is poised, Adam squinting down the gunsight, breathing firmly, calmly.

Time slows in these mists. I gaze.

The other sheep are like an audience gathered around. Grey shapes in the mist.

Meh, meh, look at him, *meh*, he doesn't care. *Meh*, she's mad. Look at them.

I put my hands over my ears, preparing for the horrible noise: like my daughter when she hears motorbikes revving or loud applause, or people shouting in crowds. Sometimes even the rattle of the cattle grids can freak out my daughter. Lyla says the sounds are black and red, scary colours: her favourite sounds are blue and silver. It's called synaesthesia. I've looked it up. Another symptom.

The sheep is waiting. I want this to stop. I want Adam to hurry up; I want to close my eyes, yet I can't.

I have to watch.

Adam squeezes the trigger. And as he does, the sheep abruptly shifts, bleats desperately, and loosens itself, entirely, from the wire, wrenching itself free—

'Adam!' I move closer, protesting. 'Adam, stop! It's free! Stop!'

The gun explodes. The noise echoes and reverberates, silencing the onlooking ewes, scattering them across the soaking grass. I feel a ghastly, sudden wetness: there is blood splattered all over my jeans. I am flailed with the blood. I stare down, appalled.

'Jesus Christ, you daft woman!' He is half laughing, half angry.

I shake my head, dazed, fighting my revulsion. I am drenched with blood, and the sheep is dead, its head cracked completely in two, skull and meat and bone in pieces, mixed with the sludge of brain. There is a tinge of burning which taints the air, and I look as if I have waded through a mire of gore.

'Adam.' I put a shuddering hand to my mouth, regaining myself. 'Adam, it was free, you shot it for no reason.'

'It was going to die. The wires had cut too deep.'

I have both hands over my eyes. I don't want to look at the sheep, or my husband. 'I'm sorry,' I say at last, because I am so very tired of fighting. 'I'm sorry. You were right. Look at me, my jeans. Ah.'

'It'll come out in the wash. Blood does that.' He offers me a brief, sympathetic smile, the first hint of real warmth in days. 'Look, Kath. I've got to bleed this ewe, that's a lot of good mutton. Can't go to waste. That *would* be wrong. Do you really want to talk right now?'

I *really* want to go back to the car and drive home, sit in a hot bath for an hour. But I must be stronger.

'Yes. I came here to talk to you.'

'OK.' He grunts as he stoops to the sheep, the shotgun replaced by a knife. 'OK. Please. Carry on talking as I work.'

'While you butcher a sheep?'

'You're the one that came up here, Kath. You're the one that interfered. You're the one that—'

. . . *that drove yourself in the water*. But he doesn't go there. He shows mercy. Instead he puts the knife to the throat of the sheep and with one practised, deft movement, opens a violent red gash. The head is yanked back and the blood pours out, glistening and hot, ready to be drunk by the receptive earth. Red pools form on the sods: a pink, steaming foam.

'Talk,' he says. 'Talk to me now, if you want.'

'All right.' I kneel down next to him. The cold earth seeps through my jeans. 'I want to go back over those days, Adam. I've been racking my brains. I can't remember anything. I mean, I can remember Christmas, Boxing Day, then nothing. My first memory is waking up in the hospital. But I can't trust those memories, Adam. Because I know I invented others, like – like the patch of ice. Like the idea it was an accident.'

'What do you want me to tell you? If you can't remember.'

'How was I found? After the crash?'

'I told you that weeks ago.'

'Tell me again!'

He wipes the knife with a cloth. The bleeding has almost stopped so that tiny scarlet drops form and fall, one by one, with a jewel-like delicacy.

'You were found at Burrator, by some waterworks guy, helping the search, in the middle of the night. You were very wet, must have fought your way out of the car, underwater, swum to the banks. Climbed out.'

'But why would I do that if . . . ' I can barely say it; yet I have to say it: 'If I wanted to die?'

He sighs. He rubs his forehead. Perhaps rubbing away the pain, the sadness, the grief that I could do such a terrible thing.

'I wish I knew, Kath. I really, really wish I knew why you did any of it.'

He might not know anything, but I do know something. I've been researching suicide, Googling it. Suicide. Survivors of suicide bids, people who jump off bridges, buildings, cliffs, but who do not die, talk of regretting it even at the moment they leap, the first moment when it is too late.

And perhaps that was me: perhaps I regretted it as I drove in, as I watched the dark waters crash through the windows. Maybe the image of Lyla came to me at that final moment: Lyla alone in her little den with her chains of paperclips, looking at a card she made for Mother's Day: a drawing of a dinosaur saying *rawr* and a big red heart for her mummy – her dead mummy, who drove into the water and left her behind.

I am shuddering with the cold, and the remorse. The pain of contrition, and yet the burn of doubt, too: I still cannot believe I would kill myself. There must be some other explanation. Yet all my thoughts are gurgling into blackness, like a moorland stream disappearing into a marsh down at the Belstones. Where the villagers used to sleep with bibles on their chests, such was their fear of the fogs and the mires.

Sometimes, these days, I begin to understand their superstitions. And their rituals.

Adam puts a hand on my arm. 'Hey. Kath. Please. Whatever happened, you're still here, and Lyla needs you to get better. Come on.' It feels as if he is throwing me a lifebelt.

'Let me walk you back to the inn, Kath. I've got to skin the sheep, it's a horrible job, but it can wait. Foxes won't get her, I don't think. Go home and have a bath, and get yourself changed.' He lifts me to my feet. 'We can talk more as we walk back, if you want.'

Slowly we trudge the sodden path back towards Warren House Inn. The mist is lifting, slightly, showing the undulant moors ahead. Acid turf, wet desert.

'So I was conscious when I was found? By the reservoir?'

'Yes, Kath. Go left here.'

'And did I say anything?'

'Apparently not. Just *help me, help me.* Then you fell into a coma, in the ambulance. And you woke up in hospital. Your brother was the first to come in: they couldn't reach me.'

'Daniel came in first? I thought it was you?!'

He shrugs. 'You've forgotten that too. You were very hazy that first day. Slowly recovered, over the next week.'

So Tessa was right, again. My memory, in trying to heal, has invented facts. I remember the moment Adam walked into the hospital ward, with flowers, peaches, books, poetry. How I cried with happiness that my first visitor, after my accident, should be my lovely husband come to see his miracle wife.

But that was all nonsense. My first visitor was actually Daniel, my brother. Why Daniel?

Because Adam could not be reached.

My husband points ahead. 'There, Warren House. You can make it easily from here. Just follow the stream: always follow the stream, darling, when you're lost. I better go back.'

My husband could not be reached. He was unavailable. He wasn't there. All those days after Boxing Day.

I sense a need in me, to get some perspective, to examine this objectively. Shattering into helpless pieces doesn't help Lyla, or me. I am being too timid. I put a hand on my husband's wrist. 'Adam, I know you were doing up that hut: you left the house day after Boxing Day, right?'

'Yes. We'd planned it,' he says, his voice flat and calm. 'I told you before Christmas, you were fine about it, said I deserved some time away, on my own. Like we do.'

This is true. Adam works longer hours than me, earns more than me. His summer days can last from dawn to dusk. And we long ago decided that the quid pro quo would be him having some time out, away from his intense and sometimes wearying family. This is our dynamic, this give and take; it's the machinery of our marriage, why we're still on the road.

But we came off the road. Down at Burrator.

'But where exactly were you, Adam, that week?'

'Old rangers' hut. Parks Authority premises.'

'But where?' I realize I've never asked him this.

'Dixworthy.'

'Where's that?'

'It's hard to describe.'

'Why?'

He sighs, exasperated. 'Does it matter? It's wilderness, up on the northern moors. Between, I don't know, Manaton, thataway. Do you want a postcode? Google Street View? What's the point?'

I get his drift. We are man and wife, standing in a dwindling mist, on a slope of grey moor, arguing about the exact position of a rangers' hut, to explain why the wife attempted suicide. It is ridiculous. And yet I do need to know.

'Wait,' I say, 'I think I've heard of Manaton. It's quite near Kitty Jay's grave, isn't it? Towards Chagford?'

He's silent. For a moment, his expression changes. I see a hint of something: then it is gone. But I saw it. I saw it. I'm sure of it.

'OK, I've got to skin a bloody sheep! Say hello to Ron for me. Ask if he wants some mutton chops.'

He returns the way we came.

I turn, and walk downhill, following the stream. In a few minutes I reach Warren House. I am the only soul about. Just one, small, black-faced sheep loiters, skittishly, by the whitewashed wall. It looks at me: at the blood-stains on my jeans, at the mud and damp smeared across my stupid cowardly face. It doesn't even bother saying *meh*.

For a moment, I am rooted to this dark Dartmoor earth. I am a standing stone. Cold and hard. Because I've known Adam for twenty years. And I've realized what I saw on my husband's face. That expression, just glimpsed.

Guilt.

Salcombe

Saturday morning

Everything was unnaturally quiet. Saturday morning usually meant weekly Peak Noise for the Kinnersley household, as Charlie and Oscar woke up, realized it was Saturday, whooped with delight, and decided to re-enact a light-sabre fight from *Star Wars* with bananas.

Today Tessa Kinnersley sat at her desk in her little study, in a converted attic on the top floor, and listened to the blissful silence. She sighed with something approaching contentment. Her main work for the day was done: she'd written up the research for her set of lectures next year. The Psychology of Evil.

Now she sipped her organic coffee, cupped its warmth in her hands and looked out of the Victorian window at the sailing boats in the little harbour, the woodlands over the water. Dog walkers were exchanging pleasantries on the waterfront; a young couple strolled hand-in-hand, gazing in the windows of estate agents, and moving on with a frown.

It was a mild winter day on the south Devon coast.

The sun was slanting through the study window: if you stood in its warmth and closed your eyes, you might imagine it was spring.

She wondered how many hours of peace she had before her. Dan had loaded the boys into his big Lexus at about ten a.m., the movie the boys so wanted to see started around noon, so they'd all be back by three. Or four. She had the house all to herself for almost the whole day, which was a pleasant feeling. Later she might go down to the deli, buy some of that amazing Spanish ham, the *Jamón ibérico de bellota*, make a lunchtime sandwich.

But first she had a different hunger to satisfy: an appetite for the truth about her sister-in-law's suicide bid. It vexed her intensely. Delivering the awful truth to Kath had only deepened Tessa's worries. What would happen to Kath when her memories returned? And why had she done it in the first place?

The sums didn't make sense. Every time Tessa added two plus two, the answer seemed to be three. Some ingredient was missing from the story, dark matter that she couldn't discern. How could a woman go from a noisy, cosy family Christmas, with kids happily squabbling over the two-pound coin in the pudding, to the darkness of suicide four days later?

Tessa poured herself some more coffee from the cafetière, and returned to her desk, staring at her black computer screen. Had there been any clue in that Christmas of what was to come? She couldn't think of anything. It had been a notably happy Christmas, if anything. Dan and Adam, who didn't especially like each other, but who rubbed along when necessary, had bonded over some abstruse argument about rugby – and some of Dan's cigars in the garden. Kath had seemed relaxed, smiley, delighted, that Lyla had kids to play with; Kath's occasional sibling friction with Dan, the favoured son, was also absent.

And the kids had really *played*: hide and seek all over the house, up and down five floors, from cellar to attic, squealing in mock terror as they discovered each other in the second bathroom, behind the shower curtains.

Lyla had twirled on the spot as the three cousins, the three mischief-makers, planned the next game. The psychologist in Tessa had long ago recognized these unusual body movements as a kind of stimming – self-stimulation – the repetitive physical tics of kids on the autistic spectrum, but this spinning like a top was Lyla's happy stim.

When Lyla was unhappy she would grimace, or even bark. Or flutter her hands like little birds, up and down, up and down. Sometimes Lyla's stims were quite distressing. Eerie faces, manic flapping. But there had been no unhappy stims at Christmas.

Christmas had been good. And on Boxing Day the Redways had said goodbye and a big thank you, and had loaded up the battered National Park Land Rover with a box of leftovers for Felix and Randal. As they'd reversed out of the drive, Lyla had waved giddily at Charlie and Oscar, the dogs panting by her side. On the back seat.

Four days later Kath Redway had slowly and carefully driven her car into the drowning blackness of Burrator.

Two plus two equals three. Where was the dark matter?

Swallowing more coffee, Tessa turned on her laptop, and clicked to a site she had already bookmarked. Suicide. Causation. Warning signs.

One in four people who attempt suicide leave a note. If a note is left, it significantly increases the likelihood that the suicide bid will be successful . . .

Kath had left a note. And she had very nearly succeeded. Which meant this next information was especially troubling:

A third of people who attempt suicide will repeat the attempt within one year, and about 10 per cent of those who threaten or attempt suicide will eventually succeed in killing themselves.

Was there a genetic explanation? It seemed not. There was no history of insanity or suicide among the Kinnersleys, according to Dan. His mother had enjoyed a happy childhood, as had her parents in turn. The worst family trait was a hint of alcoholism, but, as Dan said, while cracking open another bottle of Rioja, everyone before 1950 was alcoholic by modern standards.

Dan certainly liked a drink, and whenever he drank, and Tessa quizzed him about it, he would tell her that Winston Churchill drank forty-two thousand bottles of champagne in his life, and in between silver tankards of Pol Roger Reserve, he had defeated the Nazis and won the Nobel Prize for Literature.

As for their father, the passing American, he'd died in a car crash. No drunks, no drink, just bad luck, and a ludicrous funeral, as much as Dan remembered it, with Hare Krishna and pagan ululations, devised by Penny K. herself.

Paging through the website, Tessa searched for the facts she wanted. Here:

During pregnancy and the first year afterward, there is a three- to eight-fold decrease in the risk of suicide.

And here:

One Swedish study (Berglund, 1992) showed that having children is notably protective against suicide; instances of suicidality amongst parents appear to be half those of nonparents. This is especially true of parents of young children (under 12) . . .

Tessa sat back from the screen. This was why two plus two made three. The missing one was Lyla. Tessa simply did not believe that Kath Redway would leave her only child, her only daughter, even more alone in the world. Kath adored that child: who loved her mother right back. If anything, Lyla gave Kath her purpose. *Lyla* was crucial to *Kath*.

And Lyla was very lovable, in her own way. When Tessa had visited Huckerby in the run-up to Christmas, Lyla had proudly shown off all the bird feathers she'd collected, and had enthusiastically recited the names of all the species. Perhaps thirty or forty names in Latin, word perfect, yet laughing at herself as she did it, mocking her own obsessions.

It was touching, and sweet. If you let that lonely little girl be herself, the smiles came, and the wit and the laughter, and her pretty face glowed. If you could break through the intense shyness, little Lyla Redway had an inner loveliness, and what mother would forsake that? Certainly not Kath.

The coffee was cold. Tessa drank the bitterness anyway, staring, hard, and unseeing, through the window at the sunlit roofs of Salcombe and the blue of Kingsbridge estuary. An idea was forming.

Could it be something to do with Adam? His disappearance, right after Christmas, was a little abrupt. But the Redways sometimes did that. They had periods apart, the odd week; also, they loved each other, and they both loved Lyla. Things were solid between them. Adam had endured that illness a few years back, and Kath had nursed him through it.

Infidelity? Tessa considered it for a moment, and dismissed it. Yes, Adam was very handsome and women surely desired him, but Tessa hadn't heard a whisper of anything like infidelity. Not even a rumour, and Dartmoor in winter was full of rumours of unfaithfulness. There wasn't much else to do.

What else?

Closing her laptop, Tessa went through the facts of the day itself. The afternoon before her suicide bid, Kath had left Lyla with a friend. Emma Spalding. The Spaldings were the nearest neighbours, and also the Redways' landlords, the owners of Huckerby.

According to Emma, Kath's request had been unexpected, but not unusual: she quite often asked Emma to help out and Emma liked having Lyla stay over. Sometimes Lyla wandered all by herself, in her feral way, from Huckerby across the wild moors to the Spalding farm, always trailing her protectors, Felix and Randal. And when she did this, Emma would give Lyla biscuits and milk and they'd all go to the stables, where the Spaldings kept their horses.

Lyla loved those horses. She would spend hours grooming and feeding them, combing their manes, looking after them when they were ill. Emma Spalding once told Tessa she was convinced the sick horses got better when

Lyla was there, as if she had special gifts. Something uncanny, something magical.

But Tessa didn't believe in gifts, or witchcraft, or the uncanny. The mind was a machine, the human soul a programme. Her lectures on the nature of evil were designed to show this: that genes and the environment, nature and nurture, the parents and the planet – and their complex interaction – were always responsible for human cruelty and criminality.

Which meant that there had to be a logical explanation for Kath's apparently meaningless yet callous decision to kill herself, and leave her little daughter without a mother.

And the answer was up there. On the high moorland. Hidden but findable.

Tessa stared out of her arched study window. A large seagull had suddenly landed on the neighbouring roof. A huge grey bird, shaking its head violently, like it was silently saying NO NO NO

Saturday afternoon

Tessa's mobile rang, interrupting her novel. The screen read KATH.

With a needling of anxiety, she took the call. Sitting up on the sofa, putting the book down.

'Hey, Kath? Everything OK?'

'Yes. Yes, I'm fine. I just wanted to ask something. Ask Dan something. But he's not answering.'

Kath's voice sounded strained. But it had sounded strained ever since Burrator. Unsurprisingly. Tessa glanced at her watch, 3.20 p.m. 'He's probably driving, Kath. He took the boys to Plymouth, some space movie, or maybe dinosaurs. It's in 3D – that's all they cared about.'

Kath chuckled. Tessa went on, 'So he's probably got his phone switched off, he's religious about it when he drives with the boys.'

'Yes,' said Kath. And nothing else.

'What is it, Kath? I can ask him when he gets here, or get him to ring you – won't be long.'

'OK, OK.' Kath trailed off. Unconvincingly.

In her mind, Tessa pictured her sister-in-law in the longhouse, high up on the moors. It might be sunny down here, but it could be raining, hailing, foggy, even snowing up there. Only thirty miles away, but such a different world. A colder, harder world.

'Kath?'

'I just wanted to ask him about that day. You see, I found out that Dan was the first person to come to the hospital.' Her voice cracked at the edges.

Tessa said gently, 'And you'd forgotten that?'

'Yes! I really genuinely thought the first person to come in was Adam! Oh God, Tessa, these memories, they're all over the place, I feel as if my mind is scattered, like – like a load of toys, like when Lyla was three, you know how toddlers can ruin a living room in five seconds? That's what my mind is like. And I want to put the toys back in their right places, the proper boxes. Does that make any sense?'

'Of course. And it will happen, Kath. The memories will return: the brain heals over time. But you do have to give it time.'

'OK, yes. I know you're right.' Kath sighed. 'Thank you, Tessa. I've got to go fetch Lyla. God knows where she is, it'll be getting dark soon. But—'

'Go on.'

'Could you ask Dan what time he came to see me? I need to get the chronology right. In my head? Maybe ask him to call me?'

'Sure. Of course.'

They said goodbye. Tessa lay back on her sofa, picked up her novel, got through two paragraphs, at which point her unusually peaceful Saturday was shattered by the noise of her boys returning with Dan: an eruption of energy, the shouts and flinging of coats. *Mummy, Mummy,*

Mummy! The film was brilliant, they had helmets made of light and and and . . .

It took her an hour to get her husband on his own. The boys had settled to some computer game in the living room. She and Dan had retreated into the big bright kitchen for cups of hot tea.

'So after the film we went to some corner shop, with a lottery machine, and Oscar said, apropos of absolutely *nothing*, if we won the lottery he'd buy a snowy owl and three micro pigs, for you and me and Charlie, and mine would be ginger and sleep with me at night.' Dan laughed. 'Honestly, where do they get this stuff? It's like children are brilliant French surrealists. Shame they have to wake up.'

Tessa chuckled, too. 'I got a call from Kath.'

'Oh yes?' His smile faded. 'Anything wrong?'

'No, no. I mean, she says she's OK. But she had a question, about, well, that night, or rather the next day.'

'Ask away. I'd do anything to help her, you know that, Tessa. But I feel so absolutely helpless. There's no solution to this mystery. But ask.'

'She says that you were the first to see her, not Adam, in the hospital. But she says she forgot that – another aspect of her amnesia, of course. And she wanted to know the chronology, to fill in the gaps. What time you visited, that kind of thing.'

Dan frowned. 'Good question.' His frown deepened. 'God, I dunno. It was all so chaotic, it's a blur.'

'You were in London, that business trip,' she prompted.

'Yes, let me work it out.' He paced to the kitchen windows, looked out at the back garden, the swing, the winter twilight, the fine day dying into rose and darkness. 'So I got the call in the morning, from the hospital, and I hammered the car down the M4, yep, yep, I remember

114

that, I think I did Chiswick Roundabout to Plymouth in about three bloody hours. Fuck. Lucky it wasn't speed-cammed. So, yeah, it must have been about noon.' He shrugged. 'Does that help? I'll call her. I'll call her later, I promise. I've got to talk to her about the birthdays anyway. Charlie and Lyla.'

Tessa winced. *The birthdays.* Normally Lyla and Charlie had a joint birthday party up on the moor or down on the coast, as they were born two days apart. It made sense, and Tessa knew it helped Lyla *and* Kath, because it disguised the fact Lyla had few if any school friends. Her loneliness was diluted by the presence of her cousins and their friends. But this year Dan had different plans. Tessa shook her head. 'Do we really have to do this? Can't it wait another year?'

'I promised him Disneyland Paris. God knows why. Stupid. But I can't go back on it, and he's so excited, as is Oscar: they were banging on about it in the car. And it's all arranged, on our way back from the holiday, the Canaries, some nice winter sun!'

'But Lyla—'

'I'll pay for them to do Disney, they could come for the weekend.' Dan's smile was expansive. 'I'll pay for them all! Lyla and Kath, even Adam, of course I'll pay.'

'You know Adam won't accept. He'll see that as charity, he's proud. And he'll want to be with Lyla, for her birthday treat. Like any dad.'

Dan shrugged. *Yes, I know.* 'Perhaps we can have a second party when we get back from holiday?'

'Hmm,' Tessa mused. 'I guess we could do Two Bridges Hotel again; they always like having parties there, that creepy walk to Wistman's Wood. I don't know.'

'OK.' Dan glanced her way, and frowned again for a moment; then he turned, distracted. 'Jesus, what the fuck are they doing now? Boys! Foxtrot, Tango! Stop it!'

He paced out of the kitchen to break up the fraternal squabble in the living room. Tessa could hear Charlie saying *gimme it back gimme it back gimme it back*. The fight didn't sound too bad. It was the silent fights that were the worst: they usually meant Charlie was throttling Oscar leaving him nearly asphyxiated. Or vice versa. It was amazing how these two brothers could so obviously love each other yet so frequently assault one another.

Tessa took the mugs and put them in the sink, thinking about Dan's answer. Kath's chronology. Something had clicked, there was something here. Information. What was it?

Methodically, she washed the first mug, placed it on the metal dish rack. She looked out at the garden as she rinsed the second mug, at the swing and the footballs and the big plastic toy car, big enough for a kid to sit in, though the boys were fast growing out of it now.

The car. That was it. Dan said he had driven so fast from London to Plymouth to see his sister, he could have got caught by the police, snapped by a speed-cam.

Tessa stopped rinsing, the mug suspended in her hand. She stared out at the sunset. Dan said he had driven the car too fast, but that was all wrong. *Because he didn't drive to London.* Tessa distinctly remembered the conversation, late on Boxing Day. How he couldn't face the holiday traffic, the gridlock on the M5. How he'd decided to take the train to London, instead.

Why was her husband lying, on this of all subjects? Was it just the confusion they all felt?

Tessa put the last mug down, pensively. She could hear the boys, still fighting in the living room.

Gimme gimme gimme.

Burrator

Sunday morning

I am here, I have returned. The scene of the crime.

The waters are a tranquil black under a very grey sky.
My hands are thrust in my anorak pockets, hidden from
the wintry cold. I am staring at the break in the granite
wall through which I drove on that night, three weeks
ago.

This gap is barely wide enough for a car. Which means
Tessa was right. You'd have to steer carefully to get
through this space. Which also means: I must have done
it. I deliberately drove myself between the broken-
toothed brickwork, right into the deep, dark, freezing
water, just so I might die.

I step closer. Nervous. As if I might fall in. As if I might
find the truth.

I want the truth; but I am so scared of it.

Someone has lashed grey metal caging across the fatal
gap. Presumably this is to prevent copycat suicide bids,
to prevent all the other thirty-six-year-old Dartmoor
mothers-of-one from driving into the reservoir for no

apparent reason; but I wonder why they haven't simply finished the rebuilding.

It's like one of those churches gutted in wars, kept in a state of burnt disrepair, as a sobering memorial.

Or maybe the council ran short of money, or the builders are on holiday. Because this isn't a memorial: no one remembers. I know this because I've finally discovered the courage to browse my mysterious suicide bid, and I have found one tiny original report, on a local news website.

It is algorithmically repeated in other places, but not elaborated or pursued. I also know Adam kept it all off Facebook: he curated our social media, to save my reputation.

So this article is *it*, apart from gossip that might have spread from police or nurses.

Taking out my phone, I read the stored news item.

Accident at Burrator Reservoir

A 36-year-old woman, believed to be local, survived a serious accident on 30 December when her car veered into Burrator Reservoir, a well-known Dartmoor beauty spot. The incident is thought to have occurred around 9 p.m., though the victim was not rescued until the early hours of 31 December. The victim is now in Derriford Hospital, Plymouth, in a stable condition . . .

There's one more brief paragraph, but that's it. That's my fate, the vivid cruelty of my life and its near ending, summarized for the world.

I walk right up to the wall, place my phone on the flat, cold, Victorian capstones, and stare at the placid waters.

The stunned calm of deep winter stills everything. No birds sing, no ducks quack, the water is a silent mirror to the oppressive ceiling of empty sky. The woodlands over the water, gathered under the high granite knuckles of Sheepstor, are intensely dark and motionless. There is no one looking at me from behind the old trees, no one watching. No one sees me.

It is difficult to imagine this place as a scene of drama. But it was. I try to picture that night; to picture *me*: slowly driving off the B3212, passing the little Spar in Dousland, and heading down the Burrator side road, all the way down here, the night before New Year's Eve. What was I wearing, did I have make-up on, how did I prepare for this date? Was I excited, shivering, zombie-like? Was I hungry, thirsty, crying?

An icy breeze stirs the Burrator waters, combing them with black ripples, which plash against the brickwork. Then it dies away, and the stillness returns. Like the world is waiting for me to work things out.

I try to invoke my expression in that final second. Was I thinking of Lyla?

I know I wasn't drunk. The hospital tests showed barely detectable levels of alcohol in my blood, and no evidence of illegal drugs. So I was sober. When I did it. I don't even have *that* excuse.

Picking up the phone again, I stare at the words as if they will magically transform into an answer. But all I get is more questions. Why did I sense it was icy that night? I've checked and rechecked the weather. It was mild and dry, as Tessa said. No ice to skid on, no frost, nothing like that.

Completely dry.

The mysteries deepen like the dark waters of Burrator.

And deepening them further is Adam. I definitely saw guilt on his face. And Adam is, usually, pretty much an open book. An honest man. He rarely, if ever, lies.

It's one reason I love him.

So why does he feel guilty? What isn't he telling me? Perhaps it is guilt related to my suicide bid, that feeling of *I should have done something*. The stuff everyone feels when someone they know attempts self-murder. *I should have talked, should have been there, should have called after Christmas*. It's one reason I find suicide so detestable, one reason I cannot really believe I did it: suicide infects everyone around it with a lifelong sense of self-reproach that can never be erased. And I would *not* do that to Adam, I would *not* do that to Lyla.

A cronking noise distracts me and I look up. Five ravens are wheeling across the whiteness, five black cruciform shapes, spiralling repetitively. Are they hunting, or mating, or something else? I don't understand their behaviour; Lyla would surely know. She likes crows and ravens, rooks and magpies, the birds of winter. She says they are collectively known as *corvids* and they are clever. So perhaps the *corvids* understand, maybe they were there that night, the winter birds, the crows and ravens. Because no one else knows, and no one else saw.

But someone can see me now.

There is a dark figure on the hill to my left, staring down, in my direction. I think it is a man. The figure is silhouetted by the grey clouds, a black shape of a human; but his stance suggests he is holding binoculars. Observing something. Could be a birdwatcher: Burrator gets a lot of them. Twitchers looking for raptors and waterfowl.

The man moves further along the lip of the hill. He moves in a distinctive way. I know that walk, that stance, the set of the shoulders.

It's Adam.

And he is definitely watching me, not any birds. He must have followed me. My husband is stalking me. Perhaps he thinks he is doing me a favour, protecting me from myself; perhaps he was worried I would drive into the water again.

Anger seizes me. This is wrong. He might have been doing this for weeks! It's disturbing. Sinister.

Flushed with fury, I jab at my phone as I stare at him, high on the hill. Let him see me calling him. Let's see how he reacts.

But of course there is no reception. Wherever you really need reception on Dartmoor you can't get it. As if it's an ancient law, made by the stannary parliaments, the medieval laws of Methral Brook and Great Week Mine. No Reception When You Need It. So instead I stand here and shout up at the hill, like a madwoman. 'Adam!' The figure does not move.

'Adam, I can see you! Adam!'

My desperate shouting fades to nothing. The figure is moving away.

'Adam!'

Could he even hear me? Now he's gone. Possibly it wasn't Adam after all. But I am sure it was. Yet what was he doing? Looking after me? Watching over me? He said he might have to drop Lyla at the Spaldings', because sometimes he has to work Sundays. Sometimes he has to work *every* day.

Whatever the case, I don't need looking after, and I certainly don't need to be followed, as if I am some criminal. Or someone who requires handholding, as if I am going to jump in the water all over again.

But the confrontation will have to wait; I have another, more pressing task. Which requires a different kind of courage. Seizing the moment, I scroll to the end of the report on my phone, to that vital name. The solitary eyewitness to my self-murder.

Brian Angove.

Venner

Sunday morning

It's not hard to find his house. There are only about six cottages in the tiny hamlet of Venner, a mile from Burrator. The hamlet is so small, it has no church, no pub, no shop, just a few thatched cottages sending wisps of smoke into the cold white sky, like graphite doodles on blank paper.

Brian Angove's cottage is called The Mallards, according to Google.

And there it is. A little black plaque bearing a blue duck, beyond the garden, a red-painted cottage. On a bright day it must be very pretty, the sort of place that makes tourists slow down for a minute to take a blast of photos on their phones, before heading on to the gastropub, five miles away, the one that does Exmoor lamb.

Smoke curls from this cottage too. So Brian Angove is in. Swallowing my anxieties, I creak open the tiny gate and walk up the path, count one two three, in time with my vigorously beating heart, and knock on the door with the cast-iron handle.

There is no immediate response. I glance at the windows. The glass is so thick and antique it is hard to tell if anyone is inside. A solitary crow watches me from a telegraph pole, its head tilted in curiosity. Perhaps it followed me from Burrator.

I knock once more, to no effect. There's no one in. Sighing with a mixture of dismay and relief, I turn, and head for the car.

'Hello? Can I help you?'

It's him. I recognize his image from my internet search. He's a retired county councillor. Sixty-seven, but seemingly hale and hearty. Brian Angove is wearing a pale-blue cardigan and brown corduroys; I hear the yapping of a dog in the dark interior of the cottage.

He squints at me. Comprehension dawns. 'Oh my word. I know who you are.'

I shrug.

'Please,' he says. 'Come in. I've got a pot of tea on the go. It's Darjeeling.'

I accept his invitation and step into his fragrant little cottage, full of old photos and sun-bleached gymkhana rosettes and fading photos of children. He takes my coat and delivers it to some closet, then returns and guides me down the hall to a neat kitchen table, where he pours the tea into floral china cups, stopping for a moment to say, 'We could have something stronger if you like, Mrs . . .'

'Redway. Kath Redway.'

'Yes. That's it. Redway, yes of course.' His smile is kindly: he wants to help, but I see pity too.

'Tea is fine,' I say. 'It's very nice of you, thank you. I'm so sorry to bother you.'

'It's no bother,' he says. 'I'm all alone here, on Sundays especially. I'm more than happy to talk if it helps. If that doesn't sound too peculiar.' His face flushes for a moment. 'In the circumstances. Ah.'

'No it's OK, it's OK.' I hurry on, because I am worried I will stop and walk away if I pause, even for a moment: I have dreaded this meeting since I discovered the identity of the witness.

'Mr Angove—'

'Brian.'

'Brian, I don't know if you know all the facts surrounding my case. You know. My . . .' I can barely say the word. 'Suicide. The facts surrounding my suicide attempt. All that kind of thing. Um.'

His gentle eyes meet mine and I see the pity again. I suppose it's better than hatred, or contempt. The woman who tried to leave her daughter alone in the world.

'All I know, Kath, is what I saw. What I told the police when they asked. That's all.'

'So I better tell you more about me.' My words rush out like young Dartmoor rivers. 'I have mild retrograde amnesia, because of the brain trauma, from the crash. That means I can't remember much or even anything of the few days before—' Again, I cannot say it. 'What I did that night.'

'I understand, I do understand, rest assured. My wife had memory loss before she died.' His voice is soft. Sad. 'She had Alzheimer's, very early onset. I understand these things, I do not judge. And I'm presuming, in the light of what you say, that you want to know exactly what I saw?'

'Yes,' I say, very quietly. 'Yes please.'

He pours more tea. And he tells me everything I expected, everything they say. A mild and dry December night. No ice, no frost. He was walking his dog around Burrator, across the dam at River Meavy, into the

125

oakwoods. Then he saw me and my car. An old Toyota. Parked on the tarmac. Next to the dam and the reservoir.

'I was parked?'

'Yes. That's why I stopped and looked. Not many people come to the reservoir at night, in the winter.'

'And it was just me in the car?'

He frowns. 'You, ah, really want all the details?'

'Yes.'

'Very well. I remember thinking it was a little peculiar. A person alone in a car, at the reservoir, in the dark. Looking at the water. And you were sitting up straight, perfectly still. As if you were thinking very hard.'

Something puzzles me here. 'If it was dark, how could you see anything?'

'It was a full moon, and the clouds were broken. You had a hood up, an anorak, or something. But I saw your profile.'

'Definitely me?'

'As the police said when they interviewed me, who else could it be?'

I stare at my Darjeeling. It's nice. Posh tea. Posher than the tea we have at home. Made with real tea leaves. I have an urge to swill them around, like my mum in one of her pagan moods, in the candlelight of a Salcombe evening, with all her hippy friends gathered around the Tarot cards, the African masks smirking on the wall. The only difference is that I want to see the past. Not the future.

I look directly at Brian.

'And what happened next?'

He shakes his head, slowly, regretfully. 'You drove your car nearer to the reservoir. Which did slightly alarm me, as there was that temporary gap in the wall. But you stopped again.'

'And after that?'

'I watched for a while, but you simply sat there. And I'm afraid to say,' he blushes and sighs, 'well, I got a bit bored. I reckoned you were meditating, thinking about something. People do that, come down to Burrator to think. The water is calming, isn't it? Peaceful. So I carried on walking Delilah. Our usual route. I thought no more about you until I reached the top of the reservoir, where you can look down. And then I saw it.' He shrugs, and looks quite pained. This is the moment. 'I couldn't quite believe it.' He closes his eyes as if he is saying a brief prayer; he opens his eyes and looks at me. 'I watched as you drove quickly through the gap, into the reservoir. Into the waters. Just like that. It was horrible and strange, I'm sorry, almost like a dream. A nightmare.'

I wonder if he is going to cry; I wonder if I am going to cry.

We both drink our tea. He continues, 'What struck me was the silence, the quietness of it all. It wasn't loud or dramatic: it was a quiet, mild evening and you quickly drove into the water and the car sank, so silently, so fast. And seconds later it was as if you'd never been there.'

If I hadn't seen it, no one would have known. Gone forever, in the blink of an eye.'

I say nothing. My quietness is painful. Brian says, 'Kath?'

'Sorry. Uh. Sorry.' I want to block this out, to retreat from this terrible image, the car sinking so quickly. *In the blink of an eye.* 'So what happened then, after I drove in the water? What came next?' He looks at me, mournfully, and sympathetically.

'Well. I was quite paralysed. I stood there for a while, a minute or so.'

'Why?'

'I was so *shocked,* I'm sorry – but then I ran straight home. I hadn't brought my mobile, there's no mobile reception down there anyway, so I had to run home. I don't run very fast, I'm afraid, not these days. I got to my house and called the emergency services and they took it from there.'

'And this was about nine p.m.?'

He nods. 'I hear they searched, and they brought divers, but of course you were found hours later, on the other side of the reservoir. In the woods. You must have swum, I suppose.'

'Yes, I suppose I did.'

His pain is still evident, his regret at not coming over to check on me. Before I did this terrible thing.

I look across my tea at my solitary eyewitness.

'Brian. It's not your fault, none of it. How were you to know? How was anyone to know?'

He nods. Our eyes meet, and then they avert. The teacups squeal awkwardly in the saucers.

My fierce anxieties deepen. What Brian says makes total sense, and makes it worse. I drove down to Burrator; *and I thought about it.* I hovered, I cavilled, I had doubts. I must have sat there in the car, silently thinking about Lyla and Adam, wondering if I could do this to them, go through with this, deliberately destroy my family. And I decided, Yep: I could do this to them. And I drove my car into the water, and it is now at the bottom of Burrator, where the police divers found it. It will probably stay down there forever, become a place for eels and trout. Rusting away to nothing.

'Thank you,' I say to Brian, and there must be anguish written in my face because he says, 'I'm sorry. I'm sorry I didn't think more, didn't go up to you when you were

128

parked, and, and . . . Well, I'm sorry. And I'm so glad you are alive.'

'Yes.' I don't know what else to say. This new silence is awkward, and terminal. I push back my chair; but Brian delays me with a gesture, says he will go and get my coat. And with that, he disappears.

Standing up, I am drawn to the window at the far end of the kitchen that looks out on to a humble garden. I feel, again, as ever, as if I am looking for something, but not knowing what.

Without warning, it hits me. There is a smell here, sweet verging on sickly, and I detect the source; a small reed diffuser on a shelf next to some ancient cookbooks. A heady, lemony scent. That scent. What is it? I am not sure. But it jogs a memory. A piece of the mental jigsaw puzzle; a fragment from that night. The memory is of a man, in a car, with me. The man is angry, shouting, his eyes piercing. Is this memory from the night I drove into Burrator? I am sure it is; it must be. It feels right. The doctors said memories would return, unbidden, and this could be the first important piece.

I lean my hand on the wall of the kitchen, feeling unsteady, my knees weak.

'Are you all right?'

I turn. It's Brian, carrying my coat.

'Yes,' I say. 'Sorry. I actually just thought I remembered something.'

'From that day?'

I blush. I don't know why. 'Yes.'

Brian helps me into the coat and we pace down the hall and I step out of his cottage, about to say goodbye. He stays me with a gentle hand on my arm. 'Is this the first time you've had any memory of that day?'

'Yes, but it was nothing. A tiny fragment. A face in a car. Nothing.'

'But the doctors say that all the memories will eventually return?'

I nod, hesitantly. 'Yes. But in pieces. Random.'

Brian gives me a half smile, sympathetic. 'In the early days of my wife's illness she found she could retrieve her memories with some, ah, techniques. Meditation. Photos. Associations. That is,' he looks me in the eye, searchingly. 'That is, of course, if you really *want* these memories to return.'

With a handshake we say goodbye. The door is closed, and I cross the road to my car. I am thinking about Burrator. I used to go there sometimes when I was younger, I used to love that view, over the water, to the woods, and high Sheepstor. It was a place I went to contemplate things. And that night in late December I went to contemplate my own death, and how to do it. Because there was no one to stop me. Because Adam was away. Because he'd left me with Lyla, in the darkest corner of the year.

Adam.

I'd almost forgotten. The figure on the hill. That really *was* Adam. I wonder, again, and angrily, how long he's been doing this. Following me.

I check my phone. There's a good signal. Urgently, I dial Adam's number, waiting for the inevitable voicemail: *Hi, this is Adam Redway, I'm probably out on the moor, leave a message.*

He picks up. 'Hello, Kath.'

'Why are you following me?'

My husband's silence is prolonged. Stunned or guilty. I cannot tell. He says nothing. I rage on, '*Tell me!* Why? I saw you today. On the hill. Why are you following me?'

'What the bloody hell are you talking about?'

'You were there, on the hill. It's creepy. It's wrong. Stalking. Stop it!'

I can hear him breathing heavily as if he's formulating a lie. I can hear wind in the background. He is still outdoors.

I want him to say the word *Burrator*, without me saying it. So I know he is guilty.

'I'm not following you, I'm not doing any such thing, Kath. Jesus Christ. This is crazy shit. I'm not stalking my own wife! I don't have time! I'm at work!'

'I don't believe you—'

'Listen. I'm up at Throwleigh, helping Nigel, we've got more fly-tippers, that frigging roof insulation kills the ponies – I can take photos if you like, would that be enough proof?'

'I saw you! Looking down at me, with binoculars!'

'No you didn't! Christ, not unless you've been in this farmyard. Jesus, Kath – stop it!'

I hold the phone hard in my hand, so hard I feel I might break it. Or break something else. My knuckles are white with anger. Why wasn't my husband the first one to come see me in hospital?

I have to press this now. 'Adam, what were you doing that night? Why did you have to go away for a week? Right after Christmas?'

'I was restoring the rangers' hut. Told you.'

'Just you?'

I hear the whinnies of ponies in the background. He goes on, talking above the weather. 'Dez was meant to join me. Dez Pritchard. But he didn't, he had some Christmas shit, you know.' He pauses, I hear a curt sigh. 'You know the kind of shit that happens at Christmas, Kath, don't you? Eh?' His sarcasm is laboured, but it still hurts. 'So, yeah I was alone. Got some peace to myself. For once.'

The phone is pressed so hard to my ear it hurts. I am angry, and also confused. My husband was not merely uncontactable for the entire period after Christmas – *he was alone*. I didn't know this. I had presumed he was with others, that was certainly the plan, I didn't know it hadn't panned out. This surely means something. He could have been anywhere. He could have been doing anything. He *could* have come home. He has no *alibi*.

Before he can ring off I ask again, 'Let me get this right. You preferred being alone up there, all week, sleeping in some hut, to coming back home, at night, to me and Lyla?'

Wherever he is, the wind is loud; his voice is louder. 'For a few days, Kath, yeah. So I got some bloody time to myself, away from Huckerby. What would be the point in coming back anyway? It's a long drive from Manaton, in the deep of winter, half the roads were flooded: it would've taken hours. And besides, who bloody cares, why do I have to explain myself? You know I haven't had a damn holiday away from Dartmoor for three years! Three years straight! You do know that, Kath, eh?'

I can't help wincing as I stand here in the speckles of rain. This is true. For the last three years I've gone to sunny Portugal with Tessa and Dan and the cousins, for summer holidays. Dan pays for me and Lyla.

Adam refuses to accept the charity, to come with us: he won't take Dan's money. But he reluctantly agrees that we can go, so Lyla can have fun with other kids, otherwise she wouldn't get any summer holiday at all.

And when we're gone he stays on the moor, and

works. Fifteen hours a day. The long, exhausting summer shifts.

My anger abates. Or my willpower.

I tell my husband we will talk about it later, and I ring off, before I damage our marriage further.

Opening the car door, I sit for a second and stare sadly at the spots of rain on the windscreen. I fiercely want to believe Adam. And yet I fiercely don't want to believe him. I am sliced precisely in two by the sharpest of dilemmas. Because if I believe him and he wasn't there at Burrator, that means I am getting worse, not better. I am starting to imagine things, as I surely did at Hobajob's. And if I *don't* believe him, that means my husband is not just a liar, he becomes something else entirely. Something worse.

And I cannot help but wonder where he was, the night I drove into Burrator.

Enough. Clicking my seat belt into place, I twist the key in the ignition. Foot to the floor, I race away. As I leave the village, a further, even darker thought intrudes. Brian Angove said that I drove that night as I am driving now: he said I drove *quickly* into the reservoir. What if I didn't actually mean to press the accelerator, what if I meant to do something else? Hit the brakes? Turn away?

One man would know, the only man who fixed my car.

Adam.

He was always tinkering, keeping the Toyota going, saving us money. We can't afford proper garages and mechanics, and he knows all about engines. Everything. He grew up on a farm fixing tractors, and trailers, doing up old motorbikes.

Is it conceivable he did something, over Christmas,

to the brakes, the throttle, something to make my car more dangerous? I do not know enough about cars to judge, and the car is now deep underwater and cannot be examined. But it is surely possible. Adam would only have done it when he knew I wasn't carrying Lyla. So he would have had to return to Huckerby, that week, that day – or perhaps, with this knowledge, he got someone else to do it at the precise moment, someone who was watching me. Maybe I never intended to drive into the water at all, but the car was altered that way.

My hand goes to my mouth, as if I am saying something terrible.

No. I *cannot* think this of my husband. What possible motive would he have, why would he want rid of me? Or *want* me to have a fatal accident? The thoughts are a whirl of snow in a Dartmoor gale, a white-out up on Skir Hill. And still, as I drive, as I race away, the crows are watching me, from the telegraph poles.

Black feathers. Black eyes.

Princetown

Monday afternoon

Adam stood, blowing warm air between cold hands, waiting in the chilly schoolyard for Lyla to come out of Princetown Primary School. The same way his nan would once have waited for him, when she could still drive.

His mother rarely came to collect him from school: too sad, or too drunk because she was sad, or taking those pills that made her sleepy and apathetic and unable to drive, but which made the humiliation of her marriage tolerable. His dad never came for him either: he was always away, working on some site, or more likely with some woman. Grinning when he came home, but never sharing the joke. Because it was never a joke for anyone else.

Nodding at some of the other parents chatting in the schoolyard, Adam wondered if he had broken the pattern. Of bad fatherhood. The repeating cycle, like the endless churn of water in a mill-race. Until this past Christmas, he would have said yes. Because he was a *good* father, a *good* husband: he worked every hour he could, he provided and protected, he hadn't kissed another woman since the wedding kiss with Kath.

But now? Ever since Kath had driven into Burrator, Lyla had occasionally behaved as if this calamity was *his* fault. She would sometimes push his hand from her face when he went to comfort her, flinch when he tried to kiss her. Sometimes she did this with a look of real fear, as if she knew something about Adam that he didn't.

Adam desperately wanted the old days back. He didn't want to be here in horrible Princetown, glancing sideways at the prison, looming over the end of the town, like the mad black palace of some tyrant.

You could never ignore the prison in Princetown. As he rubbed his hands against the bitter cold, Adam thought of all the ageing criminals in there. The rapists, the paedos, the murderers. The prison had long ago been downgraded from Category A to Category C, but plenty of the worst villains remained inside, because they were deemed too old and inert to attempt escaping. Too rotten inside, too morally eroded. Harmlessly evil.

Perhaps these guys were staring out at him now, from their cells, wondering what he was doing. Perhaps they were simply waiting to die, waiting for the moment when they might be buried alongside the Napoleonic soldiers in gloomy Princetown Church, where the damp was so bad weeds and ferns grew inside the nave, sprouting from the two-foot-wide stone walls.

When they had lived here in Princetown, years ago, the prison used to obsess Kath, gave her bad dreams. And so Adam had done everything he could to find somewhere new, somewhere better than Princetown for them to live. He'd searched and searched, with their limited budget, until a friend of his Uncle Eddie put him in touch with the Spaldings, and they'd offered to rent them Huckerby.

He'd done that. Him. Adam. The man of the family. He'd saved them. And now he was being blamed. Now he was becoming estranged from his only daughter, his only child?

The emotion threatened to choke him. He tried to fight it. He looked at his watch, then glanced up at the noise. Kids were pouring, early, out of the school, rushing like a torrent, like the joyous, falling waters of the West Dart, singing its way under Crockern Tor, and Adam knew he would have to wait.

Because it was *too* early.

Lyla was a rule-follower. If there were rules or codes she *had* to follow them, rigidly. Anything else panicked her. It was another reason why they all lived much more happily – or happily until this Christmas – out in the wilds, in the longhouse he'd found at Huckerby, the house he'd spent weeks, months, years making watertight and comfortable, a home where his girl could roam the wild moors at will, unworried that she might be trespassing, breaking rules.

Rules made her anxious. They had to be obeyed. Especially the school rule which said that school finished at 3.25 p.m. And for some reason the kids were pouring out, today, at 3.16 p.m.

He gazed about him. The other parents were dispersing briskly, ushering their offspring into cars.

3.17.

3.18.

The supervising teacher strolled back inside. The last cattle farmer took his bonny daughter by the hand and left the yard, with a nod Adam's way.

'All right, Adam? Cold weather comin', I hear?'

Adam offered a polite smile. And now he was all alone. 3.20. He could see a curious face in the window of the school office, looking out at him.

Quickly the face turned.

3.22.

3.23.

3.24.

Everyone else was gone now. Apart from Adam, and the killers in the prison. Finally, Lyla appeared at the painted school door, gazing out at the empty yard, her face puzzled. She shuffled over to her father.

'Where are they? Why've they gone early? It's not allowed.'

Adam reached for her hand but she was flapping her fingers. Stimming anxiously. 'They shouldn't let people go early. It says school finishes at three twenty-five. I tried to stop them going.'

'What?'

'I tried to tell the other children. They were breaking the rules!'

Adam gazed at his daughter, inwardly wincing, but as they walked to the car he attempted a smile. 'It was probably a teacher. Letting them go. Maybe you didn't hear. But,' he paused, pained, 'what did the other kids say to you? How did they react?'

'Oh. The usual. They laughed at me.' Her voice was almost a whisper now, softer and sadder than the summer breezes at Skaigh Woods, so quiet it tore at his heart. 'It's OK, Daddy. They always laugh at me, I'm used to it. Do you know what they call me?'

Adam wasn't sure he wanted to hear this. 'What do they call you, Lyla?'

'The Girl Who Isn't There,' she said. 'Some boy said it, and now they all say it. I'm The Girl Who Isn't There.'

The stab of pain was sharp, but deep. 'Sweetheart.' He kept his voice as casual as possible. 'You will tell me if anyone bullies you, won't you?'

'But they don't bully me, Daddy, they ignore me. That's why I always spend playtime by myself, by the water fountain. Or in the corner where no one can see me.'

'You don't ever play with anyone else?'

'They play so strangely, Daddy. I did try to understand, I did, I tried to join in but they laughed at me.' She was smiling brightly but sadly, up at the sky, following some bird, smiling bravely at something Adam could not see.

'But it's not their fault I can't understand their games. One of the boys said I was like a witch who lives at the end of the village, who no one talks to. They were joking, Daddy. Weren't they?' She looked up at him and he could see the troubled thoughts she was trying to hide.

Adam strived to conceal his own pity. *The Girl Who Isn't There.* It was cruel and it was raw. It was also accurate. Sometimes when Adam looked at his beautiful, eccentric daughter, when the two of them were out hiking on the high granite tors, or standing in the oakwoods of Soussons, with her pretty head tilted, and her blue eyes half closed, he could see her listening to the imperceptible noises, the sounds of the moor: shrews under the witchbeams, butterflies in the honeysuckle, and sometimes he would think, she's not here. She's somewhere else. And no one knows where.

They climbed inside the Land Rover. Adam started it up and they headed out of Princetown, Lyla mute now. Adam checked the mirror. She was staring at something in her hand. With a faint throb of anxiety, he realized what it was.

A hag stone. A polished stone with a weathered hole

through it. A stone against evil. He hadn't seen one of these in years.

'Where did you get that, darling?'

Lyla looked up, caught his gaze in the mirror, and shrugged. 'Somewhere.'

'Tell me?'

She shook her head. Turning the stone. Over and over.

'You know that's a special stone, don't you?' No answer.

He pressed again. 'People used to hang them on doors, or put them in special places. They believed they were magic. Silly stuff like that.'

Lyla muttered as she turned the stone. 'I find them all the time.'

The tension quickened inside him. 'Where? Where do you find them?'

Another shrug. 'Places.'

'What places?'

The monosyllables turned to silence. Her eyes were averted. He knew she wouldn't speak now. Not for a while, not for a day. Nothing to be done. Adam gazed out across the landscape as he drove the moorland road, as the sunlight and cloud-shadows chased each over the grey slopes, the wind sighing in the ferns and heathers. The frail winter sun always gave such a shifting light: one minute glittering on the silver sprays of birch trees, then gone again, thrusting all into darkness.

The silence was too much.

'You know your granny collected those special stones?' Lyla did not reply. Adam was talking to himself.

'She knew all the legends and stories. You should have met her: she was a grand woman. My nan. Molly Redway. You'd've loved her, Lyla.'

Lyla did not reply. Adam drove on, he knew the road so well he could practically close his eyes and drive it blind. So he let himself drift into memories. He was seven. Granny Molly was telling him stories in her cosy little cottage near Doccombe, with Adam's bike leaning against her garden gate. Sometimes he went to see her with his cousins, Jack and Harry and Neil, but usually he went alone.

Because Adam was the only one of the family who took a real interest in her stories. The stories were great: they distracted him from the unhappiness of home. So many stories. Stories about the Walla Brook, the stream of the strangers, stories of the voogas, the little caves used by miners near Lydford, where the pixies lived; stories about Amicombe Hill on the coldest winter nights. It was said that on those still winter nights, when the deep wells of moorwater gave back a reflection of the curving moon, you could hear the howls of the Devil and his witches. It was also said that the Devil once stopped at the Tavistock Inn on his way to Widecombe, and paid in money, which turned to dead leaves in a day.

On and on the tales went. A different one every evening. Stories of spells, of drownings and mires, stories of the River Dart as it took another life: *Dart Dart, every year thou breakest a heart*; and after that came all those endless winter stories of phantoms: ghostly highwaymen, ghostly hands, ghostsoldiers, ghost-trees, ghosts from Sheepstor to Lustleigh. After telling these stories Molly would laugh uproariously and make another cup of tea, and Adam would laugh too, feeling safe, because it was all a joke. Everyone knew the stories were silly fairytales: there weren't any witches under Vixen Tor, not any more.

So Adam would laugh and eat his nan's fruit cake, and feel happy and safe in her home, the same way he felt happy and safe in Uncle Eddie's farm, the way he never felt safe in his own home with his mum crying quietly, a bottle of something in her hand, falling asleep on the sofa, drooling on to a cushion, his dad out all hours, and his older sister having left home to go work in Bristol.

And then, years later he'd told Molly's stories to Kath's mum, because she was always so curious about all that stuff. But Penny Kinnersley didn't laugh, sitting there in the pub in Chagford. She ordered more expensive wine and listened earnestly to these tall Dartmoor tales as if she was learning something important. Penny Kinnersley, who liked to do astrology charts, and pray to the moon. Penny Kinnersley, who had her ashes scattered at Kitty Jay. Penny Kinnersley would have known all about hag stones. And Vixen Tor.

Briskly, Adam parked the car. His last chore of the day: paying in cash for the winter firewood. Everyone in Dartmoor liked to be paid in cash.

He turned to his little girl, strapped in the back of the Land Rover. She'd placed the hag stone on the seat, arrayed in a curving row with her pens and pencils and rubber. A pattern, of course. She was always making patterns. But this hag stone. This was new. Where had she got it?

'Got to pop in this farmhouse. Won't take a sec. You want to come?'

Lyla shook her head. Moving the hag stone to the left, perfecting the pattern.

Adam kicked open the door. The day was cold, bitter. He jogged to the door, rang the bell, but the Pritchards' isolated farmhouse looked dark and empty so he shoved the envelope of cash through the letter box. The money he'd earned. Again the resentment churned, as he recalled Kath's latest prosecution. *You're stalking me.* What exactly did she expect? What was he meant to do, not watch out for her? Not check up on her?

So yes: he was following, checking, watching. He was doing his job, the farmyard task, the moorland chore. Shooting the dying sheep.

Processing the carcass. Protecting Kath from herself. Saving the family. Getting them through the bad times. Because he was a good husband, and a good father. And sometimes good men had to do bad jobs.

And sometimes men had to stay silent as they did these jobs, even when they knew they'd been wronged.

But his resentments still surged. Thaw-water from a moorland winter. And he couldn't stop it. He wondered if *this* was the time to tell Kath what she had said when he came into the hospital, while she was still very woozy, before she fell asleep again. The words she had since conveniently forgotten.

The words he had never forgotten.

Adam, I'm sorry, the sex, I never wanted it. It was the eyes, they were such a memory, it was my fault.

But he still couldn't say this, despite his jealousy. Because it might break her entirely. And Lyla needed a mother more than ever, because his daughter was behaving more strangely than ever. But who had Kath had sex with? And why had it made her drive into the water? Was it even related? Adam wondered about that old car. He was always checking it, it was always so close to being a wreck. But that week he was away.

The cold was biting, as he opened the door.

'All right, Lyles?'

His daughter barely acknowledged him. She looked down at the hag stone.

Taking deep breaths, Adam started the engine and drove down narrow stone roads, past the sign saying *Take Moor Care*, raced over the rattlebone clatter of the next cattle grid, that noise which made Lyla put

143

her hands over her ears. He drove on, eating up fast corners, checking the mirror. Lyla was staring out of the car window over the rainy emptiness towards Blackdown.

Following her gaze, Adam realized his daughter wasn't gazing aimlessly. She was watching a moorland pony cantering across the wild grey grasses about half a mile away. He slowed the car and joined her reverie. Because he loved the ponies as much as she did. They'd been here so long, these creatures, longer than men probably. The hillies were a law unto themselves. Sometimes hundreds of hill-ponies would scatter, stampede, for no reason. Adam had seen it for himself. It was always such a sight, a great herd galloping away from something invisible, as if they had seen a ghost on the moor, something prehistoric, long gone, which only the hill-ponies could remember.

He shuddered inwardly, as a related memory returned with a sharpening pain. The ponies. That was the *one* job he'd found too much. The killing of the ponies.

It must have been fifteen years back, more, when they were all in their late teens. Adam and his uncle and his cousins – Neil, Alec, Jack, whoever was around – had all been recruited to shoot the hill-ponies. Because Natural England wanted it. They culled the half-breeds to preserve the real hillies, and to save the moor from overgrazing. It was grisly work and no one wanted to do it; but the Redways needed the cash. And this kind of bloody work was their business.

Jack was especially keen, he always needed money.

So his uncle and cousins and Adam had spent a week driving out to Kes Tor or Grimspound or the old quarry tracks south of Princetown, way off road, following the packs of ponies, cornering the terrified horses, mares and stallions, in dark quarries, rocky cul de sacs. And then he and his uncle and his cousins had climbed out, with their boltguns, to do the job.

There was a tried-and-tested technique. Cruel and grim.

First, you coaxed the horses with a mint, a Trebor mint on the flat of your palm, then you waited, and eventually one of the ponies would relax and come over, out of sight of the herd, and after that, when they stooped to eat the sweetie from your hand, you put the boltgun to the soft forehead, three inches above the eyes, under the hanging and beautiful forelock. That was the blind spot. The sweet spot. Bang.

They all wore their shittiest clothes, because the blood and brains went everywhere.

Sometimes you had to do this to foals, and the mares would run over and see the foals slump to the mud and sedge, and their desperate, urgent maternal whinnying was the worst: like a hideous wail, yet fiercer. Sometimes you had to kill the mothers, too. The sounds of suffering were too much to bear.

Adam stirred himself from this atrocious memory. The horse was gone now, and Lyla was no longer looking out of the window. Adam drove on, glancing at the mirror.

'Lyla. I want to ask you a question.' She grimaced but said nothing.

'Why are you acting a bit, like, strangely with me, sweetheart?'

Lyla shook her head. 'Mmmnot.'

'Yes,' Adam insisted. 'Yes, you are. Ever since Christmas, and Mummy's, um, accident. You behave differently. To me. As well as Mummy.'

As he changed gear, she said, 'I don't.'

'Yes. You do.'

'No.'

The pointlessness felt like wading through boggy ground. 'Lyla, please. I only want to help. If something is worrying you, tell us, tell me. We love you, don't want you to be anxious, you can tell us.'

She shook her head and looked quietly away, looked past him, at the vast draperies of distant winter rain; her averted face hiding the shine in her eyes. She looked even younger than her years. Soon she would be ten, soon it would be her tenth *birthday*, and Kath, against all his advice, was organizing a party. But who would come? Kath claimed she'd had verbal confirmation from a dozen parents already, that they'd attend, and Kath had told this to a surprised and then excited Lyla; but this initial enthusiasm, Adam reckoned, was just the parents feeling sorry for the strange little girl.

In time the kids themselves would object. *We don't play with her.* And then the refusals, the mind-changes and apologies, would duly arrive. Hurting Lyla more.

He decided to have one more go.

'Lyla, like I said, it helps if you tell things. That's all.'

'What?'

'Tell us if you have any worries—'

'No, Daddy. Please.'

'What?'

'*Please* stop asking things. You don't want to know. You don't want to know!'

He was at a loss. What did he not want to know? What did *she* know? He wondered if Lyla had witnessed whatever it was Kath had done that night? Perhaps she had witnessed that infidelity, the key to it all. His daughter appeared to know more than she was admitting. Maybe it was too awful for her to tell.

'Lyla—'

'No, Daddy. Stop it!'

He abandoned the questioning for now. It was clearly pointless, or actively counter-productive. And they were nearly home. The liquid sunset over Hexworthy was a wild and pretty sight. A violent orange bleeding into red and black. He parked the Land Rover and they squelched across the farmyard. Kath's car was nowhere to be seen.

Lyla ran ahead. Such a fast runner now. He called out to his disappearing daughter, 'Remember to change out of your uniform!'

She'd opened the front door and run inside. They never locked it. Adam went to the back of the car to take out the shopping in the last of the wintry twilight. As he hefted the Lidl bags he paused: he could hear his daughter singing in the kitchen. A distinct song. Lyla liked singing. She had a sweet voice, though she was usually too shy to let anyone hear it. She loved all the Seth Lakeman songs, especially: 'The Streamers', 'Band of Gold', and her favourite, 'The Warning of a White Hare, her eyes burning bright'. He was glad she never sang the Kitty Jay song. The tune was too harsh, the words too much. Way too much.

But this wasn't a song he recognized, anyway: these words were very different.

Weren't they?

Adam hoisted as many bags as he could, trying to do this boring chore as quickly as possible, staggering to the door of the kitchen. He looked down. A dead rat was lying there in the yard, close to the front door, grinning fiendishly, as if it had died in severe pain. Poisoned, no doubt. But who had left it here? Right here, by the door?

His girl was still singing.

And now he realized what she was singing. And the

liquid cold entered his fingers and his arms, and headed for his chilling heart.

O little blue light in the dead of the night,
O prithee, O prithee, no nearer to creep

Adam felt a rush of irrational fear. For the first time in his life, he was scared of something he could not comprehend, as if he was hearing his nan tell one of her silly ghost stories, and he actually believed it. First the hag stone, now this.

Lyla sang it again:

O little blue light in the dead of the night,
O prithee, O prithee, no nearer to creep

His heart pained him with its thumping. Because this was an old song Molly used to sing, just once or twice. An old Dartmoor tune. And he'd quite forgotten it, and the fact that his nan used to sing it. He was sure that no one else would have remembered it. He recalled Molly telling him the legend of the blue-flamed corpse-candles: floating blue lights that appeared at night at a window, presaging a death. You only sang this song if you thought someone was about to die. His nan had sung the song to him, the song of the blue light, in the dead of the night. He had been seven, or eight. And no one else had ever sung this song to him since that day. And Adam's mother had died a few weeks later after Molly sang it. The death was from a sudden undiagnosed cancer, the kind that eats you up, in weeks, like you were never there. A candleflame snuffed between two casual fingers. And a few years later his dad had moved to Exeter, with some new woman, who he'd probably been seeing all along, and Adam had moved in with Uncle Eddie, and been glad to do so.

And in time Adam had forgotten this funny old song, and Molly's singing of it, yet now he was being reminded. Now his nine-year-old daughter was singing this same song very wistfully, standing in the middle of the gloomy kitchen, staring out of the window at the last light of a dying winter's day. Singing the song of a death rushing towards them.

O little blue light in the dead of the night,
O prithee, O prithee, no nearer to creep

Suppressing a shudder, Adam turned to shut the kitchen door. As the door closed, the dead rat grinned at him, its yellow teeth bared.

Hexworthy

Tuesday afternoon

I am watching, thoughtful, self-absorbed, as the dogs gallop ahead of us across the open moor. It's a vigorous walk. Emma Spalding has come better dressed for this hike than me: Hunter wellies, green Barbour, a thick scarf. She looks a proper countrywoman, tall and stout, fifty-something, striding the moors confidently as if she owns them all, from Ashburton to Bridestow.

I'm in jeans and blistered walking boots that let in the water. We can't afford new ones. But I don't care. It's good to get out of the house. I spent the whole of yesterday designing invitation cards for Lyla's birthday party. I offered verbal invitations days ago, and got lots of interest, but I wanted to remind everyone, make it official. So I took hours and hours drawing little birds and fishes on my laptop, something Lyla-esque, trying to remind everyone that my daughter isn't just the geeky, awkward girl no one likes, but that she is special, precious, funny, adorable, if you give her a chance. Then I put them all in envelopes, sealed them and stamped them and took them to the Princetown post office, said a little prayer as I popped them in the slot. I've invited practically everyone at her school, thirty or forty kids, in the hope that eight or nine will come, from the twelve mums and dads who initially agreed.

I look up. Emma is marching on. I race to catch up, striding over the rolling hills of fern and bracken. I can see the thatched roofs of Hexworthy village from here, the whitewash of the Forest Inn. Further in the distance I can see the heights of Buckland Beacon, with its Ten Commandment stones, the words of God, chiselled into granite by some mad landowner way back.

Thou Shalt Not Murder.

As we walk on, I gaze at the Beacon. Remembering the time when I went to church for a few years in my mid-teens. I think I did it solely to annoy my mother, as a feeble act of rebellion. Christianity! Abrahamic religions! Patriarchy! Mum had been suitably scandalized: she'd probably have preferred me to summon demons. Or dance naked around the stones of Scorhill, like her and her friends from Totnes.

But now the memories of that period, my churchgoing, my tambourine-bashing, return to haunt me. Because it reminds me that I am a mortal sinner. An attempted self-murderer.

Here it is to be noted, that the Order for the Burial of the Dead is not to be used for any that have laid violent hands upon themselves . . .

'Kath? Are you with us, dear?'

I turn to Emma and force a smile. 'Yes. Just wondering where the dogs have gone. Ah, wait, that's Randal!' I call for him but he ignores me and paces on, his ears pinned back. He is probably scenting a rabbit or a hare. Or some doggy memory of a scent, something long gone.

'Minds of their own, your dogs,' says Emma Spalding. 'Except when they're with Lyla, of course.' She laughs robustly. 'Your daughter commands them with a single word, like a fairy queen.'

I nod, glancing back. I do that these days. Glance across the moor, as if something is coming for us, something fast and determined. Right now it looks as if rain is coming: the black clouds form their winter regiments.

'Thanks for the company, Emma, it's not the nicest day.'

'Think nothing of it,' she says. 'It's great to get off the farm. I've been on the phone all morning, trying to get permission to swale. You don't know how hard it is!' She puts on a comically formal voice, mimicking some stiff civil servant: "Areas of bilberry exceeding twenty hectares can only be burned once every seventy-eight months."' She swats at some gorse with her walking stick. 'They don't *understand*. Commoners have been tending this moor for *thousands* of years. We *made* the moor, then Defra comes along and says it knows better? Pff! Look at all this ling: it has to be burned back.' Emma pushes her greying hair out of her eyes as the breeze kicks up. 'Sorry, Kath! Ranting again, hah! Farming on this moor is so *damnably* hard. But we love it. Don't we?'

'Yes. Yes, we do.' I'd like to agree more sincerely, but I can hear the voice of my daughter in my head. Lyla hates the swaling, she sometimes cries about it: the way it kills the animals, the tinier birds, and the way that for weeks afterwards, whenever you walk through a swaled moorland scene, everything is black, and you get covered in ash, the ash of dead things.

'Kath?'

'Sorry—'

I am doubly distracted: even as I think about Lyla, I am also scanning the grass for signs of our exuberant yet lethal dogs. I can hear them barking, but I cannot see them. They are probably halfway down a rabbit hole, cornering some terrified doe. On Dartmoor the casual cruelty of nature always intrudes, even on an everyday afternoon walk.

'You wanted to ask me something,' says Emma, as one the dogs – Randal – canters into view, and disappears again, barking excitedly.

'Yes.' I stiffen, gathering my weakening resolve. I have to do this. Drain the waters. Reveal the tors and hills. I believe I am getting there. But I need more help, more facts. 'It's about that day, the day I . . .' I swallow the dry taste of my shame and embarrassment. 'The day I did it.'

Emma looks at me, unflinching. 'I was wondering when you would ask, to be perfectly honest, Kath.'

'All right,' I say. 'Can you please tell me what was I like when I came over?'

'Which time?'

I stop and stare at her. Perplexed. 'Sorry, what? What do you mean, which time?'

'You came over twice that day.'

Her eyes widen at my blank look.

'You don't remember?!'

Helplessness surges. This is another thing lost at the back of my mum's endless cupboards. Another jar of Manuka honey I had forgotten I ever possessed. 'No, I don't remember. Oh God, it's freaking me out. Please tell me: I'm trying to fit it all together.'

'All right, ah, shall we sit here, out of the wind? Your

154

lurchers will come back soon enough.' She points to a ledge of exposed granite, part of a humble tor to the left. We sit on the cold, damp stone and I listen. Hard. As she explains.

'At about noon Lyla came over to our place, by herself, with Felix and Randal. You'd called me beforehand, asked if it was OK. You said you had to do some shopping or something. Tavistock, was it? Anyway, Lyla didn't want to go with you.'

I nod: it is logical. Lyla doesn't like big towns, madding crowds. In the past she would kick up silent tantrums before a big shop, hiding in her den. She would go rigid and foetal simultaneously, refusing to move. Sometimes we had to pick her up, force her into the car.

'So,' I am keen to fit this new information into the old, though I don't see how it squares. 'How long was Lyla there, the first time?'

'A few hours. Perhaps four? We mucked out the horses together. It was nice. George and I had been away for Christmas and we'd only been back a day and we'd missed her!'

'And after I'd been shopping, I came back to collect her.'

Emma confirms, 'Yes.'

'I don't quite get it.'

Emma says, very patiently, 'You left Lyla with us twice that day, Kath. First in the afternoon, then later on in the evening.'

I shake my head, looking across the gorse. I think some farmer is already swaling down towards Scorriton. I can see billows of white smoke, a long, slender line of burning orange flame. I imagine Lyla staring at this, I imagine her thinking of all the little moorland animals, the field-mice burned alive, birds trapped in fiery thorns.

155

My confusion is deep as a Dartmoor mine. If I dropped Lyla off once, I'm not sure why on earth I would do it again, and ask so much of Emma. The Spaldings are very kind to us, they cut our rent in half when Adam was ill. I hate to impose on them too much. I turn to Emma.

'So I brought back Lyla again, in the evening? How did I seem?' Another uncharacteristic pause. My friend is silent. I'm not.

'Emma, please, I need to know. I tried to do that thing, that terrible thing. And I can't remember why. I don't care how bad it is, it can't get any worse.'

She answers quietly. 'Well, dear. All day you were, um, a little odd. *Distrait*. Is that the word?'

'I don't know. What does it mean?'

The wind whirrs in the bracken, restless and impatient. Waiting for something bad to happen. Emma smiles, uncertainly, reassuringly.

'You were agitated, Kath. I knew you'd been alone with Lyla since Christmas. We knew Adam was away, so I put it down to that. Loneliness and isolation: there was a lot of rain after Boxing Day – we came back to floods in places. Raybarrow was like the Bristol Channel.'

'But, I can cope with rain. I'm alone with Lyla a lot. We like being alone at Huckerby. I don't see why I would be agitated.'

The grey-white smoke from the swaling is obscuring the view. I cannot see. I cannot see.

'Emma, there must be more. What did I say, what did I look like? Give me something, anything.'

'All right, Kath, dear.' She puts a maternal hand on my shoulder. 'You seemed agitated, but also a tad, well, *excited*.'

The perplexity grows. I open my mouth, but say

nothing. The silence extends between us until Emma feels forced to say more.

'What I mean is: you looked rather giddy, and girlish, especially the first time, when you walked over to collect Lyla at 4 p.m. You'd had a drink, I think; I saw wine stains on your lips.' She shrugs awkwardly. 'But you weren't drunk. Rather, you know. As I say. Excited.'

What is she saying? I go on despairingly: 'And the second time, when I dropped Lyla off again? How did I come across?'

'You looked smarter.'

'I changed into new clothes?'

'Yes, you had a new shirt on, um, smart boots, new jeans.'

'What?'

'Look, Kath. It's got absolutely nothing to do with me. You're my friend. I'm not going to judge anyone, especially not you or Adam. Every marriage is different, every marriage is difficult. God knows George and I have had our differences.' She stands. 'We really ought to be going, here are the dogs, right on time.'

Felix and Randal are galloping back, ears flapping excitedly.

I won't let this drop. As we hike back to Huckerby, I press it again.

'Emma, you were going to say something else?' She remains silent.

'Emma, please, I'm going mad. I need to know what happened that night. No matter how painful, *not* knowing is worse.'

She sighs, repeatedly thrashing the bracken with her stick as if she wants to kill it. 'Must get back,' she says. 'Those horses won't feed themselves!'

A hearty panting to my left interrupts us, and makes

me turn. It's Felix. He has blood on his teeth. He and Randal must have got a rabbit, chewed a leg or an eye, left it bleeding to death. Or they simply killed it. Everything is bleeding out, and I don't have much time left.

Adam likes the fact the dogs hunt. He likes that they kill.

Adam, Adam, Adam. Is he the man on the moor, or did someone else come to see me? And what did they do to me?

I do not know. And soon I must face my daughter's birthday party. The panic and confusion rises, all around me, like black water. I feel as if everything is watching over: the dogs, the birds. No, they are not. I have to get a grip, hold my breath, escape the car as it sinks into the blackness.

Again I run to catch up with Emma, and take her by the hand.

'Please, Emma. Please. Tell me everything. I have to know. Or I will go mad.'

Her sigh is enormous, but she nods. 'OK. Very well. But please don't take this as gospel, Kath! As I said: you were acting oddly, rather giddy, talking to yourself really – I couldn't be *absolutely* sure, but you were muttering.'

'What was I muttering?'

'You seemed distracted. You said you'd talked to Adam, or you needed to see him. Something had happened.'

'Like what?'

'I don't know. But you said you were going to meet someone. You mentioned Two Bridges. The Two Bridges Hotel.'

The wind dies. At precisely the right time.

I look at her. 'Who? Who was I going to meet?'

Emma is barely able to meet me my eye. She looks

over my shoulder as if she can see down to the coast at Brixham and at last says, 'Your brother. You said you were going to meet your brother.'

My mind swirls; the wind catches dead bracken and flings it into the air.

'My *brother*? But he was in London. And Adam was away. Dan. My brother?'

Emma walks on. I stand here. Thinking.

Daniel Kinnersley. My brother. Who dislikes Adam. Who got the house. My mother's favourite. My handsome, rich and generous brother, of whom I am sometimes jealous, despite myself.

Why would I be excited about seeing him?

Nothing quite fits, yet the pieces are clearly all here. There is either another man in all this, or there is an aspect of my brother, or of my husband, that I never suspected.

And now I begin to suspect. Both of them.

Salcombe

Tuesday evening

Tessa watched her husband pour more wine. Daniel Kinnersley watched her watching him.

'It's an Imperial Reserva. I'm not going to leave it to evaporate.' He swivelled the bottle on the dining table to show her the label. 'Look! Compañía Vinícola del Norte de España – 2004! This is the stuff they serve *in heaven*.'

'I'll take your word for it,' she said, smiling, and sipping her own white wine. Tessa didn't like red wine, but she liked Dan's enthusiasm. She loved his drive, his hunger, his ambition, his appetite for the world, and for her. Being around Daniel Kinnersley was exciting, and sexy. There were a lot of sexless marriages out there: she knew enough to know that she was lucky.

'Here,' he said, 'let me clear these plates away. You spent hours cooking a delicious dinner, seems only fair I should spend three or four minutes loading the dishwasher.'

He disappeared into the distant kitchen, carrying

the dessert plates, with their last smears of tiramisu. Whistling.

Tessa sat back, halfway satisfied. The boys had already gone to bed, ready for the early flight tomorrow; so they'd taken the chance to have a proper supper with candlelight and silver cutlery and good wine and sword-fish steaks in caper sauce. She'd never cooked the recipe before, and it was, she thought, a definite success.

The world seemed a pretty good place. The big house gleamed. Through the dining room windows the pretty lights of Salcombe harbour sparkled brightly in the deep winter darkness. Their holiday clothes were packed: sunshine beckoned in the Canary Islands, and on the way back, a weekend at Disneyland Paris. They were to fly out tomorrow at 10 a.m., so they'd have to start the drive at 6 a.m., but it was worth it. Winter sun!

The only jarring note was, firstly, the nagging thought that would not go away. *Kath*. Up there in that rented house, marooned on the moors. Kath. Having to organize a birthday party for her lonely girl. And there was that niggling but persistent lie: Dan's claim that he drove back from London, when Tessa knew he used the train.

With a happy whistle, Dan came back into the dining room, sat down at the shining mahogany table and tipped the last of the red wine down his throat with a gasp of pleasure. Languid and relaxed, he reached behind him, for another bottle. 'Yes, yes, yes. It's the second.' He smiled mischievously. Carelessly. 'You do know Winston Churchill drank sixteen pints of whisky every day, and a bucket of absinthe, and still became pope. After flying to the moon?'

Despite herself, she chuckled, and felt an urge to kiss him. But then it nagged again. *Kath*. How could she feel happy and contented, how could she joke with her husband, sitting here in this big house, with nice food and good humour, and a winter holiday barely hours away, when the other half of Dan's family was mired in confusion, and misery?

And that poor little girl.

And that brooding, sometimes menacing, husband.

'Dan.' She watched him as he flamboyantly uncorked the second bottle, sniffed the cork, carefully half-filled his glass. The wine made a *luxurious* sound as it was poured: the glugging sound of money, the sound of Dan's success as a property developer, the sound of their good luck. Too much good luck, perhaps.

'Dan, do you think we could do more, to help Kath? They're in such a state. Can't we do more?'

He flashed her a sharp little glance. 'Like what?'

'I don't know. Pay for therapy. Anything.'

'There is no therapy, you said so yourself.' He sighed. 'Can't we have one evening when we don't talk about this? Can't you ever leave it alone?'

'Dan, she's your sister! I worry about her. And Lyla. I'm trying to help them: Adam asked me to get involved and you said it was a good idea that I should break the news to her.' Tessa raised her hand in protest, as Dan made to speak. 'We can't let it go. These memories will return and it could be horrific. Whatever caused her to attempt suicide. What if it tips her over? What if she is already having another, deeper breakdown? I want to know why she did it, before the returning memory hits.'

He looked at her, his eyes heavy with alcohol. But still bright. Cynical. 'OK. Sure. Good for you.' He yawned. 'But, Jesus, Tessa, this endless meddling, this endless Sherlock crap gets us nowhere. Why did she drive there, who did what when, how does it help anyone?' He shook his head. 'Maybe we should all accept she had a spazz-out. She's lucky to be alive, move on.'

'I will, Dan, I will stop all my' – she made air quotes with two fingers – '"meddling". When I've exhausted all avenues.'

Dan sighed. 'OK, darling. Whatever.'

He tasted the wine and nodded to himself, happy at the fineness of the flavour.

Across the table, Tessa watched him. A man relishing the sweetness of life. And fair enough, she thought. After all, he'd earned it. He'd worked insanely hard as a younger man, building the company. Seven days a week, barely seeing the boys. Now he had underlings and the business wasn't quite so demanding, so he was kicking off his shoes, stretching out, and being a better father, too. Football at the weekends, proper holidays. Off to the Canaries tomorrow, a villa with a big blue pool. They were so lucky. Too lucky. It nagged at her, once more.

'Dan, do you ever feel guilty, about getting this house from your mum? When Kath got virtually nothing?'

He flashed her a sharp glance. 'Sorry?'

'This house. We got such a kick-start compared to Kath and Adam. Do you ever feel guilty about it?'

He regarded her levelly. And he nodded. 'OK, yes, I do feel guilty about the house. Of course I feel that. Although I also wonder. Perhaps Mum had her reasons.'

'Reasons?'

'Reasons of her own.'

'Like what?'

Her husband blithely ignored her. He was lifting the beaded redness of his wine to the candlelight to examine the ruby colour, with the light behind it. 'Exceptional,' he said. 'Quite exceptional. Tempranillo, Graziano. Marzuelo. Like a line of poetry, in the form of liquor.'

164

Tessa interrupted. 'Dan? What does that mean? *Reasons?*'

'What I mean is, who the fuck knows why Mum did it? She could have had any number of reasons. That was Mum, that was her charm. She was scatty. Perhaps she genuinely thought those shares and paintings and creepy antiques were worth as much as the house, who can tell? By the end she was *scrambled*, Tessa, a real mess, painting herself orange in Goa, dying of cancer, talking about the Devil.'

He shook his head and set his glass down. 'Besides, darling, I do try to give them money, I do try to help them, but Adam's proud: he simply won't take it. And I respect him for that, and I don't want to disrespect him. Therefore, in that light, what can I possibly do?'

Kath nodded in thoughtful agreement. It was true. What *could* they do, more than they did already? During Adam's illness they'd quietly given Kath some cash, to help out, but you could only go so far with that. Kath didn't like it. And Adam would be furious if he felt they were being subsidized; the antagonism with Dan would get much worse.

She took another sip of Sauvignon Blanc. Thought about Dan's mum, his family. Then Kath again.

Dan reached a hand across the table, took her fingers in his. 'Hey, babe, look. I know you worry about all this, but Kath is tough, way tougher than you think. Really. She'll be OK.'

'But that's it, she's tough, she's smart. *I don't get it.* Why would she try and do that? That terrible thing?'

He grimaced, with a hint of irritation, her fingers still entwined in his. 'Maybe she just had a bit of a meltdown, over Christmas. I mean, who could blame her – the fucking weather up there, the endless winters. I'd have a noose out by November.' He squeezed her hand. 'Can we not talk about this any more? It gets exhausting. Shall we clock out, go to bed?'

'It's ten p.m.!'

'Or I could fuck you in the kitchen if you prefer?'

Again, he made her laugh. Also, he turned her on. Tessa grinned. 'Let me finish my wine, you terrible seducer.'

'You've got ten minutes.'

Her mind was hazy. The wine, and the idea of sex, was blurring her thoughts. She remembered she'd wanted to ask one more question. His lie about the drive down to see Kath. When he'd really got the train. Yes. That lie. Why did he lie? But her mind was fuzzy, her mood was good. It didn't really matter, it could wait.

Yet it couldn't.

'Dan, there's one more thing I've been meaning to ask.'

'Mmm?'

'It's about the day Kath was, you know, found, when you rushed back to see her in hospital.'

'Uh-huh.' He was sealing the bottle with the cork.

'Well, it's just that you said you drove down, like a madman, but I don't see how.'

She wished she hadn't had that third glass. But she had to go on, now she'd started. 'Thing is, Dan, you didn't drive to London, the day after Boxing Day, you got the train. Remember? We discussed it. You wanted to avoid the M5. You left the car here. So how could you drive back?'

Dan had his back to her, checking the cork was firmly back in the bottle. Slowly, he put the bottle on the shelf behind. Now he swivelled, and smiled. 'I drove down with Alex Delaney. One of the developers in Truro. He's got a bloody Aston Martin, gave me a go behind the wheel!' Dan laughed. 'He was driving down anyway and

I thought, that will be faster than the train. Remind me to buy an Aston Martin when I'm fifty-eight. It's almost better than sex. Almost, darling.'

Was he lying? Again? She thought so. She couldn't tell. Perhaps she didn't want to tell. Perhaps she should leave it alone. He was right. They were off on holiday first thing tomorrow. Sun and cocktails and the boys, laughing in the pool.

He pulled her to him and his lips met hers. She felt her doubts yield when he kissed her the second time. Her phone was ringing, spinning on the dining table. From this distance she could see the word KATH on the screen. Maybe, however, it was time to forget about Kath, for a week or two. She'd call her when they got back from holiday.

Yes. It was time to devote herself to her sons, to her husband, to his kisses. Because he knew how to kiss her. Dan Kinnersley always knew how to kiss her. And she was a lucky wife. She really did have it all. So why did she want to ruin it?

Tessa didn't want him to stop kissing her. He'd brought her into the kitchen. Almost carried her. He was still kissing her, expertly, even as he stripped her. And he was pushing her against the fridge freezer. Lifting her up on to the marble counter. More forceful than usual, way more forceful.

Like he wanted her to forget everything they'd said.

Two Bridges Hotel

Saturday morning

Sitting in my car, outside the hotel, reading my emails, I stare at the last of my hopes draining away.

> Dear Kath, I'm afraid to say Daisy is really rather poorly this morning, so . . .

> Hey K. Apols for late notice!!! Nancy's sister has got ballet and . . .

Nancy wants to go and there's this other—

And one quite comically formal,

> Dear Mrs Redway, it's with regret I have to say Gabriella is, despite our prior hopes, unable to accept your kind invitation to your daughter's . . .

I don't even bother with the last one. The subject is enough. *So sorry . . .*

Instead, I close the phone down in quiet despair, gazing at the hotel, the little clapper bridge, the newer Georgian Bridge. Two Bridges, in the middle of the moor. This ramshackle three-hundred-year-old coaching inn, surrounded by rugged moorland, smack bang on the main road across the bleakness of the wilds, beside the chattering West Dart River, would once have been the centre of Dartmoor's bustle: the yard would have been full of mail carriages, farmers on horseback, and intrepid women travellers in peach and lilac silk shoes being assisted from their broughams by waistcoated porters in hobnail boots. Now it's coach parties and hikers, bird-watchers and adventure sports enthusiasts, and the old pub, with its vitrines of dead pheasants and old ticking clocks from Widecombe and glass engravings of Queen Victoria, is a good venue for kids' parties . . . except this won't be a party.

I count how many refusals we've had, and how many changes of mind, and how many acceptances. A couple of days ago we were down to six attendees, and that was fine, not brilliant by any means, but not embarrassing. But with these late mind-changes, these last-minute refusals (did they all get together and realize how awkward and sad this celebration might be: did they all agree not to go to the mad girl's party?) now we have a mere two kids saying yes. It's exactly as Adam predicted.

What if *no one* comes? The humiliation will be appalling, unforgettable. And it's too late to cancel. I made special cards, little bagged presents for the six kids. Now two kids will get three bags of presents, each.

If they turn up.

Taking a big hard grip on my emotions, carrying the special cake I baked yesterday with *OMG you're TEN!*

written in pink icing, along with lots of sugary birds and hares, which took me at least three hours, I get out of the car and go into the hotel.

And I look left, and wince. There's a whole corner of the lounge bar reserved for Lyla's party. The Two Bridges holds a lot of kids' celebrations, and they always do it the same way. I asked them to cater for possibly eight kids and a few adults: I had to give them a rough figure several days ago. So the big long table has twelve plates and twelve sets of see-through knives and forks and bowls of sandwiches and sausages and chicken wings covered in clingfilm and inflated blue balloons tied to the chairs, and my heart throbs with sadness. It will look dismal. Three kids huddled in the corner of a party table set for a dozen.

This is the last children's party we will throw for my daughter. She's ten, and you don't really do it after ten, do you? The next stop is eighteen.

So the last party before she grows up will be excruciating.

Can I do anything to make it better? I haven't told Lyla about the steady stream of cancellations. I thought six would be enough to distract. Six kids can still make a satisfactory amount of noise.

Now?

Setting the cake on the awaiting table, ignoring the expectant, cheery smiles from the bargirls, I step outside into the cold, slanting winter sun, and dial a number. Emma Spalding. Perhaps I can recruit adults to make up the numbers. Why didn't I think of that before?

Her answer is swift, and disappointing. 'I'm so sorry, Kath, but George and I are heading down to Exeter, meeting my daughter's fiancé. We'd love to otherwise, of course, we love Lyla, but—'

171

'It's OK,' I say. 'Really, thanks for even considering it.' I end the call and stand gazing at the moorland road that leads to Princetown. The so-called party starts in half an hour. No, fifteen minutes. And it will be three embarrassed kids – at most – on a table set for a dozen. Adam was entirely right: he warned me against this. We should have done something else: a special film, horse-riding, rock climbing, but I didn't want my daughter to be the only child at her tenth birthday, blatantly isolated. Now she will feel the loneliness even more keenly.

A tell-tale crunch of gears. It's Adam and Lyla. She's in a long black dress with lacy cuffs, matching her long black hair. She looks lovely: there are hints of the elegant young woman to come. And she's clearly excited about the party: she's jumping up and down, doing her happy stim, twirling like a dancer, balletic, and elegant. One day she will be a beautiful, willowy teenager: she will get lots of attention from boys. Will she even know what to do with it? I was awkward, her dad was awkward. I suspect she will be super-nervous and shy and stand-offish. She may go her whole life without a boyfriend out of sheer shyness; or she might accept anyone out of loneliness. A junkie, a criminal, anyone. I think of the dead birds she arranged, her growing wariness, even of me and her father. My daughter is getting worse. I have to make this better.

'Mummy, is Lottie coming? And Simon? Like you said? Are they all coming? How many are coming?'

She is giggling and happy, she hasn't had a party without her cousins to back her up for years and is understandably thrilled. This is all for her.

All these people are coming just for her!

'Did you really ask Callum? And Zvetlana? What about Ali? And Jojo?'

She is clapping her hands and Adam stands behind her, giving me a glare of pure malevolence. *This is all on you, Kath, this is all on you.*

Unable to contain her excitement any longer, Lyla runs past me into the hotel: she knows it well, she's been here before, when we've had parties with Charlie and Oscar and all their friends, and Dan and Tessa, and other parents, when it's noisy and fun and followed by the big walk to Wistman's Wood. My mum loved Wistman's Wood. I suspect she used to take men there.

Adam is in a leather jacket, black jeans, stubble as dark as his expression. 'How many?' he asks.

I shrug, helpless. 'Two.'

His blue eyes are piercing and accusatory. '*Two?*'

'I hope. They haven't confirmed.'

'Christ. You have to cancel, Kath.'

'It's too late! It starts any minute, I put eleven a.m. on the invites.' I check my watch, and cringe. 'Five minutes.'

'Jesus.' He exhales. 'Jesus Christ. I warned you.'

'I know.'

He's right. I've made another terrible error. I am a bad mother. Perhaps, with my stupid suicidal brain I shouldn't even be a mother, I'm not capable. They should take Lyla away from me. I am a danger to my daughter's happiness. A menace. A madwoman.

Adam puts a hand on my shoulder. 'Come on. Better make the best of it.'

We step inside the hotel. Lyla is already sitting at the table, bouncing up and down on her seat. So happy that today she will have friends. Lots and lots of friends, a dozen kids, breaking the winter spell of her isolation. Her new life will begin. Ten years old!

Adam and I sit to either side of her at the long, empty table. Lyla chatters about who's coming, Adam and I

173

try to chatter back, but really we sit there mentally contemplating all the food that probably won't get eaten. A bargirl comes over and says a big Happy Birthday to Lyla and Lyla smiles shyly and hides behind me and I shrug at the bargirl, and the bargirl smiles uncertainly, and she gazes at the empty table, and says, 'So you're expecting quite a few?'

I am wordless, as mute as my daughter. Adam says, 'We've certainly got enough food.'

The minutes pass. Adam and I talk about the dogs. Adam stands up and goes to the bar, and makes phone calls. Is he planning to escape? Leave me to the disaster I created?

I sit here alone with Lyla and we stare at the chicken. 'Are you hungry?' I ask her. 'We can start before they get here.'

'No,' she says. 'We must wait, it's not polite to eat before everyone is here: you told me that, those are the rules. We must wait for everyone to arrive.' Already I can hear the urgent nerves in her voice. Is everyone going to arrive?

Every minute Lyla gets up and looks out of the hotel window, waiting for cars, waiting for her supposed friends. The car park is empty. Sometimes she runs to the main door and stares out. The bar staff are looking at her.

Lyla runs back. She sits at the table and gazes at the cake. Her happy stimming has stopped, replaced by anxiety. 'Where are they, Mummy? They are coming, aren't they? Callum? Zvetlana?'

I gaze sidelong at my returning husband, he glares back, and suppresses an angry sigh. The bar staff are wondering what to do now: they are looking over at us, unsure, perhaps embarrassed, checking out the party that isn't happening, the lonely little girl at the end of the big party table with the balloons and the cake and the glittery bags of presents for kids who clearly aren't going to turn up.

'It's a long drive for lots of people, Lyla, I mean, the weather and everything.'

What am I saying? It's a bright day, cold but sunny: there's no problem with the weather at all. Lyla looks at me as if she now knows I am lying. I can see the first signs of tears in her eyes. She bravely resists them, tries to smile. It's the smile that looks like a grimace, fixed and awkward.

What can we do?

A noise drags us all to the window again. Hope rises. A big SUV pulls into the car park. It looks as if it has kids in the back. I swap hopeful glances with Adam. I reckon I recognize this car, I've seen it outside the school. Yes, I do recognize it. YES!

Lyla whoops with delight, at last: her first guests. We troop outside the hotel to welcome them. Welcome! Come and have cake and chicken wings and prosecco for the adults!

Two blond adults and two blond kids get out of the car, and Lyla stands there waving at the kids, overcoming her terrible shyness, being courageous and grown up, she's so happy to have guests, any guests, so happy to have friends, any friends. But the two boys look at her in bewilderment.

They must be a year younger than her. I've seen them at the school, but they're not even in Lyla's class.

Lyla stops waving, her happy smile fades. She stands there in her special party dress. The two boys frown and say something to their dad and the father shrugs at them, and gives us a distant, brief, puzzled smile, and

175

then this happy family sets off down the path past the clapper bridge.

They're not coming to the party, no one is coming to the party: it's half past eleven, it's a quarter to twelve. The sun is cruelly bright, the moors serene, though the distant tors are dark and brooding, even in the sun. Lyla stands, rigid, in the car park, staring at the empty spaces, staring at nothing, and no one. Adam gives her a hug, but she shrugs him away; so he turns, with a flash of malice at me, and goes back into the hotel where the table waits inside. Empty. Balloons floating. The cake uneaten.

The pain is unbearable.

Lyla's hair kicks in this subtle breeze. 'No one,' she says, quietly. 'No one came. No one likes me, Mummy. No one at all.'

I want to hug her until I can squeeze all the sadness out of her. But I can't. This is it, I think. This is the worst part of parenting, the realization that no matter how hard you try, how much work you do, how much effort you put in, you cannot guarantee your children's happiness. You cannot protect them from sadness.

A couple of tears run down Lyla's cheeks and she quickly brushes them away with the cuffs of her pretty black party dress. We stand here, mother and daughter, and she talks quickly, her hands fluttering, her face grimacing. 'People don't like me. It's OK, I like them but they don't like me. It's because I don't understand them, isn't it?' She looks up at me. 'I want to understand them but I can't. I try to smile and I try to talk but I don't get it.'

Her eyes are full to bursting with tears. Her bravery makes it even more painful.

She is sobbing now. 'If I was going to die, do you think people might like me more? Would you love me more? Just before I died?'

I gaze at her, trying not to show my horror. The pine trees bend; I feel myself bending in the winds of this melancholy. Bending, and breaking. Lyla is sniffling, staring at the ground, kicking grit with her special party shoes.

'I really tried, Mummy. I really tried to join in. But they all laughed at me. So I must have got it wrong. It's my fault.'

Another car pulls into the hotel car park. It's a National Park Land Rover. I recognize the people who get out. These aren't kids. These aren't guests. These are Adam's friends: Suzie the ranger from Ashburton, with her partner Alice, and Gavin Davidson. All laughing. Carrying things. Waving at us.

Two more cars pull in, in short order, and people emerge. Ron from Warren House. Dez Pritchard, and his girlfriend. And Tom, a sheep farmer, lives near Gidleigh, known Adam for decades. And here's Adam's cousin Harry who sold me the car, and he's obviously been via Huckerby, because he's brought Felix and Randal.

Everyone is coming across, giving us smiles and hugs. The dogs dash over to Lyla and she kneels down to hug them, and they lick the tears from her face. And all the men and women tousle Lyla's hair and for once she isn't shy: she's so wrapped up in the dogs, her beloved dogs, and Ron says, 'Hey, Lyla Redway! We hear someone special is having a party! That means a celebration is in order!'

And I stand here, smiling and tingling and feeling so grateful to my husband. He did this. He made those phone calls: he had a back-up plan. My handsome, loyal, loving, resourceful husband has saved the day. It's not the party we wanted, but Adam was right, we never could have had that party: Lyla doesn't have friends; she wants friends but can't seem to make them, she is as lonely a child as you can be, and yet adults are drawn to her, she has something that adults can see and appreciate.

And dogs. And birds and ponies and mice.

The party has changed beyond recognition. Going back into the hotel, I see that the table is now arrayed with beers and wine bottles, and a lot of the kids' stuff has gone. Everyone sits down and there are so many people the staff are not embarrassed any more; they are laughing and joking, recognizing friends, swapping gossip, and fetching more chairs.

Beers are drunk, glasses are clinked, the dogs sit at Lyla's feet and she smiles shyly at the head of the table as we sing 'Happy Birthday', and all the chicken wings have gone, and all the sausage rolls and thick ham and tomato sandwiches have been guzzled, and we order more beer. And it's all great fun.

The party mingles with the regular drinkers: I see Suzie talking animatedly with a bargirl, probably flirting, but it doesn't matter, it's all good. Adam sits at the head of the table, beer in hand, singing verses from 'The White Hare', the Seth Lakeman song that was Adam's and mine, our song as we dated, our special song. Then some other tunes – ancient folk tunes I've never heard before, but I join in nonetheless.

The good humour is infectious. I feel myself almost forgetting about everything, from the hag stones to the panic at Hobajob's, from the suspicions about Adam and the car, to the strange idea that I came here, to see my brother. For a beautiful fragment of a day, it's all gone. Obscured. We are singing. Lyla is smiling.

At the end of the sing-song, Adam says, 'OK. Come on, guys. Let's go and see the pixies in Wistman's! It's traditional!'

And we all laugh and get up and Lyla runs ahead with Felix and Randal, and the adults run after them; even Ron is running, though he's a little drunk, I think. Adam and I follow behind, and I give him a special hug, and kiss his stubbled chin as we walk from the table. 'Thank you, Adam. Thank you so much for doing that.'

He smiles and walks to the bar, his wallet taken from his jacket. He is addressing some girl, behind the bar. She is young, blonde, petite. Pretty. Tying her apron behind herself, like she is starting a shift. She has bruises on her neck; like finger bruises. Her nose is pierced with a silver ring. She is wearing one of those fashionable black lace chokers.

She takes Adam's credit card and looks at the name, as she puts it in the card machine.

'Adam Redway?' she says, casually.

'Uh-huh.'

'You're the park ranger, aren't you? The famous one, rescued the tourists?!'

My husband shakes his head, humbly. And chuckling.

'They were in about a foot of water, I'm not Superman.'

'Hah.' She smiles. 'And I've seen you hiking near here, haven't I? Do a bit of it myself, when I get the chance.'

'Possibly,' he says. 'Though it's also my job.'

The girl hands him the card, and the receipt.

'Sure I have, I saw you hiking down at Hobajob's week or two ago, when we had that freeze. I had to go home it was so cold.'

Adam takes the card. And does not blink. He must

know that I can overhear all this. And yet his innocent bewilderment is entirely convincing.

'Nah, must be mistaken. Not Hobajob's. Never go hiking there, I like it up on the moors, on the tors with the wind. That's my place. OK, talking of hikes, we've got a big yomp to Wistman's. Ta for the party!'

The girl nods, and puts away the card machine, blushing, and slightly frowning. Following Adam with her eyes, as he saunters out of the Hotel. Then she turns, and she notices me for the first time. And her face is filled with curiosity. As if she recognizes me, in a slightly unnerving way, but is not sure why. And with that, she disappears again, behind the bar, through a door.

Embarrassed, or busy, whatever.

What just happened? I am not sure. But this girl claims she saw Adam at Hobajob's. And he almost never goes there, unless it is to drag Lyla in for tea. But he was at Hobabjob's, and it seems he was there on the day of the ammil, the freeze – I am sure that's what she means.

So perhaps it was him. Scattering my rubbish. My blood, my hair, my tampon, even though I know this is absurd. Why would my own husband want to frighten me? And his daughter?

I walk out into the cold, half-hearted sun. The rest of the party is already over the road, climbing stiles, heading up the slopes towards Wistman's Wood, tucked away in its little green valley. Half an hour away, but worth the trudge. I can just about see Lyla, amongst them, skipping happily.

My daughter is happy. The dogs to either side of her.

I am about to follow, when something else alerts me. There's an old bus shelter here, plastered with peeling adverts: a memory of when Dartmoor had proper public transport. There's a rusty bench inside the shelter: hikers use it to hide from the rain.

And today, through the cracked and dusty window, I can see there's someone sitting inside, staring out. It's not a hiker, though: not some rambler in a cagoule, not some birdwatcher with expensive binoculars.

I can the distinct profile of a lady. A rather old lady.

The recognition makes me reel, once more. A hand lifts to my trembling mouth.

It is my mother.

I know this is a hallucination; I know this is an apparition, some vapour of my damaged mind.

But I am, nonetheless, looking at my own mother, through the cracked glass panel of a concrete moorland bus shelter. She is staring blankly out at the road: waiting for a bus that will never come. And now the horrifying face of my mother turns and gazes my way. Her expression is curious, as if she is surprised to see me, but not overly surprised. She stands up. She is coming outside the shelter, to talk to me.

No.

This must not happen. A sickening cold overcomes me. I look away, hiding my eyes with shivering hands. When I look back, the face is gone.

But I saw it, I know it: I saw my mother. I am hallucinating dead people.

And now I hear that voice. Frailer now, but so distinct.

'Katarina? Darling?'

No. Too much. Too too much. I am running now, running running running, running across the road, running away from Mummy, running over the little bridge, running back into the warmth of the pub.

I can't face Wistman's Wood. I can't face anything.

Slumping into a burst leather sofa, curling into a foetal position, I try to calm my drumming blood. I don't know how to explain this terror to myself. I have seen a ghost; my mind is cracking open.

The bargirl with the bruises stares at me, inquisitively. Slowly drying a glass.

Morrice Town, Plymouth

Wednesday morning

Tessa and Kath stood together, and looked out at the huge and brutal walls, and the rolls of steel razor wire, coiled along the top, like Christmas decorations in a nightmare. Naval ensigns flapped, eagerly, in the wintry breeze; oversized concrete hangars squatted above the dark waters of the Tamar: the home of the nuclear submarines, with their missiles ready to destroy the cities of the world. Yet hidden from sight.

'It looks like Princetown Prison,' Kath said quietly.

'Exactly what I thought,' Tessa replied. 'They moved a load of us here a month ago, while they're doing up the main campus. And as soon as I walked in, I looked out of that window and I thought, *Oh My God, I'm right back in Princetown.* Big high walls like a jail. Do you want some coffee?'

'Sorry?'

'Before we chat, Kath. I can send for coffee. There's a little place right outside does a great flat white.'

Kath's face was pale. Her expression puzzled, 'What's a flat white?'

Tessa called to her assistant, in the room next door. Who appeared, promptly: keen and cheerful.

'Sara, could you nip down to Drake's and get me a flat white and . . . ?' Tessa turned. Kath was squirming, tugging nervously at the sleeve of her baggy jumper.

Tessa yearned to help. To do anything. 'Kath? Would you like some coffee?'

'Uh, oh, uh, uh yes, I'll have, um, a cappuccino. Thanks.'

Kath was offered a seat. Tessa pulled her own swivel chair from behind her desk, to make it all seem less formal.

Whatever reason Kath had for coming here, Tessa wanted Kath to feel relaxed, if such a thing was possible: she didn't want this to appear like some kind of interview, or, even worse, a consultation, therapy, *psychiatric assessment.*

Kath smiled, unhappily. 'Thanks for giving up your time, Tessa.'

The idea was waved away.

'Oh God, don't worry. Wednesday mornings are good for me, no seminars, no lectures, I usually use them for watching cat videos on Facebook.'

Kath's eyes widened. 'Really?'

'That was a joke.'

'Oh. Oh. OK.' Kath forced a timid laugh, 'Ah God, Tessa. I don't even do humour any more. I don't notice sarcasm, or irony. My brain is a mess, so much has been happening, and I haven't been able to tell anyone – all these things, everything,' she paused, flushing slightly – and rushed on, 'I have to talk. Have to tell someone, tell *you.*'

'OK – try me – please.'

'I will, I really, I mean, there's so much, like, OK, like there was this time in Hobajob's. The woods near Huckerby, similar to Wistman's? It was a freezing day, there was an ammil, a proper ammil, and I was with Lyla and the dogs and we got to the clearing in the middle, and, and there was all this rubbish in the frost, but it looked like it came from our *house*: a hairbrush with my hair, bloodstained tissues, things like that, worse than that, and Lyla thought she saw someone, and she keeps seeing some man on the moor, sometimes says it might be Adam, I don't know how, but this girl, at Two Bridges, said she saw *Adam* at Hobajob's around the same time, so what does that mean? *And* I reckon Adam has been watching me. Following me. I saw him at Burrator. And there's so much more, Tessa, too much, way too much. Everything is in pieces.' A pause. 'Everything.'

Tessa was numbed. Silent.

Kath looked across, her face white. 'And you know what makes it worse, Tessa? I actually thought I was good at coping with this stuff. I've coped with Lyla, I coped when Adam was ill, but this time I just feel pathetic. Loving people isn't enough. Not this time.'

The sad, stiffening silence was interrupted. Sara had returned with the coffee. The cups had pictures of Sir Francis Drake imprinted on the cardboard. And the slogan, Our Mocha Will Bowl You Over.

Grateful for this intrusion of normality, Tessa took her flat white, and sipped, confused and pained; wondering how to react. Kath was tugging nervously at her bobbly sleeve. The jumper looked as if it needed replacing. The winter coat she'd hung on the hook had seen better days, as well. Tessa felt the pang of her usual guilt.

She and Dan had everything, Kath and Adam had

185

almost nothing, and struggled even for that. She and Dan had two happy, bouncy boys; Kath had one beautiful but difficult daughter. Tessa and Dan had at least three holidays a year: a week of skiing, a fortnight of Mediterranean sun, a city break in Barcelona or New York or Siena. And last night they'd got back from a winter holiday in the Canaries, via Disneyland Paris.

Kath had spent most of Christmas alone, and had tried to commit suicide. And was now possibly falling apart, once more.

'So what do you think?' Kath shook her head and put down her coffee. 'Maybe I just need more medication?'

'Well, that's the one thing I cannot do, I'm afraid,' Tessa shook her head, 'I'm a psychologist, not a psychiatrist, only psychiatrists can prescribe. But I *can* give advice, and I can refer, and,' Tessa gently touched Kath's arm. 'I can really listen, I've got all morning, I will cancel the afternoon as well, I want to help. You and Adam and Lyla. We love you guys. Anything you want, just ask. It's often good to simply share. But, Kath, I need to hear it calmly, and slowly and in order, as best as you can remember.'

Kath offered a quiet nod, and finally, at last, in a halting but reasonably lucid monologue, she talked about the memories of a man, in a car, an argument, or some vivid interaction, and how the scent of lemon was connected. She told Tessa about Lyla's new wariness towards both her parents, but, strangely and especially, her father. She told Tessa about Adam watching her at Burrator.

And then Kath told, in a more coherent way, the peculiar tale of the spooky afternoon in Hobajob's wood, with the pattern of rubbish, tissues, a hairbrush, even a used tampon. She described the way they both panicked, imagining a man, pursuing them, when there was no one at all. Except for the fact that a bargirl at the Two Bridges had claimed she saw Adam, in the wood, around that very same time, the afternoon of the big freeze, the ammil.

Kath shook her head. 'And the thing is, Tessa, even if Adam wasn't there, even if we totally imagined a presence, that hairbrush could still have been mine, it looked like my hair, and I think I lost one like it a few weeks ago. But who would have taken it to Hobajob's? Lyla? Me? Adam? Maybe it was Lyla. She loves that wood, goes there all the time. But why that stuff? It was just so creepy, and Lyla is acting even more strangely in other ways. A while back I caught her making a pattern, in the yard, out of dead birds.' Kath visibly shuddered. 'It was so eerie. These little dead eyes, arranged in rows and spirals. It reminded me of the books Mum used to read, on witch-craft, spells and symbols. Those rubbish antiques she left us. The masks from Namibia, in the hall, all that. The stuff we couldn't sell.'

Tessa nodded, not knowing quite what to say. Searching for a source of rationality, to stabilize her sister-in-law. 'And what does Adam think of all this?'

'He denies everything. Says he's not following me. Denies he was at Hobajob's.'

'The rubbish in the clearing?'

Kath shrugged, 'Fly-tippers, he says. Perhaps he's right. And he reckons Lyla just made a random pattern. It's what she does, she likes patterns.'

'Which is true enough?'

'Yes.' Kath sighed. 'Yes. It's true. But even Adam is a *little* bit troubled, because Lyla is singing songs that we don't understand, we don't understand where she learned them. Songs about death. An approaching death. And anyway I don't know if I can even trust Adam, trust my own husband, because he seems guilty, and it turns out he was alone over Christmas, he has no alibi. And Lyla says she sees him, on the moor, near the house, she said it when she was arranging those birds.'

Tessa went to interrupt, but Kath rushed on. 'And I've also realized Adam was the last person to touch my car, to fix the brakes, did Adam do something? Did he come back and do something around that day, did he want me to have an accident? And why am I even using the word *alibi*? It's all ludicrous – yet it's all frightening me, Tessa. Frightening, and destabilizing. Horrible.'

Tessa's concerns deepened. She tried to hide them. 'What else, you said there was more?'

Kath closed her eyes tightly for a few seconds, as if trying to block a memory. Then she told Tessa about the birthday party that went horribly wrong.

Tessa winced. 'Ah. My God. I'm so sorry, we should have been there.'

'It doesn't matter,' said Kath. 'It's done now, and anyway, Adam saved the day – he called up all his friends and rellies. They came over and made it fun for Lyla. Ironically, that was when the bargirl said she saw Adam at Hobajob's, and after the party they all got lost in Wistman's Wood like you're meant to, under the mossy trees.'

'That's good. I love Wistman's, we really will take the boys up there again soon.'

Kath looked at Tessa, directly, as if none of this mattered. 'Yes, thanks, thank you, but this is one of the reasons I need to talk, to someone, to anyone, but most of all to you – this isn't all of it. There's a couple of *other* things. But they are much harder to say.' Kath's words stumbled into silence.

Tessa sat in the quietness, which was prolonged. Kath clearly needed time.

To take the pressure off, Tessa swivelled in her chair and gazed out of her window. A huge warship was making its way out of Devonport towards the open sea. These boats always surprised Tessa. They were so big, bristling with antennae and aggression. She had been working in Plymouth for six years, and still hadn't quite got used to it. War in peace, evil behind walls.

But that was it. Evil was kept behind walls: submarines were kept in concrete bunkers. Tessa simply could not believe Adam was somehow implicated in Kath's suicide bid – this stuff about the car, the need for an alibi, it didn't add up, there was no motivation, he wouldn't risk Lyla's life – but she couldn't believe Kath had attempted suicide for no reason, either.

Moreover, Lyla's confusion about her father, and wariness towards him, could be discounted. It was, Tessa reckoned, simply the distress of a child who nearly lost a mother, subsequently looking for someone to blame. And the other parent, the other carer: that was the obvious choice. Not the beloved and threatened mother herself. So it was Dad who got the anger.

The warship was almost gone. Heading out into the cold and furious Atlantic.

At last Kath spoke, once again: this time whisperingly quiet.

'OK, here goes. I have to tell. There's two more things, and I want you to hear them both.'

Tessa felt her own nerves tingling, as her sister-in-law explained, 'Remember I said I was with Emma Spalding?'

'No. But go on.'

'Well. I was. And I tried to call you straight after, wanted to tell you this as soon as I heard, but you went on holiday, and it didn't seem right.'

Tessa leaned a little closer. 'What did Emma tell you?'

189

'She said that I went to her twice, that day, the day – I went to Burrator.'

'And?'

Kath looked down at her scuffed trainers.

'I was excited. Made up. Agitated. And I was – I said something, about that day – said something to Emma.'

'What?'

Tessa leaned closer still, as Kath's muttering got even quieter.

'Kath?'

'Emma said I'd told her, that day, that I was off to see Dan, your Dan, to see my brother, at Two Bridges, that evening I drove into Burrator!' Kath's eyes were wet and wide, gazing at Tessa. Helpless, apologetic, and hurt. 'How can that be, three hours before I tried to commit suicide, I went to meet *Dan*? Where? Why? How? He was in London, wasn't he? What the hell does that mean?'

Tessa gazed at Kath. She gazed through Kath. Around Kath. Trying not to react, to show her own roiled emotions. Instead she would be her professional self. Somehow.

Kath was sitting straight, still needing to speak.

'And there's one more thing, Tessa. This is the worst of it all. I know you're going to think I'm crazy, and maybe I am.'

'Please.'

'I saw my mother. On the moor. My own mother. I know it was a hallucination, an apparition, but it's what I saw.'

The stiff silence returned. Tessa frowned. 'You saw a ghost?'

Kath looked at her hands, examining her slightly dirty fingernails.

'Yep. I did. It was after Two Bridges, the party, I was following the big hike to Wistman's. And I walked past that old concrete bus shelter. The one with the broken windows, and I looked through the window, and I saw my dead mother, but much older, she was sitting in the bench and she turned, to look at me—'

Tessa sat back, holding her breath.

'And I couldn't cope, Tessa, simply couldn't, I just raced – as fast as I could, back to the Bridges. Because I had seen a ghost. My mind was that far gone. And you're the first and only person I've told this, because if I tell anyone else this they'll know I am not capable, they'll take Lyla away, won't they?'

Kath gazed, long and hard, at her sister-in-law, saying nothing.

'I *am* having a breakdown, aren't I, Tessa? My brain isn't getting better, it's falling apart.'

'No, wait—'

'Because if I'm not falling apart, that means something is happening to me.'

'Sorry?'

'Think about it, Tessa. The hag stones, and the song about death, the patterns of the birds. The blood, the hair, Hobajobs? Doesn't it make you wonder?'

'Wonder what, exactly?'

Kath was flushing, as if she was embarrassed. 'Tessa, have you ever believed in witchcraft?'

For a second, Tessa Kinnersley said absolutely nothing. A ship's horn broke the quiet. It sounded like a big ferry, heading for the Royal William Yards.

At last, Tessa said, 'Not entirely sure I quite got that, Kath.'

Kath raised her voice. 'Don't get me wrong, I don't mean, you know, do you believe in old women flying around on broomsticks, all that. What I mean is: do you believe witchcraft could work in *some* way? A hex?

Some kind of hypnosis? So that evil or madness takes over?' Kath shook her head, and went on, 'Because I also get this sense my suicide bid, this whole frightening confusion, it's got something to do with my mum. And perhaps that's why I imagined I saw her. Because she was into all that stuff. It was one of her things for a while, witchcraft, wicca. She bought those creepy antiques from her travels. Inuit dolls, African spells. We had that stone Celtic head, that was the only one worth anything, but whatever happened to her old books on demonology, those grimoire things? Some of them were sixteenth century. We didn't inherit those.' Kath looked up, her expression deeply pained. 'Sorry, Tessa. I know I sound totally mad, and rambling, but that's the point: sometimes that is how I feel, like I've been *enchanted*. Bewitched. I feel so tired yet I get these dreams, like something is draining my energy away. The past is holding me, still got me in its grip, something to do with my mother.' Kath's tone was fierce. 'It sounds insane, and yet, if that is what's happened, some kind of hex or whatever, that would explain it all, that would explain why I drove into Burrator. Right?' Her eyes met Tessa's. 'Because there is no other explanation, apart from Adam, but what motivation does he have? What motivation would *I* have?' She gazed at Tessa, unblinking.

'Which means maybe I've been hexed and hypnotized. Something compelled me to do it. Something like witch-craft. But real. And it's still working on me. Either that or I am crazy. Or both. Oh God.'

Tessa rose and stepped forward to put a hand on Kath's shoulder. As if she could anchor her to the ground, to reality, with a single grasp. 'Look,' she said. 'Wait. You really don't need magic to explain any of this. There is a rational explanation. For all of it.'

'There is?'

Tessa forced a smile she didn't feel. 'Firstly, Kath, you need to know hallucinations are not unknown in cases of brain trauma, even mild trauma, like yours.'

Kath tilted her head, mistrustfully. 'They're not?'

'No. They're quite common. It's not especially alarming. Remember, you hit your head on the steering wheel quite badly, you were lucky the coma didn't last longer.'

'You're not just saying this?'

'No!' Tessa sat down, again, and gestured, to emphasize. 'No, not at all. Hallucinations happen. That explains Hobajob's. It, also, possibly, explains your seeing Adam at Burrator. It definitely explains the sighting of your mother. You're not bewitched: you have mild brain trauma.'

Tessa knew she was winging this, embroidering genuine theory with wishful thinking, and hiding a great surge of denial, but all that mattered right now was that she calmed Kath down.

'It's like the grieving process, Kath. It's common to see ghosts of the deceased soon after a death, it's so common it's probably normal. So, look at it that way. You nearly died. Therefore you are, in a way, grieving for yourself, and you also have some deep guilt added on top, because we don't yet know why you drove into the water. Put all that together, and it's not surprising you are so mentally shaken. But you will get better. You will heal. Trust me. It's not magic. It's science.'

Kath gazed at Tessa, a sceptical expression darkening her face. But the threatened tears had abated.

Tessa seized the moment. 'Also it's quite possible your brain is actively trying to tell you something. The memories of that night, that week, are still there somewhere in your subconscious, trying to emerge. It's possible meditation would help, something like that, yoga, mindfulness. There are techniques, I'll do some research. We'll do all this together.'

Kath nodded, this time with tentative hope. 'OK, I'll try. I'll try.'

'Good. Try and stay logical. The puzzle will only make sense when you have more pieces. Possibly you got a call from Dan in London that day, and you've forgotten. It's likely Adam feels guilty simply because he wasn't there for you, that night. And maybe – probably – everything else is coincidence, influenced by your very difficult situation.' Another forced, reassuring smile. 'So. Be calm, look after Lyla, and we can meet again if you like, very soon.'

'OK. Yes.' Kath looked at her watch, acting perfectly normally now, as if she hadn't confessed to Tessa that she was labouring under a dark magic spell. 'Thank you so much. I needed this, Tessa. Even if I do sound like a bloody lunatic. But I'd better be going.' Kath offered a weak smile.

'They've got me on half days, but I can't push it, they're being so kind. Everyone is being so kind. It hurts, it makes me feel so ashamed. The least I can do is return the favour.'

As they both stood up, Kath gave Tessa a firm hug, and said, 'I'm sorry – what I said about Dan being involved. Emma wasn't entirely sure anyway.' A pause. 'So you're probably right. It could all be in my head, couldn't it, and I need time to heal?'

'Yes! That's the spirit,' said Tessa, and immediately regretted saying it: she was trying to hide her own panicky feelings with cliché. But Kath didn't notice the cliché. She gave Tessa a second, warmer hug. And then she was gone.

Tessa sat in her chair, thinking hard.

She really could explain most of this. The absurd idea of witchcraft, the hallucinations of ghosts. Lyla's resentment and fear of her father.

That was all neurologically and psychologically explicable, if sad, and disturbing.

But Tessa could not explain one other thing.

She could not explain the actions of her own husband.

Wednesday lunchtime

Clicking on her last favoured website, Tessa scanned her laptop screen urgently. She'd already visited five sites and looked in half a dozen books, plucked from her shelves. All said essentially the same as this site:

Confabulation, disorientation, delusions and hallucinations are more pronounced after severe brain injury, but are not unknown after mild to moderate brain trauma . . .

Loneliness and social isolation can also be contributing factors, and should be ameliorated . . .

If these symptoms persist or worsen after three months the trauma patient must be re-assessed, and potential complicating factors considered . . .

Many of Kath's problems, as Tessa had supposed, were therefore explicable, even predictable. Especially being stuck up there at Huckerby. But the symptoms might also be ominous. Signs of a deeper malaise, or a hidden neurological issue. Perhaps Kath might need another MRI. Perhaps, instead, a psychosis was developing?

Tessa fervently hoped not. The Redways would never survive if Kath had a proper breakdown; and what would that do to poor little Lyla? And her worsening symptoms of ASD? The new phobias and fears? Pensive, troubled, Tessa tipped back in her swivel chair, as the unavoidable doubts returned.

That word Kath had used: *alibi*.

It was a word Tessa had used herself. Of her own husband. The other day, in her thoughts. Just as she was falling asleep, after they'd had sex that night. *Alibi*.

At the time she'd actively gone along with the self-deception: she had *tried* to forget it, but now she couldn't. Not after what Emma Spalding had said to Kath.

Alibi.

Did Dan really have an alibi for that day he was meant to have driven down from London in his colleague's car, as fast as he could, to see his sister in hospital?

She needed the truth. But how to source it?

Asking Dan was clearly pointless *if* he was lying. Yet she couldn't ring that colleague and check because if it were a ruse, a fib, a BIG FAT LIE, Dan would have prepped the guy. And by calling the man Tessa would make herself the guilty party, snooping, undermining their marriage. Dan would get angry. Especially if he might be telling the truth after all. Which was entirely possible.

Was there some way of corroborating his story, without arousing suspicion?

Tessa looked at her screen, at the medical website. Pictures of stethoscopes, doctors, ambulances.

The hospital. Derriford Hospital, Plymouth.

197

She knew the number by heart, she'd called it so many times the days after Kath's suicide attempt. She had it stored in her phone. Abbey Ward. Acute Medical Unit.

For a moment, Tessa paused, and held the phone motionless in her hand. Like she was weighing her marriage in the balance.

Another warship was sailing the waters outside. Ready to defend the nation. Grey and implacable.

Tessa dialled the number.

'Hello?'

'Hello, is that Abbey Ward?'

Tessa could hear the busy sounds of the hospital, a slightly distracted nurse.

'Yes, who is this?'

'It's Dr Kinnersley. Dr Tessa Kinnersley. I used to work with Exeter General Health, in psychology. I'm a professor at Plymouth University.' The doctor bit was actually a doctor*ate*. Tessa was shamelessly and mendaciously pulling rank, but she didn't care. 'I need to speak to Nurse Sally Davis, if that's possible?'

'Dr Tessa Kinnersley, you say?'

'Yes.'

'OK. Um, I think Sally was taking a break actually – oh, no, there she is, let me get her, wait a sec?' The voice disappeared.

Tessa waited, a pencil in her hand. Tapping on her desk. *Tap tap tap.*

'Hello, this is Sally Davis?'

'Hi, Sally, this is Dr Kinnersley, Dr Tessa Kinnersley. Psychology at—'

'No, it's OK,' Sally's voice was softened by a lyrical Welsh accent, warm and eager, 'I remember you! Of course I do. Gosh yes, Kath Redway wasn't it, the accident at Burrator? Is she doing OK? I remember her poor

198

daughter, that beautiful little girl. How is she now? How is the family?'

'Kath's doing fine. But she's still struggling with some memory loss. Piecing it all together. It takes time with brain trauma, as I'm sure you know, time and care.'

Sally Davis murmured her sympathies, and asked, 'How can I help?'

'Well, that's why I'm calling. Kath can't remember the very early hours of her recovery, and we think it would help if we knew exactly what happened, if we could pin it all down.' Tessa blushed as she told these lies, gazing at her framed doctorate on the wall. 'That is to say: we'd like a timeline, like who came in to see her first, that kind of thing.'

'But that's easy!' Sally answered brightly. 'I was on shift! She was my patient, I've got the notes right here.'

Tessa tapped her pencil again, faster. Accompanying her heartbeat.

What was she about to discover?

Sally came back on the line. 'Yep, here it is. Took us a while to identify her, but as soon as we did, we started making calls. We called her husband of course, but couldn't get through, and then—'

'Yes?'

'I guess, looking at this number, ahhh, we called you? You're in Salcombe, right? But again, um, we got no answer.'

'Yes. The kids and I were away,' Tessa wished she had more coffee, her mouth was so dry. 'I'd taken them to see my folks, ah, their grandparents on my side, Shropshire. For New Year.'

'OK, yep, yes, as you say – so then we tracked down her brother Dan, um, your husband, on his mobile?'

'What time was this?'

'About eleven thirty a.m.'

11.30 a.m.

Eleven thirty.

Tessa drummed the pencil, ever harder, and faster. Tap tap tap, *tap tap tap*. She had an almost irresistible temptation to snap the pencil in two and throw it in pieces at the fucking wall.

11.30 a.m.

'OK,' Tessa said, as calmly as she could. 'Eleven thirty. And what exact time did he come in? He must have been her first visitor?'

'Yes, about noon, about half an hour after we rang him. He said he was nearby.'

Tessa repeated, with theatrical calm, 'Nearby?'

'Oh, yes. I remember him telling us he was staying on Dartmoor, at that hotel near Princetown. Er, Two Bridges I think it's called.' Sally paused, and went on, 'Does any of this help?'

Tessa was no longer tapping the pencil. Two Bridges? This was too much. The sense of something dark and bad, yet formless, was now palpable. Something very wrong was coming into view. Tessa set the pencil down. And she asked, 'Sally, has anyone ever asked you this before?'

'What do you mean?'

'About that phone call, with Kath's brother, Dan?'

'Erm,' Sally hesitated. 'No, come to think of it, I don't believe they have. Why? Is it relevant to her memory loss? We were all so panicked, so glad to get hold of anyone, to be honest. We were all focused on Kath.' She sighed. 'I so hope she's getting better, that lovely little girl. How're they coping, is she getting better?'

'Yes,' Tessa replied. 'She is, and this could be really helpful, too. Thank you so much for your time.'

With a brisk click, Tessa finished the call and set the phone down.

Dan had been on Dartmoor the night his sister had tried to kill herself. And he wasn't merely on Dartmoor, but close to the Redways. Staying at Two Bridges Hotel. And he'd been lying about it all along. Lying to everyone: to Tessa, to Kath, to everyone. So Kath was right. There really was a pattern. And it was being progressively revealed. Like a mosaic covered by soil, slowly scraped away.

Another noise made Tessa look out of the window.

The little Cremyl ferry, which had been serving this estuary for a thousand years or more, was crossing the harbour. Making its way from the Barbican to the Royal William Victualling Yard. Past the vast concrete bunkers where they kept the nuclear submarines. Dark and concealed.

Black Tor

Thursday afternoon

I must go where the ponies go, as Adam always tells me: watch how the wild ponies walk the moors, moving from tussock to tussock, thereby avoiding the sinks of fetid mire, the sudden, tendon-snapping ditches.

So that's what I do, I walk diligently, stepping from clump to clump. And as I do, I look across the rolling green moors, at a distant spire of a church, surrounded by a huddled village. I am following Tessa's suggestions. I am trying to discover the solution by lonely walking. And meditation.

Today I am hiking a loop, from Huckerby Farm, over the hills, to Black Tor and back. It's a walk I've done many times. I know this step-wide stream that bars my way. As I jump across I scatter dark birds from the nearest hill; they look like soot shaken across the sky.

The birds crawk in alarm, as they flee, even further. As if I am the predator, come to kill them, come to kill them and arrange them in lines and rows and circles. Yet I do not feel like a predator. I feel anything but. I am simply a figure alone on the bare moor. A woman bewitched by memories, and the lack of memories.

Yet of course: I am *not* bewitched, this is insane. I have to stop thinking this. I have to remember what Tessa said and get a grasp. I used to be logical: I was a scientist, an archaeologist. There must be a reason why I drove into the reservoir, but – I feel like screaming this into the sky, frightening all the birds from Yelverton to Salcombe – *I still don't know why I tried to kill myself*. I still can't *believe* I tried to kill myself. Somebody did something to me. Was it Adam, was it someone else?

Taking deeper breaths, trying to get my proper bearings, I stop, and look north. A mist is forming around Princetown radio tower. How quickly mists and fogs roll on to Dartmoor. I can only see the top of the tower: the rest is cloud underneath. That means the whole town, as so often, will be wreathed in a cold and vile fog. Forcing the prisoners, the rapists and childkillers, to stare at a chilly grey nothing. Like an extra punishment.

My pace quickens. I used to like walking the moor, these days I begin to loathe it. Who is out here? Anyone could be out here. Some random man, some killer; or another ghost. But there is no one visible. There aren't even sheep saying *meh*. The solitary noise is the squelch of my boots as I walk towards the next hill, and as I consider the facts in my possession – all the fragments in my mind. They are like potsherds from an archaeological dig. But I am a trained archaeologist. I can piece them together.

One of the few facts I possess, which I haven't really addressed, is that suicide note.

I shouldn't have done what I did; shouldn't have let this into my heart

204

So I am going now. Going away forever
Forget me if you can, I know you won't forgive

I can vaguely remember writing this. In Huckerby. I have a visual memory of my hand putting these words on paper. But that is all. I have no further context, no scenario. I do not know what I was wearing when I wrote it, let alone what I was thinking. So what did I mean? What is 'this' that I let into my heart? And why is it, or was it, so unforgivable?

I am near the top of the next hill. And as I crest the rise, the fog parts dramatically, down to the south: in that abrupt Dartmoor fashion.

The clouds above me are still a grey coffin-lid, sliding over the moors, but now, down there nearer the coast, the sun is bright: shining on the rich golden patchwork of fields, on the soft and lovely lowlands. And for a second it feels as if I am surrounded by a promised land. By Eden. The whole moor might be a prison, with cattle grids for jail bars, but out there all is loveliness.

And I have been there before, and I will get there again. I will get out of this. I am resolved. I will do it for Lyla.

Determination fills me. I am keen to be home now. Keen to see my family. Give Lyla a hug.

And I know a shortcut. It's not my planned walk, it takes me along Devonshire Leat, and on past Whiteworks, with its desultory ruins of chimneys and old spoil heaps, then through a scatter of ruined barns.

There are so many abandoned buildings around here. Some are original longhouses, like Huckerby. Six hundred years old. A thousand years old. Places where laughing children used to live with nursing lambs; now it's weeds and thistles, and dead rabbits.

The barns stare at me. As if they know me. Know of me. Or I know them.

Ducking past the last black-eyed cottage, I hop over another stream, walk around a small copse of conifers, which trap mist in their topmost branches, like cold smoke. Soon I will be able to see Huckerby. My home. Where Lyla waits. The girl I will save. By working it out. By solving the mystery of myself.

But I don't see Huckerby. As I trudge around the last grey palisade of firs, I see the figure of a man, barely discernible through the drifting mist. It looks as if he is wielding a tool, an axe, or hatchet, and he is hacking wildly at a hedgerow. He's got his back turned to me, the blade swings. Manic, brutal, ruthless.

It's Adam.

I am sure it is. The shoulders, the stature, the thick, dark hair.

But why? How? The fear stirs. Why is he out here? Where's Lyla? He's meant to be at home. My black-haired husband is out on the moor, with a big axe or hatchet. And I have to confront him, I cannot run away, I've had enough of running away: so I run towards him, through the curdling mist, towards my mad husband who is hacking away as if he is killing a pony, cutting off its head.

'Adam?'

I feel as if I have caught my husband doing something awful, something that might explain everything. The next few seconds might change my life.

The man turns, in the fog.

It's Harry Redway.

'Kath?'

I feel like a fool: but not like a lunatic. It is not *that* insane an error. Harry has the same build as Adam. Same dark hair. Similar leather jacket, different boots. Different jeans. In the mist, from a distance, he does look pretty similar. Now I get close, I see that, of course, this man is younger.

But there's still something wrong. Harry looks furtive. Adam's cousin is one of the most likeable of the Redways: normally. He's quick with a joke, quick to buy a round in Warren House, quick to find a new girlfriend when he gets bored with the last. He's never alone for long.

But he's alone out here.

With a big hatchet hanging from one hand, in the middle of the moorland bleakness, and he looks evasive.

'Hello, Kath.'

'Uh, hi Harry.'

'Car doing OK?'

I nod. Say yes and thanks. Mention the clutch. But the conversation feels absurd. The blade in his hand is so big.

'What are you doing, Harry?'

Harry looks down at the hatchet in his left hand, and his eyes widen, as if he is surprised to see it there. 'Ah yeah. Swaling.'

'What?'

'Got a gig from the Bowens, neighbours of the Spaldings, to help 'em out.'

'Sorry?'

His characteristic grin returns, though it seems forced. 'Gotta make a firebreak, cut back the gorse, you know. So it doesn't burn all the way to Brixham. Before they start the swaling.'

A firebreak? This makes a kind of sense. I've seen men doing this before. Swaling is so controversial, hated by so many: the assiduous winter burning of the moor, the deliberate destruction, the grand and raging fires: it is hedged about with endless rules and by-laws.

But I've never seen anyone making firebreaks around here, and I've seen a lot of swaling. Ever since I was a kid I've seen swaling: because my mum used to love it. She actually loved the ritual winter fires: she used to drive us all up to see the really big swales. She'd stand there in the glow, entranced. Worshipful. She thought it was so *authentic*. A three-thousand-year-old tradition, pre-Christian but still enacted. She loved the old stories of how the kids were sent out to collect the burned gorse afterwards, the blacksticks, to use as fuel, how the monks would pray for the success of the fires to drive away serpents, to drive away the Devil.

And I can vividly remember the smell of those fires, that looked so enormous to me, an eight-year-old girl confronted by ten-foot-high flames: the mix of that sweet coconut scent of gorse-flower, with the acrid smell of ash, and soot, and cremated things. Torched animals.

Harry lifts the hatchet. 'Sorry if I scared ya.'

'No no, it's fine, it's really nice to see you.'

'You, too. You too. Anyhow, Kath—' He nods at the gorse. 'I'd better get back to work – bloody toilet of a day. But tell Adam I'll be round for a pint, end of the week, probs.'

I nod. 'Yes, of course, sorry. Man at work! I'll give Adam your best.' We wave goodbye, and I jog on. After a few hundred yards I turn. Harry has his back to me again. Cutting and hacking at the gorse and the ling. Making a firebreak.

Harry Redway?

My mind is stirred. I am tempted to run all the way back to Huckerby. Because I have the sense of memory returning, of my mind trying to fix itself, as Tessa said it would. I want to grab the moment, rush through the opening window. I'm not far from home: I'm past the last muddy path. I have to make the most of this opening brightness, like the fog that parted, briefly, over Black Tor. Showing the Promised Land.

The kitchen is warm, and empty.

Fumbling water into the kettle, I hear a noise from the living room and Adam walks in with a bottle of beer in his hand. He looks at me with a level, contemptuous expression. And then he walks away again, back down the hall, towards the living room. As if I don't even deserve a greeting.

As if I have done something new, and bad.

Whatever. Right now I don't especially care.

Sipping my tea, I lean back against the sink, thinking. Breathing deeply, meditatively: as Tessa recommended. I am remembering that smell, coconut and ash. The dark smell of the moorland, tortured by fires. I can picture it all: I am a little girl like Lyla, staring into the meaningless flames, alongside my mother. I am holding my mummy's hand, and not quite understanding why men would set fire to the beautiful moorland, deliberately.

I can picture the moment so vividly: because smell is so deeply interlinked with memory. Smell *invokes* memory.

Here is my chance. Why didn't I think of this before? I have mild brain trauma, and it can be healed.

Crossing to the larder, I pull the old wooden door open. There it is. An old plastic lemon, full of juice. I've been avoiding the smell of lemon ever since that moment in Brian Angove's house, because it made me so uneasy. But what if I *force* myself to inhale that smell?

Snatching a tea towel from the cooker, I squirt lemon juice into the towel, soaking it. Pressing my nose deep into the wet cotton I breathe in the sweet citrus scent.

At first, nothing. Blurs. Nothing.

Lemon.

I breathe deep, again and again. Inhaling the lemony perfume. Breathe in, breathe out, breathe again. And now there's something. It's working. I can see me, and it's not what I expected. Not what I expected at all.

Nothing to do with Adam.

I am in Two Bridges Hotel. It is lunchtime. It is the day I tried to kill myself, I am sure.

I am drinking a glass of wine, and then I am not. Why? Because I am hurriedly leaving the pub. And as I leave the pub, and go to my car, I see another car pulling in. Yet I do not go over to the driver, even though I know him. Instead I duck down and run to my own car, so he can't see me.

Why?

I don't know. The brief, generous tumble of memory has ceased, like a fruit machine that stops paying out. I breathe deeply, in and out, inhaling the scent, but all I can see now is a standing stone. Somewhere on the moor, with an unusual shape, thicker at the bottom. It's not a stone I recognize.

And that is it. The image of the stone melts away, and I am left here, in my own kitchen, holding a tea towel soaked in lemon juice. But I am also holding something else, in my mind. The first crucial piece of that puzzle.

I was at Two Bridges the day I tried to kill myself. And so was another man I know.

My brother Dan was the driver of the car. And I was running away from him.

Huckerby Farm

Thursday afternoon

Trying to work it out, I drop the tea towel in the sink, and start rinsing out the lemon juice, gazing around, lost in my thoughts. Wondering about Dan, and Harry, and all of it, and the standing stone I do not recognize. Where is that?

Dartmoor stares at me from the calendar on the wall. The photo of snow and flowers on Kitty Jay's grave. The last resting place of the legendary suicide, the place where my mum's ashes are scattered.

I've *always* wondered why my mum chose Kitty Jay's grave. She never really liked it there. She much preferred Wistman's Wood, or the sea at Salcombe. Yet she was quite explicit. *Scatter my ashes at Kitty Jay's grave.*

Did she believe the legend? Was that it?

Perhaps. Thirty years ago some archaeologists dug up the grave, and found the skeleton of a young woman, about two hundred years old, implying that the legend concealed a truth. That the girl who killed herself, from unrequited love and shame and a guilt-ridden pregnancy, really *was* buried there: interred at a crossroads. Suicides were traditionally entombed at crossroads so that when they woke up and went to haunt people, they wouldn't know which way to go.

Kitty Jay's grave is the kind of place they would once have buried me, if I'd finished the job at Burrator.

But what am I doing? I have a vital new piece of information: Tessa needs to know. Going closer to the window to get the best signal, I dial Salcombe.

She answers at once.

'Tessa, I've remembered.'

'What?'

'Remembered the day I did it. I used a memory trick. With lemon. Associations. And it worked, a memory returned, and I am sure it's true.' I pause.

'And?'

I take a deep brave breath, and go on, 'Dan was there. At Two Bridges. The day I drove into Burrator. I know he was there – because I was there. But he was there in the *afternoon*, Tessa. And for some reason I didn't want to see him, I ran away to avoid him.' My voice is tense, but it is clear. 'And I've no idea why. So—'

'She knows.'

I turn, startled. It's Adam, leaning against the frame of the hallway door. I nod. As if I understand what he is saying. I do not.

He takes a swallow of beer and says it again. 'She knows.' A glare, as he adds, '*She knows what you did.*'

This feels significant, and ominous. I tell Tessa we'll talk later, and I turn to my husband. 'Sorry, Adam, what do you mean?'

He wipes beery lips with the back of his thumb. 'Have a guess.'

The bottle of cheap Lidl beer is nearly finished. I look

212

at him, and at the drink. My husband never drinks alone, at home, and rarely in the afternoon.

'Lyla,' he says simply. 'Lyla knows. Think someone told her at school.'

He swigs from the bottle, his eyes still fixed on me.

'I tried to tell her it wasn't true. But she doesn't believe me. She's been doing that thing again. What d'you call it, that thing. Stimming. Doing it all day.'

I look at him. My darling daughter. She knows about my attempted suicide. Oh God.

'How bad is it?'

'In the car coming back from Lidl, this afternoon. She was rocking back and forth. Like a robot. Even banging her head against the window.' He glares, relentless. 'So, yeah, Kath. I'd say she's stimming badly. Pretty pretty pretty pretty pretty bloody *badly*.' He sets the beer down, picks it up again.

He looks so coiled and malign, I wonder if he wants to crack the brown bottle against the sink, make it into a jagged weapon, and grind it into my guilty face. I refuse to cower. Though I want to cower.

'How do you know she knows, Adam? Has she said anything explicit? Where is she now?'

'She's out with the dogs, she wanted fresh air. She'll be back for tea soon, so you could ask her all this yourself. Spend some time with her.' He sucks the beer bottle. 'When *was* the last time you and Lyla talked, about this shit, eh? Since that fuck-up of a party?'

Despite my guilt, I bridle at this, because this is unfair. He did nothing about the party because he seldom does anything like that. Sure he was right it was a mistake, but at least I tried. It's always me that *tries*: he always leaves that kind of organizing to me: anything formal to do with Lyla.

From school uniforms to school days out, that's all down to me. Plus all the various attempts to get her to learn music, or enjoy drama, or ride a bike, I tried them all – and I failed, because all she loves is jam jars filled with April tadpoles from the Taw and looking at kestrels over Chinkwell. And sitting in her den, listening to the blue and silver sounds.

I gaze at Adam with deepening despair. My minor victory with my memory and the scent of lemon seems trivial now. I am despairing, but I am also angry. My outrage rises to meet his. 'At least I *am* having a go, Adam. At least I am trying to socialize her. When was the last time you took her to a play-date or a movie, did something normal like that?'

'I don't bloody do that,' he says. 'Because she doesn't bloody like it. There is no damn point.' Another slug of beer, but it doesn't stop him talking. Fast and hard, almost shouting. 'She's a loner, that's our beautiful daughter, let her be what she is, let her be herself, let her wander the moors, let her climb the bloody hills, look for nightjars: it's what I did – she's my girl.' He is speaking so fast the beer spits from his mouth. 'She's her father's daughter – is that what offends you? That I'm her dad? Did you want someone else? Someone richer? Like your brother? Did you want to fuck someone else?'

'What? Don't be ridiculous.'

How have we got to this? We used to love each other. But now I am bristling, defensive. Yet I have nothing to fight with, no weapon. All I have is suspicions. Adam on the hill, Adam working on my car. Emma Spalding's comments.

I am a suicide. I have woken at a crossroads and brushed the soil from my face, and now I don't know which road to take.

Adam reaches into the fridge for another beer. Clunks the door closed, beer in hand. How many has he had? It doesn't take much to get him drunk: though he doesn't usually let it get that far. I think of the sheep he shot on the northern moors so casually, with that laconic violence. I look at the calendar on the wall again, that sad, pretty grave in the snow, near where he stayed over Christmas.

'Adam . . .'

He opens the beer bottle, and tosses the metal cap into the sink. It clatters. 'What? What now?'

'When you were up at that place. Over Christmas. Man . . . something. Up by Kitty Jay – where Mum is scattered—'

There it is again. Guilt.

He pauses, briefly looks away, at the kitchen door. I can hear the dogs barking in the distance. Lyla coming home, probably. He looks back at me.

'Were you there all the time, Adam? All that week? Because I keep having a memory. Of a man, in a car. On that night. Was it you?'

For a moment he is silent. Then he slaps the beer bottle on the counter so hard it clangs. The dogs are barking in the yard, but Lyla has not reappeared. She's probably gone to the den. I hope she's gone to her den. I don't want her to hear this. To hear her father, ranting at her guilty mother.

'Hell with this, Kath! Stop this crap! Please! I was not there. I am not following you. I did not come back. What is this idiotic shit? I work sixteen hours a day.' He wipes his lips and snaps again, 'Fuck this. I can't pretend any more. I can't pretend I'm not angry. My daughter, my only child, is traumatized. She's rocking back and forth in the car, she's scratching herself. She's scared of me, her own dad. She blames me for the state of you. Why? Why

215

is she doing that? Because of what *you* did. And now someone has told her the whole truth, so it's even worse.'

His eyes blaze, I am cowering, backing away. He looms large, beer bottle in hand, ready to swing.

'You. You're the one making it worse. You, Kath. *You.* Because you tried to kill yourself. That's why our daughter is helpless and scared, that's why she's stimming, and rocking, and flapping her hands. That's why she's sad and frightened and arranging dead birds and feeling even more lonely. There is no other reason. It's all on you. Because you decided we should suffer, Lyla and me. Because you drove your car into a lake. Because you decided Lyla and I were worthless. You did it. YOU.'

Huckerby Yard

He has me pinned with guilt. I cannot stay here. Flinging open the door, I escape into the twilit farmyard, the tears bright in my eyes. Adam is right: it is my fault. I have to go and find my daughter. Hug her. Say sorry with an embrace. I heard the dogs return, so she must be in the den. That's where she goes when she wants to be alone.

Lyla's den is past the old, ruined barn; she cut the space out of brambles and witchbeams and hazel. Adam helped her. They spent hours and days slashing the greenery, making a leafy, twiggy little cave for her where she could be alone. Adam put up planks and plastic to keep it dry, I brought cushions and blankets. Adam even made a little wooden gate, on squealing hinges.

I knock at the barred gate. 'Can I come in?'

Her voice is so very quiet. 'Yes.'

I open the gate, and crawl into her den. She is sitting cross-legged in a red T-shirt, a thin blue hoodie, black leggings. She looks so small and vulnerable. She must be

217

freezing but apparently she isn't. Felix and Randal are there, on either side of her, snoozing.

Her eyes avoid mine; she is reading a book, in the fading light. It sits open in her lap.

Lyla is surrounded by all her collections. A couple of gorgeous kingfisher feathers. Last year's wildflowers. Rocks, stones, and tiny shells. On a shelf there are neat long rows of birds' eggs, all pale blue and cream and yellow, all cracked and split because she would never take a living egg. To her left there are books, encyclo-paedias in clear plastic bags, so they don't get wet. An open matchbox contains the skull of an adder.

As the soft winter breeze shivers her den, the chains of paper clips make her favourite tinkly-tankly sound, subtle and ghostly.

Lyla loves making these chains of paperclips, linked and looped together, which she hangs from the branches of her den. They are her very own windchimes, making her favourite noise.

Tinkle-tankle. Tinkle-tankle.

Abruptly, she looks my way. 'I've been reading lots of things today, lots and lots. Shall I tell you?'

'OK.'

She brushes black hair from her blue eyes. Now I realize that she's been crying. There is a pinkness to her face. I want to hold her and hug her, but I am scared that my guilt and my evil will seep into her, the pox of Plague Market.

Felix is awake, looking at me.

'What have you been reading, sweetpea?'

Her voice is level, and oddly calm. 'About suicide. All facts about why people kill themselves.'

Her wet sad eyes meet mine.

'Gladiators. I read about gladiators: they used to kill

218

themselves by putting their heads into the spokes of moving cartwheels. That's what I read on Google. Because they thought that was a better death than obeying the Romans and fighting to the death in the arena. Sometimes they stuck javelins in their throats.'

'Lyla.' I don't know how to stop this. We try to keep a check on her access to the Net, but really, these days, what can you do? And Adam is clearly right: someone has been talking to her. About me, and what I did. But I need to avert this, distract her. 'Please, darling, it's getting dark. You can tell me everything later.'

She shakes her head and starts to lecture me again, her voice fast and quick. And as she speaks, she flutters her right hand. 'There was one man who stabbed himself to death with spectacles. And there was another – another man who did it by drinking boiling water, and someone pushed a broom handle down her throat, and someone stuck darning needles into her stomach, to kill herself, and I read about one person, one person in America he tried to kill himself by drinking acid, but it didn't work, so he tried again and he killed himself by swallowing lighted fireworks.'

Her hands flutter, up and down, up and down, and she grimaces at me, and hisses. 'Mummy. *Ssss. Sss.* Mummy, think about it, that must have been amazing, I think, I mean, what did that look like, he would have had sparks coming out of his mouth, fireworks in his mouth, exploding inside him.' She clearly sees the concern on my face, but she goes on as if in a trance. '*Ssss.* And I read there's been suicides in England since the sixth century. The first were reported on the South Downs – that's in Sussex – and some animals commit suicide too, pigs can do it, and macaques, *ssss* I read that macaques will kill themselves, they're monkeys, and most suicides happen very suddenly, people only think about it for five minutes. *Sss. Ssss. Sssss.* And then then then, I read about China and in old days the Chinese people had this this thing when the man died the widows would choke themselves to death on gold leaf, because they didn't want to live any more. They had no one to love so they swallowed gold leaf, crinkling in their mouths. Swallowing gold, swallowing gold to make themselves die, and and and—'

Her hands are fluttering so fast, she is trembling and shaking, and then she clenches her hands and her eyes are tight shut, and her fisted hands lash out. Suddenly she is attacking me, hitting me hard, as hard as she can, smacking me on the head. Eyes wide open and furious.

I try to fend off her blows. The dogs scatter, out of the den. And still she hits me.

'Why did you do it? Why did you do it why why why why why, Mummy? Why did you leave me, why did you try and leave me? Don't you love me? You don't love me, you can't love me. I love you but you hate me, you don't love me. You're my mummy but you can't love me, can you, because you left me here! You hate me, you left me and you tried to go away forever because you don't even like me, you think I'm strange, you wanted to leave me alone in the corner you're like everyone else you tried to go go to go go to go! Why why why why WHY?'

And then she pushes me away and looks up at the tinkly-tankly chains hanging from the roof of her den and there are tears rolling down her face, and she is howling, and sobbing.

And I cannot do anything. Because she is right. I tried to destroy myself, I tried to destroy her, I tried to destroy everything. And now I am destroying this family all over again.

Salcombe

Tessa Kinnersley sat in her lovely expensive, steel-and-granite kitchen and waited for the Two Bridges receptionist to reply. The seconds ticked by.

'No,' the woman said, 'there's definitely no Kinnersley registered that night. December thirtieth, right?'

'Yes.' Tessa frowned, looking at the kitchen window. The February darkness was now total outside. 'Are you sure? Perhaps my husband used a company card, we really do need a copy of the invoice. And he's sure he stayed that night.'

The woman sighed, clearly irritated.

'I'm sorry, but yes, I'm sure. The only guests on that night were a couple from Germany, Schwartz, a single woman, name of Dickinson, and . . .' The woman tailed off, presumably trying to read something. 'Another couple, from Japan. No Kinnersley, and no company booking. Sorry.'

The *sorry* was emphatic. It said, *Please go away and leave me alone.*

Tessa took the hint.

'All right, thank you. I hope I haven't troubled you too much. There must be some mix-up.'

Tessa rang off. This information made it even more mysterious. Kath had remembered Dan being at Two Bridges in the afternoon, and that memory was probably reliable, triggered as it had been by the scent of lemon. She had read all the literature: people with brain traumas, and returning memories, commonly had troubling associations that only made sense when the mental networks healed. And scent was *particularly* associated with memory: the use and application of specific scents was a known, professional technique when attempting to retrieve deep memories.

So Dan had probably been at the hotel on the day of Kath's suicide bid, and he was there the day after. But the night was missing. Where had he been in the evening hours, the early morning? What did he do? During those very hours when Kath drove into Burrator? And what, in particular, made Kath run away from him?

Tessa looked at the clock on her expensive cooker. The date, the time, in glowing red lights. A week ago they'd all been on a scary ride in Disneyland Paris, looking at animated pirates with the boys. Laughing at Captain Hook and the parrot that said *Arrrrr*.

Yet in minutes her marriage, that family, everything, could be over. The house, the life, the happiness. Gone. She estimated her husband would be home in about three minutes: he'd called from the petrol station. His two-day business trip was complete, he was happy to be coming home.

She looked at the clock again. The vivid red glow, slightly pulsing. She was precisely right. Three minutes had passed and she could hear the big car pull into the drive, the smooth grumble of the garage door. The engine turned off. The key would be going in the door. The happy, successful husband returning to his lovely family.

Tessa gazed down at her glass of red wine. It was entirely untouched.

If her marriage ended she wanted it ended soberly. For the right reasons.

She needed to be sharp. Didn't she?

Tessa took a big gulp of the wine.

Dan was coming down the hall. She could hear his footsteps in the living room, the sound of him probably looking for her.

'I'm in the kitchen!' Tessa called out. Loudly. Too loudly.

Hiding her fears.

Moments later he appeared, smiling, good-looking: the man she had desired, until recently. Another image from Disneyland rose in her mind from nowhere, Dan and the boys buying ice cream from Mickey Mouse, and giggling. Dan tousling Oscar's hair. Could this same man really be involved in Kath's suicide bid? What had he done that made his own sister run away?

'Hello, darling.' He raised his hands to tousle his hair, dark and wet from the rain. 'Bitch of a day. Horrible trip. I *sooooo* need a sharpener.'

As usual, he made straight for the cupboards, took out a big tumbler. Then he went to the shelf, grabbed a bottle, poured a generous shot of Williams gin. Turning to the fridge, he grabbed a tray of ice, clunked his tumbler full of ice cubes, and drowned it all with Fever Tree tonic. The sugar-free kind.

This was his evening ritual. He thought this was a normal evening.

Tessa stared at him as he rummaged in the fridge. He had no idea.

'Where are the lemons? Where do they go? Ah, wait, here you are, you citrusy little slut. Flaunting yourself by the milk.'

He turned as he dropped the lemon slice in his drink; he smiled and glanced at her wine as he sat down at the wooden counter.

'I can make you something stronger, as well, if you like. Keep out the winter blues?'

She ignored his offer, without a smile. He shrugged. She looked him in the eye. 'Dan,' she said, very calmly, 'Tell me what really happened that day, the day after Kath had her accident.'

He gazed back at her with a puzzled frown. And a puzzled chuckle. The ice cubes rattled in his glass as he laughed, and sipped.

It's fake, she thought, *it's all bloody fake, the frown, the laughter, the sense of bewilderment.* She said nothing but waited for him to realize.

His chuckle faded. 'What? Why the fuck are we back to this?'

'Tell me.'

He took another swift hit of his gin. 'Oh God. Enough. *Ça suffit.* I told you. Jesus Bleeding Christ.'

'Told me what?'

'I drove back fast, with the guy with the Aston.'

She nodded. 'So if I call him, call this rich guy in Padstow, he will back up your story?'

The frown returned. 'Yes. Of course. Because it's the damn truth. Jesus, what is this detective crap? You know, you should buy a magnifying glass. Deerstalker hat. Try injecting cocaine.' He looked at her. 'Oh come on, Tessa. This is a joke. I'm joking, can we move on?'

Tessa shook her head, bleakly. 'When you first told me that story, you said that this rich guy, Alex Delaney, lived in Truro, not Padstow.'

Dan was silent for several seconds. Then he laughed slightly drunkenly, the gin beginning to hit. 'For fuck's sake. I forgot! And who gives a scintilla of a shit, anyhow? Padstow. Fowey. St Mawes. Somewhere with yachty idiots in deck shoes. Somewhere rich, on the Cornish coast.'

'But where?'

'I don't know! And I don't bloody know, my beloved wife, because he dropped me off, he had another hour to go, down the A30—' Dan sighed, loftily. 'Christ, Tessa I'm not lying about this, I'm not bloody lying about the day my sister nearly died. That's not my style.'

Yes, you are lying, Tessa thought, *I know it. I need to prove it. And then I might have to leave you.*

And yet, even as she thought this, Tessa's resolution began to crumble. She thought of her boys, having their sleepover: did she want them to come back to a broken home, to a fatherless house, to a divorce, or something much, much worse? She thought of the parrot that said *Arrr.*

She thought of Charlie, laughing, at the parrot, and Dan ruffling his hair.

Tessa drank some more wine. She was scared but determined. 'It's not just your lies,' she continued. 'There are witnesses. Eyewitnesses. I have proof.'

And now as she said this, she saw for the first time something different in Dan's eyes: a brief and passing hint of fear.

Tessa hastened, seizing the moment: 'Your sister Kath says she saw you in your Lexus, driving into the Two Bridges. That day. A memory that's come back to her. So you were there, at the Two Bridges, that day. December thirtieth. And when she saw you, she ran away. Why?'

Dan shook his head. Rather contemptuously, he finished his gin, and went over to the counter to get the gin bottle.

This is what he did before, Tessa thought, *this is how he buys time to concoct lies, to fashion explanations, he's like an actor using a prop.*

Here it came. His glass was refilled, and he turned back to the table.

'For God's sake, my sister has amnesia, Tessa. You're a psychologist. She has brain trauma. She's not herself.' He sank some cold gin, half smiling. 'You told me she has hallucinations: she actually thinks she saw our dead mother hanging around bus stops – maybe she sees fucking witches flying across Huckerby during the full moon, how can you possibly rely on her—'

'Because she was telling the truth, I am sure of it. Because, as you say, I am a psychologist. It's what I *do.*'

'Sure, but you're not a fucking mind-reader, Tessa. Holy Christ, enough of this DCI Kinnersley shite. Put down your evidence bag and get a grip.' He was almost shouting now, and there was real fury in his voice, fury designed to scare her off, to make her drop it. 'Stop this, Tessa. Stop it!'

Was that an actual threat? Tessa steeled herself and sat back, in case. He was quiet, scowling. Waiting for her to yield. But she would not yield. It was time for her to finish this off. To present him with evidence he could not wave away.

'Dan, you need to let me speak, and you need to listen, because there's *more.*'

And this time she saw it for sure. A flinching, a glimpse of deep anxiety. A faked smile of confidence he did not actually feel. And he was drinking gin too quickly. He always drank fast but this was different. He was unnerved. She went for it.

'I spoke to the nurse at the AMU in Derriford Hospital. Nurse Davis. Do you remember that name?'

Her husband blinked, once, twice, then firmly shook his head.

'No.'

'She's a young Welsh nurse. She was the one who phoned you, Dan, who phoned you from the hospital to tell you Kath was in a coma. She first phoned you, apparently, *at eleven thirty a.m.* And you were at Kath's bedside by noon. I suppose it is possible you drove from central London to Plymouth in thirty minutes, but that would mean your friend's *Aston Martin* averaged, ooh, *six hundred miles per hour,* and in that case, yes, you're right, I do think you would have got speedcammed once or twice, don't you?'

His smile was entirely gone. Dan looked queasy. A tiny tremble disturbed the corner of his mouth. Tessa calmed herself, and prepared herself. It was time for her exaggeration, but she needed it, so she could get his confession. The truth. At last.

'I confirmed with Nurse Davis, Dan. She has all the official hospital case notes, written down at the time. She quoted the conversation with you, as it's all on record. Because you told her where you were when she rang, you told her where you'd stayed.' A big deliberate pause. 'And you were at Two Bridges Hotel. On the night Kath drove into Burrator. It's all written down. At the hospital. In a file.'

The refrigerator hummed. It was the only noise in the room. Dan was wholly silent. He finished his gin and gazed into his glass.

Tessa waited.

Dan went back to the counter and poured a third large glass of Williams, but this time he did it with a distinct air of resignation, leaning over, his palms flat on the counter. He was defeated, she'd got him, she'd proved his lies. She'd *won*.

But still the worst remained to be uncovered. *Why* was he lying? She still didn't understand the depth of his involvement. Did he meet Kath that night, and if he did, what did he do, or say, or reveal? And why had she run away from him?

'Sit down, Dan. This is very, very serious. You need to be entirely honest now or I will never speak to you again. I will ask for a divorce and I will fight you for the boys and I will get them. I'll take the house. I'll take it all.'

Dan sat down. Obedient, and subdued, like an admonished child. A different man. 'Go on,' he said, quietly.

'I need to know,' Tessa said. 'This isn't any old marital lie, Dan Kinnersley. This is a lie that involves the near drowning of your sister.'

He squinted at her as if trying to work something out. Then he gasped. 'Oh my God! You really *do* think I was actually involved, don't you? You think that somehow all this links with Kath's suicide attempt. You think I caused it, you think—'

'Of course I bloody think that!' Tessa was shouting now, she didn't care if she got the neighbours calling the police – the police were probably coming anyway, they might be coming for her lying husband. 'What do you expect me to fucking think? The night your sister drives into deep water on Dartmoor you lie about your whereabouts, you say you were in London but you were on Dartmoor!' Tessa slapped the table hard: so hard it stung her hand. 'And, what's more, there's no record of you actually staying in that hotel. I checked with their reception, so your movements that night are a total mystery, except we know that from late evening to mid-morning you were somewhere around Kath, *the very same time* she made her fucking inexplicable suicide bid. And we know that she was scared of you, because she ran away from you.' Tessa leaned forward, spitting her words. 'So what *did* you do, Dan? Did you meet her that night, did you say something, do something? What did you do to your own fucking sister that would make her try and take her own life? What did you *do*?'

As she shouted these last words, Tessa swept her arm angrily, sending the wine glass spinning on to the slate kitchen floor, smashing it into a thousand satisfying shards, the way she wanted to smash this marriage.

There. Done. Broken. Fuck it.

Yet the noise and shock seemed to purge something in her. She felt herself calm. And as she calmed, she noticed that Dan was looking her right in the eye, with an expression she had not seen before. Ever.

Sadness. Resignation.

'OK, you're right.'

'How am I right?'

'I lied about that night.'

She stared at him. 'How? Tell me everything!'

'I lied. I'm sorry. I'm sorry. I lied. I've been lying. And I've been lying for a year.' He searched her gaze, imploringly, looking for sympathy. 'But please, believe me. I had absolutely nothing to do with what happened to Kath. I didn't see her that night, that afternoon. I didn't see or talk to her at all.'

'So what bloody happened? Why were you at Two Bridges, yet there's no record of you staying? Why and how are you lying?'

He picked up the glass again, sipped more gin. Slowly. Steadily.

'I've been seeing that bargirl in the Two Bridges. The blonde one. I've been seeing her for a year. I met her at the kids' party there, last year.'

Tessa sat back, utterly stunned. She didn't know whether to feel hurt or relieved. So this was it. This. This thing. This crap. This was the feeble explanation. It was simply an affair?

Yet: it was an affair. He was sleeping with that girl, the one with the piercings, the tats, the short blonde girl. Tessa recalled her, from her many visits to Two Bridges.

Dan shrugged, his face flushed. 'Usually I take her to anonymous hotels, places by the motorway, Tavistock. Okehampton. That's where we go. Sometimes I take her to the cottage in Brixham. When it's not rented out.' He had the sense to wince as he admitted this. 'I picked her up that afternoon, and we went there. Brixham. But she had an early morning shift, so I brought her back to the moor and I stayed in her room. She has a room at Two Bridges cos she works there and it's so remote.' He sank more Williams and tonic and closed his eyes, rubbing his eyes with weary fingers, and then he looked at Tessa once more. 'That's why I'm not in the register. But that's why I was there in the morning.'

Tessa was momentarily silenced by too many emotions. Hurt, grief, dismay. She'd loved Dan, she probably loved him now. Love didn't disappear in a minute. They'd had a good relationship, until now. She'd thought they were happy; they *were* happy. They had a satisfying sex life. Or so she had presumed. And it was all lies.

'Why her, Dan?'

'Sorry?'

'I want to know. Why her? A girl. A bargirl. That girl.

She's barely out of her teens. Is it the intellectual conversation?'

'Please don't do this.'

Tessa snorted. 'Fuck you. Tell me. Why her? Just because she's younger, got a nicer body than me, no kids, no stretchmarks, is it that? Am I getting too old for you?'

'Please!'

'Tell me.'

He shook his head. 'Stop.'

Tessa raised an angry hand. She was close to slapping him. He looked at her, at the hand, the threat of violence; and she realized: it was the piercings, the tats, the black choker with that little ring.

'Oh fuck, it's kinky sex, isn't it? You're having rough sex with her, aren't you? BDSM, all that. Bondage, whipping. You always wanted that from me, I never liked it enough. So you went elsewhere?'

This time he couldn't even look her in the eye. She was clearly right.

Tessa pictured her husband, probably in their Brixham cottage, tying the girl up, locking handcuffs to the bed. The bed they had bought together.

Bastard.

Dan was still averting his eyes as he drank his gin. The kitchen suddenly felt too big. The whole house felt huge and hollow with sadness. All that money, yet all this sadness. What could they do now? What would happen to them all? Tessa felt the most intense weariness.

'Go sleep somewhere else,' she said. 'Get out of here, sleep in the spare room. Don't come near me.'

Her husband paused as if he had something more to say, but he obediently picked up his drink and meekly made his way out of the kitchen.

When she was sure he was gone, Tessa went to the

cupboard under the sink, and pulled out a dustpan. Very carefully, she began to brush up the shattered glass. There was so much of it everywhere, glittering and lethal. Just one broken glass, making all these needles and shards; just one broken glass, and you could sever a thousand veins.

Saturday morning

They met in the kitchen. Dan had spent the night in the spare room. Tessa had spent the night barely sleeping, turning her pillow over and over, seeking the coolness of a solution; finding none.

Now they moved around each other, in the kitchen, like members of a different species mistakenly put in the same cage at the zoo. She made toast. He made coffee. It was 8.30 a.m. In an hour he would go off to collect the boys from their sleepover; as he did that, she would climb the stairs, to her study, her desk, her beloved window, to her work and books and normal life.

Except it was no longer normal. Everything had changed, even as everything looked precisely the same.

Tessa contemplated her husband as he plunged the cafetière. Could she ever forgive him? She had no idea, not yet. Did she believe him? Probably, maybe, possibly. Dan seemed sincere in his declaration of innocence regarding Kath. So it was just an affair. A pitiful little thing. But it was still infidelity. A year of horrible lies.

Tessa ate her miserable toast; Dan filled a coffee mug. Tessa wondered how many marriages ended in kitchens. Probably quite a lot. She thought of Dan in the cottage they'd bought in Brixham. Did he and his little slut cook together, in the kitchen? Of course they did. Perhaps he kissed her over the table. Perhaps he roughly fucked her on the table. Tied her to a bloody kitchen door, or whatever kinky people did.

She imagined them together. The man twice her age. The teenage bargirl with issues.

Bastard.

Dan broke the silence first. 'Tessa. This is intolerable, I have to know. Do you believe me?'

She shrugged silently, trying to restrain her anger. She was simultaneously exhausted yet furious. She wished she'd put more marmalade on her toast. Yet she couldn't be bothered to go to the cupboard and fetch the jar again. Overnight everything has become so tiring, so pointless, so wearyingly predictable: the rich, handsome husband fucking the kinky little bargirl. How disappointingly ordinary of Dan Kinnersley to be that pathetic man.

And he was trying again. 'Please, Kath, I need to know. I have to know. I can understand if you hate me, I can understand if you want a divorce: I was seeing that girl, it's all true, all that is true. What can I say? I did it, you're right. But I can't have you thinking I had anything to do with Kath's accident.'

She looked at him wearily. 'I don't know.'

He sighed, frustrated. But Tessa wasn't going to let him off so easily. She wasn't going to let him off at all. This was all too serious. There was too much evidence against him that had yet to be explained.

She asked, outright, 'What about Kath running away from you?'

'We discussed this. I have no idea. I didn't see her.'
'Discuss it more.'

'Look.' He raised his hands in surrender, 'What the fuck can I do? I don't have footage, all I have is the truth—'

'The truth?'

'Yes. The truth. OK, I've been lying about the girl, yes, I've deceived you, go ahead and divorce me, I can't blame you. I am sorry for what I did and I know sorry will never be enough – but what possible motive would I have for hurting my own sister?'

Tessa finished her toast, shook her head, and frowned. 'There's always been a bit of friction between the two of you.'

'Because I got the house? Sure. But Kath got over it. I've tried to be generous ever since. And it was hardly my doing. It was Mum.'

'Hmm.'

He pressed on. 'Yes. Yes. We have our differences, me and Kath, but I love her, and I adore Lyla. Why would I hurt that family, Tessa? My own flesh and blood?'

'I don't know. But Kath claims she was running away from you. Why?'

'I don't know. I didn't see her!'

Tessa sat back. She examined her husband, the way she would look at a prisoner in Princetown. Applying psychology. It felt as if he was telling the truth about Kath. But there was something else here, something lurking.

'What about Adam?'

'Sorry?'

'You dislike Adam. You always have. You hide it, you rub along, but we both know it, he knows it. Why? Why do you dislike him?' He said nothing, so she pressed the issue.

'You've disliked him from the off. As long as I can remember. Haven't you?'

At last, he nodded. 'Yes.'

It felt as if she was approaching the centre of the maze.

'So, why? Enough bullshit. It's time to explain. What is it with Adam? Why have you always irritated each other?'

He poured the last of the coffee as she went on.

'Is it because he resents us, because of the house? Is it just that?'

Dan was mute. She leaned closer.

'There's something else, isn't there? Tell me. Why *did* you get this house, Dan? Why did your mum favour you so much over Kath? Was it really because she was mad at the end, the cancer reaching her brain? Or is there something I don't know?'

Dan gazed into his coffee mug, and sighed, fiercely, then looked at her. Eye to eye.

'There is something. I've never mentioned it before because—' He offered a long, regretful shake of his head. 'Kath and Adam were so happy, it's not my place, I'm her brother, I want them to be happy, and he's a very good dad to Lyla.'

'But?'

'Tessa, wait. I've never told anyone this. For very good reasons.'

'It's something to do with Penny, isn't it, with your mother, and her death?'

Dan looked at the ceiling, as if seeking the forgiveness of God; then he looked back at Tessa.

'Remember it was Adam and I who went out to India, to get her ashes, so they could be scattered at Kitty Jay's grave? The ashes they hadn't already dumped in the

236

damn Ganges. Kath was in too much of a state, so Adam and I flew out.'

'Yes. And?'

'Well, there's stuff I never told you.'

'Such as?'

'She'd left letters for us, for Adam, for me. After her death.'

'Not Kath?'

'Nope. Just me and Adam. I'm not sure Kath ever knew. I never told her, I doubt if Adam told her.'

Tessa tried to work this out. Failed. 'What did they say? The letters?'

Her husband shrugged. 'Well, I haven't a fucking clue what was in his, he didn't exactly spill the beans. But I will never forget what was in mine.' Tessa felt her anxiety deepen.

'A lot of it was mad. Most of it. Stuff about death and nirvana, Shiva and Kali. She was always pretty alternative, and by the end I think the cancer *was* in her mind, but—' he sighed, awkwardly. 'There was also one alarming, yet quite rational, passage where she said she could never trust Adam. She hated him, or feared him. I don't know. And she started raving about evil and witchcraft, and that she wouldn't let him live in her house. Ever.'

'Why not?'

'I don't know. She didn't spell it out. It was implicit in what she said. And it was mad. But she clearly meant it. That's why she fled to India.'

Tessa gazed at her husband. Eyes wide and clear, as if she could see through him, see through everything, finally.

'Evil? Really? She really said that?'

'That was definitely the implication. I can't say for sure. But she clearly believed that there was *something*

237

evil or bad about Adam, or something terrible had occurred, because of him.'

Tessa reeled with confusion. 'You never thought to mention this?'

He raised a hand, defending himself. 'Wait, wait. Wait and think, Tessa. Remember how loopy this sounds. Evil. Fire and bloody brimstone. Either way, this is why we got the house, the whole fucking job lot. She hated Adam, didn't want him living here, didn't want him to get any of it.'

'But . . .' Tessa was at a loss. And she wasn't sure Dan was telling her everything. He had that look. He was toying with his coffee. There was something more. 'Why didn't you do anything?'

'Like I said. Because my sister was so happy with Adam, and I was already unfairly favoured. Was it really my job to wade in? Was it right for me to fucking wade in and trash her relationship, and then her marriage, on the basis of my mum's final ravings?'

Tessa mused. 'Possibly not . . . But now it's *different*. We *have* to do something, Dan. Because it's all returning, it's all happening again. Kath thinks she is bewitched, and she is seeing ghosts, and she's losing her mind, and if Adam is at the root of it all . . .' Tessa felt a fearful despair. They needed to intervene. But she had no idea how. The despair deepened. 'Jesus. Think of it. And that poor little girl is in the middle of all this insanity! Up there on the moor.'

The Spaldings' Farm

Monday evening

I am here. Amidst the glory of a clear winter evening on Dartmoor. The moon is a single silver claw above old Black Tor; the stars are like the tiny ends of a million shining filaments, blindly feeling their way towards the darkened earth. I can hear the call of a big white owl somewhere, hunting, and killing.

Usually I can be entranced for hours by beautiful Dartmoor nights like this, the clear cold winter nights of a million galaxies over Haytor, but after one brief glance at the godless sky, I am oblivious to it all.

Now I sit in the darkness of my car outside the Spaldings' farmhouse.

I'm here to fetch Lyla. Emma agreed to collect and keep Lyla, after school, as I had extra National Park work to do from home, without distraction. It is beginning to pile up: normal life is reclaiming me, like a mire sucking me down, even as my life spins out of control.

But I am not ignoring the beauty of the freezing,

cloudless Dartmoor heavens because of work, but because of the email I am reading, as I sit in my car.

It's one of those Dartmoor moments when the mobile phone signal around Huckerby is stupidly bad for no apparent reason: so this email, sent ages ago, only just pinged on to my phone as I pulled up at the Spaldings' big, handsome, foursquare, Georgian farmhouse.

The email is from Tessa. It's marked Urgent. It explains why I saw Dan at Two Bridges. Why he was lying. He was having an affair, with the Two Bridges bargirl. He's been doing it for a year. My own brother.

Yet there is more. And it is even more puzzling and disturbing; but enigmatic, too. It says:

> Dan is worried about Adam. He thinks he knows things about your mother that he hasn't told you. He got a letter from Penny, when they went to India, accusing Dan. Of something evil. And this might be linked with you at Burrator. Kath, I know this sounds strange but Dan certainly knows something. Please come and see me as soon as you can.

What does *that* mean?

It's unusual for Tessa to be ambiguous. She is normally straight, and to the point. And this letter from Mum? It is so conveniently timed. My doubts rise. So my brother claims he was having an affair, which explains his presence at the Two Bridges. Is this really true, or is he disguising his own, deeper guilt? I wonder if I can even trust Tessa. They are, after all, both enjoying my mother's inheritance.

Why *did* he get the house from Mum?

The image of my mother returns to me. And Lyla, hissing in her den.

You you you you you.

My mind is a chaos of voices and horrors: one of those medieval paintings of Hell, with demons in the corner, pitchforking the sinners. The self-murderers.

I have to focus on the here, the now, the life of today. My motherhood. Duties. So I silence the voices – the shrieks of the suicides, the sound of my lunacy, suspicions, and guilt – by clicking shut my smartphone, and putting it in my pocket. Then I step out of the car into the stinging, fir-scented cold. A bracing east wind is scouring the sky; it will be shuddering the gorse at Blackaller Quarry, and rattling the slates back at Huckerby.

Tightening the scarf around my neck, I sprint to the front door and ring the bell. A few moments later it swings open, revealing warmth and light and roast cooking smells, and a smiling Emma Spalding, with Lyla in her school uniform at her side. Emma's customary smile barely conceals her ongoing concern. There's always a hidden frown of anxiety when Emma looks at me these days.

'Here you go, Kath, she's had her supper.'

'Thanks so much. Work's beginning to pile up.'

'Quite a night,' says Emma as she leans out and stares up into the frigid, windy darkness, as Lyla runs out and hugs me. 'Beautiful night for stars, but must be minus ten on the tors.'

'Thank you, yes, thank you. Come on Lyla-berry, let's get you home.'

Emma closes the door on both of us, as Lyla races to the car, clutching her school bag and *Jungle Book* lunchbox.

The drive home is brief and noisy, the wind slapping the car. I have to actively fight the weather with my steering wheel, as if I am at the tiller of a ship in a swell. At one corner the road veers past a swathe of open, moonlit moorland. I can see those ruined barns in the frosted distance. I can, with a squint, make out the row of gorse where I came across Harry Redway, whom I mistook for Adam.

Harry Redway. Could he be significant?

A shiver trills inside me. A need to question my daughter. Slightly too fast, I pull into Huckerby's muddy yard. I know that as soon as I open the door Lyla will run inside and hug Felix and Randal, and run upstairs to lose herself in books and games and daydreams, and fall swiftly sleep. She looks tired. Everyone looks tired. Winter drags on, and on.

Wearing us out.

In a fortnight, down near Salcombe and the coast, there will be daffodils in the hedgerows; up here winter could last another two months.

I have to ask my daughter about this. But she asks first.

'Why are we still here, Mummy, why aren't we going inside?'

Turning from my seat, I regard my girl. Her blue eyes stare back at me. In the darkness. In the car. Who was that man in the car, staring at me? In my memory? Adam? Dan? Harry? Why did Harry look so furtive?

'Mummy, are you all right?'

I fight the warring voices in my mind, but it is hard now; they are deafening.

'Mummy?'

I stare.

'Mummy?'

I am thinking. Dark hair. In a car.

'Mummy?'

'Yes, Lyla, darling. Thinking of Daddy, and things. I have to ask you again.'

Lyla clutches her *Jungle Book* lunchbox closer. Like a defensive shield. A talisman to ward me off. I know she sees herself in Mowgli, and why not? She is a kind of Mowgli of the moors.

I almost close my eyes, ashamed of what I am doing; yet I do it anyway. 'Lyla, are you really seeing someone I know, out on the moors? And if you are, are you sure it is Daddy? Or someone else? Could it be someone else? How about Daddy's cousin, Harry?'

The lunchbox is lifted higher. Her eyes glisten, but tears do not fall.

She gazes at me and says nothing. Her eyes express pain, and sadness, and all that she must think of me. The mother who tried to leave her alone in the freezing world. I reach across the car to brush the hair out of her eyes but she pushes my hand away and sits as far from me as possible, in the extreme corner of the car. Gazing at me as if I am mad, bizarre.

A man's eyes. Angry. In a car. Dark hair, on a dark moorland night.

Why do I remember that?

Dart, Dart, every year thou breakest a heart.

One more go.

'Lyla, I know this is upsetting, but I really need to ask, to make sure: who did you really see in Hobajob's? And who did you see the day you arranged the birds?'

Her voice, when it comes, is monotonous. Her hand is beginning to stim, fluttering up and down. 'Daddy,' she says. Her lips tremble, her hands quiver.

'You saw Daddy. How many times?'

'Three times. Four. Three. It was him. It was dark, it was him. Always. Daddy. He was scary. And then . . .

Then maybe it was another man. I'm not sure. Like him. But Daddy really.'

'Another man?'

'Maybe. Not sure. Not sure. Not sure. Daddy, I think. Please stop.'

Her hands are shaking wildly now, as if she is fitting, having a spasm, and she is rocking backwards, forwards, backwards, forwards. I've gone too far, pressed it too hard, making her autism worse. But she saw Daddy three or four times? Does that really make sense?

'Lyla—'

'No, Mummy. LET ME GO IN!' Her scream is unignorable. I accede.

Kicking open the car door, she runs for the warmth of Huckerby Farm, and I follow behind. Inside, she makes straight for the dogs, who stir from the baskets and blankets, and race towards her with delight, she hugs them, and they all scamper upstairs.

It is 9 p.m. Suddenly it feels weirdly normal. Adam is on the way home from the rangers' meet at Moreton-hampstead, which is twelve miles from everywhere, and always a hassle to get to and from. But he will be back soon.

I hear Lyla upstairs: running to the bathroom, brushing her teeth, as I warm myself some onion soup.

Is she asleep? Feeling a need to make sure, I climb the stairs to her room. She is flat-out unconscious, the book she was reading – *Nonsense Verse* by Edward Lear – has fallen from her hands, and spilled the blue plastic cup of water she keeps by her bed.

My lonely daughter of the moor.

Kissing her gently on her frownless brow, I inhale the peppermint smell of her toothpaste. My kiss makes her murmur in her dreams, her dreams of the moor, her dreams of dormice and dogs and days at Fingle Bridge, her dreams of Vellake Corner, the Valley of Rocks, the grassy banks of the West Okement, the days in the Gidleigh gardens in the summer, the picnics down at Dartmeet. I kiss them all, and whisper, 'I love you, darling,' and her dreaming blue eyes move under her veiny eyelids. But she sleeps, soundly, exhausted. Felix and Randal snooze at the foot of the bed. Knowing I will need to walk them soon, I rouse them, and quietly shoo them from the room.

The dogs linger by Lyla's door. I follow my own shadow down the landing.

Right on time, the Land Rover returns. The engine is killed. The door opens. Adam flings off his fleece and blithely sits at the kitchen table with barely a nod in my direction. He opens a local paper. *The Moorlander*.

I stare at him. Adam is reading the paper as if he is a Bible scholar with an early version of the gospels. *Buzzard Shot With Air Rifle. Hit And Run Driver Admits Knocking Girl Off Pony.*

Crossing the kitchen, I grab the newspaper from his hand. 'Adam.'

He shakes his head, and tuts. His teeth grind but he does not speak. But I hear his thoughts. *Not this again, you mad bitch.*

Am I going to say anything about Dan, the bargirl, or the accusations from Tessa? Yes. No. I'm not sure.

'Adam, what if Harry Redway is involved in this? What if Harry Redway did something to my car? What if Lyla saw him, but thought it was you?'

Now, at last, he looks right at me. Blue eyes colder than I have ever seen them.

'My cousin Harry? *Seriously?*'

I rush on, I must not stop: 'Think about it. He looks

like you. He's all over the moor. We know he likes the ladies. Maybe I got drunk that night, and Harry came to see me. And something went wrong. Because—'

'Kath!'

I ignore him. 'No. Because, get this, Adam: I found Harry out on the moor the other day. With a big axe. Under Black Tor. He said he was cutting firebreaks, but no one does that there, do they? Never seen it before. Ever. Not there. And he looked so guilty, it was weird – and I thought at first it was you—'

Adam is almost snarling with scepticism. 'If Harry looked *guilty* it was probably because he was *poaching*. Though he usually does it with Jack, because Jack likes the killing. It's Harry who likes the cheap meat.' Adam smiles, bitterly, and shakes his head. 'Really. Kath, are you saying Harry, my little cousin Harry Redway, was with you the night you tried to kill yourself, that's it all his fault and he's been following you ever since? Are you now blaming it on him?'

I stare back. Defiant. 'Yes, I am!'

Adam waves the idea away

'Harry Redway was not with you on the night you drove into Burrator.'

'How do you know?'

A pause.

'I just know.'

I swallow my anger.

'But there's too much that is unexplained, Adam. I'm sure I saw things. Burrator. Hobajob's. The hag stones, my hairbrush. And you heard Lyla singing that song. About death, the little blue light. The light which means there is a death approaching, someone is meant to die, very soon—' I realize I must sound borderline crazy, but my anger is rising. Why is he ignoring my

246

evidence? Why should I spare him the rest of the truth?

He glares at me. I glare right back.

'And what's more, now I've had an email from—' I hesitate, but I have to say it – 'from Tessa. She's been talking to Dan. She said Mum accused you of things, of, of, of evil things. In a letter. When you and Dan went to India.'

His eyes glow with real anger 'Evil? Me? Evil things? Jesus wept! You saw your mum in a fucking bus shelter, and she's been dead nearly twenty years. You saw her because you have brain damage. You need help, Kath. We need to get help. You're destroying your daughter. You're killing all of us. Drowning us the way you tried to drown yourself.'

He clenches a fist. He wants to use it. I almost want him to use it. Go on, punch me.

And he is lying anyway. I remember his guilt. Whenever I talked about him staying up at Manaton, near Kitty Jay's grave, he looked guilty.

It all connects here. And I think I know how. Like a dazzling chorus, like sunrise over Buckland Beacon.

It was when I mentioned the place he was doing up that he felt guilty. But it wasn't when I mentioned it was near Manaton. It was specifically when I mentioned it was near *Kitty Jay's*. Where my mother's ashes were scattered.

I've got him. I've found the lie.

Kitty Jay.

'You *do* know something about Mum, don't you, Adam? Tessa said that. It's something to do with Mum, isn't it?'

'Don't be stupid, woman.'

'Mum and you, Dan, or maybe Harry, somehow you're all involved. A conspiracy. I know it. What the hell did you all do to me, what could you all have done to me that night? You did something, somehow—'

He comes close, looking as if he is going to slap me, hard across the face, and yet there is also guilt in his eyes. I am right: he is lying.

'Please,' he says, and he sounds desperate. His voice is cracked, broken. 'Please, Kath, please. Stop this right here, right now.'

'But you're lying! You are, all of you. That song. Harry looking guilty. My brother. My *mother*—'

He speaks, very fiercely. 'For fuck's sake! Lyla's song was a song. No one is about to die. And as for your mother – who cares. Your batshit mother gave the house to them because she was a *bitch*, and because she was crazy from the *cancer*, and she died, and they burned her by the river, and your lovely brother got all the house, and we got half the ashes, and a lovely doll from Greenland: *that's all there is to it.*' Adam is growling now. 'And, really, no, there isn't some huge conspiracy. For God's sake. It's ridiculous, stop it all, please. You have to *stop it* for LYLA.' A howling stops us both.

The dogs.

It's a howling I have never heard. Felix and Randal?

We swap glances: everything changes. Adam goes first, running up the stairs, I follow him. It is all dark: he snaps on the lights, and there are the dogs, howling at the end of the landing. They are outside Lyla's door. It is shut.

It is dark in there too, judging by the lack of light under the door.

Adam yells; I scream, 'Lyla!'

But a sense of dread tears me up as we run towards the bedroom. Pushing the door. I turn on the light. The room is so cold. Bitterly, nightmarishly cold. The harsh, winter, moorland smell of rotten silage fills the little bedroom, with its glittery pictures of the Disney princess from *Frozen*.

The window is wide open. The bed is empty. Lyla has gone.

Dartmoor

Monday evening

Two heartbeats. One bedroom. No daughter. We stare at each other, run to the window.

She's climbed out the window. Or someone has taken her.

Whatever the case: she is gone.

And the dogs keep howling, howling so loudly they can probably hear them in Princetown. And I fear I will hear this howling for the rest of my life.

Adam stammers, 'She – she must have climbed out. Jesus. Christ—'

'Or someone took her.'

I fight the desperate tears. Panic is our enemy. I point at the window.

'It's easy to climb down, so it's easy to climb up?'

'Lyla!' Adam shouts into the blackness and the slender mists and the rolling moors, shouting all the way to Hexworthy, shouting for our lost daughter. 'Lyla!'

There isn't even an echo. His voice is swallowed in the

dark. I am probably the only human that heard it.

'The den!' I cry, turning. 'If she's run away, that's where she'd hide.'

Adam turns, calling to the dogs, 'Felix! Randal! Find Lyla! Lyla! Find her.'

They look at him, puzzled. Heads cocked. They've stopped howling.

What did they see? Or sense? As we all run downstairs, I work the scenario. Lyla could have climbed out, no problem. It's a ten-foot drop, if that, with lots of handholds. Easy easy easy. And she's a good climber, excellent even, with all that clambering up the tors on the moors. She is proud of her climbing skills.

But why would she run away? Did she hear us arguing? We only shouted right at the end, but that was it, probably it was our fault. Guilt stabs me, brutal, and hard. First I try to kill myself – whatever my excuse – now I make my daughter run away? What did I expect? A reward for my behaviour?

I pray that she is in the den. Out into the dark, across the yard, we sprint towards her little cave of thorns, eggshells and kingfisher feathers, and Adam pulls open the wooden door.

Tinkle tankle, say the chains of paper clips, *tinkle tankle.*

A soft, cold wind stirs the silvery chains.

The den is empty, there's no sign she's been in here.

'Lyla!' Adam shouts, his desperate call a cloud of frozen vapour. He turns to me. 'Could be she's at the Spaldings'.'

He might be right but I have the horrible sense he isn't. What is she wearing, out here in this icy darkness? Pyjamas? Dressing gown? Did she get dressed or was she taken? Her bedroom door was shut. At some point the dogs, just outside, realized she was gone. By her scent, or lack of it, perhaps.

'Lyla!' Adam shouts again. Louder than I have ever heard him shout. 'Lyla. It's all right. Don't be scared. Lyla! Come back!'

I am phoning the Spaldings. My hands shake in the cold, the signal is feeble, it comes and goes, but here, if I walk to the top of the yard, I get two bars. Enough.

'Lyla!'

The Spaldings' phone rings. Please let them be in. Please let them have her. Please please please. I realize, as their phone rings and rings, unanswered, that we have no idea how long she has been gone.

My daughter could be anywhere.

'Lyla!'

The Spaldings' phone rings, and rings.

'LYLA!'

There is no answer. She can't be there.

Adam is running back into the longhouse. Does he have some new idea? Is she hiding in the house?

My hands are hurting from the cold as I try Emma Spalding's mobile.

Maybe they are already bringing Lyla home to us.

She answers immediately.

'Emma!'

'What? Hello? Kath?'

'Emma, where are you you're not at home I've been desperate, we're trying to get hold of you, Emma—'

'I'm in the bath, Kath.'

'Emma, please—'

'Was that you on the landline, ringing just now? We're going away tomorrow, off to London. Sorry, Kath, what's wrong?'

'So you're still at home?'

'Yes.'

I force the words. 'We've lost Lyla.' A momentary, awful pause.

'What?'

'She's run away, or just gone. Disappeared. Is she there? Is she there with you?'

'God, oh my God, Kath, no, she's not. There's only me in the house. George is on his way back from Okehampton. The place is empty – but I'll go and check the outhouses, the horses – you never know – she could be with the horses.'

The phone shakes in my hand. Emma rings off: I'll have to wait. The phone shakes so hard I nearly drop it. Cold, and nerves. Cold: and terror. The moorland stretches all around us, with its terrible emptiness, sedge and turf, tors and mire, leats and quarries and deadly shafts. The tin mines at Whiteworks, the reservoir at Burrator. The sky is cloudy, the quarter moon will not help us find my daughter. She is lost.

Unless she is at the Spaldings', she is gone.

Adam re-emerges from the house, carrying two torches and two coats and no daughter. He runs to me and gives me a torch and coat. Our argument is forgotten. We are a marriage again. Team Redway, trying to find Lyla, and I have the dreadful, plunging expectation of failure. This is it, I tried to kill myself, and my little girl is doing the same thing.

Or someone took her?

The phone rings, Emma Spalding. Hope soars to the clouded moon, somewhere over White Lady Falls, Raddick Hill, Lookweep Estate.

'Sorry, Kath. No sign of her. So sorry, so so sorry.'

Adam shines a torch in my face. I shake my head,

and give him the news. 'Lyla's not there, not at the Spaldings'.'

'I'm calling the police.' He takes out his own phone. The nearest police station is probably Yelverton. It's an hour's drive, or longer in the dark. How many men can they assemble this evening, how many square miles of moorland could they search, how long can my daughter survive in this cold? There won't be time if she's in pyjamas. She could be dying NOW.

Shivering in some field, by some dry-stone wall. Her eyes slowly closing, her heart slowly stopping. Blue beginning to tinge her lips.

O little blue light . . .

'I'm calling everyone,' I say, and I do, while Adam starts exploring the yard, shining his torch into thickets, over bent wooden fences, forlornly hoping she might be hiding nearby. I don't think he will find her. The dogs would have scented her. Felix and Randal are sitting in the doorway, halfway to whimpering. They've lost her, too. And if they've lost her, she is really, truly, properly unfindable.

I call everyone from anywhere who might know anything, or anyone who has ever encountered my daughter. I call parents from the school.

'Yes, it's Kath Redway, we've lost Lyla. If you know anything – please please help – please call me.'

I call pubs. 'Is that Two Bridges, yes, it's Kath Redway, remember, from Huckerby Farm? We can't find our little girl – Lyla, remember, blue eyes, black hair.'

I call my brother. For all our distance, and mistrust, he is still my brother. Her uncle.

He listens in awful silence And says, 'Oh. Jesus, Kath. Fuck. Fuck. I'm at a garage on the A30, not far away,

I'll turn round now. Oh my God. Be there in thirty minutes. Jesus.'

My mind spins, as the world spins. Lyla is on the moor: right now, shivering in the dark, in the bird-killing frost. I feel something like grief, already. Grief and anger and hatred: of everything. I will not let the world do this.

'Adam!'

He does not hear me. He is yelling down his phone, calling cousins, friends, rangers. Soon there will be people here, scouring the moor, but the roads are so long and narrow it could be ages before they get here. And it will take many hours to search the moor in darkness, and how will we find her in the dark: how do you search three hundred and sixty-five square miles of swamps, drowned quarries, ancient impenetrable woodland, and bottomless tinning pits? Three hundred and sixty-five square miles of places for a child to fall. And die.

'Lyla!'

Adam is screaming into the frosted mist, his voice sharp with outright desperation.

'Lyla?'

Now he turns to the dogs, calling them over; bending to their upturned noses; he has something in his hand. He shines his torch on it, and I see it's a T-shirt, one of Lyla's, with a big picture of Mowgli on it, smiling. My little feral jungle girl. My collector of shells and snails, and feathers and claws. Could she survive out there, for an entire night?

'Here, boys,' he says. 'Here. Smell this. Lyla. Find Lyla. Find her.'

The dogs sniff at the T-shirt. But they are not blood-hounds, so scenting is not their first instinct: they are lurchers. They hunt and they kill. Dutifully they bury their noses in Lyla's T-shirt, then they look up, forlorn and scared, and puzzled.

Felix snarls. As if it is our fault she is gone. And he is right.

Randal rests his head between two paws. Whimpering.

'This is no good,' I say, biting back my grief. My sadness and desperation surround me, like the endless grasses. We cannot find her in the dark, if we can find her at all. She is gone.

This desperation gives me an idea.

'Hobajob's.'

'Surely not. After the scare.'

'You have a better idea? If someone hasn't taken her, she'll go to one of her favourite places, and she still loves Hobajob's.'

I dazzle him with my torchbeam. His mouth is set and grim. But he nods. 'All right.'

We run out of the farmyard gate, on to the open moor, the dogs following, yelping. Up the muddy track, the dogs running ahead, into the wood. There is real moonlight now: the wisps of mist are disappearing. The silvery views of dry moorland open up, but they show nothing but black tors against almost black sky, and stars that shine on nothingness.

Together we vault the little wall, our torches shining on grasping branches and hanging moss and rotting leaves. I can hear the dogs, but nothing else. They are making the strangest noises, of grief, or fear. Nearly human.

We call and shout, 'Lyla! Lyla!'

Nothing. I have an overwhelming urge to turn and run back along the deepening shadows of the path to the longhouse. The dogs are making such strange and terrible noises. Eerie yowls. I don't need to know what the dogs have found. I really don't. We should go. Lyla must be somewhere else.

She is not here. Why are the dogs yowling so oddly?

Because they have found Lyla?

That must be it. She is in there: dead. Frozen. The song my daughter was singing, about the blue light, was a prediction of Lyla's own death, hurtling towards us.

Adam runs after her dogs. Their howling gets even louder. I can barely see a thing: the winter night is dark and grey, and the mossy, crowding trees make it darker still.

A wooden cage of night and cold.

Pushing through some icy brambles, I step into the sombre glade. The dogs are still circling, half demented. I prepare myself for the sight of Lyla dead, and naked, her throat slit. A white body in the cold, a smear of mud on her face. Raped and killed. Of course.

And now I see. The dogs are loping repeatedly around the corpses . . . . . . of two hares. Laid tail to tail.

There are always lots of dead hares on Dartmoor. Dead hares, dead ponies, dead sheep, dead rabbits – the moorland specializes in death. Dartmoor sometimes feels like a year-long, 24/7 Exhibition of Death, and you get used to it. You get used to finding the bodies of ponies broken in streams, or the reek of decomposing mutton on the air. You get accustomed to finding bleached skulls sitting on natural granite plinths like ritual objects.

But this, these hares, this is a different kind of death. Deliberate, carefully arranged. I put a hand to my mouth. Adam is staring in shock. Someone has cut off the left hind legs of both hares. These animals have been tortured and mutilated. Their eyes have been viciously gouged out, leaving deep dark sockets of oozing black. The hare on the left is staring right at us with its nightmare dead eyes, weeping trickles of blood.

And this isn't the worst. Because suddenly I see a pattern. The hares are meant to be eyes. The eyes of a face. A dove, blood red, has been laid among the dead leaves. That's the mouth. And a trail of gorse flowers and clumps of moss and of tiny dead mice streams from the mouth, in swooping curves.

And this, I think, is the pattern my daughter was trying to make with the dead birds at Huckerby. She didn't do it very well but I see it now. A kind of grinning face. A Green Man. The pagan symbol of rebirth, fertility, death. My mum was obsessed with these symbols.

Someone is repeating or copying this ghoulish pattern.

The blood thumps in my throat. Lyla has been here before and seen this, or someone has seen her. There really is someone out there.

The trees are black and the clearing is empty. Still we call, 'Lyla, Lyla, Lyla . . .'

Hobajob's merely shivers in silent response, a ghost of a breeze, cold and subtle. Nothing else. Nothing here.

'This way!'

As one, we run back through the trees on to the open moorland, the dogs loping alongside us, sensing our desperation.

Once the trees are behind us, Adam shouts again, 'Lyla!'

And now the moor answers, at last, with an echo, resounding, faintly, from the great granite rocks of Combestone Tor.

Lyla

But there is no other noise. Just a grand and terrible nothing. She is lost. I am crazed.

'Come on, Adam, come on – please think! Where might she go out here, when she's wandering?'

'I don't know. Jesus. She wanders all over! Kath, you know her, she could be anywhere.'

Adam scans the moorland urgently with his torch, a pitiful beam in the vastness, picking out clumps of brown-and-grey winter grass, and silvered patches of wetness. He shouts again, pointlessly, and again the moor answers with echoing silence.

Now he turns the torch on to the cold, muddy dogs. 'Felix, Randal, follow Lyla, follow her. Where do you go? Where does she take you? Where?'

The dogs gaze up. They growl. And suddenly they bark, as if they understand, and they start running off the track, downhill. I have no idea where they are going.

I hesitate. 'They could be taking us entirely the wrong way!'

Adam shakes his head. 'What choice do we have?'

He's right. This is our only hope. It is about minus three out here. Bone-cold and grimly damp, and with a new wind picking up. Even steelier, even chillier. We shiver as we follow the dogs.

How could a small girl in pyjamas survive in this cold?

The dogs run on, with definite purpose. My hopes rise. Panting and barking, they head down a beaten sheep track I do not know. Between tumps of turf, over tiny streams, pebbles rolling in my torchbeam. For a second I stop, astonished.

A pair of shining green eyes looms out of nowhere on my right, caught in the torchlight.

'What the—'

'It's a pony,' says Adam, panting like the dogs. 'Just a pony.'

He's right. A pony in the night, standing by a dark pile of rocks. The ponies have green eyes when you see them illuminated in darkness. Those same sad green eyes might have seen my daughter run this way. She loves the Dartmoor ponies, if this is where ponies go, at night, she might be here.

A new noise jolts me. The dogs are barking, but this time excitedly.

Have they found her? Is she alive?

'Look, some kind of shed,' Adam directs his torch beam.

I see a small conifer wood, grey and black in the freezing moonlight. But there, where the trunks begin, Adam is right. A shed. Shelter. And this is a place the dogs clearly know, so I reckon she probably brings them here, with her picnics. When I make her peanut butter sandwiches, give her a brace of apples, and off she goes, on long summer days, on her own, wandering free.

I am praying the way I used to pray, when I wanted to annoy my mother.

The dogs run excitedly up the wooden steps into the shed. They have *surely* found her. Adam runs up behind them and I follow, my heart ready to burst with relief.

The dogs stop barking. Our twin beams quickly scan the single wooden room. Smelling of old planking and mould.

There is no one here. Lyla has not been here. Felix and Randal sniff around the shed as if Lyla might have come here many weeks ago. But there is no sign of any recent presence. Nothing else at all.

I sink to my knees. I am not crying. I have crossed some horizon, beyond emotion. I am hollowed out: there are no more tears.

I have lost my daughter. It is what I deserve. For what I did at Burrator.

Lyla has done to me what I tried to do to her. Here is my righteous punishment. My death is returned to me, with interest.

261

Dartmoor

Night

Adam has his head sunk in his hands. I listen to the wind rattling the windowpanes of the shed. The glass is broken, the cold cuts through. Lyla might have survived if she'd found her way in here, but she didn't make it—

No. I say the word aloud. I shout at myself.

NO!

She is not dead. It is 11 p.m. and we know nothing. We will find her. She is a child of these moors. I will fight for her as I fought for my life, in Burrator. I may have made that terrible decision, but I also got out of the car, swam to the beach, because I love my daughter.

Pacing to the door, I look out into the severity of a cloudless black night, and a moon that curves in on itself; a foetal spine of silver on a dark ultrasound. Lyla aged five months in my womb.

The moonlight illuminates a standing stone. There are so many standing stones on Dartmoor. Hundreds.

I look at this stone. It vaguely reminds me of the stone I remembered, the stone that didn't look quite right, that

I have been unable to identify, even as I google endless images.

'Lyla!' Adam is calling by my side, through the door. 'Lyla! LYLA!'

I ignore him, keep gazing at the standing stone. An image from that terrible night returns. I remember seeing a different standing stone, from the car; but where? I remember thinking how impressive it was.

'You're right.'

I turn. Adam is pointing at the stone. He says,

'There. That bloody stone. Lyla loves them, doesn't she? I've seen her sit next to them. Merrivale. Scorhill. Dance round them. If she came this way, she went to the stone—'

'But the dogs?'

'They're guessing. They're lurchers. She may have left a better scent, by the stone, and we can try again: it will be fresher, the dogs might pick it up.'

There is no argument. This slender hope, my husband's idea, is, once again, all we have. Wherever she is, if Lyla is outdoors, she cannot survive much longer, not in this winter blade of a wind, this icy scythe slicing the uplands.

'Felix, Randal!'

Together, we race out on to the moor. I stumble over a soggy hump of grass. I drag myself up. We approach the stone.

'Here.' I am gasping: harsh February air is scalding my throat. My torch shines on the granite of the standing stone, patterned with grey and silver lichen, so many thousands of years old. I say,

'Give me the T-shirt.'

Adam hands it over. I bend to the dogs, and offer it to them and they inhale Lyla, all over again. I point at the moonlit ground, making clear my meaning: now sniff *there*, sniff the grass, the watery sedge, *pick up a scent!*

Felix looks at me.

And then he sniffs the end of my pointing finger. His eyes are a melancholic brown in the torchlight. These final hopes, already feeble, begin to fail. I try once more. Offer the dogs the T-shirt, and point at the ground. 'Smell it. Find her!'

Felix gazes my way, head cocked. And again he sniffs the end of my pointing finger.

Adam pushes me aside.

'That's not how lurchers work! They don't understand that. Do it this way. Big dogs need manhandling.'

He grabs Felix by the collar, leads him a couple of yards to a kind of a sheep track. I shine my torch on them, counting the moments as Lyla shivers by a wall, waiting for her parents to find her, but failing, her fingers trembling, her white face turning whiter as her body slows to a stop.

It's all my fault. I have brought her to Merrivale. To the Plague Market. I have infected her with my death wish, despite myself. My love is gold in vinegar, and it carries my disease.

Adam firmly pushes Felix's muzzle to the earth, to the beaten grasses of that livestock path.

'Lyla,' he says, to Felix. 'Lyla came this way, your girl, our girl, she came this way. Find her. Find Lyla. Find Lyla. LYLA.'

A frozen moment waits. The starlit darkness gazes at the drama. Felix barks. Then he barks again, very loudly. And he is off, running, and now Randal is barking too, like proper bloodhounds, carrying the intrinsic DNA of all dogs. I whisper, to myself, *You can do it, boys, you can do it,* as my ankle bends in a ditch, as my knees knock against the skinning rocks.

I can see a stream, and a clapper bridge.

And the dogs go straight across. No hesitation. Noses to the stones, definitely following a trail. The moon shines on the four of us, but every silvery fraction of a second sends Lyla nearer to a shivering end, barefoot in pyjamas on the frigid hills, or stumbling, falling over, breaking her head on a jagged boulder—

'There!'

Adam shines his light on a kind of corral. A ring of dry-stone walls, erected to protect moorland livestock – cattle or sheep or ponies – from exactly this kind of ferocious winter weather.

The dogs are yowling, crazily. Are we too late? Adam climbs the stone wall, using a granite stile, I follow him. The dogs leap over. I never knew they could jump that high. The two of us, two terrified parents, direct our torches on to the circle of grass.

Wild ponies are sleeping at the other side of the corral. And that is all. A team of wild ponies, lying side by side.

'Jesus,' says Adam. 'She's not here. That's it. What else can we try? What else??'

His voice is cracking, with a despair I have not heard before. But I am not despairing. I have a sense.

'Wait. Let's go nearer. We can't see properly from here.'

Slowly, painfully slowly, we walk towards the sleeping ponies. Adam holds the dogs by their collars, keeping them quiet. A few steps from the animals, I shine the torch down. And now I see a flash of pink, the bright pink of a child's dressing gown. Lyla is lying right between the sleeping ponies, hidden in the middle, as if the animals chose to huddle around her. Like they found her lying here, and lay beside her, to keep her warm, keep her alive. Like dolphins that support and save a drowning swimmer. My daughter has become one of them, one of

266

the Dartmoor animals, a feral child, lost in patterns of stones and pelt, and darkness.

'My God,' says Adam, very quietly, as he reaches gently between the sleeping ponies and puts his arms around and under our daughter, lifting her away. She does not wake. He carries her in his arms.

'She's cold,' he says. I see him hiding his emotion. 'But she's alive. Let's get her home.'

I don't know how we ever got here, in so many ways. I don't know if we've wandered for hours and miles, but the return journey feels like bare euphoric minutes, the dogs yelping ecstatically as Adam carries Lyla home, across the moors, back to Huckerby, back to warmth and safety. While we walk the torchlit path, Adam calls all his friends, authorities, calling off the search. His voice is faintly trembling. Overfull of emotion. We have made it to Huckerby. When we push the gate, I see Dan, climbing out of his car.

'You've found her!'

He looks delighted, but still very frightened. 'Oh Jesus,' he says. 'Oh Jesus Christ. Thank God. How? Where?'

'She was sleeping with the ponies.'

Adam kicks open the longhouse door. 'Inside.'

We carry our daughter over the threshold into the soft-lit living room, where Dan piles more logs on to the woodfire. Hearth and safety.

We found her. Adam found her. The dogs found her. The ponies saved her. Her father saved her.

There is no one out there to threaten her. We have survived.

I look down at my sleeping daughter in her slippers, pyjamas and pink dressing gown. 'Do you think,' I say, quietly, my throat hurting from all the cold, 'we should get a doctor now, or wait until tomorrow?'

Dan shrugs. 'Who can say? She looks all right, but you never know—'

We are interrupted. By Lyla. She is awake, and staring, First, she looks at her uncle, and at her daddy. Finally she turns to me, and speaks.

'I woke up, Mummy. I woke up like it was a dream and I looked out of the window and I thought I saw Daddy waving to me, in the moonlight. Pointing to Hobajob's.' Her eyes are fixed on mine. 'So I climbed out, to go to him, but when I got there, he wasn't there. You can never get there, it always changes.' She looks towards the fire, and back at me. 'And I was climbing back into my room and I heard you arguing, you and Daddy, and I couldn't bear it any more. I can't pretend, I ran away.'

'Pretend what, darling? What are you pretending about?'

'Them.'

'Who?'

Slowly, too slowly, she turns. And she screams, at Adam, 'You, Daddy! YOU. You were there. In the car. With Mummy. You! You were shouting at her, that night, when she drove there, into the water. Like you were shouting tonight. That's why I ran away. You shouted, that night, and you were shouting again!'

Adam steps back, utterly bewildered. He looks as if he is about to cry. I have never seen my manly husband do anything like cry. Not once in our relationship. He *never* cries.

Lyla is shrieking again, at her father. 'Get out!' Her face contorts into a demonic leer. 'Get out! Get out! Get out! Get away from me and Mummy! Get away!'

'Lyla, darling—'

Adam looks astonished and distressed.

'Get out get out get out! Daddy! Ssssss! Sssssssss! Get away from us! You were there in the car SSSSSSSSSSSSS!'

Her ferocity is untameable, unnerving. She is going to hurt herself, unless we somehow calm her.

My husband seeks my gaze; I shake my head, telling him: we have no choice. Adam closes his eyes, as if in brief but silent prayer.

'What about Hobajob's?' he says. 'Someone did that. Who will look after you?'

It's a good question. I shrug, despairingly and he holds my attention, and says, 'I'll go down the road, find a bed at the Huntsman. I'll be close by.'

He turns and leaves the room; the door slams as he exits into the yard. The engine rumbles, and dies away.

Now I look at Dan and remember my memory of running away from him, at Two Bridges. He cannot be trusted either. And yet I feel a need for a man here, if only for tonight. And Adam has been expelled.

My brother clearly senses my mood, and my decision. 'We're all so tired, shall I use the spare room?'

I hardly have time to say *Yes* when he ascends the stairs.

And now it is down to me, and Felix and Randal, who sit at either end of the sofa on which Lyla reclines. The applewood logs crackle joyously in the hearth. And Lyla lies there: staring hard at the flames. The fire is a rosy glow on her white, determined face.

Huckerby

Night

I cannot sleep. I feel like I will never sleep. Not again.
Not after the trauma of this evening. My daughter is now
safely in bed in her room; my brother snoozes in the spare
room. My husband is banished. And something about it
feels wrong. More than wrong. Eyes tired, and dry, and
wide open, I lie on my pillow and watch a small black
spider crawl across the whiteness of our ceiling.

There was something *too* vehement about the way Lyla
accused her father. How can she simultaneously be so
certain it was him, yet so unsure of things when ques-
tioned closely? After all, I misidentified Harry Redway,
but I realized my mistake. She is certain she is not
mistaken; I presume she just didn't want to accuse her
own father, her beloved Daddy, of something so awful
– involvement in her mother's near-fatal accident – not
until she was emotionally unable to hide the truth.

Yet she has claimed she sees other men as well, who
look like Daddy, yet they simultaneously *are* Daddy. This
confusion is too much. It feels like Lyla being Lyla.

Silence fills the longhouse. The spider has reached the edge of the ceiling. It waits for me to realize. To make the guess.

And now the idea forms so quickly in my mind, it is like a speeded-up film of ice forming over a pond, a lake, a bay. The crystals that grow, like creatures, until the glistening sheet of silver is complete. And you can walk across to the truth.

Sitting upright, I lean to my left, for my laptop, lying on the carpet. The blue glow of the screen is spectral on my face, as I quickly type in the words.

Identity. Faces. Asperger's. Autism.

It takes me exactly 4 minutes. 240 seconds to solve the conundrum that has been torturing me for weeks. And the answer is a word I have never seen before, I word I cannot even pronounce, but a word that explains the world. Much of the dark world I have been inhabiting since December.

Prosopagnosia.

There's a hundred thousand references on Google. The definitions are largely identical:

Prosopagnosia is a relatively rare neurological disorder, the primary symptoms of which are a tendency to misidentify people, or a failure to recognize faces. Prosopagnosia is also known as face-blindness. It is often linked with other disorders . . .

A more precise piece of Googling gives me the rest of the answer.

Prosopagnosia is significantly more common in people on the autistic spectrum. It can range from very mild and sporadic, to debilitating, persistent and severe. A particularly distressing scenario is when the sufferer misidentifies close relatives with similar-looking family members, e.g. siblings, or cousins. This commonly happens when a person with prosopagnosia meets the relative out of context, at a place or time they're not used to seeing that person.

Here it is, black and white on my screen. My Aspergerish daughter clearly has this symptom, too. A mild form maybe, but she surely has it. I'd probably have guessed sooner if we had decided, in the end, to get her treated. The psychologists might have spotted it, and told us. But we opted not to get her statemented, we didn't want to *label* her. But now we have another kind of label.

Prosopagnosia. I try to say the word to myself, here in my cold and quiet bedroom, but I don't know how to pronounce it. Yet that doesn't matter.

My daughter thinks she has been seeing her father. But probably she isn't. Because of her condition, her place on the spectrum, she's seeing someone who looks like him, out of context. Someone who resembles Daddy, someone with his blue eyes, that distinctive, handsome, cheekboned face. Those broad and capable shoulders, the Redway walk. Aggressive. Used to hard work. Men of the moor.

So there *is* someone out there. Someone who has been stalking, lurking, someone who looks enough like a relative, someone I know. Someone who did something, or said something, so terrible, it led to my suicide bid.

Laptop shut, I seize the solution with relish. Because it means I am not bewitched, and I am not mad, and I am likely not suicidal, and it means my daughter, being just a little bit different, is making mistakes she can't help, and it also means my husband is at least exonerated,

273

of being there on that night, in that car: and so it all begins to make sense.

And then my relish turns to dread. This all, in a way, makes it worse.

Spells. Witchcraft. Hag stones. And now face-blindness? Whose face is she blinded by?

Out there beneath the tors, an evil has burbled out of nothing: like a black moorland burn, springing unexpected from the rotten sedge.

Bellever Tor

Wednesday afternoon

I see a man who is trying to understand me, even as he tries not to hate me. And yet we are a couple who have been deeply in love since he was eighteen and I was seventeen. Father of my beloved daughter. The child who has expelled him from his own home.

'How is she?'

The winter sun is spangling cold on our faces. But I can see long acres of grey cloud in the west. The afternoon dies.

'She's all right.'

'That's it – all right?'

'Yes.'

And it's true. She's all right. Considering.

Adam falls quiet in his taciturn way, and as he gazes at the rolling waves of the moor, the monstrous green swells, I recall the day following Lyla's disappearance.

The doctor came first thing the next morning and checked her. He told me she was remarkably intact: a tough girl. Used to being outdoors. For all her strangeness

275

and vulnerabilities our daughter Lyla Redway, it seems, has some serious strengths, both mental and physical. The walls she has built around herself to survive her social *failures*, the jaunts and jeers, the lack of friends, have also protected her. She has an inner resilience. He even said she was fine to go back to school.

But even now, two days later, I cannot bear to think of when she went missing. We haven't yet discussed it. Lyla and I haven't discussed her father, either: the only passing mention of Adam came when a car pulled up in the yard. Lyla and I were stacking firewood, the winter fuel so diligently sawn and split by Adam. Lyla and I were loading the logs in the wicker basket by the wood-burner when I heard the grind of brakes.

It sounded like Adam's Land Rover.

Lyla grabbed at my arm, and said in terror, 'Is that Daddy? It's Daddy, isn't it? Please don't let him in, please don't let him into the house. I'm scared of them all, they'll make you do it again, they'll make you drive in the water.'

I told her to sit on the sofa, and snuggle under the duvet, then ran out into the yard.

But it was just a delivery guy, a smiling young man from Amazon, with a load of books I'd ordered for Lyla a week ago and quite forgotten. He handed me the cardboard package, and laughed. 'You're quite out of the way here, aren't you? Don't you ever get lonely?'

'Hah no,' I said, attempting a happy smile, accepting the package.

He gazed around the yard, at the naked black trees, the thorny grey fence. 'Guess it must be great in summer?'

'Yes, it is. We love the moors, we love the way we're lost, all alone out here,' Even as I said this, I realized my words betrayed my feelings: we are all alone out here.

And for the first time since we moved here I felt that we were too isolated. And now it seems that the moorland wastes stretch on, ever further, and I don't know the exit roads any more.

The young man gave me another smile, this time with a squint of doubt, as if he didn't quite believe me, or felt sorry for me. Perhaps he discerned the disguised anxiety on my face. And he got in his van and drove the winding miles to Princetown, and the main roads, and people and pubs and places with life.

Adam interrupts my thoughts. 'Why did you want to meet me out here?'

'Well, I want the fresh air, and, also: you've been busy all day—'

'Relaying paths, up Lakehead.'

'Anyway, it's OK,' I say. 'This is fine here. Lyla simply won't have you back at the house, not yet, and here we can be private.'

He nods, frowning. The two of us walk across the grasslands, towards Bellever Tor, a soaring outcrop of dark, malignant rock. Whatever the weather, Bellever Tor, of all the tors on the moor, always looks the most lonely and forbidding. Like a fortification from a terrible, long-ago war, not quite forgotten. Like a ruin they couldn't level.

Dartmoor ponies roam around it this afternoon, cantering and random, their eyes wild and sad, and strangely inconsolable: like a cavalry with all the soldiers dead, leaving the steeds to linger bewildered on the battle-field.

I turn to my husband to confront our domestic war. The home front.

'This is far enough. Let's sit.'

I point to a fallen tree covered by moss so thick it

resembles upholstery. Adam sits, waiting and obedient. The exile. He's told me he stayed in the Huntsman the last two days, the pub nearest Huckerby, looking out for us. Ready at a moment's notice to help. But we haven't needed help. Nothing has happened. Less than nothing.

I go first. The stiffness between us is intense. 'Did you speak to the police about Hobajob's?'

He nods, picking up a random moorland stick, and throwing it into the dimming light. It twirls and falls. 'It was what I suspected.'

'And?'

'They said it was some teenage Satanists, the usual, kids up from Plymouth, torturing animals, having a laugh. They get it all the time, all across the moor. They found some spliffs, whatever you call them, skunk, in the area, round the clearing. Sniffer dogs found them. Bottles of vodka, too. Usual shit.'

'But – but it was so *creepy*, Adam, those poor blinded hares. It was a definite symbol, Adam, the Green Man. The same symbol that Lyla made with the birds, weeks ago. My mum loved those pagan symbols.'

He looks at me and sighs. 'Well, the police aren't so fussed. And there's no real damage, unless you're a blinded bloody hare, so they're not exactly calling in Scotland Yard. Is Dan still at the house?'

I've been waiting for this question. Dan left this morning. He has a job to do, and a marriage to save. Both are more than difficult at Huckerby, with its remoteness, and its indifferent mobile phone signals and feeble Wi-Fi.

'He's gone. Finally. Went back to Salcombe this morning. And to be honest, Adam, we wanted him to go, there's some awkwardness there, too, with my brother, between me and him. Oh God.'

I pause. I think it's time Adam heard about Dan, unless he has heard already. I have no idea. Our lives have diverged so quickly. Preparing myself, I look across the roiling billows of turf: gazing at a stretch of mire-water, leathery brown, glistening in the uncertain winter sun.

These are the blanket bogs, where the rivers Avon, Plym, Erme and Swincombe all began their seeping descent. Down the coast to the sea, like Dartmoor villagers dutifully carrying their dead to Lydford Church.

I speak. 'Adam, you know I had a vision, a returning memory, of seeing Dan at Two Bridges, the afternoon I drove into Burrator?'

I wait for him to answer. The wind whirrs in the sedge. Like a quiet engine. At length, he shakes his head, bemused.

'Did I know that? To be honest, Kath, I've heard so much, so many stories, seen so many things, these last weeks, I can't remember.' His shoulders are slumped. I do not like seeing my big strong husband like this. Even if sometimes I resent him, fear him, wonder what he did to me, I don't want him broken. Not yet. Anyhow. Not until I *know.*

I persist. 'Well. Don't you want to know why Dan was at Two Bridges?'

He grunts. 'Sure.'

And he listens as I explain: how Daniel Kinnersley, my handsome, rich and oh-so-fortunate brother, has been lying to Tessa for a year. Lying to everyone. Screwing some girl from the Bridges.

The wind ruffles his dark, dark hair, and Adam laughs, coldly. 'A year, you say? With that little bargirl? Blonde one, with the piercing and tats? She used to sleep with my cousin, Jack.'

'Yes. Her.'

'What a predictable wanker. Dan fucking Kinnersley, having an affair with some teenager. At Two bloody Bridges. I remember Jack saying she liked it rough. But that's Jack's scene. Is Dan into that as well? The posh middle-class property guy, likes to tie a girl up, give her a slap?'

I interrupt. 'But that isn't all of it, Adam. There's a lot more. The point is, I now know that these returning memories are real. And I have other fragments of memory. I remember a man in a car that night. He was angry, I think. Lyla said it was you. But you say it wasn't.'

My husband shakes his head. 'Where's this going?'

I ignore him, and continue,

'And there's that line, that song Lyla sings. I heard her singing it again, yesterday.' I sit closer to Adam, like someone might overhear our secrets. 'She was standing at her bedroom window, like she was in a trance, it was evening, a full moon, and she sang that folk lyric about death again: *O little blue light in the dead of the night, O prithee, O prithee, no nearer to creep . . .*' I shudder as if I am cold. 'She didn't even know I was watching. Her bedroom door was open and I stood there on the landing and looked in and there she was in her pyjamas, barefoot, singing it through an open window, her room all cold from the wind, and it made me – well. It was so odd. Where *did* she get that song? Does she still think someone is going to die?'

At last, as if he has had enough of this, Adam grasps my shoulder. Nearly shaking it.

'What are you trying to say, Kath?'

I take out my phone.

'I read something. Discovered something.'

'What?

'Have you ever heard of prosopagnosia?'

280

I feel oddly triumphant. He shakes his head; I say,

'Adam, I think I've worked it out. I keep sensing a man on the moor, someone stalking me, but you say it's not you. And Lyla says she sees you, but you say she doesn't. And I think I've worked out how this all makes sense, how it can all add up. It's because Lyla is Aspergery. And she's got some related condition, it's called proso-pagno . . . sssia.' I stumble on the words again. I don't care. 'See. Here. Read these two definitions. I screen-grabbed them. See!'

He takes the phone from my hand. I watch as he reads, waiting for his reaction. His face, however, is blank. The wind tugs at the grasses, the ponies run away from us forever.

Returning the phone, he is wordless. I am not.

'You get it, right? It means she sometimes misidentifies people, especially people close to her. That's why she keeps thinking she sees you. If you'd let us get her state-mented before, we'd have known this. But anyway. Look! This is it! The answer.'

He gazes at me. He has read the words I read. He frowns. He turns his head away, grim-faced, as if I am disappointing him. Or upset about Lyla? I am not sure. I carry on anyway:

'So we know it's someone that looks like you. And that someone was in Hobajob's. And it's someone who hangs around here, who resembles you. Which means,' I wait for a moment, I want this to have an impact. 'It has to be Harry. Your cousin. I'm sorry. Whatever you say, it has to be him. He's involved, that's who Lyla is seeing. If she saw someone in the car with me, it was him.'

He opens his mouth, and he speaks.

'No. It wasn't him.'

'Why?' I search his face, the air is so cold. 'You keep saying this. How do you know?'

'Because I was with him that night. The thirtieth. We were drinking together. Warren House.'

The confession stings, it hurts me hard inside. I gaze his way.

'But you said you were alone?'

My husband shrugs. Stiffly. 'So I lied. A little white lie, is all. The roads were flooded that night, I was bored at the hut, so I drove a few miles to Warren House, had a drink with Harry and some of the guys, drove back to the rangers' hut. No mobile signal, all the way. Too remote.'

I feel a kind of allergic reaction.

'You didn't tell me this? You didn't tell anyone? Really?'

He sighs, vehemently. 'I was drink-driving, Kath. *Don't you see?* I was using a Dartmoor Park Land Rover. If I'd told anyone, especially the cops, I'd have lost my job as well, and my car. And then where would we have been? What was the point? We'd have had no transport at all. Not your car, not my car. So I told a little white lie to save this family but, y'know, I begin to wonder, perhaps we are unsaveable—'

A despair rises in me. There must have been eye-witnesses in the pub. My husband is clearly telling the truth, so it can't have been Harry Redway. Or Adam. Not that night, anyhow. Or could it?

'And what time did you finish drinking? What time did you drive home?'

His eyes try to meet mine, but they don't quite make it.

'About . . . six, half six. I got there mid-afternoon. Downed about four pints, then drove home at two miles

282

an hour, so I wouldn't hurt a fly. Ron told me they all carried on boozing till late, Harry included, so that's why I know he wasn't with you.'

I let this information settle. And what it implies.

'So,' I say, quite carefully. 'You still don't have an alibi, do you? For where you were later? It could still have been you, at Huckerby in the car. The night I did it.'

His eyes are narrowing. In anger. 'For God's sake. Make your mind up. One minute I'm innocent, because of this – what was it prosopo— something. That thing. Face-blindness. One minute I'm innocent, the next I'm your bloody murderer again. This is just useless, Kath. Pointless. Blaming it on Lyla, pretending she mixes up faces? She never does that. Never . . . I've never . . .' Without explanation, he looks up, and gazes at the tor, over my shoulder. And then his expression changes. Profoundly.

Abruptly he stands. Different, angry, determined. But determined to do what? His demeanour unnerves me What has happened?

'Adam. Are you OK?'

'Yes.' He is marching back towards the cars. 'Lyla's with the Spaldings, right? So she's safe, yes?'

I try to walk as fast as him. 'Of course.'

'Good,' he says. 'That's good.'

I give up chasing and watch him as he gets into the Land Rover. Without a hint of goodbye, he cranks the engine and races away, flinging mud and leaves into the stony walls of the lay-by. I get a glimpse of his face as he skids into the distance.

He is on a mission. He has something urgent but necessary to do.

I think of the way he shot that sheep.

Tavyhurst Church

I've spent another hour walking around the moors as the light dies. Trying to work out the puzzles. Where did Adam go, his face suddenly filled with fury? I definitely saw the rage, but for once it wasn't aimed at me.

The puzzle is unsolved. I walk the springy dry turf, away from Bellever Tor, towards Postbridge car park, trudging moors as Adam and I used to do, when we were young and in love.

Once more I jog around the circuit of the facts. I am sure I didn't try to kill myself. Someone is out there. Someone who looks like Adam. Or it is Adam, because he still has no alibi. Alternatively, perhaps, it is *nothing* to do with our family, could be it really is a random stranger. A random psycho. A teenager from the Devonport slums, on skunk. Wanting to kill me. To kill Lyla. For no reason at all.

And how does this fit in with my mother, and my husband's supposed evil traits? I'm not sure I can trust anything my brother says, at the moment.

The confusion becomes weariness, and the weariness drags as I climb in the car. Engine on. I drive quite fast through the closing dark and the encroaching fog. In the murk, it feels as if mine is the only car on the moor, my headlights making lonely silver cones in the mist. I imagine someone watching these lights from a hillside far away, wondering who I am and where I am driving.

The cattle grids rattle. I see a turning and the headlights catch a black-and-white roadsign. *Tavyhurst ¾ mile.*

I remember that name: I remember the village church. St Andrew's, Tavyhurst. It's where my mother asked us to hold her memorial ceremony. It was another strange request, like asking for her ashes to be scattered at Kitty Jay's grave. My mum despised Christianity, the patriarchal faiths, the conventional funeral. It seemed odd that she wanted us to assemble there. I never could work it out.

On an impulse, I take the turning. The last slants of winter sun cast upon the wintry hedgerows a brief, rich, saddening copper – which fades to blackness and darkness, as Tavyhurst appears over the rise: a cluster of thatched cottages and ugly council houses. At the centre, by a black duckpond scummed with dead leaves, is a shuttered post office, a pub closed for the winter and the medieval church.

Parking by the pond, I button my coat against the cold. This is a proper Dartmoor freeze, dry and steely. I wonder if there is another ammil on the way. If so, it will ruin the plans for the swaling. Everyone is making firebreaks, cutting notches in the gorse, getting ready for the big yellow and scarlet fires. My mother would be packing picnics.

There was certainly no ammil on the day we remembered

her. It was a classic dank grey Dartmoor winter afternoon like today. We all filed through this metal gate, walked past the Georgian gravestones and pushed open the iron-bolted fourteenth-century door.

I push it now. The interior of the church is dim and chilly, and soaked with the usual sweet, sour, melancholy perfumes of mildewed paper, old incense, wildflower water left too long. An English church in an English village, stranded by time and history.

Why did Mum choose to be remembered *here?*

Sitting myself in a pew as the final winter daylight strains through the gaunt, stained-glass windows, I examine the memorials along the walls, the dusty marble tombs of the local gentry, the brass plaques dedicated to dead archdeacons, of local sailors in the Royal Navy. Remnants of Empire.

Everything feels deceased.

I look down the empty aisle, past empty pews, to the west wall of the church, where ropes hang from silent bells in the silent tower. It feels as if there is no one on the moors but me. But I am not mad. I did not try to kill myself. I will find an explanation. I will, I will, I will. Perhaps it is here. Where my mother was remembered.

Leaning back, breathing deep, I gaze up at the ceiling. And my blood runs hot and icy.

The Green Man.

All along the medieval ceiling are wooden bosses decorating the curves of the wooden arches, each one engraved with a version of the Green Man, grinning, leering: vomiting tendrils and vines. One is skeletal, another fat-faced. There must be a dozen or more. A festival of writhing mouths and eyes, death and fertility, the skull vomiting the rose.

The wind bangs the door, making me jump.

This pagan motif, the Green Man, is common in Dartmoor churches.

You can find it over doorways, under windows, even carved into gravestones. But I have never seen so many as this in one place. Leering faces laughing down at me.

This is my mother's bleak joke on all of us. Another key to her puzzle. She chose a church stuffed with non-Christian symbols. We didn't realize she was telling us something. And she is still talking to me, weaving her spell.

Katarina, darling. Katarina, Katarina . . .

Katarina.

I need to understand what she is saying and I will be free.

Something about fertility and sex and death.

Now I wonder if she is saying something specifically about her own death. Why her remains were scattered at Kitty Jay's grave, the famous suicide spot: where the shamed woman was buried – with the unwanted child in her womb.

A cold wind presses at my neck as I gaze down the empty nave to the altar and the choir. I can smell the moor that surrounds us: the sheepshit and the mires, the dead leaves and dead marriages.

The wind blows through the door that I stupidly left open. Oddly. It feels as if it is blowing in time with my breathing. The world is surrounding me. And the door creaks on the breeze, and now I realize that I can hear someone. Behind me. Someone has come into the church, with great quietness. I can hear footsteps. Stealthy and soft. Someone trying to be as silent as possible.

Creeping up behind me.

My mind freezes, my fear burns. Yes, I hear footsteps. Light, female footsteps.

I dare not look round. Because who would come to a deserted medieval Dartmoor church on a dark winter evening? Only someone looking for me.

In the chill, I hear that voice, once more, and the cold wind raises the hairs on my neck.

'Kat.'

I do not turn.

'Katarina.'

It is the breeze.

'Oh, Katarina . . . My darling, I never meant to favour him . . .'

The world is frozen. It is an ammil of the soul.

'Kat . . . Kat . . . my darling. *Katarina.*'

It is my mother's voice. Behind me.

I turn.

Kennec Farm

As he neared the cottage, Adam looked left, where the wet grey grass yielded to a line of rowans and gorse and tiny stunted trees, where moss streamed in ribbons. The rags of moss looked like strips of green cloth, clouties tied by locals praying for sick children, for the dying, forever petitioning the Lord.

Help us. Help us.

But of course, there was no one listening, no help to be had. There was no man on the moor, and no God in the heavens. Adam had to do it all for himself. Save them all.

He felt an odd sense of calm as he contemplated things. He'd solved the puzzle. This was it. Everything fitted together: he just had to restrain his brutal anger.

Kath's diagnosis, of *prosopagnosia*, was too piercing and perceptive to ignore. He'd seen it himself. Years ago, he'd watched as Lyla mistook Charlie for Oscar – misnamed them – even as they stood right in front of her, one Christmas. These were cousins she'd known,

291

essentially, since birth. Yet in Adam's presence she had misidentified them.

Of course he'd never shared this. It was just a one-off: that's what he had told himself. He didn't need to give Kath more evidence, to have their daughter carted off, packaged, put in a little box called Autism Spectrum Disorder. That's why he'd kept it to himself, at the time. Yet this new diagnosis, *face-blindness*, explained too much, right now.

Lyla has surely witnessed, that night, a man who looked very much like Adam. A man who had probably had sex with Kath. A man like Adam yet not Adam. A Redway of a similar age; one of the cousins. And Harry Redway was ruled out. He was in the Warren that night, with Adam.

This left one candidate.

Adam knocked on the door of the cottage. Night was over the next hill. The moon was already hiding behind inky clouds.

Jack Bryant answered wearing T-shirt and jeans, motor-bike boots. And that deceptive grin. 'Well, well. Hello, Cousin, whassup?'

'Can't you guess?'

Jack sighed sarcastically and wiped his dirty hands – soaked with motorbike oil – on a rag. A man who liked to mess with engines. He chucked the rag on a shelf. 'Nah, sorry. Forgot my mind-reading goggles.'

'Have another go.' Adam stepped closer.

Jack didn't budge, blocking the door.

Adam repeated, 'I said: have another go.'

Jack squared his muscled shoulders. 'What the bloody fuck are you on about, Ad?'

Adam allowed himself a half-smile. 'What did you do to my wife, Jack, the night she tried to kill herself?'

'You what?'

Somewhere in the yard the wind rattled in metal. The farmyard, as Adam had already noted, was a total mess. Cousin Jack wasn't much of a farmer, he was more like Adam's dad. Booze and gambling. Motorbikes.

Drugs.

Women.

Adam said again, 'What did you do to my wife, Jack, the night she tried to fucking kill herself?'

This time Jack shook his head. 'Ach. Fuck off, Adam. Nutter.'

'What did you do? You did it. I know you did. I can't believe I didn't work it out before. You and women, you always like it rough. Don't you? And you always liked my wife.' He pushed his way in, a hand firm on Jack's chest. Adam was taller by two inches, but Jack was not small. Was this size difference enough? No. Adam had to restrain himself. Have it out with words. Call the police. But get satisfaction first.

The hallway smelt of mud and dogs and rain and beer. This was the house of a bachelor farmer, who liked the girls.

Jack stared at Adam's hand on his chest. 'Get your fucking hands off me, Adam.'

Adam stepped back a few inches, preparing. He made fists of his hands, but resisted the urge, for now, to punch his cousin. Very hard. Though he'd always wanted to. Ever since that night back in Chagford, all those years ago. Jack had always teased him with that knowledge of the past, used it, manipulated Adam with an air of joking devilment, yet with malignance, too.

And Adam had never forgotten the way Jack teased the ponies with the Trebor mints before putting a bolt in their brain, laughing at the blood, at the desperate, whinnying mares.

The two men stood in the darkness of the hallway, breathing heavily.

'Look, calm the fuck down, you melt,' said Jack at last.

'What did you do that night? Where were you? Not at the Warren, like everyone else.'

'Sorry? Am I going mental, or is it you?'

'I *was* in the Warren that night, with Harry and the other guys. They all said that they hadn't seen you for a while. Since Christmas. Dez said, at the time, you were in London, maybe, but you never go to London.'

'Really.'

'Yes,' Adam growled. 'Yes. Fucking. Really. So where were you?'

Jack glanced quickly around him as if looking for a weapon. A wrench, a blade, a hammer. Then he stared back at his cousin.

'Listen up, Adam. Get this clear.' Jack shook his head angrily. 'I literally have No Fucking Clue what you are talking about. I had nothing to do with whatever shit your crazy wife did.' He folded his tattooed arms.

Muscles bulged in his biceps.

Adam wondered who would win, if they fought. Probably he would, but he couldn't be sure. Jack Bryant was definitely the kind of guy who'd use a blade, if it came to it. Adam wondered what kind of guy *he* was: could he use a blade on this bastard, the man who had been tormenting his daughter, cutting up hares, seducing his wife, or worse?

'Why do you think I had any involvement with Kath, you nut? It's bollocks. Total bollocks,' Jack scowled dismissively. 'She's too old for me now, anyway. Like 'em younger. Sagging tits and a drooping arse don't do it for me any more.'

Adam raised a hand, close to punching, to killing, even. 'I know it's you, Bryant. Been you all along. Because you love all this shit: joking, teasing, cruelty. You're a sadist. You liked killing the ponies, you loved tricking them. Didn't you? I remember the way you grinned, with the blood and brains all over you. Sometimes you'd do it in front of the mothers, wouldn't you, bolt the foals, let the mothers foam and whinny. So you could kill them too. My uncle despised you for that, everyone despised you for that.'

'Jesus.'

Adam moved closer, before Jack could find a knife. 'What's more, this is when I realized it was you. This afternoon. Talking to Kath. You're the only one who knows all those ghost stories, all that folk stuff, from Nan in Doccombe. Aren't you? Especially that song. Because there are only two people who might know that song.' Adam stiffened himself, readying himself. 'We both know one of them, and she's dead, so that leaves you. You went to Doccombe with me the day she taught us that song. You and me. I've remembered. So it's you that's been freaking Lyla out, teaching her that song about the blue lights. It was you that blinded those hares. It was you left that rat there, with the teeth, poisoned, and it's you that's been putting down those stones. It's been you all along, playing some stupid game. This is the shit you do. And you did something to my wife that night. You drugged her. You fucked her. You've always got drugs. And then you messed with her car, the brakes, the throttle, and made her drive into the water. It was you.'

'Jesus.' Jack smirked in the gloom. 'You've got it bad.'

He turned his back on Adam and pushed open the door to the kitchen. Adam followed, his fury contained. But violence was coming. He could sense that Jack sensed it. Jack didn't have his back to him for long.

They were face to face again. The room was brutally austere. Some cheap cans of beer stood on an old wooden table. A stopped clock hadn't been fixed. A few dirty plates were piled in the sink.

Jack grabbed one of the cans, cracked it open and drank, and offered another to Adam. 'Seriously, mate, fresh out the fridge. Have one before you bust a fucking blood vessel.'

Adam waved the beer away. He surveyed the room again, looking for proof, for anything, before he beat the living shit out of Jack Bryant. A large photo of a young woman, pretty and blonde in a summer dress, with long, tanned legs was pinned to a corkboard.

'Not bad eh?' Jack smiled, watching Adam. 'Lives in Okehampton. Name's Amy. Dental nurse. Arse on her, Jesus.' He tilted the beer, drank, burped loudly.

Adam felt the urge to smash the can from Jack's hand, put a knife to his throat, force a confession. It was coming, it was coming, the violence was coming. Now, now, now. Beat the truth out of him. Because if he got some confession out of him, any kind of confession, his wife wasn't mad.

Somehow Jack Bryant *must* be responsible, someone *had to be* responsible. If it was Jack Bryant it would explain things, and they could go back to being happy, him and Lyla and Kath. It was all Adam wanted.

Jack slugged another mouthful of beer, and pointed, once more, to the photo.

'Remind you of anyone?'

Adam snapped. He swung a punch at Jack. It was a

good punch: he felt his knuckles crunch into Jack's chin. He felt teeth and muscle yield and crack under the weight of his fist, felt the kind of crunch that turns into proper pain. Bruises and blood.

A good first punch. Almost a knockout blow. Practically a jaw-breaker.

Jack staggered back, dropping the beer can, coughing blood. He grabbed a tea towel to wipe it away. Adam knew he should go in for more: he had the advantage. He could finish him off, beat him to the ground, kick him till he was unconscious. Kick the sludge of brain out of his ears and nose. But he couldn't. He was a father. And a National Park Ranger. He'd lose his job. However much he wanted to take revenge, he had to obey the law. He needed to go to the police. He had his proof. Jack Bryant was the man.

Adam reached for his mobile phone, but as he took it from his pocket Jack flung the tea towel away, and smirked. He *smirked*.

'You know, Adam . . .' Jack coughed, and spat a glob of blood into the sink. 'Before you call the cops with your fucking theory, maybe you should hear something. About that girl in the photo.' Adam stared at him. What was this?

'Because, funnily enough, she's your answer, mate. Adam. Cuz. Her with the legs and the tits. Between her legs is where I was, December thirtieth, the night your mad bitch of a wife drove into the water. I was with Amy Royle.' Jack had regained himself, no longer slurring, no longer coughing blood. He took up another can of beer and grinned as he drank. 'Yeah. I was with Amy, in *Florida*, a winter fucking holiday. We went via London, all right, but we went to Florida, and got back New Year's Day. We kept it quiet cos she's got a fiancé, she didn't want him to know, but she thinks he's a dick, prefers me in bed. Cos, you know, I know how to fuck a girl. Do it properly. Shove her face in the pillow, force her legs open – they love it, they love it rough, with a proper man. They say they don't, but they do.' Another shot of lager. 'Perhaps you should try it on your wife?'

Adam wanted to punch again. But he held back.

'You ever been to sunny Florida? You could take your poor little girl. Y'know, Disneyland. Cheer her up. Get out of that pit of a longhouse.'

And now Adam stood there. Not knowing how to react. Jack Bryant was cruel, selfish, uncaring – but he wasn't an idiot. He wouldn't say any of this if he couldn't prove it. Airline tickets, hotel receipts, it would all be on record. Jack Bryant was too smart to make this up if it could be easily disproved.

Adam felt the weakness in himself. Like a weakness in the knees. He'd been so convinced. He felt dizzy with disappointment. If it wasn't Jack Bryant it was probably no one and his wife really was mad, and so was his daughter, and it was all getting worse, and there was no way back. This time winter wouldn't end. This time they were finished.

Silence filled the kitchen. Adam could hear the skitter of rats in the walls.

Jack stepped closer to the corkboard, unpinned the photo of the girl, and threw it on the bare kitchen table, nearer to Adam. For him to see. 'She really does, doesn't she? You know what I mean. She looks a bit like a younger Penny Kinnersley, don't you think? Right? Same hair, same smile, same come-and-get-me look? Sexy.' Anger coiled inside Adam.

'Because,' Jack said, 'this is what it's all about, innit?

You think I've got some mad obsession with your wife, don't you, you dull cunt? But I haven't.'

'But—'

'There are no fucking buts, Adam. Sure, I fancied Penny, we all did, her in the pubs up in Chagford, buying drinks for all the boys, and all her witchy friends dancing naked. Remember that night? Mayday. Sure you do. Who could forget it? Certainly not you. Because, let's face it, Adam, it wasn't me that fucked Penny Kinnersley, was it?' He leaned closer, leering. 'It was you.'

Huckerby

Sunday evening

I haven't heard from Adam in days, apart from the odd
text when I tersely reassure him that Lyla is OK. We've
spent all weekend, my daughter and I, pretending that
all these terrible things haven't happened. Mostly we've
been watching TV, silly movies we've already seen six
times, nothing surprising or agitating, cuddled up together
on the sofa under duvets. I've been trying to forget the
fact I hallucinated my mother's voice, in the church. I
am now hearing ghosts, not just seeing them.

And what are they trying to tell me?

The dogs have been on walks, but nowhere near the
valley where we found Lyla. We've baked cakes we don't
really want or need, just for the sake of baking, for the
scent of flour and sugar, butter and cream, simple sweet
things: the smell of loaves in the kitchen, the ordinary
goodness. Because an ominous blackness surrounds us.

We are marooned on the moor, and our ever-present
anchor, Adam, has been ripped away. I don't even know
where he is now: he might have moved on from the

Huntsman. Who knows? We don't talk. Meanwhile, Lyla and I are two people stuck on a listing boat, watching the waters rise, not even bothering to bail: not really knowing what to do.

It is Sunday evening. The last clear daylight of this cold, dry winter day turns a delicate mango, a faintly tropical glow over the sullen moors. I am standing at the kitchen sink, washing dishes, staring out at the bracken and the quickbeams beneath that florid sky, the orange now dimming to a creamy, blowsy rose. Normally I would find this scene beautiful but today I wish I was looking at houses. Offices. Car parks.

Lyla is still on the sofa, watching *Jungle Book*. Again. My mobile rings, spinning excitedly on the kitchen counter.

ADAM.

So he's still trying. He won't give up.

ADAM.

Shall I even bother answering this time? Perhaps he has something practical to say.

'Hello,' he says, and his voice is urgent and strained. 'I've been trying to get through.'

I check the top of the screen. One bar. The signal comes and goes inside the granite longhouse. 'Must be my phone. You know what it's like behind these walls.'

We are talking about the thickness of the granite walls? I don't want to talk about anything. Not yet. Possibly not ever.

'But I tried the landline too,' he says, as if this makes everything OK. As if he hasn't been lying about that night, all along. How many more lies does he have?

'I unplugged the landline, Adam, like we always do. Lyla hates the jingle. It scares her, and right now who cares? What else is there to say?'

302

'I just wanted to check on Lyla again, is she OK?'

'I would have called you if there'd been an issue, you know that.'

And I would. Whatever has happened, however much I begin to hate or despair of Adam, he is her father, and a loving father: I would not keep him in the dark about his daughter. Even if he has been keeping me in the dark in so many other ways.

I wait. He says nothing. This is a long, pained pause. I hear him breathing as he wonders what to say next. I wonder where he is calling from. Staying with his cousin in Chagford? Sitting in the snug at the Oxenholme Arms, with its Stone Age menhir in the wall? Maybe he is all alone in his Land Rover, parked on some lonely road near Aune Head, Rattlebrook Works, or the total bleakness of Naker's Hill, where the treeless nothingness sobs far into the distance, as he misses his beloved little daughter—

No. I cannot allow myself to feel sorry for him. Not yet. Not until I know what happened. My mother's fear of Adam, Kitty Jay, how it all fits together. And Lyla knows *something else.* And I feel she will tell me soon.

'Has she mentioned me?' Adam asks. 'Has she said anything?'

'No, not much.' I don't care if the truth hurts him. 'She's only repeated what she said before, she doesn't want you here.'

He falls silent again. I tilt my head and regard the moors, watching a line of white-grey smoke in the distance. One of the farmers must be swaling: burning the dead gorse and bracken. It has been quite dry around here for a week, everyone is swaling. Soon they will be swaling Hexworthy.

It feels right. Emotionally, metaphorically. Burn down

the old, make room for the new. Perhaps that is what I will have to do with my marriage. I don't know.

Adam tries again. 'We could meet somewhere neutral, somewhere—'

'No,' I say, hard and cold. 'No. Enough. And stop asking if Lyla is ready. She's not ready. She is scared of you. Even if she's mistaken, that's if she *is* mistaken.'

Another pause. And here it comes. His voice finally rises, with his anger. It comes roaring out. 'Scared of me? *She* is scared of *me*? Why the fuck is she still scared? We saved her, I saved her. I carried her home. I rescued her. I've been looking after this family all along. I've been doing my best. Why is she bloody scared?'

'I don't know, but—'

He doesn't give me time, he doesn't want an answer, he is shouting now. 'Fuck you, Kath! You've done all this, to me, to us, you and your brother and your mother, not me, and she's my daughter too—' A tiny pause for breath; I hold the phone away from my face, he is shouting so loud. 'It was you that drove into the fucking water, it was you that sent her over the edge, it's all been you, all of it, all of you Kinnersleys, you're the ones to blame. And now my own daughter is scared of me, when I've done nothing! You're even sending me mad. I thought it might be my own cousin, Jack, but it's not. It's you. It's been you all along, Kath. Fuck this shit.'

I am not sure how to answer. Half of me believes he has a point; half of me is terrified of him.

He rants, on and on with a violent anger that I have never witnessed before. 'You've turned my own daughter against me. I will never forgive you for this. Just you wait. You fucking, fucking—'

I end the call. I simply cut him off. The horrible swearing echoes in my mind, as my heart hurts in my chest. I can sense his burning anger, right across the moor, divided from the daughter he adores. He really thinks that I am the guilty party, that it's all me, because it was me that drove into Burrator. And part of me cannot blame him.

Yet he is still lying about something, and some of it is to do with my mother. And I am scared of him. We must get out of here, me and Lyla. This must surely be the end of us, at Huckerby.

I put the phone down on the counter, and gaze out of the window. The white smoke of the swaling resembles a twilit Dartmoor fog. But this is a fog full of fire. A fog that burns, and kills.

Monday morning

Again this odd, forced, staged normality. I make Lyla's favourite breakfast: scrambled eggs. She munches the toast and eggs, in her school uniform, as she reads her latest book. The pages rip by. *Hyperlexia.* Her brain is a fire that I have to keep feeding, or it might go out. So many words, so many thoughts in there I do now know.

But then she closes the book and looks at me as I dry my hands on the *Come to Dartmouth* tea towel. The cartoony sailor smiling between my fingers.

'I am sure it was Daddy.'

Anxiety tightens, quick and hard, inside me. I stay outwardly calm.

'You really are sure?'

'Yes.' Her voice is small, but she seems ready to talk. 'I know I get confused sometimes.' She blinks rapidly. 'But I saw him a few times, near the farm, near our home. And on walks.'

I remember the figure I saw on Burrator hill. The man who stared at me. Had it really been Adam, even though he denied it? I have to seize this moment. 'OK. Let's talk about Daddy. What about Daddy, Lyla? Where did you see him?'

She looks away from me, blushing. She looks down at her empty plate, the crusts of toast. She looks at the window, at the calendar, at the photo of Kitty Jay's grave, which refuses to be turned. She looks everywhere but at me. I can see how difficult this is for her. She hisses briefly, in her agony. Her left hand flickers, nervously on the table.

'Lyla . . .'

She shakes her head and grimaces at the table.

'Lyla, we don't have to talk about it.'

The stimming stops, apart from one hand, twisting, twirling, faintly. Suspended in the air, but moving gently. And then she says, 'First I saw Daddy by the barns, under Black Tor, just once. I saw him in Hobajob's, I think. But mostly I saw Daddy in the car with you.'

I pull up a chair and sit down at the kitchen table. She still won't look at me. Her hand twirls, doing rigid little twists in the air.

'After you left me with Auntie Emma. I saw you in the car with Daddy.'

'Where, Lyla, and when?'

'At night.'

'Where? Exactly?'

She shakes her head, staring at her plate, as if she disapproves of the crusts. 'The back of Auntie Emma's house, that little road, Mummy. That little road – you took me there.'

I know where she means. There's a tiny lane behind the Spaldings' house: it leads past a disused stables, Conybeer's. They went out of business years ago but we took Lyla there when she was an infant. She learned to ride when she was five, maybe before. We thought it might help her socialize. But what was I doing there on the road to Conybeer's? And what was Adam doing there, if it was him?

'How could you tell it was me and Daddy, darling, in the dark?'

The right hand drops, the left hand quivers in mid-air. 'You parked your car and you had your light on and – and I saw, for a second, Daddy's face, his blue eyes. He was shouting at you and you looked scared, Mummy, and then – then he – then you—' Now both hands come up again, shaking violently, opening and closing, and her grimacing returns.

This is clearly very painful. I try to calm her. 'Lyla, you don't have to tell me.'

'No, I must tell you. I didn't say before because it is Daddy and I love Daddy but I hate Daddy because Daddy makes you do that. I should have told you before, Mummy, but I didn't want you to do it again, but this is what I saw, this is it this is it this is it—'

She looks as if she is about to cry, to fall apart. I get up and go round the table and give her a hug: a big warm Mummy hug. 'It's OK, Lyla. You've said everything now. It's all going to be all right, you and me and Daddy: everything is all going to be OK.'

I'm not sure she believes me, I doubt that she believes me. But her hands stop shaking, and her grimacing slowly goes away: the act of confessing is perhaps enough to calm her. Quietly she pushes back the chair, and says, 'We have to go to school. I mustn't be late.'

In the middle of all this, she still has that urgent, rule-following need to be punctual. I struggle to be normal. Choking the words out.

'Have you got all your things?'

'Yes.' She lifts her *Jungle Book* lunchbox, and her school bag. 'Ready.' The drive to Princetown is silent. Lyla really does seem calmed. I am, in contrast, even more roiled and anxious.

After I have dropped Lyla at school I pause with my head resting on top of the steering wheel. Eyes closed, sensing the plastic on my skin. My mind is ablaze. The swaling season has begun.

Taking deep, long breaths I follow the road homewards to Huckerby. But at the last junction, where the old oak bends over the broken gate, and a shaggy brown Dartmoor cow munches thistles, I swallow my piercing fears and I turn right. Heading for the Spaldings' elegant house.

But I don't stop there: I go right round, on to the Conybeer's road.

Slowing the car to a stop, I look at the rocks and rusty brambles that line the weeded road, a road almost no one uses. It goes nowhere. Or so I always thought. A typical Dartmoor dead end.

There is a gale of smoke on my right: the swaling is getting nearer. Chasing the plovers and the dunlins. These burn-outs are so close I can see the dirty yellow flames of scorching grass, the black silhouette of a farmer, and a beater, managing the swale.

Fire breaks. Warnings. Danger.

My heart pounds, my throat hurts, but not from the cold.

Did I really park here, with Adam, or someone else, that night?

I regard the narrowing road ahead; and a big untrimmed bush that flourishes out of the tumbledown granite. What is that bush? I recognize it. The little yellow flowers are probably near enough to the car for me to pluck the white-and-yellow petals. I think it is some sort of winter honeysuckle. I have a memory of Mum growing it in Totnes, or Salcombe, because it brightened up the grey winter garden, with vivid colour and a distinctive scent.

Winding down my window, I lean to pick a flower, but before I can pluck the bloom the perfume hits me. *Lemon.* A sweet, almost citrusy aroma. This is it. This is the lemon I remembered. We must have parked here, with the windows open. It was a mild evening. The scent would have filled the car.

Reminding me of Mum, perhaps.

I wonder if it will remind me of anything else. I do not want to know. I want to know. I am frightened, but I have to do this; it worked before.

Stifling my fears, I lean out of the car window, grab a big handful of the soft creamy little flowers, a dangerous posy, the nosegay of my suicide bid, and I crush the petals and stamens to my nose and close my eyes and breathe in deep.

At once another memory returns, like a bright piece of colour falling through the darkness, a section of a glowing, stained-glass window. I can see Lyla sitting at the kitchen table singing the Kitty Jay song. We are in Huckerby and it is a winter afternoon. *That winter afternoon.*

I am sitting opposite her. Thinking about Kitty Jay's grave, where my mother's ashes are scattered. And here's the other part of the memory: I am holding my pen, writing some lines. It is a poem. *A poem.* This is what I was writing that very afternoon: one of my stupid poems that I never show anyone. It was a poem about Kitty Jay, the woman who killed herself, after she was impregnated and cut adrift by some blackhearted gentleman, some handsome cad.

My suicide note wasn't a suicide note at all. It was the first lines of a poem:

I shouldn't have done what I did; shouldn't have let this into my heart
So I am going now. Going away forever
Forget me if you can, I know you won't forgive

I did not write a suicide note. I wrote some amateur verse about Kitty Jay and left it on the kitchen table, in my usual way, never satisfied with my work.

Which means the only evidence for my suicide bid is the glimpse of me in my car, at Burrator. And the fact that someone was possibly parked with me in this car. Where we smelt the winter honeysuckle.

Half of me feels intensely relieved: I surely didn't try to kill myself. Half of me is even more scared. Adam looms larger. But I still can't work out his motivation. If it wasn't Adam, then who was it? If Lyla misidentified someone so closely in the car I reckon it would have to be someone who looked *extremely* like Adam. *Not* like a cousin. Not Harry, or Jack. More like a brother. Yet he has no brother. He has a much older sister. That's it. So it's Adam. Has to be.

Closing the car window, excluding the lemony scent, I press the accelerator and drive on, ignoring the urgent beating of my heart. I drive slowly past the disused stables.

The Conybeer's sign is still there, but it hangs by one nail from its rotting wooden post. Clearly, no one has bought the business. The buildings beyond are black and empty. Dead windows. Shattered glass. A single tractor tyre lies on its side in the yard gathering brown rainwater. Ravens wheel above, watching me. Seeing if I can follow through on my suspicions about my husband. About the world.

Hands on the wheel, I gaze down the narrow lane. I have never gone beyond here. I do not think. But I did continue down the Conybeer's lane, on 30 December. Perhaps Adam came here, drunk, to see me, after his session at the Warren.

The smoke from the swale drifts over the road in a pungent mist. Part of me hopes the smoke will get so thick and bad I cannot go any further, so that I cannot find the truth, cannot reach the end. But the smoke lifts, and my excuses vanish.

The lane is so absurdly narrow the brambles scratch the paintwork of the car on either side, as I inch forward, five miles per hour. If I met someone coming the other way I'd have to reverse a mile. But I won't meet anyone coming the other way: there is nothing down here. No one ever comes here.

It is a dead end.

The brambles get thicker. The road turns from asphalt to mud. The winter birds are watching as I near the conclusion. I can see a rusted iron gate ahead of me, but it is open, and the open gateway leads to brown, unbroken moorland.

The end.

Way out there on the moors I can see standing stones. They are far away so they must be big, to be so clearly visible. Very big. Giants. Three metres or more. The sight of them makes me faintly nauseous. I've seen these stones before. Especially that one at the end: it has a strange shape I remember, yet it doesn't. Not quite. How does that work?

I get the sense of an evil, returning, a sudden rotten evil that is so intense, I think am going to be sick. In the car. I don't want to be sick in my own car. Kicking open the car door, I stumble out into the cold air, taking deep breaths, nearly retching.

Gasping in my fear, I lean back against the stone wall, beyond the gate. Closing my eyes for a moment, I hear the cawing of crows. When I open my eyes I feel like a hunted animal, as if I am being watched. By the man on the moor. Or from the barns under Black Tor.

Ahead of me I glimpse a sign, one of those Dartmoor signposts that gets lost in the undergrowth, and slowly becomes part of the foliage. One of the arms of the sign points ahead, through the gate. It says BURRATOR. The other says DRIZZLECOMBE. Beyond the gate I see there is a grassy parking space, and yes, at the other end of the space, half hidden by gorse, a moorland road begins again – another tiny, barely used lane, winding up a hill.

So it appears you can get to Burrator from here. And therefore it is possible I came this way when I supposedly tried to kill myself. When I was with Adam. Or Adam's double. We were arguing.

Perhaps I found out what he did to my mum, that made her think him evil.

Yet still the leap from all this to suicide – or murder – is way too much.

I would have simply left Adam, if I'd discovered he was not the man I knew and loved. We'd have separated. Surely.

The roads still lead nowhere. I am still lost.

Yet I have a vision of myself, staring up at that sign to Drizzlecombe.

And I was definitely staring up. Why would I be staring up at it?

An idea occurs to me. Perhaps I am looking at that standing stone from the wrong angle. Turning to the horizon, I tilt my head left, and right, and get nothing. And then, with a cold and profound shudder, I understand the perspective I need.

Lying myself down on the cold mud, uncaring of the dirt and wet, I stare across from this new vantage: and now I clearly recognize the shape of the stone. This is how I saw it. From flat on my back, looking up.

And I was flat on my back because I had been dragged from the car, and I was being raped.

Drizzlecombe

Monday morning

Lying here, on the cold Dartmoor soil, I close my eyes, and I can picture almost the whole thing. Someone above me, furious, shouting, laughing. A handsome blue-eyed man. *Adam.* And he is raping me, beside my car, in this place where I saw the standing stones. I remember a struggle in the car, a knife at my throat, being dragged by my hair. My legs being forced apart.

My own husband?

I sit up, abruptly. The heaving in my stomach starts again. I place a cold, shuddering hand over my mouth. It is as if my body wants to expel the truth, this toxic memory. Someone raped me here. It certainly feels like it was Adam. And then what? Where did he go? Did he leave me here, beaten, unconscious? Perhaps I woke, and he was gone, and in shock or horror, I got back in the car and drove to Burrator. And looked at the deep black waters, strafed by the winds of winter, and decided I could no longer live.

But I still do not comprehend this final movement – I

315

cannot bear to believe – that I could do that to my daughter, even if *that* was done to *me*.

I survive, I get by, I cope: it's what I do. I would have gone to the police, not to the reservoir, to take my own life. Unless I am a much weaker, sadder, more fragile person than I thought. Unless Adam, if it was him, not only raped me, but did something else. Perhaps he told me something so bad, it tipped my already unbalanced mind into self-destruction. Perhaps he raped me in revenge for something I had done.

The footpaths stretch across the moor, mazy and unmappable, ancient and modern, they march in all directions: from tor to leat, from combe to lake, from the stones of Stalldon Row to the firing ranges on Willsworthy, to the great old alignments I see here.

Drizzlecombe.

It's a part of the moor I have never visited. So very very remote. Yet it seems I came here on 30 December: presumably my rapist chose it for its total, silent isolation, a perfect place for his purposes, there are no houses for miles, the roads are barely passable. No chance of witnesses. No one to see what he did.

The acid taste in my mouth is vile. I want to spit it out yet I sense that won't get rid of it. The cold is acute: my fingers are numb as I get to my feet, open the car door, start the engine and retrace my route, past Conybeer's ruined stables, past the Spaldings' farmhouse. The windows are dark, the house looks empty; I guess they are still having their break in London. As I drive, I look to the right, beyond Black Tor. Great lines of smoke from the swalings rise behind it, as if the entire moor has been ripped open, revealing the fires of the earth always raging beneath us.

Slowing the car, I gaze through a break in the

316

tumbledown dry-stone wall. I can see the barns that stared at me when I drove home that night. As if they knew me. The ones Lyla talked about. *I saw Daddy by the barns under Black Tor.*

I sense I am close to the very last facts, and I desperately need them, because once I have made the final accusations everything will be broken. I have to be sure.

Stopping the car, the engine dies and the moorland silence engulfs. Climbing out, I zip myself as warm as I can and, ignoring my shrieking fears, begin my march across the moors, towards those ruined barns.

The smell of the swaling taints the air. Burnt gorse and dead birds. Smoke billows to the grey chilly sky; I hear shouts in the distance as the farmers manage the dangerous burning. Shouting and beating, shouting and beating. Dartmoor people are not easily deterred from their ancient traditions. Like my husband.

Now the anger begins. My first reaction was shock, but now I feel anger. If it was Adam, I won't let him win. He didn't kill me that night; he shall not win now. I won't let him do to me whatever he did to my mother.

The barns are barely a mile away. But the moor beneath my feet has turned to mire, the grass to silvery water. If I sank to my knees in this, I'd be in trouble. This is impassable. I will have to go right, climb the nearest hill, go the long way round.

The wind bites as I haul myself over a row of stones, and scramble up the next pile of wind-sawn rocks. It's an impressive tor, a serious crag of cracked and battered granite; but I like the exertion: it stops me thinking. Of the future. Of Lyla without a father.

One more heave, one more handhold – on a cold spur of quartzy granite – and I attain the top of the tor. It's high enough to give me a view beyond the moor: the glimmer of the distant coast, which drags the rivers from these moors.

I must go down to the barns.

Gathering myself, fighting my fear and fury, which come at me from both sides, I stamp down the hill. I am running now, running off the anger, running like the Dartmoor ponies, leaping from tump to tump, jumping the puddles.

Here we are. I am approaching the first ruined barn. The swaling smoke drifts like poisonous mist between the buildings.

Fear tightens itself around me: telling me not to look inside this hulk of a building, with its black and glassless windows, like the gouged eyes of that hare in Hobajob's. But I have to know. So I push at the door, which creaks on ancient hinges. I allow myself one moment of hesitation, to quell my fears, and I step inside.

The stench of mould and damp is oppressive. Finger to my nose, I gaze around. There is a bird's nest in a corner. Shattered eggs. Droppings. But no sign of humanity. Nothing.

Something.

I can hear the screech of something alive. The noise is sudden, loud, strange. I turn, terrified. It's a big crow, flying in through the window, not expecting me, a crow nearly in my face, black feathers in my eyes, hysterical, frightened. The bird flutters away, half falling to the floor. I wonder if it is hurt but it screeches again, and flees out of the window.

I stand, taking deep cold breaths, sensing that the whole moor wants me to leave. The winter birds are trying to frighten me away; but I will not be deterred.

Dabbing my face, checking there is no blood, I step outside. A stronger, colder breeze stirs the pelt of the land. In the hints of winter sun the silver-green mires seem to move like something enormous struggling into life.

The next barn waits. I must try them all.

This neighbouring barn is a little bigger, yet it has much smaller windows; one of the windowpanes is intact, the glass unbroken, though choked with dust and cobwebs and dead spiders. The door also appears to be in better condition, perhaps because it has been used recently.

A strange sensation grips me as I push against it. As if someone *wants* me to enter this hulk of a building. As if I am being manipulated.

Turning quickly, I scan the faraway hills and rolling moors. The road to Huckerby. There is no one in sight.

Swallowing my irrationality, ignoring my cowardice, I twist the squealing doorknob.

Inside it is very dark, because the windows are so tiny. It is also deeply cold. I can barely see a thing. I want to leave at once, yet I sense a human presence. Someone has been here. No ghost. Someone real.

The scent of mould is not quite as pungent as in the other barn. The floor is cold and hard, plain concrete, perfectly dry.

My eyes slowly adjust to the darkness.

There is a sleeping bag in the corner. It looks new. At the end is a pillow made of a second sleeping bag. Someone has clearly been bedding down here. Rough camping.

Hikers? Shepherds? Adam? Possibly it is soldiers: they use the moor for training: *Get from Yelverton to Okehampton, use what shelter you can, carry everything on your back. Fifty pounds of kit.*

Yes, soldiers – that makes sense. Stooping to the sleeping bag, I examine the material. It looks quite serious, designed for low temperatures. So that could be military kit. By the pillow there is a plastic Aldi shopping bag. Picking it up, I look inside, and see a couple of apples. Fresh. Unrotten.

Someone has been here in the last day or two.

Under the bag is a single, sad-looking book. *In Watermelon Sugar*, it says, on the front. I've never heard of it. It looks old, secondhand, well worn, much loved; in the darkness of this freezing, half-ruined barn, I can just about make out the cover: a monochrome picture of a bearded man sitting on a railway track.

He looks sad. As sad as the apples in the shopping bag, as sad as the dead spiders in the window. The whole thing, this place, my mind, the moors, it all sings with sadness. My broken family, my broken life: how will I protect Lyla now?

Calming myself, I open the book. The spine is old and the pages part immediately: falling naturally open, to reveal a photo, loosely inserted either as a bookmark or as a way of protecting the image.

It is an old colour photo, very faded, tending to sepia. In this meagre light I can't quite make out the faces. But something about this group of figures chills me, something about the house behind the people in the photo, the sensation of this thing in my hand. I know what it is, and it fills me with dread.

Stepping to the unbroken window to make use of the grey winter light, I lift the photo close.

I am looking at a picture of my mother. She is about thirty-six or seven, smiling in a summer dress, painfully dated, yet so new then. The house behind is Salcombe. It must be a sunny day: shadows are deep and rich. There are two children with her on either side of her. On the left is my brother. And on the right, is me.

320

The photo trembles in my hand.

I must be about nine. Roughly Lyla's age. I'm not entirely sure, because the face – my face – has been viciously scribbled out with black ink.

A doodle of hate. Erasing me.

Huckerby

Tuesday morning

This seems to be where I will spend the rest of my life, standing at the sink, gazing out of the kitchen window. Gazing at the cold and muddy yard, remembering when Lyla laid out all those dead birds. Perhaps that is when it all began, or when it all began to go wrong. Perhaps my daughter cast a Dartmoor spell on us all that afternoon, a hex made of bird bones and icy feathers.

She's out there now, playing with the dogs, throwing a stick up the lane into the Dartmoor fog. She refused to go to school this morning, for perhaps the first time in her life: she said she was too sad about Daddy.

I didn't have the heart, or the strength, to argue with her and, in truth, the last thing I wanted to do was drive through that fog to dismal Princetown, then go to do another pointless half-day of work in the National Park Office when I can do the very same work from home, and be close to my daughter, which is where I want to be. I feel an urgent need to protect her.

'Catch, Felix, catch!' Lyla seems cheerful enough,

hurling the stick from one side of the yard to the other. The delighted dogs are even happier, gnawing and shaking the stick until the rat in their heads is surely dead.

Opening the door, I call out to my girl, 'Don't stay out there too long, will you? That fog is freezing.'

She does not turn, she does not respond. She's in her special place: focused on Felix and Randal. I try again, calling her; I don't want to go out there, I haven't got any shoes on. 'Lyla.'

The stick is hurled towards the rowans. Lyla jumps up and down as the dogs canter away.

'Lyla!'

At last my daughter stops, tilting her head my way. Her face shows confusion. Then she gives me another strange smile. As if she is wearing a mask of her own face. 'Mummy?'

'I said, please don't stay out there too long. This weather, it's freezing, I know you don't mind the cold, but . . .'

I gaze at the fog. It's a killer even by Dartmoor standards: a cold, damp sky come down to smother us. To hide us all, each from the other.

'No, Mummy, I promise.' The grimace has gone. Now she looks blank, expressing nothing at all. She picks up the stick. I can see her quietly talking to herself: her lips are moving, but she says nothing aloud. She does this more often every day. She will say a sentence, then quietly – silently – her lips move afterwards, forming words that only she can hear. I don't know if she is checking her own sentences, or silently contradicting herself. Or casting more spells over Huckerby.

The fog is so intense that I can barely see her now even though she is fifty yards away. She and the dogs are mere shapes in the grey, figures from a dream already half-forgotten, and her voice is muffled by the damp.

'Felix, Randal! *Over here.*'

Closing the kitchen door, I lean against the warmth of the iron stove. And now the storming questions return. Who is out there on the moor? Who had that photo of me and my mum and Dan? Why is my face the one scribbled out so viciously? I look at my phone on the kitchen table. It is inert. I've turned it off.

Adam has been trying to ring me all morning, since 8 a.m. Probably he wants to apologize for his ranting. Perhaps he wants to rant some more, to threaten me. Maybe he wants to admit to me what happened with my mother.

I have no desire to talk to him. Until I know what I am doing. Soon I will have to go to the police: I simply must. But what is my accusation? I have a vivid memory of being raped. I have no proof. Just a fragment of returning memory: which is probably of my husband. Probably. Also I think someone who knows me, or knows of me, has been camped not far away, on the moor. That could also be my husband. And my probably-autistic daughter is still predicting a death by a song that no one taught her. And, by the by, I hallucinated the ghost of my mother on the moor the other day, and heard her dead voice in a church.

And, yes, all this was after I possibly tried to commit suicide, for reasons I still cannot deduce. Leaving behind a daughter who is pathologically incapable of identifying her father.

I can picture the policewoman's face as I deliver this incoherence. She will sit there with her recorder, and she will politely shake her head, and turn the recorder off. They will think me a madwoman. And I will have accused my own husband of rape, with no evidence, and Adam and I will split, and my daughter will be damaged further, perhaps broken forever.

Deep down, Lyla still adores her daddy. She wants him back. I know this. And if we split, we would have to live in some grisly flat in Princetown. It's all I could afford on my income. Or in a tiny studio flat in Salcombe, where my brother and sister-in-law have their own divorce drama, and I will make things worse.

I'm entirely stuck, like one of those hikers, trapped in the sucking black mud of Fox Tor Mire, the tourists that Adam has to rescue on a weekly basis in the summer. I am up to my waist, and every time I try to struggle free, to work out the problems, I sink further into confusion and fear.

Because I am also very scared.

That photo I found on the moor. The *way* my face was so violently erased. Someone hates me, for reasons I don't know. I sense that danger closing in, faster now.

Picking up my mobile, I switch it on, counting the damned seconds as it slowly comes to life. There is no signal at all. My stupid mobile. My dumb, feeble signal. So I cross the kitchen and put my feet into chilly wellington boots and I go out into the frigid yard. I can hear my daughter, and the dogs, but they are entirely lost in the fog, up the wintry lane.

Who do I call? Why don't I have more friends?

Because I chose to lead a solitary life, to move down here with my husband and Lyla. Because we exiled ourselves: quite happily at first. Now I am not happy. Now I need to call someone. Anyone.

I stare at the phone in my hand. Only one name comes to mind. I press the keys; she answers at once, as if she has been waiting for me.

'Tessa?'

'Oh my God, Kath! Are you OK?'

'Yes, yes I'm fine.'

'Dan told me about all about it, Lyla running away. Everything. You know you could have called me, any time since?'

'I know, I know,' I shrug, inwardly. 'I've been kind of hibernating, hiding away in denial. Avoiding people. It's all so difficult, Tessa, you know.' I don't want to say I've become suspicious of everyone, including Dan, including *her*, however unfairly. So I wait for my words to catch up with my thoughts. 'Did Dan tell you what Lyla said, to her dad?'

She hesitates, and then says, 'Yes. I don't know what to think. Nor does he.'

I don't want to talk about it; instead I ask her, 'How are you guys?'

She sighs heavily. I can picture her in her Plymouth office, staring at the concrete walls of the submarine base. 'Not that good, to be honest. Not as bad as you, but not that good. What a mess.'

'How're the boys doing?'

'We've managed to hide it, but they can tell. But look, Kath, that's enough about me, this is some boring affair, average marital crap: what's happening up there? You're all alone, are you guys OK?' She pauses, before saying, 'Don't you think you might benefit from . . .'

'Not being stuck in the fog in the middle of nowhere?'

She laughs, ruefully. I go on,

'Yes. Yes, I do think that, Tessa. There's so much other stuff happening here – it's why I rang – I was wondering, that holiday place you own, in Brixham. I hate to ask, hate it—'

'Oh God no, don't worry! *Of course* you can stay

327

there. We've got a couple in at the moment, having some romantic getaway – God knows why, in darkest February – but they're moving out late this afternoon and then it's empty till spring!'

'Dan won't mind?'

'To be quite frank,' Tessa says, 'I don't give a fuck what Dan Kinnersley thinks. Especially about Brixham. You know he used to take that girl there?' She is snarling now. 'Kath – absolutely you can stay there, stay as long as you bloody like. I won't have time to clean it but if you want it this evening?'

'Yes, yes, yes! Thank you. Yes, please!'

Relief floods through me. We will get away from here, Lyla and me and the dogs. We have to get away from here. I can sense that menace is coming at me, out of the fog, from that barn on the moor, from the scribbled-out photo of my face. Danger is homing in: truth is finally emerging from the mist, and I sense that it will terrify me: because the first time I knew the truth I drove the car into dark water.

I gush my thanks to Tessa. She tells me not to worry, eight times over. I tell her I will make arrangements, pack all our stuff: drive down this evening. We shall escape. We shall get out. We will have a little cottage by the sea, and Lyla can watch the seagulls, and she will miss days and days of school: *and I really don't care.*

'Thanks, Tessa,' I say, once again. 'Can you do me a final favour?'

She guesses before I ask. 'Don't tell Adam?'

I blush even though she can't see me. 'There are so many issues, and Lyla is sometimes weirdly terrified of him, and . . . we're a little scared, to be honest.'

'Won't say a word. Trust me. I will swear Dan to

secrecy too, if I even tell him. No one else will know where you are.'

'Thank you. Thank you so much.'

Closing the call, I turn the phone off again. If I leave it on another minute I am sure Adam will ring, and I don't even want to see his name on my screen.

Abruptly, as I slip my phone in my pocket, Lyla runs down the lane, like something magic coming into life out of the deathly grey of the fog.

'Hey, Lyla-berry. Are you all right? Where are the dogs?'

She looks at me, her lips slightly trembling. Is she scared? What's happened? Without another word, she turns and gazes at the fogbound lane, where I can hear the dogs barking. Loudly. The fog is so thick: horrible and clammy.

'They're fine, Mummy. Felix and Randal, they're fine. They're rabbiting. Happy. Happy happy happy.'

But as she speaks she lifts a hand and makes fingers as if she is working a puppet, as if her hand is shaped like a beak, opening and closing, opening and closing. These stims are almost constant now, when – a few months ago – she could go weeks without doing anything Aspergery. Now it is nearly incessant.

And I did this. I've made it worse. We've made it worse. Adam and I have wrought this damage.

Lyla gazes into the darkening fog. She sniffs, as if she can smell something nasty, and looks confused. She moves her lips, but I cannot hear words. After that, she runs past me, without an explanation, into the house.

Something is very wrong.

I follow her in. She's sitting at the kitchen table, staring at the calendar. Her lips are moving again. Faster, faster. And no words come out. Until words come out.

'I'm scared, Mummy.'

'I know, darling.' I try to hide my own fears. 'But, hey, here's some news, we're going down to Brixham. Tonight!'

Again her lips move as if she is talking but no words can be heard. So I speak for us both. 'Remember that place your cousins have: that lovely holiday cottage, in Brixham, right by the sea, with the little garden – well we're going there, Lyla! Soon as we get sorted, we'll head down there this evening. Going to stay there for a long while, have a really nice break.'

She stares right at me. And says again, 'I'm scared.' Now she slowly lifts a hand and points at the calendar. The photo for January is Kitty Jay's grave in the snow. Yet it is February. And I know I am never going to turn the page. It will always be January. Just after I died. Or just before I died.

'What are you scared of, darling? We'll be fine. We'll be fine. It's only fog.'

'Remember you talked about Kitty Jay on the day you drove into Burrator, Mummy?'

This comes out of nowhere. I don't know how to respond. Though I understand what she must be referring to: my poem. My so-called suicide note.

Lyla's lifted hand flutters in mid-air. As if she cannot control it, as if it is not part of her any more. 'Kitty Jay. You told me the story, that day you tried to go away forever. You said you would write a poem about it—'

'Yes, I did.'

'It made me remember something. And I've remembered it again.' Her hand wobbles violently now, her lips move, fast, without words, her mouth opening and shutting. 'I'm scared, Mummy, really scared.'

Her eyes are fixed on mine. Hard and blue and beautiful, like her father's. Like her beautiful, angry father.

330

'Something is coming. Something is coming to get us. Someone you know.'

'Shhh,' I say. 'Shhh. Don't be silly. We're safe in our house, and soon we will be in Brixham. We have to pack a few things and we're out.'

'That poem you were going to write about Kitty Jay.'

Her other hand hovers in the air as if she is a marionette, on a string. My daughter is mad now, as mad as her mother. Her mother who probably did not attempt suicide. I should perhaps be elated that I did not attempt suicide, that I am not that evil, selfish woman, the woman who could leave her daughter, but I am not elated. I am as terrified as Lyla.

'Mummy, I remember what I remembered. When we were talking that day about Kitty Jay, I asked why Granny was scattered there and you said you didn't know, because she never really liked the story, and never liked the grave, and never put flowers there like other people, and you told me the legend, and you went off and said you might write something—'

'Lyla.' I can smell smoke. I turn and look at the warm stove but it seems OK. Perhaps they are swaling close by. 'Lyla, I think—'

Lyla shakes her head: this is one of her lectures. 'Mummy, I remembered something. It's Daddy. I can see him, he's leaning over the cot, and he's singing me a song.'

'The cot?'

This must be one of her special memories, from before her first birthday. She might be nine months old, in this memory, or six months old, or three.

'Daddy is singing me a lullaby so I can go to sleep because I am crying, and do you know what he sang first, it was that song from his nan—' She closes her eyes and sings it. '*O little blue light in the dead of the night, O prithee, O prithee, no nearer to creep.*' Her voice trails away and she looks at me. 'I think he was singing it because his nan was dying and he was sad, and then, Mummy, then he sang another song to me, the Kitty Jay song. *O Kitty Jay such a beauty cast away and and and—*' Lyla's left hand twirls, very gently, her right hand hidden under the table, 'And after he finished the song he said to me, "Your granny was Kitty Jay: she cast her beauty away." Why did he say that, Mummy? And after that Daddy sang it again, but different: *O Kitty Jay, her baby cast away, her baby cast away.* And then he looked very sad and then I went to sleep. Why did he do all that?'

I sit here, bewildered. 'I don't know.' And I don't. Yet. But an idea forms. I am sure Adam never imagined that his five-month-old daughter would remember him saying any of this; so he was talking to himself when he sang all this, he was admitting something to no one but himself.

What was he admitting?

Lyla is trembling now, trembling all over. 'Mummy, I'm scared, because he's coming.'

'What?'

The smell of smoke has become quite intense. And yet I am fixed on my daughter's trembling face as she speaks.

'I know I have Asperger's, I know you don't want to tell me, I know I am different, I know I have synaesthesia. I know this is why I have memories from being a baby. I have read it all, Mummy, I know what people like me are like and why I do these movements that scare people, so they don't like me. I know I am stimming. I know I can't understand people, or friends and games. I read it all, I know it all. You need to know. Because I've been reading on Google and I know that 1.8 per cent of men and boys surveyed had a diagnosis of autism, compared to just 0.2 per cent of women and girls, but girls are different because—'

'Lyla! Stop.'

She stops. She doesn't have to spell it out any more. I let the silence fill the longhouse as the answers fill my mind. At last.

I may have worked it out. Kitty Jay's grave. What was my mum telling me by having her ashes scattered there? That she too had fallen in love, maybe got pregnant, and she was dying anyway from cancer: so she killed herself, with the baby inside her. She couldn't bear to tell me, or she was too ashamed, she always hated suicide – but she left clues. That was why she wanted her ashes scattered there. Where the suicide was buried, the woman ashamed of her pregnancy.

Lyla is trembling more violently. As if she guesses what I am thinking. I am terrified by her words, her movements, my thoughts, my ideas, my realizations, everything.

'Mummy I can hear him coming very close now.'

'What? Who?'

I know enough to trust Lyla's remarkable hearing. I can only hear the nothingness, the dark rustling sound of swaling, burning gorse.

'He's in the yard. I can hear his footsteps on the twigs, it's a kind of reddish sound. He's going to do it again.'

Running to the kitchen drawer, I yank it open, and urgently seize a knife. The biggest knife we have.

The moment I look up I see that the fog is darker than ever, and it is tinged with yellow, a strange, glowing yellow, at the base, where it meets the ground. And now I realize it isn't fog. It is smoke mixed with fog and fire, burning gorse and bracken.

The swaling is out of control. It is coming up the path, heading for our house.

And framed by this fog is the figure of a man, striding towards the door. He looks eerily and disturbingly familiar. Terrifyingly familiar. He has the distinct, full mouth of my mother, the set of her features, the high forehead.

But there is another, closer resemblance, too.

Panicked, rigid, trembling, I shove the knife in the back pocket of my jeans. A second later, the man kicks the door open. And looks at us both. I remember it vividly now, the blue eyes and the brutal hatred.

He has a knife in his hand, a blade that is so much bigger and nastier and shinier than mine.

'You could say hello,' he says. Unsmiling. He looks hard at Lyla. 'After all, I am your brother.' Then he looks at me. 'And your brother, as well.'

Three Crowns Inn, Chagford

Tuesday morning

Tessa Kinnersley put down her phone and gazed into the roaring log fire in its thirteenth-century hearth. The last of her coffee was cold; she pushed the cup away, and considered.

She was certain she'd made the right choice: helping Kath, offering Brixham. But what was she going to say to Adam Redway? He'd rung her this morning, begging for a meeting. Presumably, he was going to plead for Tessa to intervene.

She wouldn't do that. Helping Kath and Lyla was fine, giving them a way off the moor, a place to be safe; but she wasn't going to get more involved in their problems: she had sufficient marital problems of her own.

Nor would she mention that Kath had called. She didn't quite know how to handle Adam Redway.

'Hello.'

Tessa turned and there he was, reaching out a hand. He looked tired, she thought: tired, resigned, a lesser man.

'Thanks for meeting me at such short notice, is it OK if I sit down?'

'Of course.'

Adam sat in the big leather seat on the other side of the fire. The hotel bar was nearly empty, serving coffee to a few residents: it was too early for lunchers or drinkers. She looked at him while he gazed around.

'Used to come here when I was a kid,' he said, reminiscing. 'They'd let us drink underage. Doubt they'd do it now, far too posh.' His smile was regretful. 'Like the rest of Chagford. Have you seen the wine shop next door? Like something from London. Everyone's from London in Chagford these days.' He rubbed his face with his hands, and asked, 'What brings you up here, Tessa?'

'A friend from London.'

'Ah.' He blushed. 'Sorry. I wasn't meaning to insult anyone. God, I keep getting everything wrong.'

Tessa assessed Adam's uncombed hair and badly ironed shirt under his fleece. He was a cliché of a man exiled from his wife. Falling apart. Unkempt. At least he had the grace to look like shit. She wondered, as a contrast, what Dan looked like, right now. Working from his hotel room in London. Probably he was in a pricey suit, a dazzling white shirt, wearing a silk tie and a smile: laughing down the phone. Perhaps he was with that girl.

'Your friend here on holiday?'

Adam was trying to be amiable, but it was painful.

'Yes. We're having lunch up at Gidleigh. I want her advice,' Tessa said. 'She's a divorce lawyer, you see.'

Adam blushed, again.

Tessa went on, 'Adam, I don't want to be rude, but I haven't got long, and this is pretty awkward. Because of Dan, because I am friendly with Kath. For all the reasons you know.' She paused. 'I really do want to help you guys, in any way I can, but I'm not sure how. And I am busy.'

'I know, I'm sorry, Tessa, I know my marriage is my marriage. Not your fault.'

'So why did you want to meet me?'

Adam faltered. He looked uncharacteristically nervous. His eyes slid to the side, taking in the stones of the hearth, the huge iron tongs, the mighty cast-iron spit that would once have roasted entire hogs. Like a huge torture device. He looked back at Tessa. 'I want to tell you the truth, about the past. Does that make sense? I want to tell you, Tessa, so you can tell Kath, and tell Dan, for that matter. So I can bloody clear my name. I would have told Kath myself, by now, but she won't let me visit, won't even take my calls.'

'All right.' Tessa glanced at her watch, as a clear signal. *Hurry up. Get on with it.*

He cleared his throat. 'It's difficult,' he said, finally. 'I've never told anyone.'

'You'll have to try. Or this is pointless.'

'I know.' He took a long breath. 'OK. You see, it all relates to this mad idea, that I . . . assaulted Kath on the night she did what she did. And somehow this idea has got into Lyla's head, too. She's claiming I was in the car. That she saw me in the car.'

'Yes. I heard.' Tessa kept her tone deliberately flat. Neutral. She would hear him out, but that was it.

'Tessa.' His blue eyes were imploring. 'Tessa, it's nonsense. Bullshit. She might have misidentified me, because of her condition, ASD, we don't know. But it's crap. All of it. I *never* came back to Huckerby that night. *Wasn't* in that car. I was up at Manaton all week, until I got the call from the hospital.' For a moment he hesitated, then added, 'It's true that on the afternoon she drove into Burrator I *was* out, but I was just having a few pints at the Warren, and there was no signal, and I was drink-driving on my way back to the hut. I kept it all quiet because, if I'd told anyone I was drink-driving, I'd have lost everything. Car, job, money, everything. On top of the accident. We'd have been totally ruined. What was the point?'

'OK . . .'

His gaze was desperate now. 'Believe me! Please! I need *someone* to believe me. I had nothing to do with Kath's accident. I wasn't there.'

'I see.'

Adam abruptly raised his arms, in surrender, as if Tessa was pointing a gun at him. 'No, you *don't* see. Because there *is* something else, something important. I have been lying, in another way. About the past. About Kath's mum.'

Tessa leaned forward. This was new. What was he going to say?

Adam shook his head.

'Truth is, something . . . did happen. To the three of us. Way back. I did do something. Something very stupid. I had sex with Penny Kinnersley.' His blush was fierce, but he continued: 'It was just one night! I was nineteen, bloody nineteen. Just a boy. Kath was in her first year at uni, living in halls, we were going steady, I was in my job, but it was my first year. I was so bloody naïve. Not even twenty. Then one night, here in Chagford, where they have all the dancing, drinking, boozing all night, I ended up alone with Kath's mum, with Penny Kinnersley.' He shook his head, blushing in shame. 'Everyone was hammered. It was the traditional Mayday party, with a lot of London people, everyone in green, doing acid, waving pagan flowers up at Scorhill, all that – and Penny was staying at the Ring O'Bells, and I was trying to be gallant: I offered to walk her home, through the dark. It was such a beautiful night, warm and sweet, and I wanted to impress her, be chivalrous, show her I would be a good husband for Kath, that was all, and—' Adam sank his face into his hands for a second. Then he lifted his gaze and his blue eyes focused hard, on Tessa. 'On the way back to the pub, she did it. She seduced me. Simple as that. I was drunk and she was a very good-looking woman, very extrovert. She knew exactly what she was doing, she had so many men, and she took me and she kissed me, and we went back to her room, and I was drunk, and we did it, and that was it.'

Adam's gaze was insistent. 'It was just that one drunken, stupid night. No one else knew, no one saw, apart from Jack Bryant, my cousin who drinks down at the Warren – he was there at the Ring that night, he saw her come on to me, he actually saw her pull me into her room. Literally pull me. And he's kept it a secret ever since: he's a bit of a bastard but he's not a total bastard. He's family. He kept it quiet.'

Adam ran fingers through his hair, as if he could comb away the guilt. 'Anyway, as soon as I woke up next morning I bitterly regretted it, totally, totally, because I really was in love with Kath, and I got my clothes on and I left Penny there. Made a vow I would never touch another woman.' Another deep sigh. 'But Penny kept coming back for more, after that night. She wanted more from me, a proper *affair*. She said she was in love. Said I was the spirit of the moor, the Green Man, crap like that, I dunno. She said we would conceive some sacred child. Crazy shit. Mad. So I rejected her. I told her to go away, told her I was in love with Kath, and then I told her Kath and I were engaged and Penny ran off to India, furious, and crazy, maybe she already had the cancer, who knows. And that's all that happened, Tessa. That's all that happened. It was one night with a woman who wanted more.' His voice was low and sad now. 'And yet it seems I should be condemned, should lose my wife and daughter for one drunken night, at the age of nineteen. Is that right?'

Tessa was silent. She refused to answer. But inside, she thought: *This is a man who is telling the truth*. And he was probably right. No one should lose everything for one error, decades past.

Adam filled the silence. 'Soon after that, Penny died, she died so quickly. But when—' Adam shook his head, as if incredulous at his own story. 'But when me and Dan went to collect the ashes, there were these, like, *letters*. For me and him. I can guess now what she said to Dan. But the one to me was horrible. Worse. Disgusting.'

Tessa looked at him, sceptically, but curiously. 'In what way?'

'Full of hatred. She said she'd got pregnant by me, that one night, and she said she'd aborted the baby. She said that she felt so guilty at what she'd done that she'd killed herself. Really. That's what she said. And therefore her death was all my fault. It was toxic. Fucking poison. I think she hated me for rejecting her. She wanted to hurt me as much as possible. She wanted revenge on *me*.' Adam frowned, his voice growing stronger, angrier. 'I nearly burned the letter. But I didn't. And now I'm glad I didn't. It's here. Look.'

Reaching into his pocket, he pulled out a crumpled envelope and took from it an old piece of paper. He handed it over. The letter was wrinkled and pale brown with age, the hue of milky tea, but it was still perfectly legible. Tessa read every word, every furious sentence, confirming what Adam said. The letter was written in a fevered scrawl, the mad words of a dying woman. Was this loathing sprung from the cancer in Penny's head? Or was this wicked madness, this malignance, Penny's real self emerging?

'See what I mean?' Adam said. 'She was nuts. That's all there is to it. I know Kath really loved her mum, I know Kath still misses her, but Kath doesn't realize what her mother was actually like: she was a fucking witch, obsessed with sex, and what she could do with sex. She could be downright evil. She liked to hurt, play these cruel mind games, manipulate everyone. And she's done that all right. She's done it with those letters, the inheritance, every way she can. By giving the house to Dan and nothing to Kath: she did that to hurt me and Kath. And still her selfishness hurts us all these years later. She's still destroying us. Was Kath's suicide bid caused by it all, somehow? I don't know. I still don't know.'

He sat back, and exhaled, his job done. He looked calmer.

'So that's my confession, Tessa. That's what happened. I did one stupid thing, as a teenager. I let a manipulative older woman use me, and now we're all suffering.'

His phone made a beeping noise. A message arriving. Adam took it from his pocket. And his frown now was not angry: it was mildly alarmed.

'I've got to go, sorry. But this is weird.'

'What? What's wrong?'

'Swaling,' he said, as if to himself. 'All over? At Cherry Brook, as well? That's odd.'

Before Tessa could ask any more, he was up and pacing out the ancient hotel, opening the door to a rush of cold winter wind. A medieval tapestry of Heaven and Hell fluttered in the breeze, making a demon dance with his pitchfork, as if he were, at last, alive.

Dartmoor

Tuesday morning

Adam sped out of Chagford, doing fifty, breaking the speed limit as he swerved around the narrow moorland road. But he didn't care. Out-of-control swaling could be seriously dangerous. It wasn't his patch but it was his moor and his friends. He needed to help.

He was in deep valleys, thick moorland, out of signal; after fifteen or twenty minutes his mobile caught some reception – and he got six or seven pings in a row. Messages. Which had been queued up, and waiting for him. Urgent messages from his friends, colleagues, rangers—

Trouble in SW now. Sherberton.

It's totally out of control, Combestone. Can someone check wind forecast.

Hexworthy village. Fire reported near church.

Hexworthy?? That was close to Huckerby – and Lyla, and Kath – far too close. And he was still so far away. He had to go right across the moor. How fast could he risk driving? His hands were damp as he took the curves at dangerous speeds. And then, when he swung the car over another tiny bridge he got another message. With a photo attached. He glanced down at the phone screen and the message nearly made him drive straight into a wall.

And it was sent about thirty minutes ago.

Hey Dad,

I reckon you deserve at least a text. And a photo. Before they die. So here you go.

I know you don't know me, but you really should. Because you made me. When you raped my mum. That's my mum who casually gave me away. Because she is a witch, because they are all witches. That's why I am going to kill them, kill my sisters, kill and rape your Kath and your Lyla. And I'll video it for you. OK? I'll send it to your phone, Dad.

I'm sending over the first pic. There will be more So you might as well slow down. I know where you're driving from. But you're not gonna make it. I did Findyourphone. I know you are in Chagford. You are an hour away You don't have time to help, Dad. You are too late, Dad

So say goodbye to everyone, before I cut them into pieces. That's how they killed witches in Greenland, did you know that? I read it in one of Mummy's books.

Adam felt a deep and intense nausea. The photo arrived in his phone with a cheery ping. Adam gazed down in despair. The photo was a selfie. Clearly taken at Huckerby,

in the kitchen. The selfie showed Lyla tied to a chair –
and standing by her was a half-smiling young man. This
man had Penny Kinnersley's chin, her jaw, the particular
set of her mouth, very full-lipped. Generous, even. But
everything else screamed *Adam*. Adam's hair, Adam's eyes,
Adam's genes. Almost a doppelganger.

The young man in the selfie was clearly his adult son
by Penny Kinnersley. And he had Adam's daughter tied
to a chair, with a big knife poised at her pale, ten-year-old
throat.

Like she was about to be cut into pieces. This very
morning. And this message was *old*. Adam put his foot
to the floor. Eighty miles an hour. Ninety.

Huckerby

Tuesday morning

'So here we are again, Katarina.'

He enters the kitchen as if he has come for coffee and choc-chip cookies. Smiling my mother's smile. Holding the knife. He points the shining tip of the blade at me.

'Got your mobile?'

I nod. Mute.

'Slide it across to me.'

I do what he says. I take the mobile from my pocket, and slide it down the kitchen counter. He picks it up, glances at the screen, reads it, pressing buttons. Looking at the screen very carefully. I wonder if he is using that app. Findyourphone. Working out where Adam might be, close or far. Perhaps he has a hunch already.

After that he takes out his own phone and types a number, without calling. Then he smashes my phone on the hard wooden surface, shattering it. Pieces of plastic and metal go spinning everywhere, clattering into the sink, on to the floor.

Now the point of his blade is aimed at the kitchen table. 'Both of you: sit down.'

I glance across at Lyla, standing under the calendar, under the snow on Kitty Jay's grave, red flowers on white. She is perfectly still. The only sign of fear is the trembling corner of her mouth.

'Do as he says, Lyla. Please, darling. Just do what he says.'

We move towards the table, scrape chairs across the floor. We sit down, slowly. I feel the pressure of the kitchen carving knife in my back pocket as I sit. It's only thanks to Lyla that I have it, but what chance will I get, against him? He sits there, silent. Waiting, thinking, apparently.

He is tall, six foot two. Muscled. Well built. Looks older and harder than his years. He must be eighteen or nineteen, though he could pass for twenty-five, even twenty-eight. He looks much older the way his dad looks much younger.

His dad.

The last shining fragment of coloured glass is fixed in the lead of that stained-glass window. The whole story is revealed.

If I was close before, now I see it all.

My mum must have had a baby by Adam, an illicit baby just like Kitty Jay, and she killed herself, just like Kitty Jay, because she had cancer and couldn't look after the poor child; and that's why she asked to be scattered at Kitty's Jay's grave. She was impregnated by the Green Man, my man of the moor, my husband.

My mum was Kitty Jay, but it was not her beauty that she cast away, it was her baby by Adam. This baby was a son. This son is now a man. This man has been camped out on the moor, he has scribbled out my face, he is here

348

for revenge. And now this handsome, jumpy, sinister young man sits across our kitchen table. Waiting, thinking. No one moves. My mind churns.

Slowly, he leans across the table, opposite us. Smiling all the time. His smile, in its shape, is very much like my mother's, but now I realize it is also a little like Lyla's, when she is particularly Aspergery. A hint of a grimace. Fixed and faked, trying to express emotion, or hiding some other emotion.

'Quite a fire, isn't it?' he says. 'Worked it out, the other day. How it would help. Cos I saw that *Adam* was away. Daddy. And I saw they were doing the burning, whatyoucallit, swaling, whatever. I knew this was it. I had to take my chance with you guys. With the witches. Finish what I nearly did at Burrator. Rape you again, the way he raped Mum. Then I will kill you. Cut you both into pieces. No one can reach us through that fire. And I set fires everywhere. They'll be totally confused. They won't even know about us, out here, not yet.'

Lyla is stimming now. Her right hand twirls in the air. The little bird trying to escape.

He gazes at her.

'You saw me, didn't you? From a distance. Saw me on the moor sometimes. Saw me in Hobajob's. Maybe going into the house, stealing stuff? But you couldn't work it out. Could you? Because I look so much like Dad.' His smile is hard and glittery. 'I did this deliberately, Sis, I let you see me, so it would confuse you. Same way I made patterns for you, on the moor, which you could copy, yet not understand. You realize that now, right?'

Lyla says nothing. I realize I was right: *prosopagnosia.* Lyla must have the syndrome – but have it mildly, because we've not seen it before. Yet her condition was enough to cause all this confusion. Leading us to this kitchen, this day, this desolate scene.

My brother sighs, in a false way. Then he looks at me. 'She's a pretty serious case, pretty far down the spectrum. Have you had her labelled yet? Eh? Got to put a label on her, Katarina.' He tuts. 'She's obviously autistic, Asperger's, freak with no friends. It's cruel, letting it go on so long, without a label. Shoulda labelled me. Then maybe I'd have been given some meds. Too late now. *Too late now.* I told you this. I told you all this in the fucking car. *Too late now.*' He looks at me, hard and direct. 'Don't you remember? I think you remember it all now, don't you?'

And he's right. I do remember. With the scent of winter honeysuckle in my nostrils, I recall it all. The whole day.

I was so bored, and so lonely. Days in rainy, wintry Huckerby alone with Lyla, trying to keep her entertained. Then a day when we talked about Kitty Jay, and it got too much. So I sent her off to Auntie Emma, and went to the Two Bridges for a drink, needing the sense of company, of adults, a single glass of wine. Anything. I remember how I sat discreetly in a tiny corner for a few minutes, looking at my silly shred of a poem. And then I was overwhelmed with guilt – the bad, selfish mother, sending her daughter away to go for a drink, in the day? – and I ran out of the pub, barely half a glass later.

That's when I saw my brother, but I didn't want him to see me. Being a bad mum. So I fled: avoiding him.

After the Two Bridges I went home. Maybe had another glass of wine. And then: an unexpected visit. From a young handsome man, with that knowing, charming smile of my mother. Full-lipped. So very distinctive. Of course, in that face, that stature, that stride there was an even more striking resemblance to Adam. Yet something blinded me to it. Perhaps I was attracted, sexually, without realizing, and the concept was too taboo to acknowledge. Or perhaps it was all too absurd.

Yet it was all there, hidden in plain sight.

And he was company for me, and we had more wine, and he seemed so charming. And most of all he had that extraordinary story, an astonishing and beautiful tale, that my mum had a baby, him, Lucas, Luke Kinnersley, a baby that she gave away, and that baby was him: so Luke was my brother, or half-brother, returned from the dead, returned from India, a final gift from my mad, crazy, lovely, quirky mother.

He didn't tell me the rest. Didn't tell me the name of his father. *Adam Redway.* My mother had so many men, after all.

We hugged, that afternoon, brother and sister reunited.

Then he told me he'd come back in the evening, and tell me the rest of his story. Of course he did this because he wanted the cover of darkness for what he intended to do. But I simply got excited. Like a teen. A new brother! A handsome young brother! A handsome young uncle for Lyla! That's why I told Emma Spalding I was off to see *my brother.* I wasn't lying. It's just that this brother was also Lyla's brother.

I got all dolled up and sent Lyla away again. My new brother Luke arrived at nine, asked me to drive us to a place he knew, towards Conybeer's. And it was there that the atmosphere changed. I began to feel menaced, to feel his strangeness.

That's when the knife came out and Luke forced me to drive on. And as I did, he told me the rest of his poisonous story, so painfully, obviously true. How my dying mother had given him to hippies in the ashram, idiots, druggies, pyjama people, vain silly dreamers like

Mum, who gave him a half-hearted home schooling, let him drink at ten, smoke weed at eleven. Neglected him the rest of the time. They had sex parties in the house, him wandering around, unwashed. Unwanted . . .

And now my mother's younger son speaks. Here. In the kitchen, as the smoke of the swaling drifts under the front door.

'You finished working it out?' He grins. But it is a sad grin. I feel almost sorry for him. For what he can't help doing.

'Nearly,' I say. And I am not lying. I am fitting the final pieces in place.

When we were in the car, by the winter honeysuckle, he also told me how, at the age of fifteen, his behaviour got so bad that his feckless adoptive parents threw him out, abandoned to the world, with a letter from his real mother. A letter waiting for this very moment, a letter telling him the truth. That he was the product of a rape. By a man named Adam Redway who lived in Dartmoor, Devon, England, Great Britain.

Go and take revenge.

And so, in the end, he came back to take revenge on Adam. To rape his wife, kill the kid, do the worst.

But even as I sit here, paralysed with terror, feeling the painful sharpness of the blade in my back pocket, I wonder: did Adam really rape her? My supposedly funny, lovely, selfish, promiscuous mother? I remember the way she used to look at my handsome boyfriend and suddenly I wonder if *she* came on to *Adam*. All those nights she would spend in Chagford, in the same pubs, buying drinks for everyone, including Adam, even as I was back in Exeter, studying and revising, so diligently and naïvely, in my Halls of Residence?

As if he can read my thoughts, Luke speaks.

'You remember the rape, Kat?'

'Yes.'

'Good. Cos I have a question. Did you come? I've wondered ever since. I mean, I know I was a bit, like, forceful, I know I had to open your legs up, get at your fucking pussy, with a knife to your throat, but . . .' He tilts his head. 'All that quivering, though? You can't fake *that.*'

He goes quiet. Lyla's hand trembles in mid-air and I try to disguise my own trembling. He looks as if he is truly enjoying our fear in these last moments, relishing our terror. He hasn't come to talk much more. He's certainly come to rape me again. And probably Lyla too. After that he will obviously murder us both. He wants the worst kind of revenge on Adam. Killing Adam wouldn't ever be enough.

I wonder if he really believes we are witches. My mum always wanted to believe in witches.

Luke turns, and winks at Lyla. Now he is cheerful, funny, rapscallion Uncle Luke. Who is also her half-brother. Uncle Luke with his knife, with which, very soon, I am sure, he will slit my daughter's throat.

I see it, in my mind, quite vividly. I see him lift her up by her black hair, slice that shining blade across her little white throat, making her blood squirt across the kitchen table. Her body slumping on to the floor, bleeding out, like that sheep at Vitifer Leat. Blood dripping on to earth, slowly, slowly, slowly; a sequence of miniature red jewels.

Lyla's hand is lowered but her mouth opens and closes. Saying nothing.

Luke grins. 'Hello, little Lyla. You do know there's a big overlap between autism and schizophrenia? There's definitely a genetic link. I checked. Funny, huh? We are so obviously *related*. Shame we won't have long to get to know each other. You do know you look like a fish when you do that gaping thing?'

He sits back, assessing us. Waiting, dragging it out as painfully as possible.

'OK, I think we're nearly done now.'

Lyla shouts at him:

'You mustn't touch my mum. You mustn't touch my mummy.'

Luke laughs, again – half bored and half amused. It has a hint of my mother's laugh. Aristocratic. Leisured.

'What exactly the fuck are you going to do, Sis? Hit me with your stuffie? Cast a magic spell with little dead birds? I'm either going to rape your mum and kill her in front of you, or I could kill you first, and then rape her, or I will rape and kill both of you by cutting you into tiny tiny tiny pieces, and we'll have a great big fucking party, the house will burn down, with you guys inside – and I'll nip away, over the mire, with time to come back for Dad.' His laughter is a kind of barking, now, barking like Lyla.

I remember him laughing like that, when we drank together, that afternoon. And again the memories return to me. How he did it, how he must have done it. He saw the poem on the table, so I told him the whole legend of Kitty Jay: the grave, after all, where his mother's ashes were cast to the Dartmoor winds.

He must have realized that my little poem looked like a suicide note. He must have seen the opportunity this presented.

So he raped me, and made me drive to Burrator with him ducked down in the rear seat behind me, a knife at my throat, so no one could see. He surely intended to knock me out in the car as we drove in. Drown me, and swim away. Then he'd have time to come back for Lyla. With no suspicion of murder.

But he was unlucky. I escaped.

Yet I will not escape this time. Lyla predicted this. The blue light comes near. My own death approaches. And my daughter's death, as well. Which is so infinitely worse.

My brother looks at me, then at Lyla. 'All right, Lyla, enough now. I'm going to tie you up, little sis. Stop you waving your fucking hands like a spaz. Then we'll have some fun.'

He gets to his feet. Lyla stands up and backs away. Faster than I'd thought possible, Luke lunges across and grabs Lyla by the arm.

'Mummy!' she screams.

I am paralysed. I have this knife. But he's already got Lyla and he has a bigger knife. If I make a move he could slice her throat open in a second. So I watch, rigid, helpless, as he takes out some short pieces of rope from an inside pocket. Lyla is trembling in his grasp as he pushes her down on to the chair. 'People use these for sex,' he says. 'I've seen them used at parties. They've very easy, very secure.' He slips a loop over her wrist, then another.

She is tied to the chair by her wrists. She struggles for a few seconds, but goes limp. Her eyes gaze at me. Eyes wet with fear, but not quite crying. My brave and precious daughter. I gaze back at her. We both know we are about to die, here in this kitchen, at Huckerby, the place where we used to make peanut butter sandwiches, for our picnics at Brentor, and Dartmeet, and Canonteign Falls. This is where we will be raped and killed.

'Here, let me take a photo. Send it to our daddy. When it's too late. Your last moment alive.'

He takes out his phone, takes a picture of himself, a

selfie of him standing next to Lyla, who is the very image of terror, tied to a chair.

What is he doing, storing the photo? Where is he going to send it? He must be very confident we can't be reached. And of course he's probably right. The fires surround us. He has completed the circle. We're almost certainly going to die.

I have one slender chance. That knife in my back pocket. But if I get it wrong?

I've never used a knife, in aggression, in my life. I have no idea what to do. I'll probably lunge at him and miss. He'll probably see my movement first. There is no hope.

Slowly, slowly, slowly, Luke strokes Lyla's hair, with the flat of the blade. His gestures are caressing, affectionate, yet he is holding a big steel knife, and lifting strands of black hair with the point. Like an old-fashioned barber with a cut-throat razor, he gently runs the flat of the blade down the side of Lyla's trembling, silent face, and softly rubs it against her neck.

It is unbearable. I cannot look. I have to look.

'Pretty girl, for a spastic,' he says. 'Pretty face. Mmmm? Shame I'm gonna chop it all to pieces.'

Again he strokes her white neck with the flat of the blade. At any minute he could twist it, use the edge, draw it swiftly across. And my brave, shivering daughter will die. Here. In that chair, in front of me. A big red gash, the eyelashes fluttering.

The blood spins in my head. I wonder if I am going to faint. The blade strokes my daughter's neck, the blade strokes again, and again. Luke is whistling, quietly. Torturing me. Toying with her throat and my mind.

Now his mood seems to change. As if he is bored. He pulls the knife away, and winks at me. Then he walks around the table towards me. A few feet away. I try to not to shudder.

'OK, I'm going to do you first, Kat. More fun for Dad. Do you from behind, and film it, before I kill you. Stand up, turn around, drop your jeans and knickers. Bend over the table, put your head flat on the table. I'm sure you've done it before, with my dad, good solid table like this.'

Does this give me a chance? I don't think so: because, when I turn around as he commands he will see the knife. In my back pocket.

I push back my chair. I don't know what to do. Luke has his phone out again, filming me, for Adam. He still has the big knife in his other hand. But he is focused on the screen, making a little movie of the rape and murder of Adam's wife, live, on camera. And then he will do the same with his daughter. I picture Adam watching this. Tears of horror.

Unbearable.

Even as I work this out: his plan, I see him look at his phone, check the hour maybe, and then send a message. It must be that photo. He is grinning. He is confident he has time to do what he likes.

I cannot let this happen, and I think my only way to escape, and save Lyla, is to do this job slowly. Teasingly. Coquettishly. Make him come close. Giving me a chance to get the knife out, and use it. As I laboriously undo the top button of my jeans, I sense Lyla, watching. Her eyes, her tears.

Pretending to fumble, I undo the second button even more slowly. Taking a long, intricate minute.

'Oh for fuck's sake,' Luke says. 'Haven't got all day. House will burn down before you get your kit off! Here – I'll do it.' He pockets the phone and marches over. Knife brandished.

We are face to face. My brother and I. My stepson and I.

His eyes meet mine.

'OK,' I say. 'OK.' And I reach around the back of my jeans, as if I am about to thrust them down, but instead I take a solid grasp of the knife handle, and as he reaches over to pull down my jeans, I do it: I whip my knife around – and I stick it *hard hard hard* into his chest.

I feel an awful crunch, a kind of recoil. I have hit bone, cut through real meat. I have a sense of butchery: I have actually stabbed a man. He has a knife, stuck in him, right in the bottom of his chest. It takes an effort for me to pull out the blade. Now blood coils joyously from the wound, and Luke staggers back, blood burbling between his fingers, which are pressed over the knife-wound.

I should do it again. Stick him, stick him again and again, finish him off while I have this tiny chance. But I can't. He's reeling, stumbling away from us, dropping his blade, which clatters on flagstones; but he is not dead. I haven't done enough, I haven't killed him, it's too low, I've missed the heart.

Yet I have bought us seconds. Luke is gasping, staring down at his wound: at the lurid rills of streaming blood. He staggers away, across the kitchen, towards the hall.

Rushing to the chair, I slash the knife over the ropes that tie Lyla to the chair. The cords fall to the kitchen floor. Lyla stands.

'Mummy – quick—'

Lyla is free, but Luke is pushing himself away from the wall. He's only wounded and he knows it. He lurches across the floor, where he grabs his big knife, and roars at me.

'Fucking whore!'

'Lyla, *run!*'

Grabbing her hand, I drag us towards the only exit route. Luke is between us and the hallway, so we sprint for the kitchen door. I sense he is standing, and pursuing; I yank the door open, desperate, but as I do, I drop the blood-slicked kitchen knife.

We have nothing now, nothing to defend us, there is no time, no time, there is no time.

We run outside into hell.

Hobajob's Wood

Tuesday morning

All of Huckerby farmyard is choked with smoke, beyond our little space, everything else is burning: fences, brambles, witchbeams. Where do we go? Our only hope is to flee along the lane, dense with smoke, the green lane that runs towards Hobajob's. It looks as if the fires aren't too thick down there, not yet. The wooded ground is always boggy, the streams are delaying the flames. For now.

In the other direction, I can hear howling. The dogs? But they are trapped behind the biggest fence and the biggest fire of all, beyond Lyla's den. They can't get through. We can't reach them.

We *have* to go the other way. To Hobajob's.

It is the worst of risks, but staying here would mean dying at Luke's hands. But where is he?

Surely somewhere close. We must run down that lane.

'Hobajob's!' I shout. 'Lyla – we must get to Hobajob's—'

Before I have finished explaining my girl is sprinting ahead of me. Running to save her life, even as I run after her, to save us both. But the fog and the smoke are drifting across the lane: if Lyla gets ten metres ahead of me I will lose her in the cold, pungent murk.

'Wait – Lyla!'

She turns. 'Can't wait, he's right behind!'

I whirl around but I cannot see anything. Huckerby is now entirely shrouded in smoke. But there he is: a figure emerging from the smoke.

The man on the moor. He was always there. Lyla was horribly right.

'Mummy, run!'

We are nearly at Hobajob's now. Smoke filters through the ancient, grasping trees as we leap the first wall. I have never seen swaling like this, wildfires engulfing the whole moor, threatening these gnarled and moss-hung oakwoods that have been here for ten thousand years. Perhaps the fires will burn everything down, this time. Perhaps we cannot escape this way, either.

I can see the shape of Luke quite distinctly. He's guessed our escape route. He's climbing the green-mossed wall, into the wood.

Lyla screams, again, 'We have to hide!'

But there is nowhere to hide. And I can hear Luke panting as he scrambles over boulders: coming nearer. So I run further into the wood, towards the clearing. Maybe the smoke will help us. It is a cloud settling on the earth. I cannot see three yards in front of my hand.

And I cannot see Lyla.

I swivel in the murk. I realize, with horror, that I've lost her. Luke is out there, somewhere, in the fog, and Lyla is just ahead, and I can't see either of them. 'Lyla!'

No. Don't let it happen this way. No.

'*Lyla!*'

My screams will tell Luke where I am, but I do not

care. Let him take me. Let him rape and kill me. Let Lyla have a chance. Just give her one single chance.

'Lyla, where are you? We have to go right through the wood – please, Lyla!'

Too late.

'Mummmmy!'

I have reached the clearing, where Luke killed the hares. I remember their empty eye sockets, filled with blood. Gazing beyond us, at something evil.

Luke is in the middle of the clearing. And he has got hold of Lyla. He stands so tall and imposing, towering over my daughter. He has a hard fistful of her black hair, lifting her up on to tiptoes. She is kicking and wriggling.

I approach, but there is nothing I can do. I have no weapon; I dropped the knife at the door.

'Hello, Katarina,' he says. And he yanks harder on Lyla's hair, making her scream. 'This is how you kill witches – chop chop chop—'

All around us, the wood awaits. The scream of my daughter echoes, and dies. I can hear the faraway crackle of burning gorse. And yet here, deep in Hobajob's, the world is quiet, politely observing the horror that is about to be enacted, even as grey snakes of smoke drift languidly between the stumps, and nettles. I see that distant branches are now beginning to burn.

Hobajob's is succumbing to the flames.

Luke hauls Lyla even higher, almost off the ground, making her weep with the pain. He is going to do what I imagined. Slice her throat wide open, like that sheep at Vitifer.

The blade is firm in his hand. He smiles at me, forcing me to watch.

'Mummy is here, baby. Look at Mummy, Lyla. Look at her standing there. Watching you die.'

He is going to slice the blade across her throat. The blood will spray into the fire. Making sure he has my attention, he lifts the blade ceremonially to her pale neck, as she wriggles, helpless.

I feel my own life draining away: I want him to kill me first. Kill me in Hobajob's, let Lyla go. But he won't let her go. The blade is ready, he is getting ready to kill my girl. Make a bloody new smile. He wants it to be dramatic. He is doing it slowly to make it worse.

I barely breathe. Hobajob stirs.

From the back of the burning wood, from the back of my head, I hear a dark, angry noise, getting nearer, very quickly. The noise is so loud and shocking that it makes Luke pause. He turns, for a second.

The dogs.

Felix and Randal.

They have somehow made it through. Somehow they have beaten the fire and are galloping across the wood: coming to save their girl, their guide, their own princess. Their fur is burning as they come belting through the smoke, like big dark black-eyed devil dogs: snarling, angry, vengeful, roaring: they head straight for Luke.

In a second, they are on him; they hit him hard, both dogs at once. He yells in terrified pain; I see their teeth sinking into his bones and now he screams for help, and drops my daughter.

Lyla is free, she falls from his hands.

'Lyla, baby, RUN!'

She runs, away from the clearing, back into the guarding woods, where the streams resist the fires. But now I cannot tear my gaze away from the dogs – and the man. The drooling lurchers have released Luke, and now they simply stand there: growling, guarding, barking: looking for Lyla, then looking back at Luke.

Waiting for orders. They are waiting for Lyla's order to finish him off.

There is blood on his hands, blood on Luke's face, blood oozing from his stomach. He rises to his feet, and fixes his eyes on me. He still has the knife. And this time he is coming for me. This time I am his prey. He has blood on his fingers. Blood streams from his scalp, his legs. He is wounded and bitten and stabbed, but he is still alive, still crazy. And coming for me, as a consolation prize.

There's nowhere to go. I am backed against the gnarled trees; I stumble on twining roots as I yield, and fall backwards, flailing. Luke takes his chance. I sense his shadow high above me. I see his hands raised aloft, the blade clasped between two palms, as if this is a special Dartmoor ritual. A sacrifice. I close my eyes, waiting for the blade to be rammed down into my heart. And I don't care if he kills me, as long as Lyla escapes. This is my real suicide: this is when I willingly give my life. For my daughter.

Have me. Let her go. I am ready to die.

But then a scream.

'Felix! Randal!'

It's Lyla: screaming through the cold and the smoke, screaming louder than I thought possible. 'KILL HIM!'

Their obedience is instant. The two dogs leap upon Luke and this time they bite him savagely, going for the throat. Tearing flesh. Mauling him, ripping at his face. He's dropped the knife, he's on the ground, at the edge of the clearing: and the dogs are finishing him off this time: they are ripping at his neck, shaking him like helpless prey. But he is fighting back, dragging them away, dragging them all into the fiercely burning bushes.

The sight and the sound is repulsive. A human screaming, dogs killing, all dying. Through the smoke I can see Luke is fighting, but he is wounded and they are big, strong, ferocious dogs. But it doesn't matter: they will all die in those flames.

Lyla shouts, 'Felix, Randal!'

The smoke is too thick to see. But the noise is fading, the screaming and howling turns to moaning, then whimpering, then nothing.

And after that there is stillness. The fire burns on. Respectfully.

Lyla stands in the safety of the clearing and she looks at the impenetrable smoke, and she does not move. Nor do I. We are both mute. And then I hear another voice.

'Lyla!'

It is Adam, his face blackened with ash.

'Jesus. Lyla, Sweetheart.'

Lyla runs across the clearing, and leaps into his arms.

'Daddy!'

Adam hugs her, so very tight.

She is sobbing, in his arms.

'Daddy – Daddy Daddy Daddy it was him, Daddy, it was him, I'm so sorry—'

He kisses Lyla again, and again, and once more, then turns to me. Here is the husband I doubted. The husband who came back to save us. Through the fires.

'Daddy. Felix and Randal?'

Adam puts Lyla down, we step a little nearer to the smoking underbrush. The flames have eaten everything, the fires have halfway dispersed. The body of Luke is a mess of red and black, of blood and soot, half hidden by a fallen branch.

Lyla ignores the ruins of the man who tried to kill us. Because two dogs are limping, slowly, out of the ashes

366

and smoke. Their fur is burned a terrible black, their bodies shake with pain. Both of them collapse on to the burned wet earth.

'Felix,' says Lyla, whispering. As she kneels by his side, Felix lifts a muzzle, sensing her touch. He licks her hand, gently, gently, for the very last time. And then he rests his head beside Randal. Who is now unmoving.

The dogs are dead.

I am trying not to cry as much as Lyla. Adam looks at us both, he puts a hand on his daughter's shoulder. Lyla is still kneeling and stroking the charred fur of Randal, and as she does this, she sings her little song,

'O little blue light in the dead of the night,
O prithee, O prithee, no nearer to creep . . .'

I gaze around.

The fires are moving on now. They are done with Hobajob's.

'Come on, girls, come on.' Adam takes us by the hand, one on each side. 'Let's go back to the house. It will be much safer there. Fires won't reach Huckerby. The wind is taking them north.'

He is pulling us, urging us both on, up the lane, over the ancient wall, out of the woods, away from the woodland fires and the pungent smoke. In exhaustion and silence we make our way down the lane, through the gates, into the house.

I lock the big front door and we all sit at the table. I think of the song. My daughter's song. The song that tells you that a death is coming,

O little blue light in the dead of the night

And then I look up, at the windows. A strange blue light shows at the windows of the longhouse, flickering and throbbing in the mist.

The eerie blue light gets nearer, and nearer: ghostly, and watery. Quivering.

It is the flashing blue light of police cars.

Dartmeet

Summer

I love this place, where the cold, chattery waters of the East and West Dart finally collide, down from the bridge, under the shading oaks, and the gracious willows. Like two awful gossips leaning together, sharing the same rumours. Like a broken family: rowdy, yet reunited.

'Try not to fall in,' I call to Lyla. 'We haven't got any towels.'

She turns, and smiles rather sarcastically; she's paddling the water with her dad, and Charlie and Oscar, and her new friend from her new school in Brixham, by the sea. Her new friend is Alice. She's as crazy as Lyla about animals, and plants, about birds and nature, as obsessive and enchanted. Alice's mum is happy for us to bring her up here at weekends, which is about the only time I see Dartmoor these days.

Dan and Tessa gave us the Brixham cottage a few days after Luke died, along with Felix and Randal, in that terrible fire, which burned out a third of Hobajob's. They gave us the whole house, just like that. Handed it over, keys and freehold.

It was their attempt to right the ancient injustice. To undo the wrongs of my mother.

Adam was persuaded to swallow his pride; he in turn persuaded the National Park to let him live off the moor. And thus it was done.

Now he drives up in the morning, from the coast, and drives home at night. And Lyla has decided she likes the 'golden-rushing' noise of the sea at Brixham. She can watch the waves from her bedroom window; she loves all the yachts and boats in the little harbour, which really do tinkle-tankle. She's gained confidence. Perhaps because she essentially saved our lives, by working out the truth, by warning me to grab the knife. I think this confidence has enabled her to gain a friend. Only one friend. But still: a friend.

We scattered the ashes of Felix and Randal in the back garden of Huckerby, by the daffodils, before we left it for the last time. We scattered the ashes of Lucas Kinnersley over Kitty Jay's grave. It seemed the right place, perhaps the only place. Mother and son reunited. Adam said a few words, as Luke's father. *Dart, Dart, every year thou claimest a heart.* And as the soft spring wind blew the grey ashes over the grass, I saw the sadness in my husband's eyes: despite it all, Luke *was* his son, a son who was abandoned and condemned from the start.

The inquest told us more of Luke's story. How he'd moved to England, joined the army at the age of seventeen. How he was discharged because he was disturbed, and because of the drugs. How he became a petty thief, smoking weed, living in squats in Plymouth, hiking the moors, reading books, grimoires, old books of magic, the valuable books Mum left to him, not me or Dan.

The inquest explained how he came ever closer to us. Trying to kill me first on 30 December, then waiting weeks, as he played his mind games, for a second attempt. A second assault when he would use the swaling to do the job. Burn the witches. Feeding the fires with petrol to bring them close to Huckerby.

But the verdict – death by misadventure – never really got to the heart of it. Never identified the source of the wrong. My mother.

All along, it was her. My selfish, narcissistic mother. Unable to bear rejection. The cancer can't excuse her. Yes, she did it just before she died, with tumours in her brain, but she did it lucidly, deliberately, and cruelly. From the stupidly unfair inheritance, to those vile and poisonous letters, some of them designed to explode decades down the line. She must have known how people would react, not least her son by Adam, a very troubled and neglected boy, given a letter on his fifteenth birthday, obliging him to take revenge for his awful childhood.

What does that make my mother? Is there even a word for her?

Nothing seems to fit.

Tessa interrupts my thoughts, my endless, babbling thoughts that flow like the silvery Teign, down to Drewe Weir. 'You OK?'

She is in a bright summer dress, cross-legged on the picnic blanket. Her sons are happily playing with Lyla and Alice. Adam is pointing at things in the water, little fishes, or eels, giving them scientific names. Lyla and Alice look particularly rapt and earnest. The boys are more intent on splashing each other.

Tessa repeats, 'You OK, Kath?'

'Yes,' I say. 'I'm fine. I was thinking about – you know – all the stuff. Luke, Mum, everything.'

She nods. 'I think about it too, quite a lot. I'm still trying to work it out.'

'What do you mean?'

Her face is turned halfway towards mine and her smile is uncertain.

'It's the evil. The concept of pure evil. It's been on my mind a while. Because I think I might have seen it a few times in Princetown jail, and now, well, I wonder if I've encountered it in Luke, or rather, in what your mother did. And it leaves me – I don't know – troubled. Sort of.'

'Why?'

'Because,' she says, 'if pure evil exists, pure goodness must also exist. Right? And pure good surely means God. But I can't believe in God. I'm an atheist, a materialist, a scientist.' She shakes her head and laughs sadly; and she changes the subject. 'Want another sandwich?'

I smile in return. 'I will, thanks, they're lovely, what is it again? Something Spanish?'

'*Jamón ibérico de bellota*,' she says. 'I'm positively addicted.'

We return to silence. Contented, familial silence – apart from the whoops of the kids. It is a happy moorland scene. We've found a slightly emptier riverside space, away from the tourists. Tomorrow the working week begins again. I have a new job, managing a little independent bookshop. It's not very dramatic, and it's not very well paid, but I enjoy it. And it means I can make the most of bright warm Sundays up on the moor, like this.

The only person missing is my brother Dan. He made a terrible error but I miss him, especially on family outings. I have to ask, 'How are things at home?'

She sighs. 'The boys want their dad back. So we think we might try again. For a few weeks, or months, you know. See how we go.'

'That's good, Tessa.' I smile, and put a hand on hers.

'Well,' she says, doubtfully, 'I still don't trust Dan, and I'll never love him the same way again. But, for the boys . . .' She looks up. 'Oh God, I think Oscar's trying to drown Charlie. That's suboptimal.'

I laugh. She gets to her feet, and calls out, 'Boys, boys! Please don't kill each other! I'll get into trouble.'

She runs down to the riverside. Charlie and Oscar are still squabbling, though I think it is good-natured. Adam looks up, and waves to me and I wave back. From a distance you can't see any of the scars, the burns on the side of his neck and right down his arm. The burns he got while walking through those flames, to save us, making it all the way to Huckerby.

Arriving minutes before the police.

In the event, we saved ourselves: or the dogs saved us. But, still, Adam proved that he loves us so much that he risked his life. And he has the scars to show it.

Lyla and Alice are climbing out of the river, wet and laughing. They make quite a pair, Lyla with the almost-black hair and piercing blue eyes, Alice the opposite, very blonde.

'We've been learning,' Lyla says, giggling. 'All about the wet grasslands, the flowers here, Dad's been teaching, showing us. Marsh plume thistle, devil's bit scabious, sharp-flowered rush!'

Alice butts in, 'Ivy leafed bellflower, purple moor grass!'

They are an act, a comic duo. I watch Lyla for stims as she talks, as she tells Alice about the new puppies we are buying to replace Felix and Randal. She does these stims much less often now. Sometimes I see her quietly repeating words; sometimes she still dances and jogs. And her hand, when she's anxious, will still twirl like a bird, like a kestrel hovering. She will always be different, eccentric, quirky, but now I see it *all* as strength. She is herself, the strongest thing you can be. We will never put a label on her, apart from her name. She is Lyla Redway.

And yet, what Lyla, for all her special gifts, can never know, what no one can ever know, is what actually happened in the car at Burrator.

The memory returned to me, a few weeks ago. Entire and complete.

Luke didn't take me to Burrator to fake a suicide. The poem was coincidental. He probably never even saw it. He took me there, after the rape, because he literally wanted to see if I was a witch. I think he believed in half of that stuff, or maybe most of it: the hag stones, the symbols, the spell with my blood in Hobajob's. And so he wanted to test me, as is traditional, by swimming, by dunking, by drowning.

The idea excited him. It was something from the Middle Ages, from the witch-hunts, something from all the books my mother bequeathed him. Luke was convinced our mother was a witch, so he thought I was a witch, and he thought Lyla was a witch. So he hid in the back of the car with a knife, forcing me to drive to Burrator. I suppose, at the end, he intended to drag me out the car and simply throw me in the reservoir.

But as we parked, I found a torch down the side of the seat, a big, heavy, old-fashioned torch, and I hit him, and knocked him out. And I shoved him on to the floor of the car, and I got ready to drive off, to go to the police, but Luke stirred, he came to; and it was then that I decided, in my panic, that I had only one choice. To guarantee Lyla's safety.

We both had to die, that moment, right there.

It was the only way to save Lyla for certain. Drive into the water. Drown us both.

So I *did* attempt suicide. To save my daughter. Yet by some black miracle, dark as the tors, both of us escaped from the car and from Burrator. And Luke made his plans to kill me all over again. By slicing me and Lyla to pieces, like they do to witches in Greenland. This time because he was, now, truly convinced that I was a witch.

Because witches float.

Lyla will never know any of this. No one will ever know any of it. But it still makes me wonder. Was Luke completely mad, and completely wrong? Sometimes I think there is something special, and different, in this family. Yet it has nothing to do with me or my mother: it is not in the Kinnersleys. No, it is in the Redways, who have been here on Dartmoor for a hundred generations.

It was probably in Adam's nan. Possibly it is in Adam, and very likely it is in my daughter. I think of Lyla's ability to summon animals. The ponies that night. The dogs, who saved us. How did Lyla do that? In all that noise and fire and smoke? How did those dogs sense her danger, across burning fields and woods?

It was uncanny. Some might call it magical.

'Alice,' says Lyla, 'shall we go and look up there? There's herons and eels, and everything.'

Alice nods happily and the two girls run off. Barefoot in the grass. Giggling in the warmth. Then gone.

Lying back, I stare up at the sky. I can hear some other picnickers, down the riverbank, they are playing a song. It's 'The White Hare':

'I heard her in the valley
I heard her in the dead of night
The warning of a white hare
Her eyes burning bright . . .'

And, listening to it, I am taken back to those early days when Adam and I were falling in love, and he'd bring me to places like this: sweet green corners of the moor. And when I think of this love, and what came since, I know that we will make it. This little family. Adam, Lyla, me. We have been tested. We survived. I reckon we will get through.

But this pretty, melancholy song also reminds me of that other side, the darkness, the winter mists on Hexworthy, the tinkling silver chains at Huckerby, those hours of cold and black and terror. The sadness hasn't gone away; the shade is still there, it chequers everything. We are certainly happier, but it isn't pure happiness. Because, in leaving Dartmoor, we have forsaken something, a part of our souls has been left behind, up here, where the grey moors rise and fall, like the lonely call of a waterbird.

We have paid a price in beauty; we have lost that daily loveliness.

As I lie here, I let the sunlight, dappled by the oak leaves, play across my face, and I daydream, sweetly, yet bitterly, of the wildflowers on the high grounds in the summer: the meadowsweet at Whitehorse Hill, the foxgloves down at Broada Marsh, the sundews and the shepherd's dials, the pennyroyals and the roses.